OTHER TERRORS

OTHER TERRORS

An Inclusive Anthology

Edited by Vince A. Liaguno and Rena Mason

wm

WILLIAM MORROW

An Imprint of HarperCollins*Publishers*

OTHER TERRORS. Copyright © 2022 by Horror Writers Association. All rights reserved. Printed in the United States of America. No part of this book may be used or reproduced in any manner whatsoever without written permission except in the case of brief quotations embodied in critical articles and reviews. For information, address HarperCollins Publishers, 195 Broadway, New York, NY 10007.

HarperCollins books may be purchased for educational, business, or sales promotional use. For information, please email the Special Markets Department at SPsales@harpercollins.com.

"The Bram Stoker Awards" is a registered trademark of the Horror Writers Association.

FIRST EDITION

Designed by Emily Snyder

Library of Congress Cataloging-in-Publication Data has been applied for.
ISBN 978-0-358-65889-4

22 23 24 25 26   LSC   10 9 8 7 6 5 4 3 2 1

For all those who have ever been
made to feel "other" out there.

We see you and celebrate your otherness.

Contents

INTRODUCTION

From the other, all terrors flow.

Since the advent of horror as a genre, fear of the unknown—and fear of what we *think* we know—has largely driven the narrative. Likewise, there is little more frighteningly unknown to us than that generalized monster commonly referred to as *the other.* You know the one—the monster with green skin and a flat head, the alien from a distant planet, the beast that drinks blood instead of red wine, the necromancer that conjures spirits in a foreign tongue. The one that doesn't fit neatly into the small boxes in which our rigid frames of reference so comfortably exist is the one we've been conditioned to fear the most.

As the film and genre expert Andrew Scahill, PhD, assistant professor of English at the University of Colorado–Denver, explains horror, "It's how we work out the difference between us and them. What we know about identity formation now is that we don't really form our identity through similarity; we define ourselves by what we are not. We're constantly forming our identity by the Other, by the monster, by *I know who I am because I'm not that.*"*

Similarly, societal bigotries coexist in this realm of otherness. Despite the fact that all humans share the same basic anatomy

---

* Oliver Ward (University Communications), "What Horror Films Reveal About Society's Fears," City Stories, *CU Denver News*, October 31, 2019, https://news.ucdenver.edu/what-horror-films-reveal-about-societys-fears.

and bleed the same, we tend to focus on our differences. Many of us have been conditioned from a young age to fear those different from us. Differences are scary and should trigger a fear response, right? Fear the other—the one who doesn't look like us, the one who speaks another language, the one from a foreign land, the one with unfamiliar customs and values, the one who is differently abled, the one who loves or worships differently. If they're different, they must somehow be *wrong*, flawed in some serious and potentially threatening way.

Society's collective disposition to suspect that something that is different must also be dangerous has been long explored in horror—in both literature and film, from the classics to the contemporary. From Bram Stoker's *Dracula* and its exploration of xenophobia in the idea of a fiendish eastern European foreigner invading polite London society to ravage its women to the queer subtext of *A Nightmare on Elm Street 2: Freddy's Revenge* and its allegory for gay panic and the suppression of sexual orientation that falls outside heteronormative boundaries, horror has long been a conduit for the coded expressions of this subconscious fear of that which is nonconforming to the mainstream. Concepts like race and gender and sexual orientation and political ideology have long been fodder for the machinations of the horror genre.

Throughout history, society has always seen itself—its condition and circumstances, its fears and collective anxieties—reflected back in its art. It should come as no surprise then—and a logical progression—that we're starting to see a tectonic shift in the concept of otherness in horror. The viewpoint is adjusting, fine-tuning to reflect a modernism in cultural evolution. As women and people of color and the LGBTQ community and those differently abled are rising up, stepping forward to demand their place at the table, the stories are recasting the other from villain to victim—modern sympathy for the traditional devil, if you will. The concept of otherness in horror is breathing, expanding its literary lungs to show the other as the oppressed, the one that must summon the courage to rise up and defeat the inhuman monsters of convention. It's no longer just us versus them; it's often them versus us in a sea change infusion of cultural context. These shades and variations of otherness challenge readers to expand their minds, to consider that the call is indeed coming from inside the house.

This recurring theme of otherness that often comes up in both critical analysis of the horror genre and discussions about the prejudices and biases people have against minority groups that manifest in myriad phobias was the catalyst, the launching pad, for *Other Terrors*. For this anthology, we set out looking for short fiction that explored the idea of fearing the other, the other as a source of terror, in both traditional and progressive ways. We cast our net far and wide, hoping to attract a diverse roster of literary talent whose backgrounds and experiences might best be suited to interpret this theme. In some of the tales curated for this collection, the other takes literal monster form. In others, the tables are turned, the concept of otherness subverted. In still other stories, the authors crafted modern retellings of traditional narratives where otherness is a defense mechanism weaponized against oppression.

Otherness has evolved and continues to evolve—and it's even more terrifying in the diversity of forms it takes.

VINCE A. LIAGUNO *and* RENA MASON, *editors*

OTHER TERRORS

OTHER FEARS

by Christina Sng

I.

There are worms in his eyes
And maggots in his skin
But they are not what I fear.

I fear his malignant presence,
His hands drawing near.
I fear the touch of his fingers

Encasing my upper arm
As I instinctively flinch
And shake them off.

His gnarled hands,
Made up of rinds
From desiccated rats

Encircle my neck
In a tight suffocating grip,
Lifting me into the air

Legs kicking frantically
A reanimated rag doll
Awakened to a dark fate.

His eyes, cold and emotionless,
Almost clinical when strangling
The woman he says he loves,

Not something he hates,
Not something he fears.
This isn't love.

II.

For over two decades,
He's chipped away parts of me:
First, the parts that were strong.

Then, the parts that were brave.
Afterward, he took away my voice
Chiseling away the parts

That made me who I was,
A person worthy of life and of love.
He left the fearful child behind,

The child he terrorized,
The child he controlled.
Until one day, I woke up

From this nightmare and
Searched for the pieces I lost,
But they are forever gone.

Only the poems remain.
The poems that remind me
Of what I have endured.

III.

His mask frightens me the most.
How often it slipped,
Yet I never saw his true face.

Or I did, but could not
Acknowledge it, just like
Everyone around us.

Most cannot imagine
Such evil exists, numbed by
The absence of overt war.

And his lies,
How easily they spill
From his mouth

Like breath and vapor,
Like smoke and mirrors,
Unraveled by a single thread.

He hates me
Because I am human,
Because I have emotions.

Because I can feel love,
And most of all, because
I see his true face now.

It is him who is *other*—
The aberration among us.
The shell devoid of fractals.

The cave without crystals.
I no longer fear him:
The hyena in the barn,

The hollow puppet
Strewn onto the ground,
The child who cannot feel love.

It is me I should fear.
How I did not realize the truth
Despite the signs I clearly saw:

Glimpses of the monster
Behind an innocent smile,
His touch that makes me cringe

And cower—my panicking heart
Smashing through my rib cage,
My gut tightening into a knot.

His blood has seeped into my hands,
His darkness etched into my eyes,
His shadow follows me now.

IV.

I learn to overcome my fear,
Use my thumbs to press hard
And gouge out his bloody eyes.

He reels backwards—
And raises his hands to hit me
But I duck under his swing and run.

A new fear:
That he will find and kill me.
There is nowhere to hide.

I grow wings so I can fly.
I grow armor to protect my body
From knife wounds and stray bullets.

I abate my fear and face him,
Despite my innards dissolving
At the thought of his presence.

Unless death shows mercy
And takes him first.
There is always that hope

But not one I can count on.
I slam his bloodied head
Onto the ground

And press hard
On his eyes
Till his head caves inward.

IDIOT GIRLS

by Jennifer McMahon

DIOT GIRLS," MR. G calls as Jaz and I run by, only he says it in a funny, shortened way, the accent he tries so hard to hide coming through like a ghost: "Idjit," he says, the word its own spark.

We've taken to the name, let it leave its mark, baptize us in some new way. We've started calling each other Id and Jit. The idjit girls.

Mr. G is standing in front of Building A raking leaves. His wife, Mrs. G, sits inside, looking out the window of their first-floor front apartment, A-1.

There's a collection of wind chimes hung up on brackets around the windows of their apartment—over a dozen of them made of metal, wood, plastic, shells, and driftwood. They tinkle, rattle, and ring in a great cacophony all day and night. Mrs. G says they help keep the evil spirits away.

We've talked about where Mr. and Mrs. G might be from. I think their accent sounds vaguely Creole and picture some swampy state with gators and Spanish moss draping from the trees. Jaz says they're from farther away than that—another country, somewhere in eastern Europe maybe—a place no one's heard of.

Their last name is long and multisyllabic—when people try to pronounce it, their tongues get tangled. When Mr. G says his name, it sounds almost musical, but with a low rasp like he's about to cough up phlegm. Everyone at the apartments has given up trying to pronounce it—they just call him Mr. G.

He wears the same outfit every day when he's out painting steps, glazing windows, raking leaves, shoveling snow: stained blue coveralls and scuffed leather boots. Mr. G is the maintenance man and groundskeeper for the Canal Street Apartments. His shoulders are slumped like he's always tired. His dark hair is slicked back and oiled, streaked with gray. The backs of his hands are thick with a pelt of black hair like the man is part bear. One time, in the summer, he had his coveralls unzipped and there, under his stained and threadbare white undershirt, I caught a glimpse of a dark shape beneath the curly black chest hairs: a faded tattoo done in heavy black lines, a geometric design that came up to his clavicle. A letter or sigil maybe. I told Jaz about it and she laughed, said it was probably the mark of the beast.

Now, as we run by, Mrs. G calls us over: "Girls! Girls!" She's waving her hands, beckoning, pleading for us to come. Jaz doesn't slow, plans to run right past, but I grab her arm and stop her, drag her back to the window where Mrs. G waits. Above us, a wind chime of large metal tubes bangs together like someone hitting a cage, wanting out. Jaz takes a step back, like she's worried the whole thing's going to come crashing down.

Mr. G calls out something to his wife, a reprimand maybe, and she shakes her head at him, responds with another phrase, thick and guttural.

Strange smells waft through the open window: smoky and earthy with a touch of spice, but pungent enough to make my eyes start to water as we move closer.

"Do you know him?" Mrs. G asks from the window, speaking slowly, annunciating carefully. Her English is much better than Mr. G's. She has a scarf tied over her hair: bright yellow dotted with tiny flowers like flecks of blood. "The boy who is missing? He go to school with you?"

I shake my head. "He goes to the middle school. We're high-schoolers," I say.

She blinks at me, eyes huge and owl-like.

The boy, Emmet Clark, is a seventh-grader. He's been missing for two days. Was last seen leaving school on his bicycle. They found his bike and school backpack under the bridge over the river two blocks away from the school. But no sign of Emmet. It's all anyone's been talking about. There're flyers stapled to every telephone pole in town. HAVE YOU SEEN EMMET? A hundred two-dimensional Emmets watching the whole town with dull brown eyes, a goofy smile revealing slightly crooked teeth.

In some places, they're stapled over the old flyers, the ones from last spring: HAVE YOU SEEN JACKSON? Another middle school kid who went missing back in April. Never found.

There have been search parties. Neighborhood watches. Curfews put in place. Last night, there was a community meeting where parents demanded to know if there's a serial killer in our midst.

"You girls be careful," Mrs. G warns, leaning out the window. I can smell the onions and garlic on her breath.

Jaz pulls me away. "Yeah, yeah," Jaz says.

Mrs. G shakes her finger at us. "I've got my eye on you," she says. I'm not sure if her words are meant as reassurance or a warning.

"That's comforting," Jaz shouts back at her. "Real fucking comforting, Mrs. G!"

"Watch your mouth, filthy girl," Mrs. G says, then mutters something, a little prayer for us maybe, or a curse. "What will your mother say, Jasmine," Mrs. G calls after us, "when she hears how you've been talking to me?"

But it's a bluff and we know it: She won't go to Jasmine's mom. Everyone's afraid of Jasmine's mom: the thick incense smoke, the giant gory crucifix that's the first thing you see when you open her door, the way she asks every visitor to kneel down and pray with her.

"Infidels," Jaz's mom hisses when Mr. and Mrs. G walk by. "Filthy people."

JAZ HOLDS MY hand tightly in hers as she leads me right through the pile of leaves Mr. G's been raking. We kick our feet and the leaves scatter everywhere. We're our own autumn wind, our own hurricane.

Mr. G shakes his rake at us. "Idjit girls!" he roars, and we laugh, swoop like crazy birds across the parking lot, leaves in our hair and clinging to my chunky wool sweater.

"Id-jit," we repeat, our own song, the pitch rising as we screech. "Id-jit, id-jit!"

We run right to the door of Building B, where Jaz lives. Instead of going up the stairs to her apartment, we go all the way to the back of the hall, open the heavy metal door that leads to the basement.

We could go anywhere, really. Jaz has a pass key—something she stole from Mr. G's key ring months ago. She'd made a copy of it, then left the original in the driveway next to his car where he found it, assumed it had been there all along, just slipped off his ring. Now she uses the pass key to get into whatever apartment she likes. Sometimes she takes me with her and we walk through other people's lives; we see who leaves dirty dishes piled in their sink, whose recycling bins are full of booze bottles, whose apartments smell like cat pee and old people. Jaz takes a little something from each apartment: a tiny figurine, a single earring, a fork—something that won't be missed, that people will think they've just misplaced.

But today there's no messing around in other people's apartments. We go straight down to the basement, pausing on the stairs to kiss because we can't wait a second longer. Her body presses into mine, and I have to hold the railing so I don't lose my balance.

Jaz tastes like cherry lip-gloss and salt water. She smells like the cheap perfume she shoplifts from the drugstore. Hurrying now, Jaz leads me the rest of the way down the steep wooden steps. The basement smells like damp cement, old books, grease, and heating oil. The furnace sits at the front end of the building, pipes snaking up to bring hot water to all the apartments. We pass by the storage units: cages of two by four frames with stapled on chicken wire, flimsy doors with padlocks. They're stuffed full of bicycles, mildewed boxes, furniture that didn't fit in the tiny apartments upstairs. We head to the one at the end—the extra unit with no padlock. It's where everything that has no place to go gets shoved: bags of salt for the sidewalks in winter, grass seed, driveway sealant, a dented toolbox with a bent screwdriver and a rusty hammer. There are things left behind by old tenants and never gotten rid of: an old chest of drawers, a worn green velvet couch, a bicycle missing the front wheel, boxes of artifacts from people long gone.

"Hello, Jit," Jaz says as she pulls me down on top of her on the old stained couch. We're safe here, tucked away behind the rusted file cabinets, moldering cardboard boxes, a ratty old box spring.

She tugs at my sweater, my favorite—chunky and black and coming unraveled at the edges.

"Hello, Id," I say, brushing my lips over her neck until she shudders. I start unbuttoning her heavy wool blazer: St. Christopher's Catholic school, where her mother sends her to keep her away from public school sinners like me. I undo the last button with my teeth, ripping it off, the smooth white circle like a worry stone I hold under my tongue.

"The id, Freud's id," Jaz explains for the hundredth time, her breathing coming fast, "is all about instinctual desire." She puts her tongue in my ear and a little moan escapes my lips.

Soon the clothes are gone and we're tangled together, bodies sticky with sweat and lip-gloss and cheap drugstore perfume. It's impossible to tell whose limbs are whose.

Instinctual desire, I'm thinking, and then, all thoughts are gone. There is only Jaz. Her fingers. Her mouth. Her breath coming faster and faster.

AFTER, SHE LIGHTS a joint. I don't know where she gets pot, but she's always got it.

She's naked, lounging on her back on the couch, smoking, watching me. I'm straddling her, on my knees, my weight keeping her pinned to the couch. She looks so beautiful, so perfect, her dyed red hair splayed against the worn green velvet couch.

She runs the fingers of her left hand up my belly, to my breasts, brushing the nipples.

Soon it'll be time to get our clothes back on, go back out into the too-bright afternoon. But I want to stay here, just like this, with her pinned below me forever.

"This isn't what I am," she says, because she always has to say it at least once, just to let me know, to keep me in check. "I'm not like this, really. I mean, I like boys. Don't you like boys?"

"Sure," I say, but the lie is thick in my throat. I grab the joint from her, take a deep a hit, let it seep into my lungs. I climb off her, slip my underwear and jeans back on.

"What do you think happened to that boy?" she asks. "The missing one?"

"I don't know. Maybe he ran away. But the fact that they found his backpack and his bike under the bridge like that, it doesn't look good, right?"

She turns, stretches like a lazy cat, takes another hit from the joint, watching the smoke drift up.

"I can't believe you bit my button off," she says, annoyance giving her voice a sharp edge. "Where'd it go?"

She's feeling around the couch for it, pulling back the filthy cushions. "Fuck," she mumbles. "I really need to find it."

I see it on the stained cement floor, glinting in the dim light like a tiny moon. I pick it up without her noticing and wrap my fingers tightly around it, tuck it deep in the pocket of my jeans, a talisman. My own little secret. A little piece of her I can carry with me everywhere I go.

"Why are you getting dressed?" she asks, her voice soft again. I shrug.

"Come here," she orders, a low purr as she reaches out her hand to pull me back down. I'm on top of her again, my mouth on hers, her fingers running up my spine, making my whole body feel electric, dangerous.

We're all hands and teeth and tongue and she's sliding my jeans back off and saying my name, panting it, saying, *Hurry, please, please, please, hurry.*

And then, everything freezes. Time stops. Her body goes rigid beneath me. The temperature in the basement, already cold, seems to drop.

She shoves me off her with a strength I didn't know she had, covers her bare chest with her hands. I land on the floor, jeans tangled around my legs, hip smashing against the concrete.

"What the fuck?" I say, rubbing my hip.

She's gone pale, her eyes fixed on some point beyond me.

I turn and follow her gaze.

There, back in the shadows, over near the boiler, a pale face watches. He's angled in a way that he can see us around the barricade of junk. He steps forward, his face framed in the dim light coming in through the tiny rectangular window.

Mr. G.

He doesn't say a word. He just stares, clenches his jaw, then turns and walks away. We hear his footsteps on the stairs, boots heavy.

When I turn back to Jaz, she's pulling her shirt on.

"Jaz," I say, putting my hand on her shoulder.

She pushes me away.

I say, "Maybe he won't—"

"Just go," she orders.

JAZ'S MOM, MRS. Fletcher, is a squat woman draped in too many layers: a housedress, an apron, a heavy wool cardigan.

"You," she says as she opens the door, eyes beady. "What do *you* want?"

The giant crucifix hangs on the wall behind her: a bloody Jesus with a crown of thorns looking at me, his eyes desperate, pleading.

"I . . . I'm looking for Jasmine. Is she here?"

It's against the rules. Me coming here, to her apartment like this, but she's left me no choice. I haven't seen her or talked to her since I left the basement yesterday afternoon. She isn't answering my calls or texts. I waited for her to get off the bus down at the end of the driveway to the apartments, but the St. Christopher's bus went right by. She wasn't on it.

I fiddle with the smooth white uniform button in my pocket, a charm I hope might have the power to call her back to me.

"She's not here," Mrs. Fletcher says.

I swallow, my mouth dry. Jesus watches, waiting. "Do you know where she is?"

"If not with you, then with some other whore," she says.

I take a step back.

"The devil wears many disguises," she tells me, moving closer, her face inches from mine. She smells like sour milk and whiskey. She touches my face, pinching my cheek and pulling at my skin like it's a mask she's trying to remove. My eyes tear up and I jerk away, then turn and run back down the stairs.

"Stay away from my daughter!" she calls after me.

I HURRY AWAY from Building B, cheek stinging, and feel my phone vibrate. Pulling it out, I see a text from Jaz: Meet me in the canal.

I practically run across the parking lot. At the north side of the apartments is the big ditch where the old canal once ran, but it's been dry for over a hundred years now. I clamber down the embankment of brown grass to the bottom. Jaz and I meet here sometimes to smoke pot. Because it's so low, when you're down here, you're out of sight from the apartments—only someone standing at the edge can look down and see you. On the other side of the old canal are the train tracks. The freight trains go by twice a day. Jaz and I sometimes walk the canal all the way into the town, looking for the bodies and bones of dead animals hit by the trains. There's a surprising amount, really: rabbits, cats, even a dog once—the poor thing was missing his head.

Mr. G has a big burn pile going at the bottom of the ditch— he's dumped all the leaves he's raked on it, added a pile of old shipping pallets, a chair with a broken back, a couple of stumps. The old Canal Street Apartments sign is on the pile too, the maroon and gold paint worn away by years of sun and rain. They've replaced it with a carved granite sign that reminds me of a tombstone.

Jaz is there, sitting on the ground beside the burn pile, her legs pulled up to her chest, red hair sticking out from under her black knit hat.

I sit down next to her. "Hello, Id," I say.

She makes a funny little sound, not quite a whimper, but says nothing.

And then, because I know she'll find out soon enough, I tell her. "I was just at your place. I talked to your mom."

"You went to my apartment?" She turns to me, snarls, "What the fuck were you thinking?"

"I—I needed to see you. You weren't answering my texts or calls."

"So you go and talk to my mother?"

"I thought maybe you were there."

"You don't go to my house. I don't come to yours. We agreed."

"I know, but it's not like you left me a choice." I stare at her. "We need to talk. About yesterday. About what we're going to do."

"*Going to do?* What's there to do?" Her face is twisted, furious. "He saw us. He's probably told everyone—my mom, your grandmother, every resident here. He probably went around like the town crier: *I caught the dyke and the Catholic schoolgirl doing it.*"

My muscles tighten. A lead ball drops down into my stomach.

"Fuck," she says. She leans down, picks up a twig from the ground, and snaps it in two.

"Jaz?"

"What?"

Do I say it? Do I not say it?

What if this is it—the last time we ever talk? I'm sure Jaz is one breath away from saying we need to stay away from each other from now on, that she's done.

"I love you," I tell her, thinking maybe these three words will be enough. Enough to save us somehow.

She laughs bitterly. "Well, that's just the fucking icing on the cake."

"And I think you love me, too."

She stops laughing. Her breathing is loud and strange. "I can't do this," she whispers. "You and me—him seeing us, it—"

"I know," I say, taking her hand. "But you're wrong. You *can* do this. *We* can do this."

She jerks her hand away from mine.

I look at the burn pile. At the ruined and broken things Mr. G is going to make disappear, turn to ashes and smoke.

My eye catches on something: a flash of red like a flag under the leaves. I stand up, stepping forward, brushing aside the leaves, and pull out a red flannel shirt. It's wadded up and covered with brown paint.

No. Not paint, I realize.

Blood.

Dried blood.

I'm holding the shirt up to Jaz, and then we hear a voice from up above. "You two get away from there!" Mr. G shouts down, a big metal shovel in his hands.

I freeze, the shirt in my hands flapping in the wind like a strange flag.

"I said *go!*" he yells as he starts coming down the embankment, moving toward us fast, the shovel raised like a weapon.

I drop the shirt, follow Jaz, who's already taking off along the canal, away from Mr. G.

"Id-jit girls!" he calls.

We run and don't look back. We keep going for nearly a mile until we're out of breath and nearly all the way to the center of town.

"What was that?" she asks when we stop at last, bent over, panting. "The thing you found?"

"A shirt. A kid's shirt, I think. And it had blood on it." I look down at my hands, wipe them frantically on my jeans even though there's nothing on them.

"Are you sure it wasn't like a painting rag or something?"

"Come on," I say, pulling her forward. We climb up the embankment out of the canal, make our way to Arch Road, and turn right. Soon we're by the rec center. Kids are playing basketball on the court outside—lunging and jabbing each other with elbows, sneakers skidding on the asphalt.

I walk up the granite steps to the building and stand in front of the bulletin board.

"What are you doing?" Jaz asks over my shoulder.

I study the flyers: youth basketball league schedule, ski swap this Saturday, youth hunting safety courses. There it is: HAVE YOU SEEN EMMET? A photo of the boy: short dark hair, a gap between his two front teeth, a smattering of freckles on his nose and cheeks. Eleven years old. Last seen leaving Strafford Middle School on October 3. He was wearing blue jeans, black Converse sneakers, and a red plaid flannel shirt. Anyone with any information is asked to call the Strafford Police Department. The family is offering a reward for any information.

"It's his shirt," I say.

"What?"

"Emmet was wearing a red plaid flannel shirt," I tell her, pointing at the flyer. "Like the one I just fucking found with blood all over it."

"So what are you saying? You think Mr. G killed him?"

"I don't know. But we've gotta go back and get that shirt. It's evidence."

WE SEE THE smoke rising in a great black cloud, smell it in the air before we even get to the edge to look down. We've run all the way back, but we're too late.

There's Mr. G, a gas can by this side, a roaring fire blazing before him. Sparks fly up, ashes floating through the air, drifting slowly to the cold ground.

He looks up at us, eyes flickering with the light of the fire, his whole face red and glowing.

And I know then that he isn't going to tell anyone about what he saw down in the basement.

Because we know a secret much worse.

WE STAND IN front of apartment A-1 with the pass key. There's a big gaudy wreath of fake fall leaves with acorns and little stuffed squirrels on their door. Jaz looks at it, reaching out like she's going to pet the squirrels, then rips it down off its hook.

"Um, are you stealing their ugly-ass wreath?" I ask.

She shakes her head, eyes fixed on the door, on what the wreath was hiding.

Under it is a drawing in chalk: a circle with a symbol in the middle that reminds me of a man hanging.

"What the hell is that?" I ask.

She takes a step back. "A magic symbol I think."

"What? Like witchcraft?"

She nods.

I remember the strange design I'd seen on Mr. G's chest. A mark. A sigil.

Jaz hands me the pass key. "Open the door."

We hold perfectly still. Outside, I hear Mrs. G's wind chimes tinkling and rattling, sending out the alarm: *Intruders!*

Mr. and Mrs. G have gone to town. They go out for the early bird special at the Sirloin Stockade every Wednesday. Mrs. G gets all dressed up and Mr. G puts on clean blue slacks and a white shirt instead of his coveralls.

I unlock the door to their apartment. "Are you sure about this?" I ask.

Jaz nods, bites her lip.

I turn the knob and push the door open. There's the smell that drifts out of their open windows: smoky and bitter, vaguely poisonous.

Jaz looks down at the threshold, at a line of what looks like ash sprinkled on the other side.

"I don't like this," I say.

"Me neither."

"You go in," she tells me. "I'll stay here and be lookout. Just in case."

"Uh-uh. No way am I going in there alone."

"Five minutes," she says. "Just go, take a look around."

"What am I even looking for?"

"Like you said—evidence. Something to tie Mr. G to the missing kid. He burned the shirt. But maybe there's something else. Something we can go to the police with."

Reward, the sign promised. A reward offered for any information.

I imagine what Jaz and I could do with the money. Run away together, maybe. Buy two bus tickets to anywhere but here. Away from her batshit mom. My Gram would miss me at first, but she'd be better off without me to take care of, in the long run. Someplace far away from the Canal Street Apartments. We could get jobs waiting tables or something. Get a cheap little apartment, decorate it with thrift-store stuff. We'd be happy, Jaz and me. I know we would.

"If he killed that kid, we need to know," Jaz says.

I open the door, take a giant step over the line of ash and into the kitchen.

"Five minutes," I say.

Jaz nods, keeps the door open, looking in. "I'll be right here the whole time. Go check the living room. And their bedroom. Check the closets. All the hiding places you can find."

I nod.

"Hurry," she whispers as I make my way through the tidy kitchen and into the living room, which is cramped and dark, the shades drawn tight.

A dingy couch with no pillows or a blanket, a coffee table with nothing on it but the TV remote. There's nothing on the walls—not a single photograph or piece of art. It's like robots live here. My heart is pounding and my mouth tastes like metal. This feels all wrong.

"Anything?" Jaz calls.

"No."

"Check the bedroom."

I make my way down the hall, stopping at the bathroom, which is clean and neat and smells like menthol. I open the medicine cabinet, find a bottle of aspirin, a pack of razor blades.

I go into the bedroom.

The smell is strongest here: smoke and spice and something acrid. I let my eyes adjust to the dark, make out a tall lamp next to the bed and flick it on.

"What do you see?" Jaz calls.

"Well, there's normal bedroom stuff—a bed, a dresser, bookshelves. A little table next to the bed. There's a brass dish of ash. Incense maybe? I think that's what the smell in here is. I see jars full of weird herbs and stuff on the shelf. There's a book on the table."

It's about nine by twelve and has an old leather cover. I pick it up, open it up to the first page, where there's a handwritten title in faded sepia-colored ink: *A Guide to Whittlers and Whittling.*

"There's like a wood-carving book or something," I say. Then I flip the page and understand that was not what the book was about at all. I scan the first few pages.

My eye catches on the lines at the bottom of a page:

We are real. We are everywhere. We walk among you. We hide in plain sight. We pass as human, but oh, we are so much more.

Why are we called Whittlers? Because of what we do with the bones.

"Oh, Jesus," I say.

"What is it?" Jaz calls.

"It's a book, more like a journal, but it's . . . it's all about some kind of monster."

"Grab the book and get out of there," Jaz says.

"What? You want me to take it?"

"There's a car coming! It might be them. Come on, hurry!"

I take the book and run out of the apartment, stepping carefully over the line of ash in the doorway.

"It's them!" Jaz says, face flushed as she runs back from the front door, where she'd peered out the window. "Shit! What are they doing back so early?" She sticks the wreath back on the door, locks it, then takes my hand and leads me down the hall to the basement door. She unlocks it, then we slip in, closing the door silently behind us. We stand together in the dark on the top step, listening to Mr. and Mrs. G come in from the parking lot. They're arguing, but of course we can't understand a word of it.

I have the book held tight against my chest, my heart pounding against the pages, making it feel almost alive in my hands.

Twenty minutes later, when we haven't heard them in a long time, we sneak out of the basement stairwell. I've got the book tucked inside my sweater. We pad silently down the hall and out the back door, the one that comes out under the fire escape stairs. We loop around the building, neither of us daring to speak.

Mr. G is out front, pushing a big broom across the driveway, sweeping up dried brown leaves. It's a battle he can't win—every day he rakes and sweeps, and the next day the maples and oaks dump more, the wind blowing them everywhere.

Mr. G looks at us, his face a mix of disgust and worry.

I cross my arms over my chest, hiding the outline of the book tucked in there. But I'm sure he knows. That he can see it through my sweater, that he knows where I've been and what I've done.

"What are you up to, idjit girls?"

"Nothing, Mr. G," Jaz says. "Just going home." She turns to me. "I've got loads of homework. I'll catch you tomorrow, okay?" Her voice is chipper, un-Jaz-like.

"Sure," I say, and she turns to go, walking over to Building B.

Mr. G is staring at me, holding the rake. "And you? What are *you* going to do?"

The book seems to pulsate against my chest.

Whittlers and whittling.

Monsters who hide in plain sight.

What *am* I going to do?

Me, I'm just a girl.

A girl with secrets of her own.

A girl who loves another girl.

Maybe, I think, standing there, facing him, that makes me my own kind of monster.

I back away slowly, keeping my eyes on him. "Nothing," I say.

He smiles a sickly sort of reptilian smile, gripping the broom tighter, so tight his knuckles grow white and I can see the bones glowing under his skin. "That's right, idjit girl. You'll do nothing."

I turn and walk back to my own building, moving as fast as I can without running, feeling his eyes on my back the whole time.

I UNLOCK THE door to my apartment—D-3. Gram's there in the kitchen making homemade macaroni and cheese—my favorite. She's frying bacon to crumble on top. "Hope you're hungry," she says. I nod, smiling at her, keeping my arms crossed over my chest. "Starved. Call me when it's ready. I'm gonna go do some homework."

"Good girl," she says.

I go into my little bedroom and do something I almost never do: I lock the door. The click seems horribly loud and I hope Gram hasn't heard. I don't want to hurt her feelings. But she has a tendency to sneak up on me. For someone so old, she moves fast, is light on her feet.

I take the book out from under my sweater and go over to my bed. I lie down and open it. The book looks old, the pages thick cream-colored paper that has started to yellow at the edges. It's handwritten but looks as though more than one person has worked on it. The early parts are in flowing, ornate cursive. Then the writing is small and messy. Then it turns to calligraphy. As I flip through, my eyes catch on certain parts.

This book contains everything I know about what we are. Stories and spells and legends passed down through the generations.

To keep up its strength, a Whittler must feed monthly. Traditionally, this is done on the night of the new moon. A Whittler requires virgin blood.

The Whittler needs to keep at least one bone from each kill and turn them into a work of art. For each Whittler, this means something different. Some whittlers build birdcages, some make spoons, some create beautiful pendants and earrings. The important thing is that the Whittler keep each trophy, turn it into something beautiful, something that can be used and admired and held in plain sight of the rest of the world. It's one of the things that gives us power, helps us to walk through the human world untouched.

I stop reading and open my laptop and do a search for the missing boys in town. I write down the dates they disappeared, then open up another tab with a lunar calendar. Both Emmet Carver and Jackson Clay went missing on new moons.

"Holy shit," I say.

I text Jaz: Mr. G is a monster. An actual monster. He kills on new moons. You've gotta come see this book!

My doorknob turns and rattles.

My heart hammers.

"Dinner's ready," Gram calls through the locked door.

"Coming," I call as I stand up, hiding the book between my mattress and box spring.

I DREAM OF the bones Mr. G collected being turned into a wind chime. Finger bones, vertebrae, slices of femur; each bone whittled into beautiful shapes: a fish, a bird, a child. They bang and rattle and sing, play a song that draws me closer, makes me sleepier and sleepier like a strange lullaby. Mr. G is there beside them, smiling at me.

What are you going to do?

I turn to run, but he reaches for me, grabs me. I look down, see his own fingers have lost their flesh; they're white bones, wrapped like a shackle around my wrist. He pulls me close, his breath hot on my neck.

Jit, he says in a voice low, familiar, teasing.

I open my eyes.

"Jaz?" I mumble, rolling over.

She's crawled into bed next to me.

"How did you—"

"Pass key," she whispers into my neck.

I look at the digital clock on my nightstand: 1:28 a.m.

Jaz snuggles up against me as I tell her everything I'd read in the book tucked under my mattress.

"He's one of them," I tell her. "Maybe Mrs. G, too. We've gotta go to the police."

"With what?"

"We can bring the book. Tell them about the shirt."

"He burned the shirt. And the book proves nothing. It's just some crazy story about made-up monsters. They'll probably think we wrote it."

"So what are we supposed to do?"

Jaz is running her fingers along my shoulder, then down over my chest.

"We watch. We watch and we wait. If we watch him closely, follow him, maybe we'll find another clue. Something to tie him to the missing kids."

"Mr. G is going to wonder what happened to the book. He'll know we were in there."

"Maybe. We should hide it. Someplace he'll never find it. Away from the apartments."

"Where?"

"Meet me in the basement tomorrow after school," she says. "Bring the book. We'll take it somewhere, hide it. Figure out our next move." Her hand is moving lower now, down my belly.

I shift, pushing into her.

"You were right," she whispers, her fingers going lower, slipping inside the waistband of my pajamas.

"About what?"

"I do love you," she says, her fingers there now, right where I want them. "I can't help myself."

I'M AT SCHOOL when I hear.

Emmet Clark's body has been found.

I duck into the bathroom, lock the stall, pull out my phone, and search for the local news.

The body showed significant signs of trauma, one of the articles says, but doesn't elaborate. *Police are treating it as a homicide.*

I stagger back out into the crowded hall by the lockers, hear a boy whose dad is a cop telling a group of kids, "Yeah, his fucking right arm was cut off. Cut cleanly like with a saw or something. There's no sign of it. That's sick shit, right? We're talking about a real psycho. The FBI brought in a whole crime scene unit from D.C. The cops here, they've never seen anything like this."

I text Jaz: They found Emmet.

She doesn't respond.

School drags on forever, but at last, I'm on my way home.

As soon as I get off the bus, I run home to grab the book and go meet Jaz in the basement.

But the book isn't there. I pull my mattress all the way off the box spring and Gram comes in when she hears the commotion.

"Did you see a book? I . . . need it."

"A book? No. I haven't been in your room at all today. I actually haven't been home much—it's Thursday and we were busy at church." Every Thursday, Gram's church runs a soup kitchen and Gram's one of the primary cooks. "It's just as well that I was out—Mr. G was in here replacing the plumbing under the sink in the kitchen," she said. "I'm sure he made quite a racket."

My heart is pounding and my mouth goes dry.

I look around my room. The closet door is slightly open—I'm sure it was closed this morning. I open my drawers and see that the folded T-shirts and sweaters look like they've been disturbed.

He knows! He found the book and now he knows that I've been in his apartment. That I've learned what he is. What he's done.

What will he do to keep me from telling?

I look at my watch. Nearly four. My phone pings out a text tone. It's Jaz: I'm here. You coming?

I leave Building D and walk across the parking lot to Building B. I look up at the windows to Jaz's apartment, sure I see her mother watching, but she ducks back into the shadows. I open the door, walk into the hallway, pass the stairs, and go to the basement door at the end of the hall. I open it, turning to look behind me, having this sense that I'm being watched, followed.

I go down the old wooden stairs slowly, the smell of damp cement and ruined things hitting me. I pass the furnace with its snaking pipes, the cages full of other people's belongings, abandoned and forgotten.

Jaz is waiting on the old green velvet couch in the unit all the way in the back.

How many times have we met here like this?

It's been our safe place, a world we created outside of the normal everyday life that happens up aboveground: family and school and strange neighbors and missing boys.

Jaz has a candle lit on the trunk in front of the couch and her face is glowing, lit up. She smiles.

"It's gone," I say. I'm scared she'll be angry, think it's my fault somehow. I've lost the book.

Then, I spot it there on the trunk beside the candle.

The book.

"*You* took it?"

Was it because she didn't trust me with it?

She smiles at me. "Come here, Jit," she says, patting the couch beside her.

I go to her. It's what I do. What I've always done.

She runs her fingers through my hair. I feel my body relax as I lean in to her. I feel, as I always do with her, like I'm home.

"He's dead," I tell her. "Emmet Clark. They found his body."

"I know," she says, whispering in my ear. She's kissing my neck, sending little electric jolts that travel down through each and every nerve. I reach for her, my fingers instinctively undoing the buttons of her school blazer. She's replaced the one I took. The one I carry in my pocket every day, smooth, polished ivory.

"We've got to go to the police," I say. "Tell them what we know. I'm sure if they search Mr. G's apartment, they'll find evidence. And if we bring them the book—"

"We can't do that," she says, her lips buzzing against my neck.

She is all I ever wanted.

My Id.

Instinctual desire.

"Why not?"

"Because," she whispers, voice husky and low. "The book is mine."

She nibbles at my neck, moves up and kisses me, her mouth covering mine before I can speak, can ask the question: *What?*

"Yours?" I say, breaking away from her.

She nods.

"But Mr. G," I say. "He had the book. I found it in their apartment."

"He took it from me."

"Took if from *you?*"

"They followed me here." Her eyes seem to grow darker. "They hunted me down. They've been watching and waiting. They think they can stop me."

I look at the book on the table, at the buttons on her jacket. See that she has the same glowing, pearly white ones on her shirt, only smaller. Some look almost yellowish in the light.

Not ivory.

Bone.

I pull away. Look at her sitting beside me on the couch where we've spent so many hours lost in each other.

Everything starts to waver, flicker in the candlelight.

Nothing feels real anymore.

"You? You're the . . . Whittler?"

"Yes, love," she says, looking sadder than I've ever seen her. "It's always been me."

She reaches down behind her, grabs something wedged behind the couch cushions.

The rusty hammer from the toolbox.

I put up my hands, but it's too late.

She's already swinging.

WASTE NOT

by Alma Katsu

TODAY WAS THE day.

Jane had come prepared. Fifty-five-gallon contractor garbage bags. Cardboard boxes, carefully broken down from the last time they'd been used. Packing tape and a tape gun. Sharpies for labeling.

She'd taken a day off work for this. Her mother-in-law, Mildred, had put her off for two years, but Jane would be put off no longer. The house had been in bad shape before Frank died but it had gone downhill precipitously since. Mildred, never a fan of housework, had ignored it completely once Frank was gone. Not that Jane blamed Mildred. It was inevitable once you got to a certain age. You stopped caring about the little things. The only things that Mildred paid attention to these days were her doctor's appointments and craft shows at the senior center, where she sold her jewelry.

In her advanced years, she seemed to have developed a blindness to squalor.

Not that Kevin had been able to help. Mildred had always been a control freak, used to having her way with both Frank and her son. It had led to a testy relationship for Jane with her mother-in-law, because Mildred had expected the same from her. But there had been times when, in good conscience, Jane couldn't go along. Kevin's requests that she humor his mother grew more exasperated over the years until it had become a sore point between them.

Not that it was a problem anymore.

They'd both hoped that, now that Frank was gone, Mildred would let herself be moved into a retirement home. There was no one to coax the temperamental furnace into life the first cold snap or clear snow from the quarter-mile-long driveway. Someone in their eighties shouldn't live by themselves in these woods, where cell service was spotty and the nearest emergency responders were over twenty minutes away. However, the months came and went, and Mildred remained resolute. She told Jane on more than one occasion the only way she was going to leave this house was in a body bag.

"I'm going to start with the closet in the spare bedroom," Jane told Mildred as she swept in with her supplies. It seemed an easy choice for a place to start.

Mildred sat in her armchair, looking up at Jane with a contemptuous eye, like a stubborn, spooky horse, afraid of what lay ahead but too ornery to back up. At least she knew enough not to argue. They'd argued over this ever since Frank died. *It was well past time to clean out. No one could enjoy living like this. It was unsafe, not to mention unsanitary.*

As the possessions accumulated, her in-laws had blamed the other. Frank had gone through hard times growing up and wouldn't let anything go. Mildred had too many hobbies, each requiring a ridiculous amount of tools and supplies. Nothing was ever thrown away, everything just added to the heap. The last time Jane poked around in the basement, what she found was enough to give her shivers. Old chemicals used for Mildred's pottery glazes or to develop photographs in Frank's abandoned darkroom, acids for Mildred's jewelry. Mix the wrong two and you might produce a cloud of poisonous gas.

When she'd brought this up to Mildred—told her that she was living above a veritable powder keg—Mildred only tut-tutted and gave her a superior smile. "Waste not, want not."

And so it had come to this. The guest bedroom hadn't seen a guest in at least a decade, Jane was pretty sure. Out-of-state family stopped coming to see them after Frank grew weaker. It had become storage, boxes piled to the ceiling.

Mildred objected to Jane's involvement, asserting her right to privacy . . . Like the contents of her closet was a national secret. Jane wasn't a gossip and had no interest in the recesses of her in-laws' house, but there was no one else to save the old woman from herself. It had been dumped on her shoulders—as she always knew it would be. Kevin never could stand up to his parents, particularly his mother.

What made it funnier was that Jane never felt part of her husband's family. She'd known the Mulligans for as long as she could remember. They had been a close-knit group, in their own peculiar way, and Jane had always been an outsider. This apartness had bothered her when she was a teenager and Kevin was her first boyfriend, the first important thing that was *hers*. She'd wanted to be accepted as part of their clan, but that never happened. Like there was an invisible membrane around the three of them that she could never penetrate.

Now, however, her status as an outsider was a bit of a comfort. "You may take Frank's shoes and sweaters," Mildred had said with a sniff, when she'd finally acquiesced. "Someone may get some use out of them." On the floor of the closet were a half-dozen pairs of men's dress shoes, arranged on an old-fashioned shoe rack. Next to it was a pile of everyday shoes, all worn to the point of exhaustion.

No point pretending you could preserve a man's life forever by refusing to remove his things. Life was more than an accumulation of possessions, after all.

Jane tried to sort through the heap, but it was pointless. No one in Whitaker County would want these shoes. Mildred would demand to know where Jane was taking them—Goodwill?

Salvation Army?—but Jane could see no option but the landfill. She filled two boxes and moved them to the hall.

At the bottom of the stairs, Mildred looked up expectantly from her armchair, like a relative at the hospital expecting bad news.

Jane went back into the guest room. Her heart sank to see that the closet floor was packed with boxes. Dutifully, she hauled one out and peeled back the flaps. It held a random assortment of Frank's stuff. Stray buttons and cuff links he probably hadn't used since the eighties. Old letters bundled together with twine. Instruction manuals for household items that had stopped working a long time ago. Eyeglasses with one lens missing. All of it dusty and old and forgotten. Everywhere she looked, more neglected items pressed forward for her attention. *Look at me. Remember me.* It was dizzying and exhausting and made her sad.

The newspaper clipping caught Jane's eye because it was the only one. It had to be important. LOCAL WOMAN'S BODY FOUND IN DRUMMOND POND. When had this happened? She searched the brittle square of paper for the date, but that part was missing. This must've happened a long time ago if she hadn't heard of it. She'd ask around tomorrow at work, see if anyone knew about it.

The body of Margaret Winston was found submerged in Drummond Pond, eighteen days after she'd been reported missing by family, according to Rochester police. Winston, of 51 Stone Bridge Hill . . .

Two doors down. That's why Frank saved the newspaper clipping. The dead woman had been a neighbor.

Jane set it beside the tape gun. She would definitely ask about it when she went back tomorrow.

She turned to the closet. The rod was packed full to bursting. She pulled out the heaviest-looking items first. Old sport coats, furred with dust on the shoulders, colors and styles that had been popular before the turn of the century. Her heart sank again; no one would want these except maybe a theatrical costume department.

Nothing to do but pack it up. The more clothing she took off hangers, the more seemed to spring forward. There was a never-ending supply, like the brooms in *The Sorcerer's Apprentice*.

A half-hour later, Jane decided to take a break. She started carrying boxes downstairs, stacking them by the front door to take out to the truck.

Mildred looked over from her chair, still clutching the arm-rests like an unhappy monarch on her throne. "Are you almost done, dear?"

"Not hardly." She started back upstairs, then remembered the clipping. "Say, do you know anything about a woman down the street who was found dead? Margaret Winston? She would've been your neighbor. Did you know her?"

Her mother-in-law looked wistful. "Margaret Winston. There's a name I haven't heard in a long time. Why do you ask?"

Jane told her about the clipping.

Mildred frowned, as she did when she was displeased, which was an awful lot of the time. "I thought I said you could take the shoes and sweaters, nothing else. I don't know that I like the idea of you poking around in Frank's things."

"We've been through this. You need"—*You need to face reality* was on the tip of her tongue but was too harsh to say to a woman watching as the last traces of her husband were being boxed up and taken away—"to make some space. Think what you can do with that closet once it's cleared. You can move your jewelry supplies in there."

Mildred averted her eyes. No one could force her to see what she didn't want to.

Jane went back to work. She pulled piece after piece of clothing off wire hangers and dropped them into boxes. It should all go in trash bags, but she would spare Mildred's feelings by pretending it was all going to a donation center.

Button-down shirts. There had to be dozens of them, most of them old, frayed, and yellowed at the collars, exuding a dusty, sour smell. Her family had shopped at Frank's grocery store her entire life, and she remembered seeing Frank in these button-down shirts under his canvas apron. Later, he switched to polo shirts. Undoubtedly, she'd find a vein of those in the closet or maybe in a chest of drawers.

Why had Frank saved each and every shirt he'd ever owned? *Waste not*, she heard in Mildred's smug tone. Her mother-in-law probably thought she'd cut them into rags or use them in a quilt one day.

Jane pulled the shirts off hangers, one by one, and dumped them in a box, too.

Then she saw it: one of Frank's old shirts spattered with brick-red stains.

Blood.

She paused. Well—Frank had worked in a grocery. Maybe he'd gotten too close to the butcher one day.

She started to take it off the hanger.

That explanation wasn't right. Didn't fit the blood splatter pattern.

She held the shirt up. The longer she looked at it, the more uneasy she felt.

She folded it brusquely and dropped it into the box with the others.

She worked for another half-hour, then went downstairs for a glass of iced tea. Mildred sat at the table, watching her drink.

"I remember that woman you asked about. Winston. The family sold the house and moved away not too long after. Young couple. One young child, a son, I believe." Mildred rubbed her swollen knuckles. "I never liked her, to tell the truth. She was pretty, but flirty. Flirted with all the men in the neighborhood. I think her husband despaired of her."

Jane pictured a young woman in capris and sunglasses. Maybe she'd flirted with a young Frank at a neighborhood barbecue, cementing Mildred's opinion of her.

Jane finished her drink put the glass in the sink. "Did they ever solve the case? Find the murderer?"

Mildred turned her gaze on her daughter-in-law like she was seeing her for the first time. "When did you become fascinated with such unpleasant things? You weren't like this from when you and Kevin were dating."

"What? No, I was just wondering—"

"It's not normal. It's morbid. I don't like to talk about such morbid things. Besides, you're not at work, you know. This is your day off." Before Jane could say a word, Mildred changed topics. "No, they never solved it. You know the sheriff's office in this town, they never figure out anything. They're just useless."

Jane bit her tongue. What she wouldn't give, at times, to be able to walk away from her mother-in-law.

Instead, she headed back upstairs.

Her job had been a long-standing sore point with her in-laws. They were disappointed when she announced she wanted a career; they'd imagined she'd stay home and raise Kevin's children. Only there had been no children. The reason was obvious: unhappy children tend not to want children of their own. Jane could admit to her own unhappy childhood, but it was up to Kevin to take ownership of his, and it had looked like he never was going to do that.

Was never going to admit it to his parents, in any case.

Then came the accident, and it wasn't an issue anymore.

Jane shut the door and pulled out her phone. Punched one button. Speed dial.

A pleasant voice answered. "Rochester sheriff's department."

"Carolyn? It's Jane."

"Hi, Jane. Now, why are you calling? Aren't you off today?"

Jane turned her back to the door; Mildred pretended to be deafer than she was. "I need a favor. Can you go into the archives and see if you can find any files on a murder that took place in, oh, the 1970s, I'd guess. The victim's name was Margaret Winston."

There was a pause on the other end as Carolyn wrote. "Sure . . . That's an awfully long time ago. What made you think about it?"

Jane skipped over her question. "If you find the files, can you leave them in my office?" She was the only detective on the team. Rochester was so small, it hardly needed more than one.

"Sure thing. Don't work too hard, now." Everyone in the office knew about Jane's in-laws, guessed what a burden Mildred might be, especially after Kevin's death. "You know, the sheriff would be okay with it if you wanted a few more days. You barely took any time off after . . . you know."

"I'm fine."

"It's just . . . You got a lot on your plate. We're thinking about you, is all."

"It's better if I keep busy." She was used to deflecting their concern. This wasn't the first time.

Jane went back to the closet, filling five more boxes before the phone rang. It was Carolyn. "Found those files you wanted. They're on your desk."

THE BOXES NEARLY filled the back of Jane's truck. There was room for a couple more, but Jane was anxious to duck into the office and take a look at those files.

Maybe everyone was right. Maybe she was a bit of a worka-holic. Kevin hadn't liked that she worked so hard, but he'd given up lecturing her, the same way he'd given up trying to get his parents to get rid of their junk.

Right now she needed a break from this house and her mother-in-law. Then there was her husband's ghost hovering in the corners, silently asking her not to do this. "I'll be back after I drop these off at Goodwill," she called out to Mildred as she left, jingling her car keys. As she drove away, she fantasized about locking her mother-in-law inside her house and throw-ing away the key.

It was right before lunch, so the office was mostly deserted. Police officers in Rochester took lunchtime seriously, spending the hour in one of the local diners. Jane was grateful for this; she didn't want to get a lot of ribbing for coming in on her day off.

For using her job to avoid addressing her grief.

She just wanted to satisfy her curiosity.

The files were sizable. Someone had put a lot of work into the case. She started with the most recent, two decades old. Nope, it had never been solved (*No surprise*, Mildred would say). She pulled out the earliest file and started skimming through the reports, the initial missing person report, inter-views, calls to surrounding sheriff departments. They had to do a lot of legwork in those days without technology, but that made it easy to cut corners. To overlook something. She had no doubt there was something useful buried in these notes.

Then there was the dirty little secret that the police didn't talk about: Some officers were better than others. Smarter, more conscientious, more dogged. Whether or not a killer was found and justice served often came down to luck of the draw.

Her eye skimmed over the pages until it hit on something she didn't even know she was looking for. *Frank Mulligan.*

Frank's name was mentioned in one of the reports.

She backed up a few paragraphs. It was an interview with Margaret Winston's husband, Dan. The husband was always a suspect in any case that involved his wife. Investigators would circle back, over and over, hoping to catch him in a lie. Dan Winston seemed to know this. On the page, he read as bitter. Bitter that the police hadn't found anything and that they kept coming back to him.

Dan Winston insisted that police speak to Frank Mulligan. Winston says Mildred Mulligan developed a grudge against Margaret and accused Mildred Mulligan of harassment: letting her dog relieve itself on the Winstons' lawn, etc. Winston claims Frank Mulligan had become belligerent and threatening . . .

Frank? Jane could see it. He could be difficult at times—hell, *most* of the time, a tendency hardened by years in retail, tired of trying to make customers happy. His patience had worn thin long before Jane married Kevin. She'd never liked to spend much time at the Mulligans' house when they were teenagers.

Winston says the dispute began over a lawn ornament, a brown ceramic owl which the Winstons purchased on vacation in Mexico several years before moving to the present address. Winston claims Mildred Mulligan coveted the owl. The lawn ornament went missing several months before Mrs. Winston's disappearance and Dan Winston believes the Mulligans are responsible.

The pettiness made Jane's head ache. It was so common in these rural communities where grudges festered like the Hatfields versus the McCoys. Except in this case, a woman had gone missing and was later dragged out of a lake. Jane flipped a few pages ahead. No indication that the police officer had followed up on Dan Winston's claim, and why would he? Frank Mulligan was a native to Whitfield County. He wouldn't open his own business and become a pillar of the community for a few years, but still, everybody knew him. Whereas Dan and Margaret Winston were newcomers. If somebody complained about a neighbor stealing a lawn ornament, the local cops weren't likely to do anything about it unless the suspect was known to be difficult.

Had she ever seen a brown ceramic owl around Mildred and Frank's house? The place always had been a jumble, the parents' tendencies evident even before hoarding was identified as a disorder. A collection of tacky lawn ornaments and planters sat clustered outside the cellar door for as long as Jane could remember. She could check them out this afternoon when she finished with the closet . . .

Wait a minute. Did she really think Kevin's parents had stolen a piece of pottery off a neighbor's lawn?

It seemed so unlikely.

Or did it? She packed the files in her tote bag to take home. She would read them after dinner.

JANE FINISHED WITH the closet after lunch. Nearly twenty boxes in all. As she drove away, she thought about how she'd deal with this avalanche of unwanted stuff. Whitfield County had few charity centers. Any thrift shop would find most of Frank's stuff unsuitable for resale.

That night, Jane started a fire in the pit she and Kevin used to burn trash. That was one convenience living in the country: You could pretty much do what you wanted on your own property, including burning a load of trash. No need to make the hour-long trip to the landfill. Mildred would be appalled if she ever found out that Jane had burned Frank's things, but Jane didn't feel guilty in the least.

She leaned on a long stick and watched the flames. It wasn't as straightforward as she'd imagined. Older clothes were mainly synthetic. Polyester and rayon. Instead of burning, they melted into a thin black shell. She poked at the pile until the flames leapt up, and then brought out the box of old button-down shirts. She began feeding them to the fire one by one. These were mostly cotton and would burn quickly. The collars were in the worst shape, yellowed and threadbare. Frank had been a hard worker, she'd give him that, putting in long hours at the store. He'd been disappointed when Kevin refused to follow him into the business, and ended up working almost to the day he died. "He never would've left," Kevin had said when he'd told Jane of his decision. They'd been in their thirties at the time. "I'd never get to run the store myself, run it my way."

She gave him credit for seeing that. She'd always known Kevin's parents would depend on him, an only child, and he'd seemed to accept it. She didn't blame him for not being more independent. He hadn't been a bad partner. He'd supported her decision not to have children and again when she joined the police force. His parents had been particularly opposed to the latter. "It's just not like you," Mildred said over and over at the time, as though repeating it would make it true. "All that unpleasantness. So tawdry. You don't really want to know what your neighbors are getting up to, do you?" Jane didn't entirely disagree, but jobs were limited in Whitfield County and it was one of the few with any kind of career progression. "If I'd known you were going to do this one day, I don't know that I would've approved of your marrying our Kevin," Mildred had said with her customary humorless chuckle.

Jane put in her application the next day.

She tossed another shirt on the flames. The sleeve rippled as the fire gave it life, like it was waving goodbye. Was it unlucky to burn Frank's clothes? she wondered. A superstitious person would say it might rile Frank's or Kevin's spirit, or release something that had been trapped in those fibers. She had to admit, looking down at the fire, that it felt a bit like she was doing something wrong. Like she was burning evidence she didn't want anyone to see.

Nonsense. She took the stick and stirred the embers.

She reached into the box and pulled out the next shirt.

It was the bloodstained one.

Light from the bonfire danced over it. The wind tugged at it in her hand, trying to take it away from her.

If she dropped it into the flames now, it would be over. Like she'd never found it.

She knew what Kevin would want her to do. But he wasn't here. It wasn't his decision.

After a moment's hesitation, she dropped it back into the box behind her, safe from the flames.

THE NEXT DAY at the station, Jane handed the shirt to a forensic technician. The sheriff's office did not have a technician, of course, but a man came down weekly from state police headquarters to pick up evidence and drop off reports.

She gave him the shirt in a plastic evidence bag. "See what you can tell me about this?"

He eyed it dubiously. "Looks pretty old."

"Cold case. I just came across it." That was true enough.

"Best I can probably do is blood type—if it's human."

"That'll be enough."

"Do you have a sample for the match?" He wanted a sample of the suspected victim's blood to match it against, but of course she didn't have that. Margaret Winston had been buried a long time ago.

This would put the whole thing to rest. Make things okay again with Mildred. Make Jane less resentful, less impatient with a difficult old lady.

She shook her head. "Blood type will be enough, thanks."

SUNDAY SHE WAS back at Mildred's house with boxes and trash bags. Her mother-in-law didn't want to let her in, but Jane didn't care. "It's a fire hazard," she said as she pushed her way in. "I can't in good conscience let you live under these conditions."

Mildred followed at Jane's heels. "If Kevin were alive, he wouldn't let you treat me like this."

If Kevin were alive. The deputies who'd arrived on the scene that night told her it was an accident. *Late night, slippery road. He lost control.* She'd suspected that they were trying to spare her. Kevin—always a little sad, always a little guarded—had changed after his father's death. Became deeply depressed. Refused to see a doctor.

In the months since Kevin's death, Jane wondered why he'd done it. She wondered, too, how much of it was her fault. If they should've had children. If she should've done things differently. If there had been anything that would've made him happy.

She suspected not.

Unhappy children grew into unhappy adults. Another reason she resented Kevin's parents. It might've even been safe to say she *hated* them for how they'd failed their son.

After Jane finished loading her truck, she went around to the back of the house. There, in front of the cellar door, was the collection of garden debris, planters and cherub statues made of cast concrete, glass bell jars for the garden. Each piece thick with dust and dirt, untouched for decades, except for the weather.

There was no brown ceramic owl. Jane wasn't sure if she was relieved or disappointed.

JANE WENT TO her mother-in-law's house every day after work. She wasn't sure what she was looking for. She told herself that she was helping the old woman, taking care of something that should've been done a long time ago. Being the dutiful daughter-in-law that she was supposed to be.

She couldn't lie to herself, however. Behind it was a niggling suspicion that she would find something—a clue to another crime buried in all that junk.

Or she was driving herself crazy, looking for a misdeed where none existed.

She couldn't ignore the feeling she got from that bloodstained shirt, however.

The forensic technician called a week later. "It was human blood, all right. Type AB negative."

Jane didn't need to check the case files. She had memorized the medical examiner's report.

Margaret Winston was AB negative. The rarest of blood types.

IT WAS TIME to tackle the basement. There could be evidence of a dozen crimes hidden in the rubbish down there. God only knew how long it had been since the furnace had been serviced. Mildred had complained it was already acting up and it wasn't even the start of cold weather. At the very least, for safety's sake, Jane needed to clear a path to the furnace.

As she chipped away at the sea of rubbish, she realized it would take a dump truck to haul away all this stuff. And that was *if* Mildred would even let her. The old woman's whining got worse every day. She threatened to change the locks or have her nephew come down from New York to stay with her. To keep Jane away, was more like it.

It was only a matter of time.

Boxes were stacked everywhere in the basement, on shelves, three-deep on the floor. Most held discarded supplies from the grocery store or Mildred's old craft projects. But Jane saw potential evidence, too. Decades of bills and receipts. Road maps from family car trips taken in the 1980s. Seemingly every letter

Mildred or Frank had ever received. So much dry kindling next to those volatile old chemicals.

Mildred came to the top of the stairs every hour, wringing her hands and demanding that Jane leave. She didn't want Jane's help. Insisted that Jane wasn't helping.

Jane had just cleared a path to the furnace when she saw it sitting incongruously behind the furnace in a dark space that no light reached. The ceramic owl. Mildred had kept it like a trophy. Couldn't get rid of it, even though it was evidence. Or maybe the decision to keep it had been Frank's. Jane recognized it from the police record, where it had sat innocently in the background of a photograph of Margaret that Dan Winston had given to police.

"Why?" Jane hadn't heard Mildred come down the stairs. She hadn't thought the old woman capable of navigating those rickety steps. "Why couldn't you wait until I was gone? Then you could tear the house apart all you wanted." Mildred's rheumy eyes blazed now. "It wasn't like we didn't think you'd find out one day. You're the reason that Kevin is dead, you know that, don't you? Once you joined the police force, he knew you'd find out eventually. He was so upset, but he couldn't persuade you *not* to. Because you couldn't be normal. Because you can't leave well enough alone."

I'm not the reason he killed himself, she wanted to say. *He killed himself because he knew what you'd done. That you weren't normal.*

"We tried to talk Kevin out of marrying you. We told him you weren't like us, that you wouldn't listen. You wouldn't put family first . . . You were so *selfish.* But it was too late. You'd snared him by then, gotten your claws into him. My poor boy."

There was such hate in the woman's face. Jane could almost say she'd never seen it before, but that wasn't true. It had always been there, just under the surface.

"I'm not going to let you destroy this family's reputation." The old woman bared her teeth like a dog and threw herself at Jane, tiny fists flailing. She fell—that wasn't entirely true; Jane had stepped aside when the old woman lunged for her, but maybe a little push was involved too. Something she'd wanted to do for years. Mildred fell behind the furnace, beside the ceramic owl. She struggled, floundering to get up.

Jane rushed up the stairs and out of the basement, her head a jumble of thoughts.

. . . *If Mildred didn't confess, she would never be convicted. At best, she was an accessory.*

. . . *Even if the judge thought she was guilty, they'd never send a woman her age to jail.*

. . . *What else was hidden in the trash?*

. . . *Kevin would hate to see his parents' names dragged through the mud.*

. . . *Kevin had known and couldn't bear the idea of me knowing too.*

. . . *Places like this are firetraps.*

She'd heard a woman in Baker had died in a house fire, trapped behind her husband's junk. The husband had gone insane with grief afterward.

She was pretty sure Mildred would choose death over dishonor.

There was a box of matches on the mantel.

They lit so easily, like they had been waiting for someone to strike them.

The strange thing was—as Jane closed and locked the door behind her, the crackle of flames rising like a Greek chorus, affirming her decision—she'd never felt closer to Kevin's family than she did at that moment.

She was almost one of them now.

NIGHT SHOPPER

by Michael H. Hanson

Mother of Otherness, Eat me.
—Sylvia Plath

S KATHI WOKE IN the early afternoon to the pulsing notes of mind.in.a.box's "Unforgiving World" bleeding from her radio alarm clock.

It looked like another day of ridiculous bragging and petty complaining on InstaBag's Shopper Reddit page, certainly nothing new to Skathi, as she had been accessing this website for at least five years. The economy had dropped through the floor half a decade ago ever since the first of the seven successive Covid outbreaks, which cost Skathi her cushy desk job in Denver and had her immediately applying for Medicaid to cover costly medical bills. With the sudden drop in available middle-class jobs, Insta-Bag's delivery service was one of the few unskilled wellsprings of available work that thousands of local laid-off office jockeys like Skathi had scrambled toward. And seeing as the totality of her vocational training consisted of nothing more than a bachelor's degree in ontology and a master's degree in noetic theory, she was lucky to get this stint.

"*I work quite diligently and wish that I were better and smarter. And these both are one and the same,*" Skathi thought with a smile. *You certainly got that right, Mr. Wittgenstein.*

As usual, she started her workday late in the afternoon to see if anything new had popped up in the biz.

The Reddit posts crawled up Skathi's computer screen like the insistent wails of Colorado's literary finest.

Sprint-n-Grab: "Christ, I hate Sprigs. Those fuckers can't keep their frigging shelves stocked. They never have canned peaches. Don't start me on their shitty produce section with its spoilt lettuce!"

Casual-Spendthrift: "Killed it today! Forty items from just two aisles at Krogers and a thirty-dollar tip. Hoo-Rah!"

Finger-Sticking-Good: "Asshole gave Minimal Tip! Mother-fucker lives over twenty miles away, and I had to hit two separate stores to get her shit, and she gives me a microscopic tip! Is my name Ben Dover?"

Kristin-Stewarts-Taint: "InstaBag cut our profit margin again? The third time in five god damned years! Christ on a crutch if this ain't the next best thing to slavery!"

Smash-N-Bag: "That's right MoFos! I just cracked it on the Boulder County Total Speed Leaderboard yesterday! Read my stats and weep you fucking pussies!"

And so on, and so forth.

It was shaping up to be another steady night on the road as Skathi prepped a quick microwave meal of chicken and rice for herself, and a large bowl of raw ground chicken and bone for her apartment roommate, Maxine, a fifteen-year-old Maine coon house cat, a small monster that was over three feet in length nose to tail and weighed fourteen pounds even. They both wolfed their food down.

"You know, Maxine," Skathi said to her cat, "it's clear Hume was right on the money when he said 'Custom is the great guide to human life.'"

THE SUN HAD gone down two hours earlier when Skathi got a New Batch Available alert on her iPhone. A special order from one of her regulars on a back road in Lafayette. Hustling out the door to her well-lit parking lot, she smiled at her ride. Skathi drove a vehicle that was both famous and infamous across Boulder County. Reaching for the door handle, she took in the sleek lines of the 1970 Plymouth Satellite she had spent over three months plating with rusted sheets of ochre-colored steel. At first glance, onlookers might think the car was a prop from a *Mad Max* film, but second closer looks took in the large number of different-sized, rusted industrial gears, at least three of them two feet in diameter, welded all over the exterior. With all this plus a working World War I trench periscope sticking out of the roof, and a small, solid bronze dirigible hood ornament, this tribute to the steampunk oeuvre was definitely a ride that no one could ever forget.

Pulling out of the parking lot, she slid in a CD containing her latest mix of drive music. Mary Lambert's "Secrets," an oldie but a goodie, started playing.

The first store Skathi hit in a dark corner of Louisville was one of several that she usually shopped at that were not on Insta-Bag's official approved list of purchase locations. It was far from off-limits, though, as Skathi had properly vetted the store after filling out four separate tedious online forms with the establishment's official contact phone number, email address, business tax number, and bank routing numbers. This was something she had done nearly a dozen times over the last two and a half years for a number of shady businesses, and it had opened the door to a steady stream of much-needed income that she never took for granted.

The building, which had no sign but whose customers called the Open Vein, was on the outskirts of Louisville, set among the ruins of some long-abandoned warehouses and the remaining foundations of a demolished canning factory. It was basically an ugly, two-story cement block with blackout windows and a single front door made of bulletproof glass and iron bars. Buzzed inside, Skathi quickly went to the rear refrigerator cabinets, snapped up five sealed plastic bags of product, and carried them to the cash register, where she immediately scanned them with her iPhone's IB app before dropping them off on the checkout counter for purchase.

Ten minutes later, about halfway through Mika's "Grace Kelly" blaring out of the rear speakers, Skathi turned off of Baseline Road in Lafayette onto an unnamed dirt road, which she followed for several hundred yards before it ended at a brand-new, beautiful custom cedar cabana home with two old-fashioned oil lamps hanging on either side of the large front door.

Skathi exited her vehicle and approached the front stoop. The evening had gotten cold quickly, and with her kicks, blue jeans, and a stylish Irish wool cardigan sweater she wore a green and blue silk and wool hijab to keep her head warm. It was the perfect attire for a chilly autumn night in Colorado. She pushed the doorbell button that formed the nose of the surrounding carving of a European lynx.

The door opened slowly, revealing a shadowed figure wrapped in a thick black robe.

"Here's your Golden," Skathi said with a smile, handing over five swishy plastic bags, "my UV-challenged friend."

"Cute as always," a deep male voice replied, taking the items and dropping a large wad of cash into Skathi's extended hand. "And here's a little something extra for you . . . off the books."

"I feel guilty you give me such lavish tips, Mr. Tepes."

"Nonsense, my dear," he replied, only his dark piercing eyes coming into focus in the darkness just inside the front door. "Reliable delivery on such short notice is priceless. Now, before you leave, you owe me a philosophical quote, young lady."

"We are asleep. Our Life is a dream. But we wake up sometimes, just enough to know that we are dreaming," Skathi recited. "Ludwig Wittgenstein."

"Wonderful," Mr. Tepes said. "You are a jewel in the night, Skathi."

"Well, thank you again," Skathi said as she started to turn away, "and please feel free to ask for me at any hour via the InstaBag website. I aim to please! Good night."

"Noapte bună!"

BY THE TIME she got back to the car, another three New Batch Available alerts scrolled across her iPhone, and she quickly calculated distance, available stores, the number of product items for each order, and the promised tip. In seconds, she accepted all three orders and accelerated her car back toward the streetlights of Lafayette. The sorrowful soft notes of Wolf Alice's "Blush" blared loudly and Skathi started singing along with it.

Five minutes later, an SUV full of obviously drunken male teenagers, probably seniors, pulled out onto a mostly empty South Boulder Road and came abreast of Skathi. Hanging out the two passenger-side windows, the two boys, jocks from the look of them, one white and one Black, started shouting.

"Hey, sweetness," the white one yelled, "ditch that piece of crap and hop into this prime real estate."

"Come on, babe," the other shouted. "It's cool you're a Muslim. We're not prejudiced."

Skathi was annoyed but did her best to look straight ahead and not give these children the time of day. True, she was only about ten years older than them, but their actions made that gap feel like one hundred years. The SUV pulled alarmingly closer to her. The white kid with red hair and pale skin suddenly frowned, then his jaw dropped and his eyes went wide.

"Oh shit," he yelled. "Dudes, it's a guy in drag! This ain't no chick."

"No way," the Black teenager shouted, "and he's white. Ain't no Muslim at all. What's up man, slumming on the main strip."

Pulling up close to a traffic light that just turned yellow, Skathi slammed on the brakes and watched the truck full of bozos continue through and beyond while she waited at the red light. She breathed deep and let it out slowly.

The world of the happy is quite different from the world of the unhappy, Skathi thought.

She'd dealt with worse over the past year as a trans woman since she'd started the estrogen treatments and began wearing makeup, a wig, and women's clothing semi-regularly.

More often than not, though, she was generally met with either indifference or simple curiosity in the vicinity of other people. It was usually just the occasional young man who hassled her. As for her regular Night Clients, they were surprisingly empathetic to her ongoing outward transformation, something that had originally surprised her and became a more welcome aspect of her job with each coming evening. Kristeen Young's "Pearl of a Girl" started playing, and Skathi bobbed her head to the solid beat.

THE NEXT STOP for Skathi was the meat department at Kroger in Boulder, where she picked up ten pounds of the warmest and freshest cut beef around. Ten minutes later, she pulled off onto a steep uphill fire road near the base of the far right of the Flat Irons as she sang along with the upbeat strains of Katy Perry's "Firework." Swerving back and forth around several species of deciduous trees, she eventually reached a decent-sized parking area (big enough to hold eight cars) situated right in front of a ten-foot-high cave whose front was an arch-shaped Victorian wall with red brick and front-facing gables laden with delicate vergeboards.

Skathi grabbed the door knocker, which was a wrought-iron sculpture of a sheep's head, and pounded on solid oak for a full ten seconds. The door swung inward without notice, and a shadowed figure of a tall, slender woman with beautiful auburn hair that hung down to her knees stood in the doorway.

"Freshly chopped from the shop," Skathi said with a smile as she handed the two large bags over, "dripping with juices as requested, Mrs. Neuri."

"Meeting all the lupine standards, eh, Skathi," Neuri replied. "Now spill it. You know you're dying to tell me a new one."

"What did one shepherd say to the other after seeing a wolf in the distance?" Skathi asked.

"I give up, what?"

"Let's get the flock out of here."

Mrs. Neuri's deep, resonating laughter made the hair stand up on the back of Skathi's neck, but she joined in for a few chuckles anyway. The client shoved a small roll of tens into Skathi's hand and backed into the shadows.

"That's really too much for a tip, Mrs. Neuri . . ."

"No, I insist," she replied, "besides, winter is coming, and I demand you replace those horrible bald tires immediately. You promise, young lady?"

Skathi smiled and shook her head. "Okay, okay, I promise. Take care."

Mrs. Neuri flashed a wide grin that displayed a mouthful of bright white and rather sharp-looking teeth before slowly closing her door.

DRIVING DOWN 287 in Lafayette and swaying to the mournful strains of Motorpsycho's "This Otherness" at eleven p.m., Skathi spotted a familiar-looking SUV barreling north on South Boulder Road.

Probably not those schmucks, she pondered, so no need to start feeling paranoid. And if it is them, they'll probably get bored and tired of cruising the streets soon enough. As far as she knew, there had not been an official reported attack on a trans or nonbinary person in the surrounding county in a few years, the operative word of course being *reported*. Rumors occasionally arose about the odd incident, but people's privacy, desire to stay in the closet, and fear of reprisal left what some suspected to the imagination. Denver, though, was a whole other story, and yeah, she had a good trans female friend who was brutally beaten by some thugs down there just a few months ago. Dana had recovered physically, but she was now more of a shut-in than ever. Skathi knew that she had to keep her own guard up at night.

Ten minutes later, Skathi pulled over and parked on the side of Coal Creek Drive next to Founders Park, an area poorly lit by streetlamps. She exited her rusty car and walked without hesitation directly to the central playground. It was abandoned this late at night of course, and she quickly made her way to the nearest of the two rockpile sculptures that anchored either side of a small rope monkey bridge. Skathi placed her right palm on the darkest of the sculpted stones that made up this façade, and a bright flash of light instantly surrounded the outline of her palm and fingers. A three-foot-high and two-foot-wide opening appeared in the rock face.

"In for a dime," Skathi said, dropping to her hands and knees and entering the darkness, "in for a dollar."

After crawling for about fifty feet (yes, the inside, like the TARDIS on *Doctor Who*, was substantially larger than the exterior could ever explain), Skathi stood up after entering a large domed circular room filled with all manner of stalls and tables on the periphery, thirty or more altogether. Each display had colorful silk and cotton banners and draping, showing off a wide variety of eclectic items. Oil lamps burning powdered oak, pine, and Irish clover incense hung from the ceiling. There didn't appear to be any other customers inside, which was always the odd case whenever she shopped at the Seelie Court Extension.

"Oh, you saw it all, Ludwig. It is not how things are in the world that is mystical," she whispered, "but *that* it exists."

Skathi walked right up to a table festooned with bright yellow and red flowers.

"Hey, Prankster Pete," Skathi said to the handsome, sinewy blond man behind the counter whose face was covered with tattoos of leaves and vines. "Here for the usual."

"Welcome back to this branch of the Summer Court, Skathi," Pete said with a shy grin, "and I've got your stash right here."

Skathi grabbed the tied-off burlap sack, used her iPhone to scan the code on the small price tag, and handed it back.

"I'll take it," she said, and handed over her InstaBag credit card, which was quickly scanned by Pete.

"You know," Pete said slyly as the paper receipt was ejected, "that offer of a date to the Shining Throne is still good, sweet cheeks."

Skathi rolled her green eyes. "You never give up, do you, Prankster? I'd think one of the Golden Ones had better things to do than troll for mere mortals to escort."

"Ohhh, we both know there is nothing merely mortal about you, Skathi," Pete said with a grin. "You are so much more than you appear, my dear."

Skathi snapped up the gunnysack and the large tip, winked at Pete, turned around, and walked quickly back to the diminutive tunnel that led the way back to the real world.

"Beannachd leat an tè ghealach agam!" Pete shouted at her back.

SKATHI FLOORED IT to her next client in Gold Hill, bouncing in her seat to the deep growling vocals of Mr. Cräbs's "Metamorphosis." Rumors abounded lately that InstaBag wanted to trim its shoppers, and she always took every effort to meet her speed goals and not give the company any excuse to drop her. This meant the occasional pullover by the cops for speeding, but Skathi had gotten pretty good at finding side streets to bypass most patrolling officers and speed traps. There was a downside to Skathi's diligence, however, and it was that her recent success at piling up well-paying Night Clients who kept asking for her services exclusively had created a temporary rift between her and all the other Boulder County InstaBagger shoppers, which currently numbered three hundred and eighty-six, but fluctuated over the past few years, once dropping to a mere two hundred, and near the beginning of the first Covid outbreak had reached six hundred.

This exclusive client list had allowed her to climb right to the top of the Boulder Total Speed Leaderboard for six weeks when it came to rank, shopper, and speed. A wildcat strike among jealous local shoppers was on the verge of happening when Skathi came up with the enlightened idea of a handicap system, one which downed her stats to more closely approximate that of her fellow shoppers. Two weeks later and things were mostly back to normal as Skathi found herself regularly sharing top rankings on the Speed Leaderboard with several others.

Standing before the gilded door of a mini-mansion, Skathi handed the heavy gunnysack over to the height-challenged, golden-haired individual with pale green skin.

"Pitcairn honey?" he asked in a mellifluous Welsh accent.

"Only the best for you, Mr. Teg."

"Priodi fi un hardd!"

"I'm currently off the market, Mr. Teg." Skathi smiled. "But I'll keep it in mind."

Mr. Teg shoved a small wad of bills at Skathi with a wide grin.

"I like your lapis lazuli eye shade, Skathi," Mr. Teg said. "It reminds me of the enchanted lake of Eire."

"Diolch yn fawr iawn," she replied.

Skathi pocketed the large tip, waved goodbye, and walked away.

BY 11:10 P.M., Skathi had made two more sets of purchases at odd locations from even odder establishments on mostly untraveled back roads in Boulder County. Afterward, she quickly dropped off a Baku pelt to a Mr. Andy Meonn in the ritzy Mapleton Street neighborhood of Boulder, and two weeks' worth of an esoteric Nigerian stew containing bat meat, dog meat, cow brain, locusts, winged termites, grasscutter feces, grasshoppers, crickets, and African palm weevils to a Ms. Alexandra Aja, who lived in a huge, elaborate all-weather Yurt bordering Arapahoe Ridge Park.

Back on South Boulder Road and listening to the soothing vibes from Assemblage 23's "Otherness," Skathi smiled, remembering Mr. Teg's comments on her makeup. Unfortunately, this brought to mind the latest set of YouTube and Twitter posts she had read by that jackass transmedia influencer Counterplots, who went on a harangue last night that all true trans people must not only come out of the closet the moment they realize who and what they are, but must also immediately commit to *passing*. While Skathi felt comfortable at this stage in her existence to dress and wear makeup that complement her true inner womanhood, she knew many others were struggling with the transition and deserved sympathy, not condemnation, for how they presently chose to present themselves to the outside world.

"How did you put it, Ludwig?" Skathi asked herself. "Nothing is so difficult as not deceiving oneself."

Skathi chuckled. Her Night Clients, as strange as they were, never seemed to have the trouble that her cisgender customers, acquaintances, family, and friends did in remembering to refer to her by her transgender identity and its accompanying pronouns. Closeted in their own way, her customers seemed to have an innate empathy for the fear, nervousness, and, well, *otherness* that Skathi had felt every day of her life since she realized several years ago that she was a woman born in a man's body.

Though she was probably now only a year or two away from sex reassignment surgery, the effect of coming out, as painful, stressful, and tumultuous as it was, became a catharsis that flooded her heart and soul with self-love. Realizing the truth of herself was akin to being blind and given the gift of sight. It gave her a bright, even brilliant, reality, where before she had stumbled across sidewalks of gray twilight and shadow. Sure, she still had the same daily problems that all people did, but now she no longer felt the push and pull, the contradiction, of perceived personality versus true personality. She was truly *herself.*

Skathi pushed all these thoughts aside as urgent pressure in her bladder had her pulling into the rear parking lot of the Shell Station just as the opening lyrics of "Salome" by Marriages bled from the back speakers.

A few minutes later, after taking care of business and touching up her makeup, Skathi exited the ladies' room on the poorly lit back side of the gas station and walked right into a solid punch to her right cheek that nearly knocked her off her feet. Her head felt like it was just stung by a hundred bees.

"Nice shot, Samuel," a male voice shouted out. "Lemme show you how it's done, Bruce Lee–style."

Skathi looked up in time to see it was the four teenagers who had hassled her earlier, their SUV parked next to her car. The driver, an Asian boy, ran forward, and after letting out a high-pitched scream, thrust his right leg out sideways where his foot struck her belly, doubling her over, knocking the wind out of her, and making her collapse to her knees.

"Sweet." Samuel laughed. "That was a bull's-eye, Danny!"

Skathi gasped, struggling to take air in but barely succeeding. She leaned on her left hand. The foursome circled her like hyenas, skipping and jumping and laughing. She tried to speak but couldn't push enough air into her vocal cords to work.

"Super Trans Man ain't coming to the rescue, princess," Samuel shouted.

"Yeah," Danny yelled, "no mercy for monster freaks."

"Just remember, sweetheart," Samuel said in a chilling voice as all four of them closed in on her, "this is gonna hurt you a lot more than it will us."

Two of them swung a foot back to kick, and Skathi closed her eyes tightly in sick anticipation.

The kicks never arrived. Two loud thuds, followed by screams, filled the air.

Skathi opened her eyes to pure chaos.

Danny and Samuel were dragged off several feet by two hulking figures barely discernible in the poorly lit area. Leaping down from a nearby tree, Prankster Pete landed next to the white boy who had yelled at Skathi from the SUV earlier.

"Jesus Christ." The boy screamed and wet his pants. "We were only—"

Without hesitation, Pete thrust a tattooed right hand into and straight through the teenager's midsection, spraying blood across the face and chest of the remaining teenager, the Black boy who had mistaken Skathi for a Muslim woman because of her headwear. He screamed and turned to run but slammed face-first into a tall, ripped, pale naked man with a bald head, and fell to the ground.

"Mr. Tepes, don't!" Skathi managed to finally speak, but it was too late.

Tepes opened his mouth wider than any mere mortal could, exposing vicious sharp teeth.

"Oh god, no . . . please . . ." The teen squealed in terror.

Mr. Tepes's mouth bit into the teenager's throat, tearing into both carotid arteries. Mere seconds of feeding left the boy drained of blood, pale and dead.

The rank smell of piss, shit, and gore filled the air.

Coughing, Skathi forced herself to stand up. She heard Samuel's voice nearby.

"No . . . please, for the love of God . . . no more . . ." he said.

Turning back toward the gas station, Skathi saw the outline of what looked like a huge wolf walking on its hind legs. Samuel's high-pitched screams were suddenly stopped when the wolf completely decapitated him with a single chomp of its large jaws. Samuel's head fell to the ground, but his body managed to keep upright for a full thirty seconds while scarlet blood jetted up into the air from his neck stump.

Several feet from Samuel's corpse, Danny was on his knees, groveling before a dark, undulating humanoid shape that looked like a solid shadow come to life.

"I'm sorry," Danny said, his eyes wide and drool dripping down the side of his mouth. "I'm sorry . . . we didn't mean anything . . . this can't be happening . . . this can't be fucking happening . . ."

"Tariaksuq," Skathi managed to yell loudly, "please don't . . ."

The shadow creature suddenly merged with Danny, causing him to shake and convulse wildly and a moment later explode in a large swath of blood, gore, and bone, spraying the area in pieces of matter no larger than a thumbnail.

This last macabre killing proved too much for Skathi's overwhelmed senses. She dropped back down to her knees and vomited. This was followed by a minute of dry heaves before she could regain some manner of composure.

She wiped her mouth with the palm of her left hand and realized she was now sitting within a circle made by four terrifying entities.

"Why . . . Why?" was all Skathi could manage to say.

"They were going to kill you, Skathi," the living shadow known as Tariaksuq said.

"You don't know that," Skathi said.

"Of course we do," Prankster Pete replied.

"Some of us see into men's hearts," Mr. Tepes said, "others into their minds. We know the truth of their intent."

The upright wolf slowly transformed into her client, Mrs. Neuri, naked and as beautiful as a runway model.

"I smelled their evil, my child," Mrs. Neuri said. "We had no choice."

"But . . . but you killed them," Skathi said, still in shock.

"Many of us like you, Skathi," Mr. Tepes said, "and depend on you."

"And many of our kind . . . love you," Prankster Pete said in a low voice.

"We will not let them desecrate one . . . of us," Mrs. Neuri said, "and you must leave here . . . now. We disconnected all surrounding security cameras before you left the bathroom. We will clean up any signs of your . . . our presence. Now go!"

WHEN SKATHI WAS within a half mile of her apartment complex, it struck midnight. Instantly, a New Batch Available alert sang from her iPhone. She pulled over to the side of West Street and put her car in park, ignoring the alert for a full thirty seconds before slowly picking up her phone. Opening the screen, she saw it was one of her best paying and reliable clients, Mr. Arges, an ocular-challenged giant of a man with a penchant for Pule cheese who lived in a secluded corner of Aspen Meadows.

Setting her phone down on the passenger seat, Skathi couldn't help but see the spots of blood that had sprayed across the back of her right hand. Shivering, she dug through her glove compartment, found some wet wipes, and quickly cleaned up. Glancing into the rearview mirror, she realized her face was paler than any makeup could account for.

The phone beeped again.

They killed those boys, she thought, *without any hesitation or remorse . . . slaughtering them like farm animals. They're monsters.*

But the way the tall white boy, Samuel, had punched Skathi in the face, and the way that Asian boy Danny had kicked her, and all their drunken laughter . . . *Yes,* Skathi thought, *they really might have been on the verge of killing me.*

The phone beeped a third time.

I can quit the night shifts right now, Skathi thought, *no more Night Clients, no more big tips, just go back to the old harried day shifts where I'll be regularly competing with PostMates and Shipt on top of my own InstaBag co-workers.*

Skathi slowly reached for her phone.

But all the medical bills, she thought, *the therapists, the estrogen therapy, and the eventual cost of surgery . . . No other job in this failing economy can give me as much off-the-record income as I need.*

Trembling, Skathi picked up the phone and looked at the screen. She felt like she was walking on a tightrope across a wide, raging river, and, halfway across, knew not whether to return to one shore or continue to the other. On one side were all the Night Clients she had ever delivered to. On the other, all of the everyday mortal kind. Did she really have to choose between extremes? Or did she have the focus and strength to maintain this precarious balance?

"Heaven and Hell," Skathi recited in a whisper, "*suppose two distinct species of men, the good and the bad; but the greatest part of mankind float betwixt vice and virtue.*"

Slowly, after the shortest hesitation, Skathi tapped the accept button on the screen, set her phone down, took the car out of park, and proceeded on a long drive to an overgrown valley just east of Apache Peak, where there awaited a family-run cheese factory hidden in a large circular copse of Gambel oak, ponderosa pine, and aspen trees.

Skathi pulled a tube of Bite Beauty Amuse Bouche lipstick out of her purse with a trembling hand to touch up her smile. Pressing both her lips together, she took another quick glance into her rearview mirror and winked at herself.

"Well, girl," Skathi said nervously, "as the great philosopher Hume might say, she is happy whose circumstances suit her temper; but she is more excellent who can suit her temper to any circumstances."

Skathi's rust-coated Plymouth, looking blood red under the bright harvest full moon, was slowly embraced by the night as Jimmy Cliff's "Give a Little, Take a Little" oozed from her car's speakers.

SCRAPE

by Denise Dumars

PINCHE CHINA. MITSUKO was tired of hearing it. Or worse: china puta. Or rarely: china marimacha. With Judy dead she hadn't heard that one in a while.

These days she wore her dark glasses everywhere. She bleached her hair, and sometimes dyed it pink, as Judy used to do. The shade she wore now had started out fuchsia and had faded to Pepto-Bismol, gray appearing now in the dark roots.

Sometimes she was taken for one of the androgynous Goth boys of Tijuana, so when people first heard her voice, and her American accent, they were surprised. Then came the wry smile, the smile that says, *I know who you are and what you are, gringa marimacha.* One disingenuous bookstore owner had told her it meant "tomboy." They had called Judy "buchona guera." Blond gueras were prized in Mexico. Pinche china. As though all Asians were Chinese. Mitsuko was Japanese American.

If only they had seen Judy when she was dying, her long blond hair going gray against the hospital pillow. Her crying and babbling, saying, "Mama, Mama," over and over again. No longer recognizing Mitsuko or her own sister and brother-in-law. The sad, desperate struggle at the end. There was nothing butch about Judy; there never had been. Damn the roles the so-called dominant culture wanted them to play.

ALL IN BLACK, her wallet attached by a chain to her belt loop, counterfeit Nikes allowing her to bounce on the balls of her feet as she walked, pink hair sticking up, Mitsuko imagined that she looked a bit like David Tennant in the *Good Omens* TV series, where he played Crowley, a demon, paired with an angel. Judy had sworn that the two actors were like a gay couple. It had been one of her favorite shows.

She rounded the corner by the shoe store and entered through the open wrought-iron gates into Botanica Mayeleo. Technically, she had come in by the back entrance to Mercado Constitución, but the mercado was subdivided into several smaller shops. At the bend in the market, when one turned left, one found the three linked stalls that made up Botanica Mayeleo.

It was still early, but a line had already formed at the one cash register that served all three shops. In line was a veritable United Nations of customers: the casual local shoppers pretending not to be buying magickal supplies with obvious uses such as bringing back a straying lover; the American tourists wanting spooky souvenirs; Indian women in braids and colorful skirts buying herbs; one Vodou priest, the only Black man in line; and oddly, two very tall white people who chatted in English with Australian accents.

Mitsuko deferred to the room across the hall until the line cleared. It was the poorest lit of the stalls, the place where she was most likely to remove her dark glasses where no one would see that she was a "china." It was a good place to hide.

She picked up a package of incense with a picture of a dragon on it. It was hard to read in the flickering light of the failing fluorescent tube.

She thought now that it was good to be anonymous, gender-fluid, although that had never been the truth either. Here, at the border, in the liminal space between countries, she sometimes felt safer than she had back home.

IT HAD STARTED with Covid-19. "The Chinese virus," Trump had called it. First it was a Latina in the park in Torrance, then a Black man at the beach. Then in random locations around the South Bay, the part of L.A. where she lived, where Asians and Asian-Pacific people had lived for generations. The hate speech. The harassment. It came out of left field, and most of the time it came from fellow minorities. It happened even in the neighborhoods where Asian Americans were in the majority: the Gardena neighborhood where Mitsuko had grown up among other Japanese Americans, the Torrance suburb that was more Korean than white.

It didn't stop. It got worse; even with the new vaccines, and the virus nearly contained, it didn't stop. An old woman at the Del Amo mall who had lived in Torrance for fifty years was attacked and beaten. A security camera caught the man and woman who had committed the crime—they told the press later on that they had done it "to send a message."

So Judy and Mitsuko were an interracial couple now; a strange target in a quasi-liberal place that hadn't minded their being lesbians, but now somehow minded that one of them was of Asian descent.

It was Judy's idea to move to Mexico. She'd done a lot of cross-border work with the art galleries. She spoke fluent Spanish. She understood the culture and was tired of being away from home for long periods of time, especially with threats against Asians happening.

"You can do your job anywhere, Mits," she'd said. "Online work is done internationally all the time. Ask Joel. He can get you started."

Joel was Judy's brother-in-law. Judy got along with him famously but Mitsuko had found him to be an arrogant know-it-all. She felt a bit differently about him now, because she found it hard to reconcile the smug mansplainer that she had known before with the broken man at Judy's bedside.

But before Judy had died of the same cancer that killed her mother, he had helped Mitsuko make the transition to working on the other side of the border. While Judy hobnobbed with international artists and critics, Mitsuko had bent over her computer, assured that there was regular money coming in, and enjoyed the occasional high-end wine-and-cheese event. Judy was happy. Mitsuko was, if not happy, at least strangely relieved. It didn't feel as bad to be dissed by people who weren't your own. It was normal, even. Not like back home. This place, Mitsuko knew, would never really be home.

Judy was her home. And Judy was dead.

MITSUKO STARED AT the package until she finally recognized that—duh—it was dragon's blood incense. Made from the sap of the *Draceana* plant, it was dark red and had a somewhat acrid smell that was an acquired taste. She put it back on the shelf.

Two men came into the semi-darkened booth, and Mitsuko stepped aside. Somehow she hadn't noticed the nearly life-size statue of Santa Muerte seated on a throne, wrapped in cellophane, back in the dark corner. Big enough that a small dolly was needed to move it, the two men in their expensive *charro* gear—complete with embroidered AK-47s on their Western-style shirts—said nothing, merely nodded and tipped their hats to an employee as they wheeled the macabre statue away.

She'd been to Santa Muerte temples. When in Rome and all that. Before going to the hospital back home where Judy would spend her last days, Mitsuko had gone to three Santa Muerte temples. At each, she left the proper offerings—a red rose, an apple, and of course some cash. In one temple, there was a depiction of Santa Muerte as the Pietà. This version, with the saint of death holding Christ's body, was supposed to be petitioned for those who were terminally ill. Mitsuko didn't know the right prayers, so she simply asked for mercy, left the offerings, and quickly left. Any gesture, any faint hope . . . well, there truly were no atheists in foxholes.

SHE PEEKED OUT of the booth and saw that the line had diminished. Stepping into the corridor, she espied Antonio. He motioned to her to come into the larger stall.

Around a display of good-luck amulets and cristales de chakras was the storeroom down a hidden corridor. Antonio opened the door to the cramped room for her. There was scant space between the shelves full of candles, statues, and more mysterious items and the larger boxes on the floor, most of them labeled Indio Products, Los Angeles.

"How you doin', Mees Mitch," he said to her. "Do we have a scrape today?" When he said it, it sounded more like "screp."

"Yes," she said.

He smiled broadly, front teeth rimmed in gold. "You came on a good day. Lots of money today."

He looked out the door for a moment, and then closed it behind him. The staff knew not to bother them.

Mitsuko sat down on the stepstool they used to reach the higher shelves. She took off her jacket and placed it on one of the Indio Products boxes. Antonio produced a black metal box, a bottle of agua purificada, and a bottle of rubbing alcohol.

How like a junkie's kit the black box looked to Mitsuko! Her heart beat faster every time she saw it. Inside, the black box looked less like a junkie's supplies and more like a Covid-era first-aid kit.

Antonio pulled on a pair of blue surgical gloves. Then he took a new razor blade from a tin, along with the kind of sample jar kept in doctors' restrooms. He wrote her name—

"Mitchucho"—on the jar, and made a show of "purifying" the razor blade with first water and then alcohol. He scrubbed his gloves with more alcohol, and then gently palpated the raised whorl of skin near the inside of her left elbow. To the untrained eye, it looked like a birthmark, or a raised scar of some kind. To the trained eye, the snail-shell-shaped excrescence matching her skin tone but for the brown freckling on its edges, was immediately recognizable.

"Hold your arm steady now," Antonio said. He positioned her arm on the knee of her crossed leg. "Hold still so I don't cut you by mistake." He wet a cotton ball with alcohol and swabbed her skin carefully so as not to be accused of touching her inappropriately.

She always looked away right before he put the razor blade to the whorl. All the while she kept thinking, *It isn't part of me, it isn't me, it really isn't me, it's best to be rid of it,* and every time she could barely keep herself from screaming, not because it hurt, since it didn't, and not because of the odd tugging feeling, which was the only way she knew that he was taking the scrape. The desire to scream came from the distinct fear that it was a part of her; almost as if a voice spoke inside her, saying, *Don't give it away, it belongs to you, it is a part of you.*

After he had taken it and placed it into the bottle, he swabbed her arm again with the rubbing alcohol. Then from the box he took gauze and tape and carefully applied it. Not that there was a wound. Not that it wouldn't grow back . . . because it would.

JUDY WAS IN the hospital for what would be the last time when Mitsuko noticed the small growth just below the elbow on the inside of her left arm. Smaller than a dime the first time, it looked like nothing so much as a small cinnamon roll, a curled spiral with dots of darker tissue atop of it. Her heightened awareness of cancer since Judy's diagnosis meant that it scared her; it didn't hurt, but "a growth that doesn't hurt" is one of the hallmarks of cancer. She immediately started obsessing online, and the only thing she could find that somewhat resembled it was a dermoid tumor. Back in Torrance, where Judy had been admitted to the hospital, she called up her old dermatologist, Dr. Yee.

As Mitsuko sat shivering in the paper gown the nurse had given her, Dr. Yee came in and took one look at the excrescence on her arm. "That is definitely not a dermoid tumor," Dr. Yee said. "So stop worrying. How old are you now, dear?"

"Fifty."

"Well, not that you're getting old, but the truth is that as we age, we produce excess skin, and a lot of it ends up as annoying benign lesions." The doctor took a closer look with a magnifier, and Mitsuko thought she saw a flicker of a frown on Dr. Yee's perfect face.

Then she smiled. "I'll remove this, and we'll biopsy it of course, but I promise you it's not malignant. We dermatologists call these sorts of things 'barnacles,' and come to think of it, this one looks a little like a seashell. By the way, you have a few skin tags on your neck and in your décolleté—do you want me to remove them?"

After removing the skin tags, Dr. Yee gave her a small shot of lidocaine and then sliced off the "barnacle." The nurse bandaged it and gave her a sample of a topical antibiotic to put on it. Back at the hospital, Judy asked if she'd lost a fight with a kitten, referencing the tiny inflamed areas where the skin tags had been.

In the morning, when she removed the bandage, she was surprised. The skin was smooth, as though nothing had ever been there. No scab, no irritated skin. The only evidence of anything unusual was a slight rash from the surgical tape; Mitsuko had always been allergic to adhesives. As for the "barnacle," there was no evidence of it left at all.

IT WASN'T UNTIL she had returned to Mexico after Judy's death that she found the excrescence growing back. This time it was fully as large as a dime. It didn't seem feasible to drive the three hours back to Torrance to see Dr. Yee; surely there was someone in Tijuana who could remove it. Ostensibly, she went to the internet to search for a dermatóloga. But she soon found herself searching Mexican websites for dermatological anomalies.

The difference between Mexicans and Americans, Mitsuko felt, was that Mexicans were completely open about their superstitions. It's not that Americans believed in them less; they just hid it better. All over Spanish-language internet there were stories about strange shell-shaped skin lesions. One website compared them to "círculos de las cosechas," which Mitsuko found out meant "crop circles." That, at least, made her laugh; surely aliens were not to blame.

Other websites, however, linked them with side effects of the Covid-19 vaccine. Mitsuko hated conspiracy theories, and against her better judgment, started looking up info on American sites. What she found chilled her; she had no patience for anti-vaxxers or the Covid-19 deniers, but both American and Mexican sites spoke of rare growths like hers and ascribed various strange causes to them, none of which made any logical sense to Mitsuko. She was sure that this benign lesion was not in any way related to the Covid-19 vaccine. Maybe such an idea would make some sense if the lesion was near the injection site, but it wasn't. For all the ridiculous theories she found, none was actually made by a doctor. In fact, perhaps more chillingly, she found no discussion at all of their origins on medical websites.

But she couldn't shake the memory of the flicker of a frown on Dr. Yee's face, so she kept searching. At last, she found that some curanderos believed that the tissue from such lesions had healing qualities. She watched a video that depicted an indigenous curandera mixing a batch of herbs to which she added the scrapings from such a lesion. Healing was healing, she told herself. After all, in a clinical trial, some people always got the sugar pill but still were healed.

It was as if someone read her mind at the fruit and vegetable stand in Mercado Constitución the next day. It was a blistering day, and she was wearing a black tank-top and regretting the color in the heat. An old Mexican woman saw the excrescence on her arm and started talking to her, first addressing her as "chica china"—now, that was a new one. The old woman told Mitsuko that the botanica at the other end of the mercado might pay her for the scrapings from the shell-shaped growth. She said "Dólares" and pantomimed counting out bills.

She hadn't worked much since Judy's death. What if she could make money on the growth instead of spending money to have it removed? It wasn't the first completely off-the-wall thing she'd ever considered doing. After all, she'd agreed to move to Mexico.

Nevertheless, it took some time before she braved the botanica. Once the salespeople were used to seeing her, she approached the young clerk whom she'd heard speaking English. His eyebrows raised when he saw the growth. Conferences between Antonio and the elder salespersons had resulted in her first sale. By that time, the excrescence was the size of a nickel.

She never specified an amount of money, and was grateful for whatever they gave her. The most recent growth, which she'd sold on the day she'd seen the big Santa Muerte statue, was as large as a quarter.

SHE WAS DEEP in thought as she passed the bookstore where she'd once been called a "tomboy" and which was separated from the shoe store and Mercado Constitución by an alley. Two young men stepped out of the alley and bracketed her. Each showed a weapon. She had trained for a long time on what to do in such a situation should it ever happen, but she did none of it. Instead, she froze.

The two young men looked vaguely familiar. "Our boss would like to meet you," said one, in an L.A. accent. "We are not going to hurt you, but you must come with us. It's nothing bad, I promise. He is a gentleman," the young man averred.

Her heart was in her throat as she allowed them to lead her to a shiny blue Mercedes. She soon found herself on the road up into the hills. Hillside shanty towns were gradually being replaced with mission-style McMansions. They pulled into the circular driveway of one of the larger ones.

Inside the house, it was air-conditioned, and a maid immediately appeared. She led Mitsuko into a spacious room. It would have been a perfect stand-in for the drawing room of Collinwood in the old TV show *Dark Shadows*.

"Don Gerardo will see you now," said the maid, as a handsome middle-aged man in a colorful silk shirt, white pants, and crocodile boots came in through another door. He smiled broadly and held out his hand to shake hers.

"I'm Gerardo Alcala, and I'm so happy to meet you, Miss . . . ?" It was clear he hadn't learned her name.

She shook his hand, still marveling at the oddness of the situation. "Mitsuko Ito. Nice to meet you, uh, Don Gerardo."

He moved to a small bar on a sideboard. "Would you like a drink, Ms. Ito? I have the best reposado, or Coca-Cola, or something else?"

"N-no, I'm fine," she said. "I'm just wondering why you asked me here."

"Well, then, please, sit down."

She sat in the cordovan leather chair, and he took a desk chair to sit opposite her. "My two lieutenants, who brought you here today, had noticed you when they went to pick up a statue for me. They thought it odd that you were, uh, 'hanging around' as Lolo says. So I told them to go down there and make inquiries. The caballeros at that shop know better than to lie to my people. They learned something extraordinary, and then I knew I had to meet you."

She didn't realize that she had been holding her breath until then. "Oh, well, that's a relief," she said, and before she could stop herself, she blurted out, "I was afraid I was being kidnapped."

He pointed around the spacious room. "Do I look like I need to kidnap people?" he asked with a chuckle. "Kidnappings do happen, so you should be careful, but no, I have other ways of making money."

She tried to swallow, but her throat was bone-dry. "I think I might like to have that drink after all. Coca-Cola, with a little rum, please."

He gestured to the maid. "Is Havana Club all right?"

"Oh, yes, wonderful," she said.

The maid mixed her drink and served it, along with tequila over ice for her host.

"So I was told that the botanica pays you for the, uh, anomalía that appears on your lovely forearm," he said.

"Yes," she said. "They give me a little money. I do it mostly to get rid of it, but it is supposed to be used for healing, and I hope it helps somebody."

He smiled. "But you aren't sure about that," he said.

She took a couple sips of the drink. "I don't know what I believe. I don't know what it is."

He leaned toward her. "Then we are in agreement. I don't know what it is either. But I have always had a keen interest in science. Chemistry, as you may have guessed, but all the sciences fascinate me. I want to study it. You're the first person I've met who actually has one."

"My dermatologist says it's benign," she replied. The drink had made her feel sweaty, even in the air conditioning.

"Why does it keep coming back? Where did it come from? Why have such things only been seen recently? These are the questions that fascinate me," he said.

She stared into her glass, surprised that she'd already drunk half of it. "It doesn't feel like it's a part of me. Each time it re-grows, I want it taken off, as soon as possible."

"Well, then, let me make you an offer. I have a fine physician. He can take samples in a clinic, not some botanica back room. And I can pay you much, much more than any shop in down-town Tijuana."

"And if I say yes can I go home now? And that's all you want, the scrape?"

"Yes, and yes," Don Gerardo replied.

"All right." She downed the rest of the drink. "As long as you promise not to cut my arm off."

He laughed and slapped his knee. "You are a lot of fun, Ms. Ito. And very beautiful. But I believe I am not the type for you, ¿verdad?"

Her cheeks burned. "Verdad."

"Then let us say buenos tardes for today. Let me give you a little . . . advance, as they say. Then I'll have Lolo drive you home. He can play Beach Boys for you in the car."

She stood, and he followed, after taking something out of an envelope in the desk. He took her hand in both of his and pressed bills and a business card into it. "Until we meet again. Just call the number on the card when you are ready."

Lolo stood there by the car. "Everything copacetic?" he asked. "You know, when I was in L.A. I went to the beach in Redondo all the time."

She realized that Don Gerardo had known all about her all along.

Back in her apartment, she lay on her bed in the heat. *Am I insane?* she wondered. *Who would agree to let a narco's doctor slice a growth off her arm? Me,* she sighed. *La china loca. Me.*

IT APPEARED TO grow back faster than before. She called Don Gerardo. The doctor saw her at a sparkling-clean clinic in an area that catered to Americans. Dr. Ochoa took her vitals and a blood sample first, and a pretty nurse brought his tray with shiny new instruments. He went for a needle of anesthetic, but Mitsuko told him that it didn't hurt so that wasn't necessary. The growth was swiftly and painlessly gone. The nurse covered the area with a pink Band-Aid.

Taking off his gloves, Dr. Ochoa asked, "Have you noticed any of these excrescences on other parts of your body?"

"No, no I haven't," she said. The very thought terrified her.

He nodded. "Very well. Please, let me know if you do. Your vital signs are excellent. If there is anything to be worried about in the blood test, I'll let you know."

On her way out, the young woman at the desk handed her an envelope. She dared not count it until she was home, but took a taxi, not worrying about the cost.

All she could think of was another of the growths appearing elsewhere on her body. The bills in the envelope added up to one thousand dollars, but did nothing to allay her fears. She undressed and examined all the skin she could see, then stood before the full-length mirror with a hand mirror. She tried to reassure herself that if there was another one Dr. Yee would have noticed, although it had been quite a while since that appointment.

She saw nothing, felt nothing. She ripped off the pink bandage and was not surprised to see that her skin was clear. Now she could think of nothing but another of the shell-like growths blossoming somewhere else on her body.

She went shopping for a few groceries, more for the walk to clear her head than for necessities. She imagined that every pair of eyes was on her.

Darkness followed. She made a rum and Coke and turned on TV Azteca hoping for a luchador movie as a distraction. Her mind went to the days when she and Judy watched *Santo contra la invasion de los marcianos* or Aztec mummies or some other monster. But instead they were showing older American movies, and she had tuned in at the middle of *American Psycho*, broadcast in English with Spanish subtitles. She turned it off, but thought, *How perfect*.

She mused about contacting some of her previous clients, then decided she felt too distracted to do so. After using the restroom, she obsessively examined her face in the mirror, starting at every small blemish and mole.

By bedtime, she had talked herself down from panicking. Just another day . . . the doctor had asked a reasonable question . . .

There was nothing reasonable in the world. Not now. There hadn't been for a long time.

As bedtime approached, she worked on reading one of the fotonovelas that Judy had bought to help her with her Spanish. They all had lurid covers; this one featured a blonde in a torn slip holding a smoking gun, the body of a man in a cowboy hat on the floor.

When she realized that she'd read the same page several times and had no idea what it said, she set it aside and turned off the lights. If she had expected sleep to come easily, she had been foolish. She thought about Judy again. One of Judy's more common ways of initiating sex was to smile and say, "You'll sleep better if you have an orgasm." But Mitsuko could not touch herself. The very idea agitated her. She considered getting the hand mirror again, examining her vulva for growths. The thought nauseated her, and she eventually fell asleep.

She awoke to hearing the phone ring. When she looked at it she saw that it was a private number, but there was a message. The message was from Don Gerardo, who said, "Stay inside. If you have to go out, wear your leather chaqueta. Don't be afraid; there is nothing happening in Mexico yet. If there is any trouble, I will send a car."

Ah, her protector, the narco. Right. In what world would she have found herself in this situation? She made herself a cup of coffee and sat down to the computer and logged in to NBC San Diego.

Someone had tried to shoot the mayor of San Diego, saying he might be "one of them."

There were riots in Los Angeles.

She switched to MSNBC. "Some are saying the second civil war has come at last, brother against brother, when a Cleveland man killed his brother, saying that it wasn't really him; it was 'one of them.' He'd seen the spiral growth on his brother's neck."

On Fox News they debated whether a person with a lesion was more likely to be a Democrat or a Republican. One commentator said, "Or if someone with the mark is a person at all."

She held her breath as she'd done at Don Gerardo's.

Maybe I should have died when Judy died . . . Maybe it's best to just die now, she thought. Her eyes brimmed with tears.

No. I will not give in, she thought. *This pinche china does not go down without a fight.*

She got Don Gerardo's business card and began punching in the number. She would not go to some man's house for protection, not now or ever, but she would ask him for something.

Someone like him surely has more guns around the house than he needs.

Surely he'd give her one, if she asked nicely.

Mud Flappers

by Usman T. Malik

CHILDREN OF THE sea, we watched in silence as they put a rope around his neck and dragged Abdul Berr twenty feet along the shore. The suited-booted man from the city, the bara sahib, looked at us as if we were vermin. Perhaps to him we were. Perhaps to rich seths all poor people look like mud flappers.

"Your boy's been causing trouble." He was a tall, block-shaped man with a mouth puckered like a crab hole. His sunglasses glinted when he tilted his head to look at his goon. "I'm a generous man, a very patient man. Isn't that so, Nasir?"

The six-foot-two goon placed his boot on Abdul Berr's jaw. "Very patient, Kamal sahib."

"But your boy's been testing my patience. Madarchod, look at his gall. He leads a contingent of activists to Karachi Press Club"—Kamal's voice rose, filled with disbelief—"gathers those newspaper chutiyas around him and actually takes names. Abay bharway, what did you think? You'd drag Murad Saeen's name through the mud and we'd just sit there scratching our balls?"

The second goon stopped brandishing his handgun long enough to kick Berr in the ribs. Berr moaned, tried to curl into a fetal position, and Nasir, grinning, dug his boot into his throat. When one of us started forward the policeman Kamal had brought pointed a shotgun at him.

"Sahib-jee!" Old Mother dropped to her knees, palms joined like a trident in front of her. We drew back at this, a murmur going through us. "Sahib-jee. Please forgive him." The wind took her words, spun them into an echo. We stopped and listened.

"What do we have here?" Kamal peered at her, sunglasses hanging off the cliff of his nose. "Who're you, burhya?"

"I told him to stop. Told him that he shouldn't stand in the way. He's young and he's a fool, but he's my grandson, sahib-jee."

"There you go." Kamal slapped his thigh, a smile dancing across his face. "Your dadi knew better, didn't she, told you to back down, you son of a swine. But you wouldn't listen."

Old Mother's hands pendulumed back and forth, as if she were praying. How many times had we seen her slice the wind with those gnarled fingers? "I'm an old woman with my legs in the grave, but by his name who holds my life in his fist, if you let him go, we'll pack our bags and leave, sahib-jee. You won't see us again."

Never see her again? Old Mother gone? The idea stunned us. If we didn't know better, it would've made us hate Berr. Why did he have to go poking his nose in business that wasn't his? Our village wasn't in jeopardy. Our waters were safe. They will come for you next, he said. Once they're done developing the two islands, once they've erected "New Dubai." But we have Old Mother, we cried. We'll survive this. They'll come for your basti, he said. Force you out, and sell the land to the highest bidder.

What did he know? Now look at him lying down, blood bubbling between his lips. Because of him, Old Mother might leave the basti. And what would we do then to stymie the tides and hold the storms? Who'd knot our ropes and blow dust to blind Enki's fish so we could catch it easily?

"If only he'd listened to you." Kamal circled the downed boy. "Murad Saeen wouldn't be happy if we returned without delivering his message. Nasir," he said gently to the goon. "Be a prince and break his arm, won't you."

Nasir's grin widened. "Thought you'd never ask, sahib."

"Hear me out, I beg you," said Old Mother. Tears streaked clean lines down her wizened face, and how could that be? In eighty years no one had seen Old Mother weep—not when two of her sons, on guard duty, were killed in the terrorist attack at Marina Club—not when Hindustani coast guards captured her husband after he strayed into their waters and then drowned trying to escape; she always did say her gifts cost a hand and a foot.

Nasir splayed Berr's arm out on the beach, grasped the wrist, and leaned on the elbow with his knee.

Rocking, Old Mother said, "Beyond the two islands is a—"

Nasir broke the boy's arm.

The snap was audible even at a distance. Berr screamed. Nasir let the arm fall, limp and misshapen, and stepped back to examine his handiwork.

Kamal grunted with satisfaction and turned to Old Mother. "What were you saying about the islands, old woman?"

Old Mother had fallen silent. She stared at the blood of her blood, his bare feet thrashing, kicking up sand.

"Nothing? That's a pity. I was hoping to hear that promise again about getting the fuck out of Karachi." Kamal pulled out a gun, pointed it at Berr's head. A *snick* as he flicked the safety off. "Nasir, let's do his other arm."

The goon beamed with pleasure and reached for Berr.

Quiet as a spell, Old Mother said, "We will leave the city tonight and never return. You will never see us again."

Kamal didn't lower the gun. "Finish what you said earlier. What about the islands?"

Old Mother rose to her feet. Her face was impassive now, stone that had weathered a century of storms. "Beyond the two islands is a third that few know of."

We gasped. Why would she say that, why would she tell? The sand beneath us shifted as lassos of water wrapped around our feet, pulling us back.

Kamal arched an eyebrow at her. "Such stories you tell. You ever hear such stories, Nasir?"

"The three children, we call them. The third wrapped in mist. Four hours by boat, the island sits in the heart of the delta, wreathed by mangroves so ancient that the fish nestling in their roots have never been seen by human eyes."

"No, Kamal sahib." Nasir eyed her, Berr's uninjured limb still in his grip. "Kaam ki baat kar, burhya. What's it to us?"

"Three times the size of the other islands. Such fishing there that you wouldn't believe. Wouldn't Murad Saeen want to know about it? And the mangroves? Richest timber you ever saw. So many treasures in its creeks."

Stop, we wanted to shout. Old Mother, mother of our livelihood, father of our grief! Settling around us like the throw of a fishnet, these city bastards may have repossessed our land, pushing us farther and filthier into the sea, but they must not capture our soul.

Kamal's gun moved from Berr to Old Mother, back to Berr. "An island of treasures." He wasn't laughing. He removed his sunglasses, hung them from his shirt collar, and lowered the weapon. "Rest of you"—his many-colored eyes gleamed at us—"got something to say, or does this hag speak for all of you?"

We said nothing. The wind sighed, spraying salt upon our tongues and eyes.

"You know, old woman, I've heard some stories too." Kamal motioned to his men. Displeased, Nasir dropped Berr's hand and moved away. The second goon bent and loosened the rope around the boy's neck. "There are hundreds of villages along the coast, but I hear only the men of this village catch a suah fish on the regular. I'm told that last year your boys caught not one but two black-spotted croakers, each more than fifty kilograms. Each sold for more than twenty lacs. Isn't that true, Nasir?"

"Jee, sahib."

"And now you tell me about this island of yours and its glorious catch? Why, I'm almost inclined to believe you. This place has a name?"

Old Mother looked at him.

"Is it in Indian waters? You trying to lure us into a trap?"

"No, sahib." Old Mother's lips were white. "It is ours."

"Tell you what, burhya." A glance over his shoulder and the policeman came padding to Kamal's side like a dog. "Tomorrow you and one of your bastard boys will take us to this island and if what you say is true"—he smiled at Berr, as if at a favored pet—"we will let this mutt live and you two can disappear to whichever hellhole your elders crawled out from. Am I clear or do I need Nasir to make you understand?"

"Clear, sahib," said Old Mother. A glint brief as the catch of sunlight on mica lit the crevasses that formed her eyes. "Clear as island water."

AFTER TAKING BERR to Old Mother's hut, where she lit candles, hung up his garments on iron nails, careful not to waste the tatters, and rolled him onto his side before settling to mend his bones, we swarmed to the sea, the withered gray-blue skin of it taut over the wounds of the earth. Our children raced in pursuit of tadpoles, dogs, and plastic bags, and cried to the gulls, and miles away Berr cried out when the hinge of his elbow wrenched into place. We waded through piles of kindling, bottles, shoes, shells, and camel droppings until we found sea-salted bones of creatures long drowned and gathered them in kid leather pouches. In silence we savored the briny smell of our ancient mother until daylight melted on the dusky lips of a star-studded evening and we returned to Old Mother's hut, half a dozen pouches richer.

She took them and shut her door.

All through the midnight hours candlelight sputtered in her window, and once in a while singing cut through the moans and clatter as if of bones on metal. Far out in the ocean, deep water creatures, wrapped in carnivorous curtains of sea slugs, bellowed. Upon a summer night Old Mother set loose sea shanties of winter, and we huddled together.

At predawn we met her by the boats, two ropes slung over her shoulders. She handed us one: Fasten it to the mast of the crabbing boat, she said. Careful with the wind knots in the middle. They must not be loosened yet.

We understood.

The second rope she gave to the lean, bare-chested, muscled boy who accompanied her, whom we didn't yet know. He had perfect teeth and the shine in his eyes was like sunlight on water. Tie it around the bow of the boat, she said. He did, tying the topknot with his teeth instead of his right arm. Then the two of them climbed onto the deck and waited for an hour before Kamal showed up with a dozen men in Jeeps, shotguns and Kalashnikovs slung over their shoulders. Three of them wore police garb. Kamal barked orders and the men swept the deck, looking for weapons.

"Burhya," said Kamal. "Time to visit your island."

"Jee, sahib," said Old Mother. "The boy is our best boatman. He'll take us."

The goon Nasir bared his teeth at the boy. The latter stepped up to start the engine, and they set off into the rising sun.

We stood on the shore, watching them turn into a speck on the horizon; then we returned to the village. A few of us went to Old Mother's hut: we wiped candle wax off the windowsill, washed away piles of ash from Abdul Berr's charpoy, beat the fish-shaped tapestry, burned the bloodstained garments pooled on the floor, and when the wind picked up and slammed the door shut and one of us looked up and said, She's opened the first knot, we nodded and went back to cleaning, while three huts down, a baby awoke and began to cry.

The day softened toward a misty late afternoon and we went to the sea, some of us dragging along chairs and charpoys. By now they must have reached the island and disembarked. Easy, easy, we murmured. We sat quietly talking among ourselves, one ear to the horizon. Other than the occasional cry of a gull, the beach was silent, brooding, as if Enki, in His house of water, had inhaled and clenched His breath, the turning of His four-wheeled chariot paused at the edge of a benthic cliff. We let the children play, but shushed them if they got loud, for it would not do to stir up the bottom of the sea now. The sea jostled against our feet, and, sighing, we burrowed our toes deeper into the sand. Some of us looked up to the sky, where Enki's shadow had darkened the clouds.

The children tired of play and crowded around us.

Mother, I'm hungry, said a child. Father, I'm starving.

We retreated to the village and fed the children and put them to bed, while on the third island some of us washed the boat, sanded the deck, and cleared away the beach. One of us, now a freshly widowed island bride, heard her husband call from the sea and we had to restrain her from launching into the midnight waters.

Then we receded to our beds and, briefly, wept.

WE WERE WAITING when the boat docked at the pier the next morning, engine off, its sail unfurled. The boy leapt down, followed by a girl we didn't yet know. She was in her teens, her skin smooth as a newborn's. She flashed us a grin we returned, and together we hauled bags, ropes, and nets filled with lobster, tortoise, crab, fish, and other meat off the boat.

What a wonderful catch, our children cried.

We looked at them, smiling.

All day we worked. Old Mother's hut was torn down, rebuilt, and thoroughly aired. A new charpoy replaced the old, fresh tapestries were hung, and the window glass polished until it gleamed. Carefully we sorted the bags from the boat, stowing away the ones with the choicest selection, divided the rest for sale or use, and cleaned the catch accordingly. Some of us went to deliver it to the fish market, while the rest stayed behind to prepare for the evening.

Here and on the island, we sat around the fire, smoking beeri and hookah, listening to the old-timers tell stories. The sea is timekeeper and time itself. Older than all our mothers, younger than the freshest babe, it sheds its skin every moment of every day. Our children played at the edges of fire and darkness, while the boy and the girl sat quiet, eyes glittering like sea jewels, like Enki's eyes glowing in the heavens. The sea gave us our ancestors and children; it must and will always protect us, said the old-timers. So long as we kept its secrets and abided by the promise.

Some of us brought out platters of kebabs and grilled meat festooned with seaweed. Murmuring our thanks, we ate, and what succulent meat it was. Perhaps it was the quality of the air or our adventure, but no salmon, rohu, trout, or shark, no crab or tortoise ever tasted this good.

One of the children stopped eating, a worried look on her face.

Eat, daughter, we coaxed.

Mother, Father, she said. Do you think the bad men will return to take away our boats, our land?

No, said the boy, a steely glint in his eyes. But the police might.

Will we be in trouble? said the child, alarmed.

No, said the new girl. She licked a finger and looked into the child's face. There's nothing to be troubled about.

Does she lie? we wondered (we didn't know her yet). Then we thought, No. We may be mud flappers, but we survived marauders, invaders, Arabs, Mongols, the Europeans, and the British. We will survive these rich seths, these developers, encroachers, occupiers, and their grinning goons.

And if we couldn't?

Then we would survive on them.

Dedicated to the fishermen and native
residents of the Karachi coast.

CHURN THE UNTURNING TIDE

by Annie Neugebauer

PREGNANCY CHANGES EVERYTHING. Every damn thing. Not just in the obvious ways, breasts and belly and hips expanding. My actual rib cage is spreading open. My face is softer. My joints are more elastic. From fuller, shinier hair all the way down to widening feet with sudden plantar warts, every part is changed in some way.

My feet ache enough that I have on orthopedic shoes even for the walk across the waterpark to set my bag on a lounge chair. I'm late on purpose, because my friend isn't coming today to grant me a protective social bubble. I squint across the broad expanse of white concrete, scanning the bright blue water of the large wave pool.

The fifty-some-odd attendees, almost exclusively over fifty years old except for me, are already scattered throughout the fan-shaped pool doing their warm-up laps. The waves are on gentle, a constant roll emanating from the deep end. I shuck my maternity cover-up and shoes, grab my giant sun hat, and hurry to get a noodle. We use the white foam pool toys as props that help us float or provide resistance. I get the last one and wade into the cool water, which feels blissful on a hot June morning like today. I inhale in relief as I get deeper, the water taking some of the weight of my bump, easing the pressure points on the pads of my feet.

I head in against the gentle tide, eager to focus and get a good workout from it. Before the extra thirty pounds of pregnancy, I was very fit. I never would've been welcome here back then, young and trim, but now I'm embraced into the fold like a long-lost relative. Not quite one of them, but also no longer not one of them.

I come up on a hind cluster of ladies as I head deeper, and although I try to keep my head down under the shade of my hat, one of the women notices me and smiles sweetly. "When are you due, my dear?"

I suck in a breath and smile back. "Just a couple of weeks."

Her smile broadens, her yellowed teeth gleaming in the refractions of the chlorinated water. "Do you know what it is?"

I can't help it; my smile broadens too. I nod. "A girl."

"Wonderful," she says, sounding equal parts honest and disappointed. "Good for you."

"Thanks," I mutter, turning my head up to the sky for something to look at. Deep, rich Texan blue: clouds smearing the distance like fierce omens. The air today is electric. Could be an afternoon storm setting itself up. But everyone seems to feel it. The buzz of the women chatting ahead of us is louder than normal, even, an almost startling clash of laughter and outcries and vocalized confessions forced loud under the breath.

The woman takes the hint and parts to the side, leaving me to push through the current. My shins already ache; I wonder if I'll get the famous varicose veins of late pregnancy. Each new side effect I get is one that will potentially never go away. They have that knack. Get spider veins once and they'll linger off and on for your whole life. Relentless time, steady blemishes. It occurs to me, looking at the women scattered around me, that this is how most of them came to look the way they do.

They're decked out in every color and pattern imaginable. Black, tropicals, pastels, neons, solids, and prints. Florals, stripes, polka-dots, geometrics, animal prints, watercolors, and more. They, like me, have on sun protection in the form of UV shirts, glasses, dorky swim skirts, and hats of every variation. Broad-brimmed floppy numbers, ball caps, visors, and fisherman's style with the flap hanging down to cover the back of the neck. Strings tied under the chin, elastics in the hair, or gravity-defying balance at jaunty angles. Others opt for bare, over-tanned shoulders and brightly dyed hair glistening in the sun. There are wrinkled décolletages, skin browned, blued, and spotted with time and elements, neck waddles, oversized noses, large moles, and heavy arm flabs waving in the open air.

They never stop moving. When they stay in one spot, they bounce and jog in place, churning the water with their noodles arcing side to side, their knees bobbing up and down as they have loud conversations over the splash. Right now, about half of the group is to the sides of the shallower end of the wave pool, using the concrete edge to do assisted push-ups.

I go deeper than most of them and do ten wide-stance push-ups with my belly bump dipping in and out of the water, then ten triceps push-ups for good measure. The cackling and shrieks of the group echo across the whole park. Maybe they're amped up because it's Friday? I can't imagine that it'd matter to most of them, though. Surely the majority are retired and don't much care which day of the week it is.

As I pause to stretch my arms, another woman catches my eye. "And how are you?" she asks.

"Good, thanks."

"No friend today?"

I smile. "Not this time."

"How long do you have?" she asks, not needing to clarify.

"About two weeks."

"Oh my," she says. "Do you know what you're having?"

"A girl."

"Your first?"

"Yes."

She smiles, nods, turns away. "They change everything," she adds, almost not even to me.

At some unspoken signal, the women spread out, clumped in pairs and small groups as they claim their area for the bulk of the class. I use the wall to get even farther in, wanting my customary back corner. I'm tall enough to need the deeper end to keep my whole body submerged—necessary for the bouncing type of moves we tend to do there. Momma doesn't jump on land anymore.

Despite having to brush past a few ladies, no one else tries to chat with me. It isn't until I finally stand still and look up that I fully register how rowdy the girls are today. Maybe it's being all clustered in one big pool instead of spread among the length of the lazy river, which we sometimes use instead. Maybe it's Friday. Maybe it's the storm clouds in the distance, lending the electricity to the bright yellow heat of the morning. They bob and churn like the bubbles in a pot, a vibrant clash of energy and gossip.

". . . no, it's my knee. I have to stretch it every day or it's so stiff I can't move it when I wake up."

". . . he doesn't really need to keep working. She just can't stand having him home all day. On Tuesday he said . . ."

". . . making a huge batch of cookies so I have extra to take to the party."

I jog gently in the deep, wedged between the side of the wave pool and the buoyed rope that sections off the deepest end where the waves emanate from. Beside me, on one of the flat-topped white and red buoys, I spot a tiny toad. He's no bigger than my thumbnail, balanced precariously on the foam, his bumpy back looking dry and fragile in the sun. My grandmother's voice echoes from my childhood, chastising, *Put that thing down, it'll give you warts.*

I crane my neck to look at the ledge above me, high enough to keep the waves in when they're turned up. There's nowhere safer for me to set the little guy—it looks pretty out of reach. I can't imagine how he made it all the way here.

In my periphery, at the head of the pool centered above the roped-off portion, I see shifting legs and sneakers. I glance up, squinting against the sun to see a new instructor. He's tall, lanky, scruffy in a charming way. He has on athletic shorts and a LIFEGUARD T-shirt, plus a blue visor that dents his poufy, curly hair. His beard and hair connect to form a dark cloud around his tan face; equally dark hair shades his wiry legs and arms, corded with muscle. He holds a bright green pool noodle and a big white megaphone that he raises to his mouth.

"All right, everybody, how we feeling?"

The women let out a raucous cheer. He grins, a brilliant flash of white teeth in his rich beard. I think I've figured out the source of the extra buzz today. Fresh blood. The other instructors we've had so far this summer have been young women, one good and two ambivalent, plus one guy who was sweet but kind of a dink. This guy is different.

I study him, and I think styles really do cycle back around. He looks like he could be straight out of the seventies or eighties, young when most of these women were young. He reminds me of pictures of my dad and his friends back when they were my age. These gals' type, I would think.

"Good to hear!" he booms through the speaker. "Everybody warmed up?"

A chorus of yeses and whoops. They love that he's playing them like a crowd. The other instructors never do that.

"Let's go then," he chants, voice carrying easily out over our heads. "What we're gonna do first is take the noodle in both hands out in front of you and push it forward and back in front of you as you do butt kicks. Heels all the way to your butt, as fast as you can. The deeper you hold your noodle, the more of a challenge it'll be."

He sets down the megaphone and mimes an out-of-water version of the exercise. I'm surprised and a little impressed by how unselfconscious he seems. He's probably my age or a bit younger, which isn't an age known for not caring. Even ten months ago I might've felt totally different if I'd been here with him instructing. I'd have thought about how dorky my long-sleeved sun shirt is, how unflattering my maternity swimsuit underneath is on my shape, the incongruity of my presence among the older group, and how generally lame it is to do water aerobics. The only reason I don't care now is that pregnancy has knocked it straight out of me. You can't be young and attractive when you're carrying a bowling ball. The bowling ball gets the youth; she happily sucks it out of you. It's a mixed blessing. Freedom from the constant pressure to look this way, act that way, yes, but also a loss of resources, a reduction in status.

So I don't care, just like all of these women, which leaves me in a bizarre and fascinating position to analyze why *he* doesn't care. Young and cute, most guys would be dragging their feet at least a little to teach this class. Just that confident, maybe. Maybe he thinks it's all a joke, but it doesn't seem like it. He seems genuinely cheerful to be here, and as he switches us to our next exercise and then our next, it becomes apparent that he's actually good at this. Far better than the other instructors so far. He doesn't stall or kill time with stupid filler moves that are too easy even for the frailest among us. He keeps us moving quickly from one thing into the next, each a decent amount of work. It's the first time my heart rate's really been up in class the whole summer.

The buzz from the ladies increases. They, too, have their heart rates up as they churn the water white with effort. They never quit talking and laughing and calling out answers to his megaphone questions. They stop shy of catcalling or flirting the way a group of younger women might. They're too old for such tactlessness. Not that they need to care. They care even less than I do what he thinks of them. Their chatter isn't overt or overtly secretive, but I sense that it's largely about him nonetheless. I wonder if he feels it, their hungry attention. Cheerful, buoyant, eager. They've been waiting for someone like him.

I notice him gesture to one of the inconspicuous lifeguards off to the side before he raises his speaker again, aims it out across the water. "Now you're going to put your noodle between your legs to float, bicycle with your feet, and breaststroke with your arms. Try not to touch the bottom. All the way from one side to the other and back!"

Keenly, the women climb onto their noodles like they are water horses and begin paddling across. I check my tiny toad friend and make sure he's okay before I start across, the noodle bumping out far in front of me because of my belly. I hug the buoy rope, skirting only the women who don't first move to avoid me. Most of them do, though. Pregnancy trumps age when it comes to hindrance; they've had more time to get used to theirs—a more gradual decline.

As I stroke my way across the pool, I keep looking up to see what the new guard's being called over for. I can't put my finger on it, but something about the way the instructor got his attention and speaks to him in a low voice, megaphone down, makes me think it's vaguely secretive.

I'm not the only one who notices. Nothing catches attention quite like someone trying to avoid attention.

The buzz of the women turns slightly softer as they run out of breath from exertion and continue, as I do, to watch the unfolding interaction with the new guard. He's younger, blonder, tanner, more muscular, and less appealing. He looks hairless and of a new generation. He doesn't flirt with the women with smiles and dimple-winks. In fact, he avoids them altogether as he crosses back toward one of the buildings and disappears.

I touch the far side and begin paddling back, dodging grannies. I wonder if maybe our instructor dude is a head guard and the other guy got in trouble or something.

By the time I'm back to my spot—the toad is still there—the younger guard has come back out with one of those incredibly long pool nets used to scoop stuff from the water. He's trailed by three other young guards, one guy and two girls, all in red swimsuits.

The women begin to mutter and mumble, asking among themselves if anyone knows what's in the water or what's going on. I have the distinct feeling, as I'm sure do all of them, that we're not being told something.

"Nice job, everyone!" he calls through the speaker. "Next up, we're going to do some crunches. Lean back on your noodle and try to bring your legs up to your chest, like this. If you need support you can back against a wall."

He instructs and illustrates as the young male guard begins sweeping the net into the deep end beyond the buoys. I strain my neck, trying to see what might be there, but it's in the middle, far from my side.

One of the ladies calls out extra loudly, "What's in the water?"

The young guy looks up at our instructor, obviously afraid to answer. Whatever it is, I have a bad feeling. Their unwillingness to tell us makes me think they think we're going to panic if we know, which makes me wonder if we should be panicking.

"Now twist with your crunches," he says, angling the megaphone the other direction to repeat, "Now twist!"

We do, watching the cluster of young guards staring down at something the blond kid is trying to scoop out. Two more guards come from the building to watch.

A louder woman calls out, "What's over there?" Her voice is undeniable; she must be answered. The mood has shifted from simple curiosity to the beginnings of discontent at being ignored.

Finally, our instructor answers her, calling down not on his megaphone, but in his strong voice. "It's a tarantula."

I hear a single gasp in the very back, near the shallows, but everyone else laughs or sighs and begins chatting again.

"Is it alive?" someone asks.

A woman in the front center, who can see what's going on, answers, "Yep, it's just floating there. Got stuck, I guess. It can't get out."

"Better than that time they found a dead rat," one woman faux mutters. She's the one who always talks too loud and pretends to lower her voice while still making sure she's heard by everyone. "Just floating by the drain in the lazy river a couple weeks back. Big old thing."

"Be careful with it," another calls up to the cluster of young guards. From where I do my careful crunches, legs wide to leave room, I can't see the tarantula in question. "They have very delicate legs!"

I nod my agreement, glancing again at the teeny toad, still holding strong. Tarantulas can't really hurt you, and they're cool and beautiful and surprisingly fragile. I hope these young guards handle it with care. I'm afraid they won't.

I'm insulted by their assumption that we'd be scared enough to cause trouble just by its presence in the whole wide pool. They're the ones who look nervous, laughing and jumping as they ineffectually try to scoop it into the net.

Our instructor switches us to leg presses, holding the noodle underwater with just one foot, and quietly talks to the teens, getting them to be serious and make a real effort to scoop the spider carefully.

"Okay," he calls through the speaker. "Now lifts to the back. One leg at a time. If you need balance, grab a wall."

One of the young male guards tickles one of the girl's necks and she shrieks. Our instructor sets down the megaphone yet again, something of his charm leaking away as he chastises them. He takes the net from the blond guy and shoos them away. Then he silently fishes into the deep end, his movements slow and careful until the ladies in the center let out a little cheer as he raises the net out of the water.

I glimpse a dark round spot that must be the spider clinging to the white webbing. Poor thing. I hope the chlorine won't hurt it.

"You should hold it," a disembodied voice from the opposite side of the pool calls up. "They hardly ever bite!"

Our instructor pauses, then grins as he walks his hands down the long pole extension toward the net. "Yeah right," he says without his mic. "*You* should hold it."

"You *should*," someone else calls, sounding offended. "Take it out of the net. Don't just drop it on the ground."

Several women raise their voices in agreement, croaking out commands and cheers and something perilously close to taunts.

The instructor's white smile slips back into his beard, but he does continue walking his hands toward the net end of the pole, creeping closer and closer to the dark fuzzy spot. If I can see it all the way from here, it must be a pretty big tarantula.

"Jog in place," he calls out, his voice almost lost over the growing murmur of the women. A filler exercise. Not his style so far. A little disappointing.

A woman near me echoes, "What?"

"Jog in place," another snips at her. "Just keep moving." But it's not the one hard of hearing she's annoyed with; it's him. He's leaving us hanging.

"Scoop it out," comes that voice on the far side again. Raspy and deep, maybe a smoker. "With your hand. Scoop it with your hand!"

A small chorus of consent rises. Some of the storm clouds cross the sun, sending a slight gray over the wave pool. The water is no longer white, but blue. People aren't moving much. We're all watching the young man as he carefully lets the end of the pole drop so he can hold the rim of the net instead. The spider is clinging not to the bottom, but one side.

The cluster of young lifeguards are barely visible clinging to the side of the building much like the spider, watching from around the corner like kids sent to bed early before a holiday.

I jog in place, holding my belly, pulse high.

"Jumping jacks," the instructor calls out, and we switch motions.

"Pick it up," a woman cries, like a chant, and says it again. "Pick it up!"

But instead of joining the phrase, the other women begin to call out other things. They agree, but they don't need a chant. "Scoop it out," they call.

"Hold it!"

"Let it crawl onto your fingers."

"Pick it up!"

I shrink back against the wall, still doing underwater jumping jacks, not bringing my arms overhead because I don't want the splash to disrupt my view. I feel breathless. Not unusual with my diaphragm crammed up under my rib cage, but it doesn't usually happen in this class.

The handsome young instructor carefully draws the tarantula out of the net, balancing it on the palm of his large hand.

The ladies cheer. Not the same cheer as when he asked how they were feeling or if they were ready for the next thing. A different cheer. A cheer made of smoke and moonlight and a lifetime of corrosion.

The instructor lets a small, close-lipped smile spread his beard, but he looks nervous. He begins walking toward the greenery at the edge of the concrete.

The graceful legs of the spider cling to his hand, nothing more than a blur from my corner. The clouds shift again and the intensifying sun blasts us all with fresh heat.

A small woman, the one with arms so thin they look like bones draped in skin, calls softly into a sudden silence: "Eat it."

There's a group pause, a silence broken only by the sounds of water lapping and swaying, as every single person in the wave pool waits for a reaction.

The instructor looks at us with wide eyes, hunched with his own hand far away from himself, as if he can hold the spider at bay. He says nothing.

"Yeah," a different lady calls, one of the more middle-aged ones. "They're a delicacy in some parts of the world. Good for you, even!"

"It probably won't make it after a dip in this chemical water. You might as well."

"Go ahead! We won't tell."

"Eat it!"

"Eat it!"

"Have a snack!"

High peals of laughter chime out like gleeful bells. I press my palms flat against the high wall behind me. My noodle floats in front of me, forgotten.

I can't tell if they're joking.

He can't either.

The women don't break into a chant, don't taunt him, don't jeer. They simply explode into delighted, wild conversations about the types of bugs and animals you can eat. Times they saw spiders in their houses and cars. Recipes that call for unusual things. How they're tired of cooking over a hot stove in this crazy summer heat.

But they don't take their eyes from him.

The young man reaches the bushes, begins to squat, his back partially to us, almost fully to me, so that all I can see of his arm is the very far edge of his outstretched hand—the one that holds the tarantula.

The overloud woman, the one with the voice that carries no matter what, repeats, once, "Eat it. Do it."

I look again to the instructor, crouched over the bushes, frozen. Finally, he twitches, begins to move his arm.

My mouth parts in horrible anticipation, and I realize that I, too, want him to. Some morbid impulse, a stray feeling of revenge. I have a flash of what he'd look like, those brown, hairy legs protruding helter-skelter from his lips, almost lost in the dark bush of his beard. I can almost hear the crunch, see the waving struggle of brittle limbs.

The thought is too real, as if I'm conjuring it. If he does it now, I'll feel complicit. I can't stay to see if he'll lower his hand to the leaves or raise it to his lips.

I glance down in time to see my tiny toad slip into the water, his back legs pumping once, twice, and I scoop him out balanced in one palm, the other cupped like a lid.

He's almost weightless. I feel his quiet, frantic movements in time with my own pounding pulse as I turn without looking back and begin to wade toward the shallow.

Behind me, around me, the women boil and bubble.

In the hollow of my hand, sudden warmth as the toad releases his bladder in fear.

There's Always Something in the Woods

by Gabino Iglesias

CARLOS LOOKED SCARED. He kept looking out the small window over the kitchen sink at the darkness outside and running his hands down the side of his jeans as if trying to dry sticky sweat that refused to leave his palms.

"Chill the fuck out, man," said Ernesto.

Carlos looked at him. A brief flash of anger creased his brow before melting back into the mask of concern he'd worn since they'd gotten together to plan this little debacle two weeks ago.

In her silent corner, Amanda observed. She had half a mind to slip out somehow and let them deal with whatever came their way. It wasn't much of a plan, especially considering Ernesto had the car keys in his pocket. Plus, she'd have to make her way to the car through woods she didn't know. Despite all that, getting the hell out sounded like paradise. She almost didn't mind having to go back and find a new kitchen gig at some other strip joint. There were plenty of those in Austin. Carlos could find construction work like he'd done so many times before. Or he could work landscaping again. He was smart and a quick learner, so those jobs never felt fair to Amanda, but he had no papers. Luckily, he'd never had a hard time finding a job. Amanda knew most business owners love cheap labor more than they hate immigrants.

"There's something out there, cabrón," said Carlos. His voice was strained. The last word had escaped his mouth like a snake slithering between clenched teeth. He was used to keeping his cool, so losing it was making everything worse.

"There's always something in the woods," said Ernesto. "In this case, it's your own fear, man. Mellow out."

"Nah, I saw something on our way here," said Carlos. "We were being followed. We were being . . . stalked."

"Bullshit. You're just paranoid."

"It's not nonsense! Ask Amanda. She saw it too."

Amanda had gotten comfortable in her dark spot opposite the cabin's door. Her back was pressed against the rear left corner of the cabin. She had her knees up against her chest. Between her legs and the two walls, she felt somewhat protected on all sides. The men kept looking out the window over the sink, at their phones, and at each other, so she'd felt invisible for a while. She liked the feeling.

The scant light coming from the small window fell on the men sideways and landed on the kitchen table. Amanda had seen what looked like sharp pieces of bone scattered on the table when she walked past it, but she was focused on getting as far away from the door as possible and didn't stop to look. Now the white pieces of . . . whatever it was were calling to her.

Ernesto turned to Amanda. The little light that came from the window reflected off the sweat on his forehead. The beads came in part from it being Texas in the middle of July and in part from his nerves. Men rely on their bodies to communicate strength, but their bodies betray them in many ways. Biology and chemistry are awful liars.

"Did you see anything, Mandy?"

She hated the nickname. Ernesto had used it to bother her for so long, and now he couldn't stop unless he concentrated on it. He seemed to enjoy bothering her, but they were good friends.

She had always made friends with outcasts, and Ernesto, a Salvadoran immigrant with no papers who escaped his country because a lot of bad people wanted him dead, was definitely an outcast. He'd also been Carlos's best friend since before Amanda met him, and that meant something to her, as if it made them family somehow.

"I . . . saw something. I've no idea what it was," said Amanda.

"See? I fucking told you. I saw it on our way here and saw it again a couple minutes ago when you were in the bathroom. It was moving out there, right beyond the trees. It was . . . big. Not wide, more long than anything . . . Anyway, we should get the hell outta here and—"

"Enough!" Ernesto's voice cut through the room like a sickle.

Amanda had been brought up by a father who liked to raise his voice and hit anyone who yelled back, so she was no stranger to explosive anger. She'd dealt with angry men her whole life. Their testosterone outbursts didn't surprise or intimidate her. She was always ready to strike first if she felt a man was about to go from screaming to hitting.

"The car is almost a quarter mile from here," said Ernesto. "The guy who's gonna come pick up the horse will be here in a couple hours. We're all about to get a nice chunk of cash, okay? All you have to do is k—"

CLUNK!

They all looked up. Something had landed on the roof of the cabin.

"What the hell was that?" As soon as the words left her mouth, Amanda felt like the dumbest character in one of those found footage films Carlos loved so much. She wished she could take the words back. She wished she could take the whole night back.

"Maybe a pinecone or some shit fell on the roof," said Ernesto.

"Come on, man," said Carlos. "You know that was too damn loud to be a pinecone."

"I don't care what is was."

Ernesto's body language told a different story. He turned and looked out the window again. When he turned back, the anger that had contorted his face a minute ago had been replaced by a crease in his brow and a tension in his lips that spelled anxiety.

"What do you think you saw, Amanda?"

The use of her full name meant more than his inquiry. Ernesto was serious. She didn't want to freak him out, but lying was out of the question. They were somewhere outside Fredericksburg in a hunter's cabin that belonged to Ernesto's uncle. They were surrounded by wilderness and relatively far from the car. Ernesto said they had to leave the car hidden in case someone reported it, whatever that meant. They'd left his Subaru somewhat hidden behind some bushes on the dirt road that led to the cabin. It was a dirt road they'd gotten on after turning off 290, a few miles after passing Johnson City's deserted Main Street. Being far from everything she knew made Amanda feel vulnerable. Honesty seemed like the best option. After all, she had seen something out there.

"I . . . I don't know what I saw. It was a bit after we left the car. We were coming up a little hill and my foot caught on something, so I stopped for a second to check my shoe and rub my ankle. The moonlight was coming through trees to my left, and I saw something move there. It was fast and . . . slanky. That's all I know."

"Exactly!" said Carlos. "Fast and fucking big. I'm—"

THUNK!

Their eyes once again flew to the roof. This time, the sound had been even louder.

Carlos inhaled and kept talking with his eyes jumping from the roof to the window and back to the roof.

"What I saw looked like a really tall man with impossibly long ar—"

"Hold on, man," said Ernesto. "Amanda, I want you to be sure. This isn't the time for games. That Carlos here is freaked out is normal, but if you think there's something out there . . ."

"I'm not playing around, Ernesto," she said.

"Fuck."

Silence invaded the cabin, a heavy, tense, tangible presence between them. Amanda pulled her knees closer to her chest and remembered something strange she'd experienced back home, something she didn't normally talk about but that struck her as a palliative for the current situation, something less ominous than the current silence. It was also as strange as what she'd seen in the woods.

"When I was about twelve years old . . ." she began. Then she stopped and crossed her legs in front of her so she could place her elbows on them, lean forward, and push her face out of the darkness that pooled in her corner of the room.

"My dad would sometimes take us somewhere on Sundays. You know, to make us forget about whatever horrible shit he'd done to us the previous six days. Anyway, one time he took us to El Yunque, a famous rainforest. As always, it was raining up there. That's what you usually get in a rainforest, right? We didn't do much. Cooked some hot dogs on one of those covered huts with a concrete table and a dirty grill that can be found all over the place. Anyway, point is, we got tired of the rain, so we waited for it to turn into a drizzle and ran back to the car.

"I sat in the front because those curvy mountain roads always made my mom nauseous, so she preferred to ride in the back with my little brother."

Amanda stopped talking. Both men were listening to her. She had their attention. That meant no arguing for a while. Too bad there wasn't much more to the story.

"We rounded a curve in the road and something ran in front of the car. My dad hit the brakes. We were going slow because of the rain and the shitty, dangerous roads up there, so the car stopped pretty quickly and didn't fishtail or anything. My dad looked at me, and I could see the question in his eyes. He knew I'd seen the thing that had run in front of the car. It'd been running on two legs. He put the car in park, threw his door open, and got out without a word. I saw him walk up to some greenery right where the . . . the creature had disappeared. Then he stopped. Way he was standing there, I knew he was seeing something. I opened my door and went to him. My mom yelled something about not being stupid and staying in the car, but I didn't care.

"When I reached my dad, his face was all scrunched up, like he was seeing something disgusting. I was going to ask him what was wrong when he lifted his finger slowly and said, 'Look, right in front of me, next to that patch of mud.' There was a lot of green, but the rain had come down hard, and there were patches of mud here and there. I looked right in front of him and saw nothing, so I kept looking. And then I saw it . . ."

Carlos and Ernesto had turned their bodies away from the window and were staring at Amanda. Carlos had his hands in his pockets. It was something he did when he got nervous. Amanda normally found it endearing, but in this context, she hated it. Ernesto had his thumbs hooked on his belt. He looked at her as if waiting for an answer to an incriminating question. She continued.

"Imagine a big gray frog walking on two legs, and that's more or less what we saw. I mean, it was slightly more . . . humanoid, but if you saw it, a frog would be the first thing that came to mind. The head was round, and it had huge black eyes. The mouth was like a slit, and its arms were long and shiny. It looked wet, but not wet because it'd been raining—more of a slimy kind of wet. It took a step to the right, still on two legs, and then bolted, moving deeper into the plants on the side of the road. It moved just like a person would."

The men stayed quiet. She was done. Telling them about getting back in the car would've been dumb. She knew a story was over when the good stuff was over.

"That's it?" asked Ernesto.

"Yeah."

"So what are you trying to say? You think there's a tall gray frog out there?"

"No, all I'm saying is that there's weird shit out there and sometimes you see something you can't explain. That's it. The gray frog was tiny, and now that I'm an adult, I know the only reason it scared the shit out of me is because I didn't know what it was. Same now. There's a thing out there I've never seen before, but that doesn't mean it's dangerous or anything, you know? Could be a diseased animal or som—"

"No," said Carlos. "No, this isn't the same. You saw some weird animal, some . . . mutated frog or some shit. This is different." Carlos walked to the table and grabbed one of the white pieces that were scattered on it. "Look at this shit," he said, holding up what looked like a curved, sharpened bone. "This is a tooth. A huge fucking tooth. They're all teeth. I've never seen teeth like this before, and I'm sure they belong to whatever is out there, the thing that was following us and trying to stay outta sight. You saw it, Amanda!"

Amanda knew what he meant. The slanky thing on two legs had moved from tree to tree with purpose and speed. The memory of its long, humanoid limbs swinging in the darkness sent a shiver down her spine. It was obviously trying to stay out of sight, but it never stayed put. It had followed them. She'd said nothing because jogging through the woods with stolen drugs wasn't the best time to entertain things like that. Now they were locked here with the drugs and some huge teeth from a strange creature until someone came to buy them, and the thing was out there, apparently throwing rocks at the cabin.

Ernesto looked out the window again, his brown eyes scanning the darkness outside. "Whatever is out there will probably go away eventually," he said. "We don't need to go outside anyway."

Carlos took a step back and pointed at Ernesto.

"You motherfucker! You knew about this!"

"What are you talking about, man?" asked Ernesto.

"You just went from 'There's nothing out there' to 'Whatever is out there will go away eventually,' pendejo!"

"So?"

"I've known you what, fifteen years?"

"Give or take. What d—?"

"You never give in so easily," said Carlos. "Amanda's story didn't convince you. This ain't El Yunque. You knew something before we came here, or at least you suspected something, didn't you?"

"I'd heard something about the area, but that's—"

"Este pinche, cabrón!" said Carlos. He turned and paced away from the window. Amanda knew that anger made him abandon English and revert to Spanish, his native tongue. He was a good man, but the dark past inside him could turn into violence if left unchecked.

"Then why the hell did you bring us here?" asked Amanda. She'd tried to push away the image of the figure walking through the trees, but now she couldn't. The memory of that amphibian thing on two legs had somehow magnified her current fear.

"I . . . It was the only place I knew that wasn't near other people. We stole about a hundred grand worth of horse from that woman. I wanted a safe place far away from . . . everything. There's only that dirt road coming here. So it's easy to see anyone approaching. It was . . . It struck me as the perfect place, okay? And it's not like what I heard sounded completely true, you know?"

"So what did you hear?"

Ernesto looked at the window again and opened his mouth, but a sound from the left side of the cabin made them all jump. It made Amanda think someone, or something, had slammed its body against the wall. Something to her left fell. The sound of glass shattering made her jump. She looked at the floor next to her. A newspaper article. She picked it up by the light brown frame and shook off some of the broken glass. She had to bring it close to her face to make out the headline: HILL COUNTRY CREATURE STRIKES AGAIN. The first lines said something about mutilated cows. She stopped reading and stood up. She took her phone out of her pocket and turned on the flashlight. The wall was covered in newspaper clippings like the one she was holding, all local, all mentioning dead animals.

A presence next to her made Amanda jump again. It was Carlos. His eyes were open wide as he scanned the wall. Carlos snapped out of it a second later and moved toward Ernesto.

"What the fuck is all that?" he asked while pointing at the wall. "If you know something, tell us now. I'm serious."

Ernesto inhaled as if bracing for some kind of invisible impact.

"You knew about this, didn't you?" Amanda sounded sad instead of angry.

"I . . . yeah, but it's just stories, you know? Weird shit folks like my uncle talk about. The motherfucker is obsessed with it. That's why we could use this place; he won't spend the night here even if you paid him. Old-lady stories that—"

"Fuck that," said Carlos. "Tell us what you know. Now!"

Ernesto took another big breath before he started talking.

"Buddy of mine who grew up right here in Hill Country told me a story about this part of the woods. His grandparents owned a farm out here or some shit. They had a bunch of acres somewhere nearby. Anyway, he said there was a thing living in their barn, a strange, tall creature with a big head and large, black eyes that hid in the woods during the day and came into the barn to sleep or something at night. Now, my buddy, Jake, he didn't hit the bottle or nothing. He was a regular dude. I had no reason not to believe him. He always told the same story time and again, too, which I've learned isn't something most liars do. You know, folks who lie all the time usually tell a bunch of lies and they get them all mixed up, but when someone always tell the same story, it's probably t—"

CLUNK!

Something landed on the roof again. This time, it sounded even harder.

"That pinecone must've been the size of a cinder block," said Amanda with no humor in her voice. "Tell your story, Ernesto. What the hell is out there? Should we be on our way back to the car?"

Ernesto took another deep breath while still looking at the ceiling.

"Right . . . Anyway, Jake told me more than once how he refused to go out to the barn at night. One time, his grandpa sent him out there to get some shit, and he says he walked in and saw the thing in a corner. A long, humanoid creature with thin arms and a very large head. Spooked the shit outta him. He told his grandpa and then repeated his story to his mom the next day. They said he'd seen the shadow of a tree or maybe a bird. He was a kid, you know? It was dark and all that. They dismissed him. Can't blame them. He was a kid talking about monsters, so I'm sure any of us would've done the same thing. Thing is, Jake kept an eye out and saw the creature a few more times, either leaving the barn or walking along the edge of the tree line behind it. It was always a glimpse, you know? Like, enough to know it was there and that it was something weird and shaped like a thin, big-headed person but not clear enough to actually know what the fuck he was looking at."

"Just like the thing Amanda and I saw out there!" interjected Carlos.

"Yeah, something like that," said Ernesto. "Long story short, Jake's room was on the second floor, right across from his grandparents' bedroom. His mom left him with them all the time because she worked night shifts at a twenty-four-hour diner right down the road in Fredericksburg. Point is, Jake's bedroom had a window and he could see the barn from it, so he became obsessed, staying up at all hours of the night trying to get a better look at the damn thing that he was sure lived in the barn or in the woods around it.

"He never saw it again, but he knew it was out there. Any time he brought it up, his grandparents or his mom would joke about his imagination and laugh at him, so he stopped talking about it. Then, when he was almost sure the thing had vanished or died somewhere out there, he and his grandpa started finding mutilated animals out on their property and in the nearby woods. Started with a few cats, dogs, possums, and raccoons. Jake told his grandpa it had to be the creature. Grandpa told him to shut the fuck up about the creature already. Animals die all the time. Disease. Other animals attack them. People poison them. They eat some shit they shouldn't have eaten. Whatever. Old man had a point, although none of that explained why the animals were all messed up or why some of them had been mutilated in weird ways. Anyway, before they could figure out if there was another animal out there attacking dogs and cats, they started finding dead deer. Then they were doing one of their rounds and found a mountain lion missing its head. Nothing out there preys on mountain lions.

"Grandpa kept up his bullshit explanations, but Jake could tell he no longer believed a single word he said. Also, they realized no animal would scavenge the bodies if they left them around. It was like they were poisoned or something.

"Jake had a good relationship with his grandpa and he kept telling him that he believed the creature in the barn was responsible. His grandpa told him to stop watching movies that were rotting his brain. I guess things stayed the same for a while, but then, on a night like any other, Jake was in bed and heard a sound like someone screaming far away, a screech that woke him up. He kept hearing it as his brain woke up for real. It wouldn't stop. Jake was facing the door and the sound was coming from outside so he turned around, thinking he was gonna get up and take a look out the window, but when he turned, he saw the thing right outside his window. He said the head was dark and had no hair or feathers on it, and its toothless, round mouth was open. The screeching was coming from it. The thing had black eyes that were larger than any Jake had ever seen. It watched as Jake moved, and instead of vanishing, it slapped a hand on the glass. Not a paw or a talon, a fucking hand.

"Jake ran to his grandparents' bedroom and dragged them both to his room, but the thing had gone by the time they came in. Jake was so freaked out about the thing somehow hovering right outside, peeking into his window, that he convinced his grandpa to grab his rifle and try to hunt the creature down. After a lot of bitching and moaning, his grandfather finally agreed. The next night, they w—"

The rock that just landed on the roof of the cabin was so big that it was followed by a crack and a moan from the wood.

"We need to get the fuck outta here right now," said Carlos.

"If there's something out there, you want to risk a half-mile jog in the woods with it behind you?"

Carlos's silence was eloquent, and it was all the answer Ernesto needed.

"So, did they see it?" asked Amanda.

"What?"

"Your story. Jake. Did they see the thing in the barn?"

"Right. The window . . . They waited by the window, but they didn't see the creature. Jake said they should try again, and his grandpa said no, but then they went out the next morning and found three dead chickens outside the chicken coop, their bodies torn to pieces by something that drank all their blood and ate away at the soft bits. The dead chickens made Jake's grandpa angry, so he said they'd spend one more night dozing off in front of the damn window.

"Well, around one in the morning, right before they were about to pass out, they saw movement to the left of the barn. Something was exiting the woods and making its way to the barn. Jake's grandpa told him to wait in the house and went out there with his rifle and a flashlight. According to Jake, he opened fire as soon as he walked into the damn barn. Then Jake heard the screeching sound from far away and then a second shot.

"The shots woke up Jake's grandma. She grabbed him by the arm and dragged him downstairs. They took another flashlight from the kitchen and ran out there. They approached the barn quietly and scared shitless, obviously. They couldn't find Jake's grandpa at first. There was blood on the floor, and the rifle was there, slightly bent as if some giant had tried to break it, but they couldn't find anyone. They hollered and looked and then hollered some more.

"Finally, they called the cops and two guys came out and helped them look. About half an hour later, one of the pigs had the brilliant idea of shining a light upward. That's when they found Jake's grandpa. The man had been attacked by something or someone, and then that something or someone had pulled him all the way up to an exposed beam near the roof of the barn. They had to get firefighters with big ladders to get the body down. Way Jake told the story, his grandpa's body had been viciously attacked. Someone had punched a hole through the left side of his body. He said you could see his ribs and lungs. There was also a large cut between his neck and shoulder that made the cops think some crazy killer with a machete was out there in the woods.

"Here's the kicker: They never found a weapon or anyone to pin the murder on. Jake kept the article that came out about it in the local newspaper in his wallet. It was short and vague as fuck, but it said the man had been 'viciously attacked by an unknown assailant.' That's fancy talk for seriously fucked up, you know? I know it said that because Jake would show it to me all the time, or at least whenever we drank together. Anyway, that happened a couple miles from here . . ."

Ernesto stopped talking. He looked deflated. Amanda felt like he'd given them a lot of information, but other than use it as an excuse to tell them to run for the car, she had no idea what to do with it.

"We need to leave. We're not safe here!" Carlos wasn't panicking, but he'd taken the first step down that road. He'd been on edge for two weeks. He'd been the one with the big idea. He knew the woman who ran the Yellow Rose, where Amanda worked in the kitchen, not as a dancer, was using the strip joint as a cover for her drug business. He planned everything. Quick hit. From the inside. No killing. Grab the stuff and vanish. It was dangerous, but Carlos was always worrying about money. He had no papers, which made things harder, and Amanda hadn't finished college and had a thick accent, which made every human resources person that interviewed her smile . . . and then give the job to someone else. They were both desperate, and when Ernesto said he could set the sale up with a friend of his cousin in San Antonio, they'd decided to go for it. Poverty is often the mother of bad decisions.

Now here they were, and they weren't willing to wait for the buyer because something tall with long arms was out there throwing rocks at the cabin. Big rocks. Anger washed over

Amanda. This wasn't fair. The plan was supposed to get them out of their hole. Maybe she and Carlos could use the money to get married. That would be an easy path to citizenship.

"Maybe we sh—"

CRASH!

The rock was larger than a melon but was more cube-shaped than round. It fell through the ceiling and landed with a loud thud a few feet from where Carlos stood. Amanda found herself on her feet with no memory of standing up.

Carlos was about to speak when something else landed on the roof.

"That's it," Ernesto said, his hand flying back to the gun tucked away under his black T-shirt. "We're—"

The screech was as loud as a siren. Their shoulders went up. Amanda covered her ears. Carlos looked up as if he expected a banshee to drop down on him from the cabin's ceiling.

Then the window exploded.

Glass shards flew into the cabin.

Amanda shielded her face.

Carlos jumped away.

Ernesto screamed.

A long, dark thing came through the busted window. It looked like a cross between a human arm and a branch covered in rotting muscles. The thin hand at the end of it had fingers that were at least a foot long. There were more than five of them. They quickly wrapped themselves around Ernesto's head and shoulders. The thing outside pulled back with surprising speed. Amanda saw Ernesto standing there and then saw the bottom of his black boots as he flew out the window.

The screech moved away and ceased. Ernesto's screams replaced the deafening shriek for a second and then stopped abruptly.

Carlos ran across the room and held Amanda's arms.

"You okay?"

Amanda didn't know how to reply to that.

"What the fuck was that?"

"No idea. We need to get in the bathroom or something. Let's g—"

"No! No, I went when we got here. There's a huge window there, right over the shower."

"Fuck! Let's run for it."

"What?!"

"Vámonos, Amanda! I think I can get us back to the car. If not, I can at least get us to the road."

"Ernesto had the keys."

Carlos's face crumbled.

"And the gun . . . FUCK!"

Amanda saw him move toward the door, stop, and turn. He was lost. She had to save him.

"Let's run for it. You sure you know how to make it back to the road?"

"Yeah . . . espera!"

Carlos ran to the small kitchen table and grabbed the three sandwich bags full of small, white heroin packets. Then he stepped back and looked at the window. The sound of insects was coming from the woods.

Amanda knew they would stay there if she didn't start moving, so she did.

As soon as she opened the door, Carlos told her to wait.

"Look around first . . ."

They looked around. Darkness and trees. Bright stars up above. Nothing else. Amanda imagined a huge dark mouth with long, jagged teeth covered in Ernesto's blood. She was repulsed and scared, but hoped the thing was busy eating . . .

"Let's do this," she said.

They were about eighty feet from the cabin, and right where the woods started looking like real wilderness and not the kind you get around places where there are people, when they heard the screech.

They started running.

Adrenaline rode Amanda's veins. She felt like the ground was coming up to meet her feet with too much force, as if it were punishing her for trying to run as fast as she could. The pain made her think about her father. It reminded her of running away to the States. It reminded her she was here because she'd made some bad decisions.

The screech got louder. The eerie, high-pitched crescendo came at them like a threat, an awful promise wrapped around a single, deafening note.

The screech stopped. Carlos had fallen behind, and Amanda heard him breathing like a scared, wounded animal. The desperation in his breathing, the fear in every frantic inhalation, jabbed at Amanda's heart.

Something moved near them. Carlos yelled. A sandwich bag full of heroin flew past Amanda's head, the plastic catching slivers of moonlight as it twirled by. Then there was a loud crunch, and Carlos's scream turned into a wet moan. Amanda dug deep and found nothing. Fear will inject your system with adrenaline, but not for long.

It wasn't fair. Nothing in her life had been fair. She deserved better. Carlos deserved better. She was tired of being poor. She was tired of being a brown woman. She was tired of angry men.

Amanda refused to look back. She doubted the thing behind her would follow her into the middle of the road. All she had to do was make it there.

An invisible knife dug into her side. Her grandmother's voice echoed in her head. *Las malas decisiones traen malas consecuencias.*

Bad decisions bring bad consequences. She pushed the voice out. Her heartbeat filled the space. She had only done what she had to do to get a fucking chance in life. Now she was running. It was the only thing that mattered.

The screech came back, a far-off siren. It came closer quickly. Amanda choked on a sob. Her body was giving up. Her calves were on fire. Her lungs were begging for mercy. The screech became so loud, it hurt her ears. Her right leg went up and found no ground when it came down. Amanda was in the air.

A blur of hard darkness covered her face. The screech stopped. The scream caught in her throat lacked the oxygen it needed to be born.

Her body turned sideways. Immense pressure brimmed right under her chest, followed by a loud crunch. Pain became the world.

Las malas decisiones traen malas consecuencias.

This wasn't fair. All they'd wanted was a break, a bit of cash, a fucking opportunity to dig themselves out of the hole they'd been in all their lives.

Darkness came, absolute and cold. It wasn't fair.

The Turning

by Hailey Piper

WEEK 1

They say the turning takes nine weeks, give or take a day or two. That's what Krissy's heard, and that's if she believes the news that the curse is real, and then she has to believe that the people in suits have a clue what they're talking about. A lot of faith to ask of a fourteen-year-old, but she's trying. Faith might be all she has left, a kind of magic that's forever dripping from this sieve of a world.

The turning begins in the feet. Her toenails have split already, talons budding at her toes' roots, and her soles stretch thin against the bone.

This doesn't get better from here, but she'll pretend it doesn't get worse. She meets her friends at school, texts them after, takes selfies for social media. If nothing else, she'll keep a record of these final weeks— Scratch that. She'll leave a record.

WEEK 2

Krissy coats greasy moisturizer over the scaly patches at her elbows and knees. Easy places to hide from friends and parents alike, and aside from her feet, nowhere else has shown signs of turning. If she can hide the symptoms long enough, maybe her body will fight the change same as a bad cold and no one will have to know.

Maybe she won't end up like those kids who get pulled out of school or mentioned on the news.

Her friends flit around her, oblivious hummingbirds. Beautiful creatures, and she envies them now, their ordinary skin that hasn't gone leathery and alien at the joints. Or are they, too, hiding the turning?

The change soon spreads to her chest, thighs, and spine, the last discovered when she turns her back to the mirror one morning and glances over her shoulder. She can't reach that far around herself to moisturize. The skin morphs unhindered.

She's still staring at her reflection when Mom opens the bedroom door. Mom never knocks.

WEEK 3

Krissy's parents pull her out of school and forbid her from seeing friends. A lump has formed on the crown of her head, and her school has a no-hats rule. There will be no hiding the budding crest. She hopes it will crumble, a brittle shell that flakes into strange, leathery dandruff.

The doctors seem less optimistic. They've seen this before, she knows, and they'll see it again when her turning has finished. Supposedly, the kids who finish then vanish without a trace.

By mid-week, her nose and lips begin sticking forward, her jaw having jutted up toward her cheekbones. No pain, only discomfort in body and soul. Heavier filters coat the few selfies she still snaps from her phone camera. A craving for fish invades her stomach, but feeding the changes will only encourage them, right? She forces down tonight's bland chicken cutlets and underbaked macaroni and cheese. Everything would taste better had it come from the water.

Mom says they'll try another specialist next week. Krissy tries to tell her "Okay," but a strange squawk rolls out instead.

Dad half chuckles into a fist, half chokes on cheesy noodles, and Krissy abandons the dining table on awkward, narrow feet.

Alone, she texts her friends about the specialist. Every word lies to them about her prospects or claws after commiseration in her parents' uncomfortable behavior.

A couple of friends respond with compulsory one- and two-sentence answers. The rest ignore her. They're probably afraid they'll catch the turning. No one really understands why it happens, after all—genetics, disease, witchcraft? The news calls it a curse, but deep down, it's a mystery.

Whatever the cause, her friends have decided they had best leave her alone. Krissy wonders if she would do the same in their shoes.

Her feet hardly fit into shoes anymore. The talons have grown too long, curling hooks that might snag every fish in the sea.

WEEK 4

The specialist turns out to be as unhelpful as the other doctors, and why wouldn't he? If some miracle cure were found to stop or reverse the turning, that news would spread faster than the curse itself. Instead, online articles only fearmonger about whose kids might turn next. Talking heads fret about social impact. Religious types of various denominations tell everyone to pray.

Krissy can't say who's right or wrong.

Non-answers aren't good enough for Mom. "Couldn't she stop it if she tried?" she asks, finger twirling her curly hair so tight that strands snap apart. Dad imitates a friendly-faced statue and stands just as useless.

"The infection isn't psychosomatic," the specialist says in a patient tone, but he doesn't understand the core of the question. Mom isn't looking for solutions.

She's looking for someone to blame.

Krissy's thumbs have grown thick since last week, but she's learning to type on her phone despite that. Once settled into the back seat of her parents' car, she logs in to her phone's Discuss app, where she's found a chatroom for other kids afflicted with the turning. She doesn't know their real names, but CatQueen, LimeSpine, BrutalCornflake5, and others help stave off her loneliness.

Unlike her school friends, they don't turn to ghosts. These friends turn like she does.

"I wish you wouldn't talk to those people," Mom says, as if the curse worsens by association. "You're not like them. They're stuck this way, but you aren't. We'll figure this out."

Krissy tries to answer, but her whine belts out in a high-pitched pterodactyl screech.

Mom glares over her shoulder. "Want to try that again, young lady?"

A tangled explanation drifts up Krissy's tongue, knotted with thoughts on community and shared experiences, but she only utters a lower, softer screech, choked at the end with a single, quiet word: "Please."

Mom turns to the windshield again, shaking her head. Krissy turns to her screen, but she listens hard.

Mom: "I can't."

Dad: "It's okay."

Mom: "How is it okay? She's turning into a fucking dinosaur."

Dad: "Actually, pterosaurs were flying reptiles, not true dinosaurs."

There is a cold, angry pause, and then a game of verbal tennis begins, one on one, with Krissy its only audience. She might as well be a ghost; her parents shout about her like she doesn't haunt the seat behind them.

More like she's inside them, nesting in their minds at all times. She's still chatting on her phone when Dad makes his peace offering via pizza and movie night. Krissy wants anchovies for the first time in her life, and Dad obliges. They make it partway through *Beetlejuice* until the scene when Geena Davis and Alec Baldwin malform their faces to scare away the intrusive family, and Mom abruptly shuts the movie off.

She doesn't have to say why. Alec Baldwin's stretched prosthetic face looks too similar to how kids like Krissy turn out in the end. How she'll turn out by the end.

This doesn't get better from here.

WEEK 5

Her parents' arguments become daily occurrences, drifting between hushed angry whispers and high-volume shouting matches. Krissy's learning to tune them out, but words crash through her walls both physical and mental. Group. Changes. Normal. Abnormal. Solution.

They don't feel her problems of a crest jutting from the crown of her head, snout stretching knifelike from her face, ears melting to earholes, or dark hair falling out in clumps on her pillow each night. Her rigid fingers struggle to turn shower nozzles, and her toothbrush snags on sharp teeth that grow unbecoming for yearbook photos and selfies alike. She's given up eating with utensils.

These are all symptoms to her parents. At their core, Krissy is the problem.

Her online friends echo the same, their parents unfeeling. That's why they have each other. They're calling themselves the were-dactyls now, with dactyl-men being vetoed for lack of inclusivity. She imagines were-dactyls would sound cool aloud if she could still speak any language but screeches.

She asks where LimeSpine has been. No one knows. Brutal-Cornflake5 suggests maybe her parents took her phone away.

Another were-dactyl suggests LimeSpine physically can't use the phone anymore. Krissy glances at her ever-thickening fingers and wonders how long she'll keep the power to tap a touch-screen.

CatQueen has theories, and they develop into group discussion. There is the always-question: How did the turning begin? Same as puzzled doctors, politicians, and clergy, the afflicted teenagers can only speculate. But those grown people with their complete yet underdeveloped brains keep clawing for solutions, not answers. They'll only consider an origin if it might provide a cure.

CatQueen suggests there can be no cure. What they're dealing with has lingered too long for any modern remedy. Archeologists used to fret about curses from dead people in ancient cultures they didn't understand. Nothing but ethnocentric superstition, especially when those archeologists should have been keeping an eye on the paleontologists, who never guessed what graves they might be digging up.

Finding the fossils of dinosaurs and the species that shared the world with them could mean looking for trouble.

There might have been magic in those Mesozoic days. The animals might have only been as conscious as crows, but every little girl who's traded food for trinkets with a corvid or three knows that, like their cousins, crows have a magic to them. They have judgment and revenge, too. Why should ancient animals be any different?

Anger might dwell in the bones of the dead, so potent that even fossilization couldn't break it. A revenge that lingers, buried in the earth until some crawling thing that dared stand on two legs and dominate the world comes digging. Finding. Unearth-ing magic that they can't feel, let alone understand, but they've freed it just the same. They had vengeance spells in prehistory, sure as they have them now.

Ask any crow.

WEEK 6

Webbing has grown down Krissy's arms. She struggles to wear shirts, the sleeves crumpling at her wrists.

Worse, her fingers have fused. Each day, their joints migrate farther down her arm. By the end, each upper limb will become one great webbed hand—a wing. She eats by sliding her snout along her dish. Grabbing at things becomes her feet's job; maybe that's why the turning begins there.

Still, she has lost the power to type on her phone. She can only scroll down the chat as her online friends wonder what's become of her, and then their discussions and questions carry on:

> How might pterosaur magic compare to crow magic?
> Did you know a flock of crows is called a murder?
> If pterosaurs knew murder, could they curse each other?
> And if so, why should we pay the price?

They talk and talk until Krissy can't keep up. She's lost to them. Goodbye, were-dactyls. This must be what happened to LimeSpine. It will happen to each of them, and then they'll have nobody, not even each other.

Every single one will finish their turning alone.

WEEK 7

Krissy's clothes no longer fit around her changing body. She drapes her shoulders in blankets and hugs them around her torso, but they come loose often and her parents shout over decency. Dad's hair thins at the crown, same as Krissy's weeks ago. Maybe he'll turn, father like daughter, the first adult in the world to succumb to prehistoric vengeance spells.

But no, he's only stressed. Mom, too. They speak softly now, but Krissy still hears them through the walls.

Dad: "What can we do?"

Mom: "I don't know. I just want our little girl back."

Can't they see that she's right here? Different, but still her. Their words hurt worse than shifting bones and jutting snout and the fish-driven hunger that burns her guts. Hasn't she been punished enough? And for what sin? She doesn't deserve wrath from the ancient world. What has she ever done but exist?

Her parents buy more blankets and hang them over the windows. If Krissy can't be decent, can't look human, then they don't want her seen.

Her world grows dark, cold, and lonely. She should sink into depression and never climb up from bed, but the turning shoves rage through her leathery skin. A pterodactyl screech shakes the air, and she flaps her still-forming wings. Her room swirls with small, dusty tornadoes.

And she gets an idea.

WEEK 8

Krissy keeps to her room by day. Her parents only whisper now, their murmurs scarcely creeping through the walls. They have a solution in mind; she can tell. They don't yet know what it is any more than she does, but she has her own projects.

By night, she clambers out the back door. It takes twenty minutes to unlock and turn the knob the first time, but she's getting faster at slipping out into the dark. Walking on four limbs has become easier than two. Her wing-knuckles help her lumber onto the porch, and her foot presses the screen door shut without a sound. Letting it crash would wake her parents, and they wouldn't understand.

She spends the night hopping off the porch railing and toward the back lawn, desperate to catch the wind. Her wings spread, flap, collapse, and she slams into the dewy grass.

And she tries again.

WEEK 9

Both Mom and Dad call out from work this week. They spend daylight hours with Krissy, haunting her bedroom the way shadows crawl from the sun, but they won't touch her. Her hide is leather and scales now. Alec Baldwin's stretchy prosthetic face in that *Beetlejuice* scene has nothing on hers, a hard, beak-like snout lined with flesh-rending teeth.

She lets her parents pretend they're better than they have been. Whether they know about her nighttime excursions is irrelevant. She can't stop.

She won't be stopped.

At mid-week, she realizes why she can't catch the wind. The porch doesn't stand high enough for strong gusts; she can't catch what isn't there. She must climb higher.

Night falls, and the rooftop beckons. Clambering from porch railing to shingles isn't easy, but her feet have grown proper talons over these nine weeks, and they help her find purchase on the way up. The turning begins in the feet, but it might end in the wings, one way or another.

The sky offers plentiful starlight and a gracious full moon. She eyeballs the chimney's silhouette and scrabbles up its shaft, onto the top, high as she can climb. To drop from its peak might break her.

But then, to never try might break her, too.

There's no point in a running leap. Her legs don't work that way anymore, and strength rises in her upper limbs. It's now or never.

She leaps.

Her wings slash to either side. Their webbing trembles. Every inch downward stretches into a small yet immeasurable unit of infinity. She has time to consider a crushed skull and snapped neck. Her parents will think she meant to kill herself. Will they be relieved?

She thrusts downward, rushing air fights her webbing, and at last her wings catch the wind. Nose-turned-snout turns upward, and she shoots from the yard, past the trees.

Toward the stars.

Once she gets going, flight becomes easy. Wind rushes around her crest, and she tilts her head in time with her wings to shift direction. She doesn't know if that's necessary, but the steering feels right. Lush trees bristle beneath her.

With air rushing around her earholes, every sound from the world below dims in the night. There's a peace here she hasn't felt in—ever? She can't be sure, but it feels good and right to fly. Like she was meant for it.

A familiar screech pierces the darkness. She turns and twists toward the clouds, and now she sees that the wind carries many riders. Winged shadows slash across the corn-yellow moon. She isn't as alone as her parents have made her feel. She screeches back, not even sure what she's saying, and the calls bounce across the sky in the greatest song she's ever heard.

Maybe this does get better from here.

An hour passes before she thinks of her parents again. She's exhausted and could really use a snack and rest. Home slides beneath her talons, the rooftop trying to catch her, and she lands harder than she meant to. Practice will make perfect. A chittering noise bubbles up from chest to throat. Is that laughter? She doesn't know, but it feels as right as flying.

She glides from rooftop to porch and is about to jimmy around the screen door when the back door behind it swings open, a rectangle of light breaking the darkness.

Dad's silhouette carves the light, and a grave smile paints his face. "We were worried," he says.

The screen door crashes behind Krissy, and she knuckle-walks onto the kitchen tiles, where a chemical stink coats the air.

Mom's awake, too, much to Krissy's surprise. She holds a glass measuring cup over a metal pan. "Hey there, sweetie," she says, jostling the pan. "We have fish. You like fish nowadays, right? We haven't been fair about what you're going through, but we want to fix that. Don't we?" She says this last question to Dad.

He nods, but his smile shows no cheer, no supportiveness. He's a grim-faced statue tonight. Something's wrong.

Hard to tell if Mom knows it. She smiles like it hurts to let her lips touch, her teeth filled with happy promises. She holds the pan out toward Krissy, arms stretched to their limit as if she's afraid to let her daughter get too close. A whole catfish lies inside, drenched in what must be cooking oil. Must be.

"Dig in," Mom almost sings.

Krissy looks to Dad, who nods again. Her fish-craving stomach dances with joy, but her thoughts hesitate. She wonders exactly what happens to the other kids who've finished turning. Are they taken by the government? Do they run away?

Or have their parents done something unthinkable?

Krissy begins to retreat, but Dad slides behind her. One flat, weathered palm presses between her shoulder blades; the other encircles her narrow neck in thick fingers. "We're sorry," he says.

"So sorry," Mom echoes. She seems to mean it, there are tears in her eyes, but she carries the pan close now. "Eat the fish, sweetie." Her voice fills with a mournful lilt, her betrayal of the deepest and final kind, a solution to their daughter-turned-problem.

Krissy flaps her wings and sends the air billowing through the kitchen. Mom grabs the fish up in her bare hands and lets the pan clatter. The oil doesn't smell like water and fish-stink—it wears that chemical smell.

"Open up, sweetie," Mom says. The fish dangles closer.

"Krissy, it's mercy," Dad says, fingers clambering toward her snout.

Mercy for who? Not for her, not when she's caught the wind and found the night. Mercy for them, then. Her family has turned into a dark egg, and now a rancid evil hatches behind Mom's eyes. She presses the fish against Krissy's teeth. The chemical taste trickles onto her tongue, as does the fish's meat. Her stomach orders her to take it, hungry like never before.

Behind her, the screen door crashes onto the porch, torn from its hinges, and wood splinters from the back door. Dad releases his grip, and Krissy feels him spin around. The catfish flops from Mom's hands and smacks wet against the kitchen tiles.

Dad: "Who are you?"

Mom, her voice cracking: "Another one?"

Glass shatters in the living room, the picture window bursting inward. A blanket writhes on the carpet, as if deciding on its own that Krissy's parents' sins must be seen, but then it shakes free of a crested head, toothy snout, and great leathery wings.

Another one. Another like Krissy.

A window cracks apart in one of the bedrooms, and two more kids-turned-pterosaur swoop into the living room through the picture window. Others follow from the bedroom hallway. Despite their wingspan, their upper limbs fold neatly against their torsos, letting them squeeze into the kitchen, snouts aimed at Krissy's parents. A pterodactyl screech bursts up one throat.

Krissy can't discern its entire meaning, but no matter what else, it's a song for her, and she answers. She returned home alone, trouble come to roost, where her parents tried to nourish her in the worst way. They thought she would always be alone. Would die alone.

But these other changed adolescents are birds of a leathery feather. Whatever angry magic swirls inside her likewise swirls inside them. Her parents have blotted up the windows for too long and forgotten that birds have flocks.

And for some birds, their flock is called a murder.

They rush at Mom and Dad, their prehistoric screeches drowning out human screams. Krissy isn't much help, but the others make quick and bloody work. Not because they're were-dactyls or true pterosaurs. Not because they can. They're quick because they're a flock of shared experiences, and they've had practice in their own houses, each forced to break free of some terrible eggshell the way Krissy has to break free tonight.

But she doesn't have to do it alone. She's never really been alone.

When the kitchen clamor settles, the flock shuffles on wing-knuckles and feet into the living room, where the night's mouth gapes wide with glassy teeth. The largest of them hops onto the picture windowsill, talons gripping tight. Wings catch the wind with ease of practice made perfect, and their downdraft gives the others a boost for thrusting themselves skyward. One by one, they glide up and away.

Krissy is the last to climb onto the windowsill. She looks to the stars and moon, where sibling shadows cut the night. Her talons crush brittle glass and brace to follow her flock toward seas and sunsets and mysterious futures. The turning begins in the feet and ends in the wings.

But the turning is just the start.

HELP, I'M A COP

by Nathan Carson

THE FIRST THING I remember is hearing laughter. I crack one eyelid to see who made the sound, but the late-summer sun is hot and blinding. The ground under my back is rocky, harsh. My parched lips are sealed; I split them to say, "Help, I'm a cop."

More laughter.

My right arm hurts. Can't even feel my hand aside from a distant burning itch. Someone kicks dirt in my face. I close my mouth, teeth now coated in a fine dry layer. I squeeze my eyes shut tighter and fade out again.

IT IS HALLOWEEN 1990. I am five years old. At my request, my mother has sawed a Nerf football in half so that I can trick-or-treat as Dolly Parton. She gets me out of the house before my father can comment on my blond wig and lipstick.

"RANDY!" MY MOTHER calls. It is four months later. I am in front of the television watching a striped puppet snake uncurl into a flute on *Sesame Street*.

My parents are wrestling fans. They named me Randy, but a macho man I am not. Not yet, anyway.

"Daddy wants to watch the news." I know better than to protest. The channel changes. I smell his Marlboro. He sits in his faded recliner. I climb onto the crumb-covered couch, idly digging my hand beneath the cushions in search of change. Normally the news is all bright colors and moving graphics. I especially like the weather report. Tonight's broadcast is dark and blurry. A Black man lies on the ground in front of a white car. He is surrounded by police with batons.

"Why are they beating him?" I ask. "Because," my father says, "he's a criminal."

"RANDY NEWMAN? LIKE the singer?" asks Mr. Coryell. He is my gym teacher. I am eight years old. "Numan," I say. "Like Gary Numan." "Hmm, never heard of him," says Mr. Coryell.

I am the smallest boy in my grade. Mr. Coryell has perfect sandy-brown hair. His body muscles make him look like an action figure. If you put him in a movie I would beg my parents to take me to see it. He sees me looking at him, follows my gaze to his tight athletic shorts. When class is over he holds me back.

"Numan." I like how he says my name. "Come to my office." I follow him. Once inside, he shuts the door. The calendar behind his desk features women in bikinis. They look like weird insects to me.

"I saw the way you were looking at me, boy," he says. "You think I'm . . . handsome?" I look around. There is no one in the room but him and me. I nod my head yes without having to speak the word.

He runs his hands down the front of his chest, over his crotch, down his thighs. "Would you like to see me without these clothes, Randy?" I am sweating. I am curious. I didn't know such things were allowed. My head is swimming. There is a deep craving I can feel but not visualize. I nod again.

He smacks me in the ear so hard that my head hits the wall.

"That's what I thought!" yells Mr. Coryell. He follows with a list of slurs I've never heard before, but I make a mental note of each one. He tells me that he will keep our little chat a secret on one condition. I am ready to agree to anything.

The next day he holds me after class again. This time we walk together into the fields beside the school. It takes a few minutes but he finally finds what he's looking for.

Dandelions wave in the breeze where we stand. There is a small bronze garter snake lounging in the grass. The pattern repeated down its body is beautiful. "See the snake?" he asks. I nod. "Catch it."

I am afraid of snakes but more afraid of Mr. Coryell. When I hesitate too long he cuffs me in the same ear that still hurts from yesterday. Fast as I can, I grab the snake and hold it wriggling toward him.

"Well done, Numan. I hoped you had it in you. Now I want you to put it back down on the ground, very carefully, and stomp its head in."

Gym class makes me feel sick for the rest of the school year.

SHADOWS STRETCH OVER my closed eyes. The sinking sun is still warm. My thirst is worse but I feel merciful drops of warm rain. I open my mouth to catch the drizzle. My body balks. A bubble in my throat rejects the salty brine. My head turns to spit and spew. I hear laughter again.

This time I open my eyes. The stream spatters against my cheek but gets interrupted by another fit of laughter. I turn my gaze up. Standing above me is a young white man, hair tied up in a man bun. He's maybe twenty. A young Black man with facial tattoos and a top hat stands behind him, reaching around, holding the dick that just pissed on me. They stagger away in stitches of hilarity.

A pretty white girl who looks like a Hilton heiress crouches over me. She is wearing a long Native headdress and not much else. The look she gives me is what I'd call pity.

"You injured?" she asks. I squint, give the slightest nod. Her eyes dart back and forth to make sure no one is watching. From a coin purse necklace she draws out a small white pill and puts it in my mouth. When I don't swallow she pinches my nose. That does it. "This will take the edge off, promise," she says.

She pulls a wad of chewed gum from her mouth and puts it in mine. Then she rushes away into the sunset.

I spit out the flavorless gum and piss-soaked dirt then fade back out.

I AM TEN. My best friend Kyle meets me in the park closest to the Forest Theater in Forest Grove. His older brother works there and can sneak us in to see an R-rated movie. This week it is *Lord of Illusions*. I am both terrified and thrilled. The song "Magic Moments" sticks with me.

I AM TWELVE. Kyle lies on my bed beneath my Erasure poster. I am kissing my way up his legs. I have just begun to unzip his pants when my father bursts into the room.

After I move schools, I never see Kyle again.

THE SUN IS down but there are other lights now. Headlights, phone lights, fires. The voices and laughter now compete with music and fireworks and breaking bottles. A thumping beat echoes down the canyon and a crowd begins to cheer. The wind is warmer than the night it cloaks.

Some details begin to return. I'm lying in the dry bed of Wapato Lake. The sheriff sent me here because it's almost twenty years to the day since 9/11. We got a tip that a big group of kids from Hillsboro were planning a rave. Gatherings of over a hundred people, even outdoors, have been outlawed for more than a year. And despite my best efforts, everyone on the force knows about my taste for electronic dance music.

Since my right arm won't comply I reach around with my left. My holster is empty. Key ring and wallet are gone too. I remember driving here in a Washington County Ford Police Interceptor Utility Hybrid SUV. It was morning then. No signs of stage construction or criminal activity. The only life I could see was an old apple tree.

DEAD FRUIT LITTERS the ground around it. A few apples still cling to their branches, though. They are red Empires with collars of green retreating into their stems. I was planning to get breakfast at the little café in Gaston after my survey. But a bite of fresh fruit won't spoil my appetite. I reach for the closest. Before I can connect the apple falls right into my hand . . . then bounces out and onto the ground, rolling under a hollow fallen tree just a few feet away.

On hands and knees I rock the log a bit and roll it over. On the soil beneath is a discarded medical mask, and a four-foot-long pit viper.

OUT FRONT OF the shop a woman violently shakes a rattle over her baby carriage. Signs in the window advertise Faygo soda and Kratom. I catch a glimpse of her kid on my way in. I am eighteen. Unless I make some big life changes I will never have a child of my own.

The clerk inside says he can't help me on-site but he gives me a number.

I keep jars of Muscle Milk on the windowsill of my apartment. An ammo box on the top shelf of my bedroom closet houses my syringes and steroids. In a few months I am still short but no longer feel small or weak.

At my gym a guy with iron cross tattoos tells me that he's signing up for the police academy. I suppress my urge to ask him out. We fill out the paperwork together and celebrate with beers. Later in the evening I think he's leaning in for a kiss. I purse my lips. He head-butts me hard enough to draw blood.

We are both accepted into the academy.

IT IS SEPTEMBER 11, 2001. I am sixteen. I'm eating a bowl of Frosted Flakes and watching the second tower fall. I ask my father, "Who's flying those planes?" He answers, "The worst people there are."

IT'S SEPTEMBER 11, 2021. I am thirty-six. I have been a police officer in one state or another for over fifteen years. I am lying on the ground while young people dance and drink, smoke and shout all around me.

"That's not just any pig," says the shadow of one masked youth above me. "Don't you recognize him?"

"How can you be sure he's the same one?" asks another. He pries his mask up to take a long pull from a bottle of white wine.

"I watched the footage thirty times. I doxxed him, too. I know who this fucker is."

I brace for the kick but just then the music stops.

"Hey," says the other. "I think someone said the Man is ready. Almost time to get this Burn started."

I AM FOUR. I am watching *Nitro* with my parents. Roddy Piper has just beaten Bret Hart and won his third United States Heavyweight Championship. We all cheer. Piper lives on a ranch in Gaston, Oregon. I think someday I will retire there.

A DISTANT REVVING engine wakes me. Sound looms down from the promontory above the canyon. At the foot is a wooden structure shaped vaguely like a person. Someone props me up from behind and leans me against the fallen tree. Torchbearers light a wreath around the neck of the Man; a burning snake swallowing its tail. I watch as the Man catches fire next. Live drums and chants throb like a heartbeat as the flames lick higher. The moon in the sky is a waxing crescent, a silver sliver that spins in my vision like a boomerang, or a scythe.

Red and blue lights whirl in the night air as my SUV sails over the cliff edge and crashes down onto the Man. A thousand people scream in elation. Fireworks sail into the sky as the gas tank of my SUV ignites and explodes.

THIRTEEN MONTHS EARLIER I am packing. It's the night before my team's deployment in Portland. For two decades I have kept myself from searching Kyle on the internet. Tonight my resolve wavers. He is married with children. His profile picture is circled by a rainbow border. His husband is a public defender. I close my laptop and my suitcase and do not sleep.

I'M HOLDING A shield behind the fence. Grenades flash amidst heavy gas and smoke. Commands chirp in my earpiece. We brace. A water bottle strikes my helmet. The fence comes down. We run as one into the crowd, swinging our batons. I connect with an uppercut swing and watch the rioter go down. As others drag her away, she pulls off her N-95 mask. I see the blood on her chin. She is Black, elderly. My baton arm hangs slack as she disappears into the mist.

MY FATHER'S TWEET reads, "I've never been prouder." The photo beneath has black borders at top and bottom in the shape of his phone screen. The picture, grabbed from a small online news site, is of me in full riot gear, smashing that woman in the face.

THE GIRL WITH the headdress is shaking me. Her pupils are dilated like two cast-iron skillets. "They're coming to get you," she says, pulling on my shirt. I cannot make my legs move. Pain lances down my arm toward my swollen hand. I feel other hands pick me up by the ankles and neck. They slide me into a white van and slam the doors.

I AM TWELVE. Kyle is in my room. "Magic Moments" plays on my CD deck. My father has not yet entered. We can escape out the window. Run away. Fall in love. Adopt children. Be happy. I never have to be internationally shamed for hitting an old woman. Maybe I will study zoology. Work with reptiles. Breed a few to make up for the one I crushed. The doorknob turns. My dream dissolves.

"WITH THAT MANY bites, he's lucky to be alive," says a man's voice. I am no longer thirsty. The bright light has returned. Is it morning? No, the light is white. The canned air smells antiseptic. I am in a bed. An IV runs from my arm. The drip is steady like a pulse, like a dance beat.

WHEN MY STINT with DHS ended I requested a demotion. No one could understand why a bruiser like me would want to subordinate himself to a local sheriff's department.

I've never been married. The women I dated told me I'd been wasting their time. They weren't wrong. How many of my own years had I wasted trying to be this person I thought my parents, the world, wanted me to be? How many embraces had I lost before the pandemic made them a thing of the past?

A DOCTOR PRIES one of my eyelids open and shines a penlight around. For a split second my field of vision is a hydra of veins. A nurse pecks at her clipboard. She caps her pen, places a pill in my mouth, then screws the lid back onto her necklace.

"The opiates slowed down the venom in his system," says the doctor from behind his surgical mask. "Not sure he would have made it here otherwise. With luck, we can save the hand."

I think about that hand holding Kyle's as we dangle our feet into cold creek water. The hospital bed feels stiff as soil under my back: rocky, harsh. The white light flickers, then begins to strobe. The beat of the drip throbs with sub-bass. A soft cry cracks in my throat.

"What's that?" asks the doctor. He leans in with his ear toward my mouth.

I say, "Help, I'm a *cop*."

The doctor stands up straight, pulls his mask below his chin. A thin forked tongue flits from his mouth. "Yesss, we know exactly who you are."

My good hand flails, reaching for . . . anything. There is a tray beside my bed with a fresh apple, and my dirt-caked badge. I manage to dislodge the tray. The apple rolls onto the floor, into the shadows. My badge falls into the waste bin with the rest of my life.

The bandages on my other hand unravel. The stump of scar tissue splits and hisses as its jaw unhinges.

I'm ROLLING IN the dirt, wrestling with myself. It is night. The music is louder than ever. So is the laughter. My boots and belt are gone. Cruel hands tug on my pant legs.

"Let's see if Porky Pig can dance!" says the boy with the man bun who'd pissed on my face. I wish I were dancing with him. That this was my property, my party, my people.

After my pants come off they take my briefs. Exposed to the night, the crowd, the throb of the bass, I grow stiff. Another snake to handle, another shame I can't hide.

The lights from a dozen camera phones ignite. The circle of the crowd's bare feet shuffles to the pulse. I am surrounded.

Laughter, screaming, music. Why couldn't I have found the strength to drop that badge in a blue box, returned the keys to the SUV, told my father just how ugly his pride made me?

More lights, more voices. The lights are headlights from half a dozen police cruisers. Kids in the crowd are shrieking. An amplified voice declares the scene a riot. I see young bodies rushing in every direction. Several are clubbed until they lay bleeding beside me. This is everything I never wanted but failed to stop.

An officer hovers over me. He lifts his mask for a moment. I recognize him. He recognizes me. Then he sees my erection and looks like he's going to vomit. His mask drops back down and he rushes back into the crowd, baton raised.

A needle scratches across the record over the sound system and the music dies. Someone is dragging me by the ankle toward I don't know where. The swollen stump that was once my hand is yawning to bite. The fangs sink into my flesh. My own venom courses through my veins.

The burning spreads. And help never comes.

Miss Infection USA

by Shanna Heath

ARTHA FUMBLED TO zip up her ball gown, and she yanked the metal zipper until—*crrrich*—a rotten chunk of skin peeled off her back. She panicked and shook the red, white, and blue sequins of her dress into a disco ball frenzy. Shimmering points of patriotic light danced on her chin and on my forearms as I stroked her cheeks. She wept.

"Relax," I commanded, and licked a tissue to blot my sister's face. "You're wrecking your lashes." I spent two days in a Stiff Girlz.net porno camp to buy those false eyelashes for her, and she'd better not cry them off her head or, God forgive me, I would be the plague that killed her this time around. "We have five minutes until places, babe." I puffed a cloud of shimmery powder onto her gray face. "Thop crying." My tongue was swelling and messing with my speech. With my free hand I reached into a small cooler and grabbed a handful of ice. I stuffed it in my mouth to reduce the bloat.

The Stiff who sat in the makeup station next to us (Contestant #13 and her barely-held-together-by-ligaments assistant) chuckled and sneered as I crunched the ice. Jerks. Mom said God gave me brains and Martha beauty, and I had to protect her from herself like Jacob should've done for Esau. I didn't need to talk pretty, and tongue draining was black-market surgery. Besides, those crooked docs took your money with one hand and sold you out the back door to a meat brothel with the other.

Unless you were Miss Infection USA.

With a rhinestone crown on her head, Miss Infection was awarded an all-expenses-paid bed at Revival and a personal consultation with the founder herself, Dr. Gross. We're talking organ transplants. Cutting-edge clinical trials. Transfusions on the daily. Skin grafts. The first Miss Infection USA maintained her original limbs seven years after her stint at Revival. I'd seen girls break apart after four months! Revival would let my Martha live with all of her limbs and even her own teeth sitting like pearls in her gums.

That is, if she'd stop freaking out. "Your blubbering is ruining everything. Chill."

"Stop yelling at me," snapped Martha.

"I'm not yelling!"

"You *are* yelling!"

Number 13 rolled her neon yellow eyes in our direction. When Martha's face was momentarily buried in a tissue, I flashed #13 my middle finger like *Bitch, back off.* She clicked her tongue at me but didn't test me further. Not here. A burly security guard stood in our dressing room with a semiautomatic draped over his white protective suit. His duty was to protect the Living, not us. No one wanted his attention. I turned back to Martha.

"Can you stick it back on?" Martha asked. She pawed at the jagged wound on her back and tried to twist her neck to see it in the mirror. "Is it active or advanced decay?"

I examined her putrefied flesh. "Active. You're a long way from attracting rove beetles."

Martha nodded, and her shoulders relaxed into the makeup chair. "We need that gummy stuff."

"Babe, we cannot pop your skin back on with chewing gum." Martha's naiveté was annoying and completely my fault. I'd stolen her away from the savagery of Stiff survival and hidden her in an abandoned McFasty's with a glitchy but working freezer.

Twenty minutes in the freezer, two hours out, repeat. No sharp objects. Doors and drive-thru window locked. Don't let the flies inside! Got it, sis?

"Chewing gum? Really, Miriam? I mean spirit gum. It's an adhesive for prosthetics."

"I know what spirit gum is. We don't have any. It's okay though. At this point, deader is better." The putrescent cavity she'd chunked out of her back was not quite gruesome enough to play the gore card. "Hold your breath and stay still." I poked my finger inside to widen it. My throat tightened with a reflex my body had all but forgotten: regurgitation. To bring ruin upon Martha's body was repellent to me, but this was showtime. Her skin could rip, or sag, or spoil, because she'd soon be gazed upon by the judge's eyes and they were the only ones who could offer true safety to Martha. And me. I swallowed down the acidic stew that lurched up from my soggy guts.

"That feels weird," Martha said. She wiggled, but I knew her limp nerve endings sent no pain signals.

I ripped off a piece of fashion tape and fixed the back of her gown to sit just below the gash, then hair-sprayed the carnage to give it a sheen that the stage lights would pick up. The gore looked grand. But, it stunk. I kicked on the AirPure unit. There was a dull tingle in my right foot, and I wiggled my toes inside my sneakers. Only four toes reported for duty. Dammit. That kick busted off my big toe. Martha would start weeping again if she spotted me tossing the toe in the trash. She'd held funerals for both my pinkie fingers. Better to let it jiggle in my shoe until after the pageant.

The AirPure sputtered to life and dispensed an antiseptic mist into the room. Number 13 pretended to hack and cough. I ignored her. Our mirror fogged for a moment, then cleared. Martha's image was centered in the square of the makeup lights, and she halted there as if captured in oils within a portrait frame. Purple veins wove delicate lines just underneath the grayish skin of her cheeks and forehead. Her graceful neck held her head without even the slightest wobble. A chartreuse mold bloomed across her chest like an elaborate tattoo (to her credit, Martha had been tending it since she spotted the first spores on her left clavicle).

"You are beautiful," I said.

I had a vision. Or, a memory resurrected.

"You are beautiful," my mother had said to the new Virgin Mary statue situated outside the Catholic mission she ran with my father in South Philadelphia. He'd found the Holy Mother at South Street Hardware. The concrete statue was small—about two feet high and weighing in at twenty pounds—but she was mighty enough to inspire devotion from my mother. Her robes and face were covered in acrylic latex paint. Her placid face was painted peach, and I informed Mom that Mary wasn't a white person and neither was Jesus, and she told me God made us in his image. We were peachy-colored, and therefore our Virgin Mary should be peachy too.

I wasn't convinced God accepted Mom's logic, because the neighborhood pigeons pooped on Caucasian Mary every hour. Mom cleaned the statue every morning, after lunch, and before dinner. Suds slid down Mom's arms to her elbows and left her with sleeves that were sopping wet and cold against my skin when she tucked me and Martha into our bed each night. Eventually, Mom had scrubbed the paint right off the statue's face. Was God happy then? Nope. As Mom scoured the cement each day, the size and detail of the nose dwindled to a nub. When Dad died and didn't rise, she'd spent a month scrubbing the Virgin's face into a smooth, expressionless egg. The doctors learned later that adults never rose—only children and almost always girls. I'd heard the news anchor explain about XX chromosomes, and Mom had said, *The Virgin Mary gave birth to Jesus when she was twelve. God shoulders you young girls with extraordinary responsibilities. The Lord always has his reasons.*

On the night Mom died and didn't rise, Martha had scrubbed so hard that the Virgin's head popped right off into her hands. She held it and rubbed it like a worry stone throughout her infection. I'd stolen it away when she died and scrubbed it clean of bloodstains with bleach. When Martha rose, in that first frightening day when a Stiff is suffering rigor mortis, I'd pried her fingers open and slipped the cool cement head into her palm and saw her relax. The moment her body regained flexibility, Martha had balled up in a fetal position with the Virgin's head clutched against her still, silent heart.

I don't know what happened to the body of the statue. It disappeared. I think the pigeons took it.

A PRODUCTION ASSISTANT blazed into the dressing room wearing a full face respirator and baby blue protective coveralls. The lady was waving a clipboard and moving her mouth, but the sounds were muffled. PAs were often newbies because no one stayed in a job working with Stiffs very long.

"We can't hear you," yelled #13 while her assistant applied shiny Vaseline to her skeletal shoulder.

The security guard tapped the speaker the PA had attached to her belt.

The PA switched it on and screeched, "PLACES. Damn, that's loud." She turned a dial. "Places."

The security guard chuckled and adjusted his grip on the semiautomatic.

"Thank you, places," I answered.

The PA looked again to the security guard. "Who do we have in here, again?"

"Contestants thirteen and seven," he replied.

She moved to write on her clipboard but fumbled and let it slip through her hands. It clattered to the seamless, aseptic flooring.

"Fuck," the PA yelled. I looked at Martha to see if she'd heard the cuss word. Now was not the time to give a lecture, Martha. She appeared unfazed. Number 13 scurried over on her shiny stilettos to pick up the clipboard like a kiss-ass.

"Let me get that for you," said #13 as she bent down. Sections of her spine were visible and it was fascinating to watch her vertebrae shift.

"No, no. Please don't touch me," said the PA, recoiling.

Number 13 grabbed the clipboard and tried to stand erect. The heel of her stiletto slid to the right and her ankle twisted. Bone crunched. Number 13 fell and grabbed for the PA, but that underpaid peon bolted back into the hallway and let #13 tumble to the ground. I put my hand up to the security guard and called out that there was nothing wrong, just a slip, an accident, we'd fix it, no problem. Martha bounced out of her chair and helped #13 stand up and balance on her remaining foot.

"Don't worry," said Martha with a lilt. "Deader is better."

So she *had* been listening to me.

"Just take it off," barked #13 to her assistant. The foot dangled on the end of her leg by a few tendons and stretches of skin. Other contestants began to fill the outside hall with chatter. "There's no time. I can carry the shoe with my foot in it." Her assistant argued with that. Number 13 steadied herself with both hands on the wall. "Shut up and do it already!" Her assistant grumbled, then pulled out a small pair of sewing scissors from their makeup kit.

I swooped in and turned Martha away. She didn't need to see that. "Let's get you in line, babe."

"Is Jackie going to be all right?" Martha whispered as we walked into the hall.

"Who's Jackie?"

Martha pointed to #13. Of course Martha had introduced herself and remembered the other contestant's name.

"She'll be fine. The judges will give her extra points for craftiness."

Martha's face relaxed and we took our places outside our dressing room door, awaiting the return of our PA and her instructions. A fly buzzed. The infernal things were always trying to lay their eggs in our ear canals or nostrils. I swatted the fly from my face and one from Martha's, too. Martha's expression soured.

"What is it, babe?" I asked.

"Group A, single file," yelled another PA as she led a line of shambling contestants down the hall.

I saw what Martha saw: Rolling past on the squeaky wheels of a bedazzled hand truck was Ruby Red. She was a supermodel head on a torso—only a torso. No legs or arms to divert attention. When Ruby Red rolled close to us in the dim hall, I glimpsed how she'd earned her moniker: Her face cradled two bloodshot eyes so succulent, round, and glistening that I wanted to suck sweet cherry juice from them and let it dribble down my chin. Girls at the camps told tales of how the StiffGirlz.net webmaster paid for Ruby to receive the first breast augmentation ever done on a Stiff. As my eyes rested on the soft bounce of those legendary boobies, I felt a prayer vibrate my lips. Ruby Red was miraculous.

Martha gripped my arm and asked, "Who is that?"

"The Stiff we need to beat."

Martha let a small huff of breath escape. "We're going to lose."

I faced my sister and gingerly squeezed her shoulders. It was best to distract her with physical touch when telling a whopper of a lie. I'd had much practice. "Listen to me. Ruby Red is a vapid torso with silicone tits."

"Don't say *tits*."

"Sorry. *Boobs*."

"Use the real words. We still have real bodies. They are *breasts*."

"Duh. I know that. I'm trying to say that she has no heart."

Martha gasped and crossed herself.

"No. Not literally. She has a heart, but not . . . love. People can't love her, but they can love you. You're going to be the first Stiff on the cover of *People* magazine. You are going to fix this world. I know it."

"I promise I will do my very best for you." She kissed my forehead with her cold lips.

"I know you will, babe."

Our PA returned and began to usher us down the hall toward the backstage area. Martha ducked her head inside the dressing room again. "Bye, Lucas," she said as she waved at the security guard.

"WAIT," I CRIED as Martha began to walk toward the stage right curtains. "There's another fricking fly." I brushed the pest from Martha's face in the blue light of the backstage. She smiled so big, it looked like the corners of her mouth were stitched to her earlobes (I had heard of such things being done). That smile kept Martha's scores high through Formal, Sportswear, and Movement. Ruby's scores would blaze ahead then fall back, and their close race earned wild applause from the audience— or boos, depending on who they rooted for.

The contest hemorrhaged participants like #13, even with her foot in her hand, and losers were hustled offstage by security. Rumors circulated among the assistants in the green room that the back parking lot was packed with refrigerated semi-trucks. No one had dared to actually look out the stage door. They whispered that the trucks hauled losers and assistants to the Zilf.com camp. I could imagine the scene—I'd been a player many times. Guys would pant behind a foggy full-face respirator. Every one of their limbs and appendages would be wrapped in a latex bodysuit. Viewers paid by the minute on Zilf to see the pageant castoffs twisted, turned on their backs or bellies, and thrusted into by the grunting, disgusting . . . (don't think about it).

Did the people watching the pageant—the moms and kids and grandpas—know what happened in the back parking lot? I'd tried to convince Martha of the apathy the Living maintained for us, even though we still walked and talked like their daughters and girlfriends and wives. During the nights I was home at McFasty's, I impressed upon Martha that this thing called the Patriarchy was what Hell was really like and it was here on Earth right now, and that if we didn't win the pageant, the Devil would be coming for us. Our death certificates were official, and they robbed us of our citizenship, social security numbers, and even from the protections of the Constitution. Our choices were meat brothels or porno camps, where we'd get (don't think about it) until our bodies disintegrated, then Asses to Ashes LLC would sell our sterilized remains in a jerk-off lotion for forty-five bucks. Or we could throw ourselves into the ocean and be chomped by great whites. Only complete evisceration like shark teeth, or maybe a wood chipper, could truly lay us to rest. Martha would stubbornly remind me that Jesus was a man, and I'd shut her up by asking, *How do you know that Martha, have you seen his dick?* She insisted I say *penis.*

APPLAUSE ROARED IN the convention center auditorium. The tuxedoed pageant host clapped his hands along with the crowd, and from inside the safety of his Plexiglas box, he announced, "Next up is everyone's favorite final round: runway! America loves to watch these Stiffs creep, crack, and crawl down the catwalk. You'll try to look away . . . but you won't be able to." The host chuckled and flashed his white teeth.

A speaker beside me erupted with the somber notes of the Miss Infection USA theme song ("You've risen from the aaaashes to be a bright flame in our heaaaarts"). I cupped my hands over my ears. The stage lights blinked out and a flurry of stage crew in black protective gear swirled around us in preparation for the finale. I looked around—where was Martha?

A sliver of natural light, foreign to the backstage, cut through the darkness. I turned toward it, as did a stagehand, and spied Martha peeking her head out the stage door. The stagehand shooed her away and shut the door again. I waved my sister over to me.

"You made it, babe," I yelled over the music. "It's the finals! I'm so proud of . . ."

"Miriam," she spoke over me, "there are trucks out there."

So the rumors were true.

"Don't worry about that . . ."

"Stop lying to me," she yelled. A stagehand hushed us. "I know what's out there. It's the Patriarchy. Isn't it?" I whisked Martha into a darker corner and away from the hubbub. A metal clip light with a blue bulb cast a sapphire radiance on my dull gray arms, and I shocked myself with the fleeting thought that I was pretty. "Will they do that to us if I lose?"

"Forget about all of that. That won't be us, babe. You're going to win."

Martha grabbed my chin. "Is that what they did to you, Miriam? In the camps?"

I pressed my forehead into hers and tried to keep my voice even. "Don't lose focus. Runway is next. Ruby Red is on a hand truck. She won't be able to walk that runway with any level of style or sass. She might be able to flip her hair. That's all. You've got this."

"My runway is shit," she said.

"Don't cuss. Nothing you do is thit."

"You're not Mom." She crossed her arms over her chest. "Tell me the truth. If I lose, are we walking out that back door and into those trucks?"

"No. We're not walking. We'll probably be carried out by security."

The familiar *kathunk* of Ruby Red's hand truck echoed backstage. Her assistant parked her next to the stage manager and they chatted while Ruby adjusted her legs. Yes, she had legs.

"Fuck," said Martha.

Ruby Red's runway costume was a marvelous machine built with gears and cords and little pipes that puffed out steam. A small control box was positioned on the edge of her mouth, and she used her tongue to move a joystick. The legs could twist and twirl like batons, and Ruby had full control of their dazzling motorized talents.

Don't think about it.

"Miriam," said Martha, shaking me. "Don't look. Focus on me."

I tried, but my eyes kept bouncing between Ruby and the stage door. I wondered if we could break through the Plexiglas and jump into the live audience—let them rip us apart.

"Listen to me, Miriam."

I looked at Martha's face. "I'm listening, babe."

"We're going to lose."

I was a corrupted music file on repeat. "You're going to win," I said again, and again.

"Unless . . ."

"Unless what?"

Martha paused. She squeezed her eyes shut. I could see her lips forming the well-worn words of the Hail Mary. Then, a revelation. Her eyebrows shot up and her eyes popped open and bulged.

"What is it?" I asked, begging to be let inside her mind.

She squeezed my fingers tightly in hers. My hands were dough in her grip—Mom's grip.

"Don't talk. Just listen," she said. Her right hand settled over my mouth. The sweaty palm pressed into my lips felt like when they'd (don't think about it) and my instinct yelled at me to make myself fast, small, and dart away. My panic was stilled only by my baby sister's gaze. "Forgive me, for letting you go to those camps."

I spoke into her salty palm. "I'd do it one hundred times over again, babe."

"I won't ever let anyone hurt . . ." Her words were muffled into my neck as she squeezed me tightly in her arms. I relaxed inside her embrace for a moment until a stagehand bashed their shoulder into us. Martha raised her head again and smiled at me—a small smile, not happy, but satisfied. "I know what we need to do."

"What?" I asked. "There isn't any time."

The host was taking his position in the Plexiglas box again as the stagehands performed mic checks.

"Promise me you'll let us win this my way."

I didn't have time to argue. "I promise." I imagined that she'd try to alter her costume in some way, or maybe she'd flash her *breasts*. It wasn't on brand for her, but it might earn her an extra photo in the souvenir eBook. We'd still be losers.

"Good," she said.

"Testing," said the host into his mic. "Testing."

It was showtime. I whisked Martha to the quick-change area and transformed her into a runway goddess. Short gold pants with a heart-shaped bustier and a long, golden, glowing tail of fabric that dragged on the floor behind her. Two sky-high gold heels and one set of candy-apple red lips. Not steam-powered, but still unforgettable.

"Places in five," said the nearest PA.

"Thank you, places," I answered. I turned back to Martha. "What else do you need?"

My sister swallowed hard and long, like a python digesting a mouse. She bent down, fished an object from our makeup bag, and held it up to me in the palms of her hands.

It was the head of the Virgin Mary statue.

She offered the small cement head to me. It was cold, like my own skin, and we felt as one. Me, Martha, and Mary. My sister searched my face with her eyes. "Will you help?" she asked.

"Places," called the PA. I heard the squeak of Ruby's hand truck wheels.

What was she asking me to do? Prayers to a decapitated statue wouldn't win the pageant. Had Martha lost her mind? I'd heard of brains going soft on Stiffs in midsentence, but Martha wasn't at that point yet.

"You don't have to think about it," Martha said. "Just follow my instructions." She took my arms and guided them to the top of her head. "Hold on to my hair like this."

I wrapped her gossamer locks in my fingers. In my opposite hand I squeezed the statue's little head. The stimuli from the two hands connected with a spark in my chest. I knew then, and the knowing was caustic, and what remained of my soul began to burn. My lips formed *no* but the sound was choked out.

Martha unsheathed a butcher knife from a bundle of Mc-Fasty's paper napkins. She plunged the knife into her neck and began to slice and hack. The delicate strands of her hair slipped gradually through my grasp, until, with speed and a sudden added weight, her head dropped from my fingers and thudded to the floor.

My thoughts condensed into small, neat, sterilized snippets of action.

I pick up your head.

Martha's body remained erect, and her arms sought their prize.

I give you your head.

My sister walked.

I guide you.

She entered the spectacle of stage lights.

I let you go.

My baby sister stomped and strutted down the runway, holding and swinging her own head like an expensive handbag. The host roared and scratched at his face in ecstasy and horror. The crowd's clapping hands were hysterical tambourines that shook the ground and rattled my loose toe in my sneakers. The stagehands and PAs and security guards crowded into the wings to gawk and cheer. Stage lights whirled and twirled to position their beams on my sister as she performed. Ruby Red's assistant left her sitting backstage, alone on her hand truck, and she screamed, but not loud enough to crumble the wall of noise made by the audience.

Even my own screams were drowned out.

The cameras and their operators raced on wheels and on foot to focus their lenses and worship every angle of Martha, burning her idol into the screens of her three million converts as they venerated at her hallowed feet. I fell to my knees, slapped my slick and sticky hands together, and offered prayers of adoration to Martha the Divine, the new Miss Infection USA.

ALL NOT READY

by Tracy Cross

Last night, night before,
Twenty-four robbers knocked at my door,
I woke up, let them in
Knocked in the head then I did it again
Two times one, one times four
All not ready . . .

ARI FUMBLED WITH the small cube as her palms sweat. The cube was the key to the future of her family. With this cube, they would be able to move to a better Quad. She could go to a better school. Everything would be perfect.

She wouldn't have to choose between eating breakfast or lunch every day. Today she chose lunch. Yesterday was breakfast. The food rations her family received didn't last long, and with her grandmother in hospice, there were few credits for food.

"Ariadne! Come get some breakfast. Most important meal of the day!" her mother called her from the kitchen.

Ari sat on the floor in her room, her legs crossed, as she worked on the cube. "Not hungry! Working on something."

She hated lying to her mother. Ariadne was hungry, but she was okay with today's sacrifice. The cube had her complete attention. She bartered for parts a few days ago, and they lay spread on the floor in front of her.

Even though she despised doing it, she frequented the junk-yard for parts for her science projects. This year was the big science fair. She needed to win.

"YOU OKAY BACK there? Been pretty quiet for a while." Her father steered the huge boat of a Cadillac onto the highway.

"Just, you know, I am almost finished." She sighed and snapped her lunch box closed.

"Right-o, kiddo. We are counting on you."

His words weighed heavy on Ariadne. She closed her eyes and exhaled as the car rumbled to a stop in front of the school.

"Be the best you can be or don't come home!" Ari's father yelled as she slipped out of the car.

She turned and saluted him before she ran inside.

Ariadne maneuvered the hallway like a pro. She kept her head down while moving past a group of bullies. These were the kids that ate breakfast *and* lunch every day. The kind of kids that didn't have to pick through junkyards for their science projects.

"Hey, Scrappy! Off to see your little Nation of Friends?" a boy yelled.

Her grip tightened on her lunch box handle. One day she would belt them one for making fun of her friends.

"You just jealous because you guys all look alike!" she sniped before the first bell rang.

Ariadne put her lunch box in her locker and ran into a few of her friends: Mai, Sudi, and Quan. They all lived near her, in the same Quad.

"Did you escape the bullies?" Sudi asked, sliding his lunch box into his locker.

"Jerks. I hate those guys. Making fun of us because—" Mai stared over Ariadne's shoulder and down the hallway.

"Forget those guys!" Ariadne said.

"Easy for you, they did not take your lunch," Quan said.

"Hey, you guys up for a game of Hide and Seek at recess? You know, my dad would say it helps to relieve stress." Ariadne fell in step as they walked to their class.

"I don't see where it would be a problem." Mai flipped her thick black braid over her shoulder.

"Always down. Are we—" Sudi nodded.

"We play by my rules," Ari said. "Meet me under the stairs by the gym at recess. Spread the word."

They walked into class as their teacher took attendance.

"Glad to see the usual suspects have joined us. Take your seats. Let's start with some math, because who doesn't like numbers?"

After lunch, Ariadne ran for her locker and grabbed the holo-cube from her lunch box. She flipped it around in her hand a few times as small bits of color illuminated. She slipped it into her skirt pocket as the teacher yelled for them to finish at their lockers so they could go outside for recess.

Ari was first in line, fiddling with the cube in her pocket. Today would be legendary. She pressed the jackpoint on her neck, sliding the sleeve on her sweater back and twisting some dials on her wrist. In her left eye, she saw a hologram of the playground, and the program titled "Hide and Seek" popped up. Only she could see it as she made a few more adjustments. She smiled as she followed the teacher outside. She gave her friends the thumbs up.

The kids ran all over the playground under perpetually grey skies. Clouds rolled in and it looked like rain, but the weather always *looked* like something. Ariadne looked around before she ran over to a set of concrete steps and slipped beneath them. She continued to make adjustments on her transparent sleeve as the others joined her in the tight space.

Ariadne crouched in the corner. She went over the rules of Hide and Seek for the umpteenth time.

"Plug in your stupid jackpoints, okay? Use this." Ariadne passed around small custom plugs for the jackpoints. "Once we get plugged in, everybody grab your weapon, okay? Y'all know what happens when you get found."

Some kids mumbled as they massaged their jackpoints behind their ears.

"Is everyone fully charged? Your jackpoints plugged in? We can't lose anyone. I programmed the game for seven, including me. I also made some changes to the game. Anything that happens in the game will feel like real life. If you are hit, it's gonna hurt."

Maya rolled her eyes and adjusted her waist-length ponytail. "Well, I'm ready. Why do you always do this, Ari?"

"Changes will keep you on your toes. If you play like it's important, then it'll be a really fun game. Plus, someone like Perri or Sudi ends up with a jackpoint unplugged and we lose the game. Like, the whole game."

Ari watched as Sudi scratched behind his ear.

"I just got these," Sudi shouted. "They itch, but my mom said they wouldn't for too long." He stopped and clapped his tawny brown hands in front of him and then looked around the group.

Mai and Tim pressed their hands to their jackpoints behind their ears and nodded at each other. They spoke in unison: "Ready."

"At least they get it," Ari sighed.

"Where are the weapons?" Quan jumped up from the group.

"The good weapons?" Perri asked.

"It's a game. You were supposed to send me new versions of your weapons. Then I add them to the game. If you didn't send me anything, then I didn't program anything." Ari stopped programming her transparent sleeve and looked around. "And if you didn't send me anything, I used what you sent me last time. This time, everything is gonna hurt."

Ari watched them stare at each other. She didn't think they understood the changes. Her shoulders fell as she looked at the ground.

"Look at this katana. I copied it from my mom. I can use it in the game. It hurts and stuff but outside of the game, nothing will happen in real life. It's only in the game."

"Wait, why does your mom have a katana?" Quan's eyebrows rose.

"Don't matter. I came prepared." Ari smirked.

"Nobody has a bat with nails? I came to win!" Quan pulled a bat from behind his back.

Everyone nodded.

"I have a mace!" Tim swung it around the tight space as everyone ducked.

"Where'd you get a mace?" Perri asked as she pulled out a pair of small, custom brass knuckles.

"Weren't you in class last week? Mrs. Anderson told us about those old-time battles." Tim pointed to Perri. "And the brass knuckles?"

Perri smiled. "My dad gave 'em to me. I made a copy of 'em for the game."

Mai pulled out two small sais and made a dramatic pose. "These were my grandpa's."

"What? How do you know about those?" Maya asked.

"Well, what you got?" Perri sassed Maya.

Maya did a few kicks, followed by a few quick jabs. "I am the weapon."

"She's out first," Tim laughed.

"I also have this." Maya whipped a small lasso from behind her back and tossed it. It looped around Tim's neck, and she pulled it until he choked.

"We didn't get to this chapter in history," Maya said. "But it's called a lariat."

Ari looked around the room. "What kind of third-graders have a thing like that?"

"Smart ones." Maya waved her arm and loosened the lasso.

"Okay, we ready? I'll be it." Ari pulled her sweater down to cover her electronic sleeve. "Let's go. One rule is you gotta stay at school, 'kay?"

All the kids stood and grabbed their weapons. They looked at Ari as she walked over to a brick wall and pressed her forehead against it.

She began to shout the rhyme,

"Last night, night before,
twenty-four robbers knocked at my door,
I woke up, let them in . . ."

Legs ran in all directions. The sound of giggles was all around as her friends ran to hide.

"Knocked in the head,
then I did it again,
two times one,
one times four,
all not ready . . ."

Ari held her hand to her ear to listen: "*All not ready.*"
No one responded.
She called out again, "All not ready?"
Silence.

Ari looked down at her shoes. She checked to make sure they were tied before she grabbed her katana and ran to the playground.

Ari knew Perri picked the best hiding places. Today, she guessed Perri hid in the bushes, like camouflage. Ari ran over to the monkey bars and thrust her katana into the bushes. She heard them rustle before Perri stood and faced her. Perri smiled like a Cheshire cat.

"Found ya!" Ari pulled out her katana before she ran it through Perri. Perri pulled herself closer and swung on Ari. She connected with a right cross to Ari's face.

Ari pulled back and touched her face. She gasped. Ari pushed the katana harder into Perri before she tried to lift it.

Perri spat blood in Ari's face. "You got me."

Perri collapsed as Ari pulled the katana out and wiped the blood off.

"I'm gonna get you!" Ari bellowed as she ran deeper into the playground.

Two multicolored domes filled the middle of the playground area. The blacktop was shiny from the rain. Ari glanced over and thought it would be the best place for Sudi to hide. He always talked about climbing things in class. The domes seemed to be meant for climbing. She slipped inside the dome and let her eyes adjust to the dark.

"Found you!" She scampered across the inside of the dome walls to get to Sudi.

"You won't win this time." Sudi laughed as he flipped head over heels and landed on the ground.

Light peered through the opening in the top of the dome. Sudi walked in a circle with his sickle sword at the ready. He blocked all of Ari's strikes with ease.

"I'm bored. Hurry up!" Sudi chided.

Ari made two swift moves. Sudi blocked one and missed the other. His head fell to the ground and his body followed.

"Two down."

As she crawled out of the dome, she saw a foot beneath the tall sliding board across the park. She sheathed her katana and ran. She tapped her jackpoint to check the amount of time left before recess ended. Twenty minutes.

As Ari leapt over the sandbox and ran toward the double slide, she sensed someone behind her. She turned right into Quan as he swung his nail-covered bat like a madman. He laughed and swung for her head as she ducked.

"You ain't scared, right?" Quan moved over her faster than ever.

"You practiced, huh?" Ari stumbled over her katana and fell on the ground.

"My mom told me she would beat my ass if I lost to you again." He smirked as he advanced over her. He raised the nail-covered bat over his head. Ari pulled out a small knife hidden beneath her skirt and stabbed him in the chest.

"Looks like you gettin' beat." Ari growled as she pushed the knife in a bit deeper.

"Aw, damn. Got me good." Quan dropped the bat and clutched at his chest.

The knife made a distinct sucking sound as Ari pulled it out. She wiped it on her navy blue skirt. "You lose. Three down."

Maya screamed as she ran up behind Ari before Ari could sheathe the knife. Her katana lay on the ground. Maya leveled her with a barrage of kicks. Ari couldn't block them fast enough and took a few to the face and upper body.

Ari liked Maya. Maya didn't talk a lot. She was also one of the best at the game. She won one time, and she may win today if Ari couldn't reach her katana.

"Maya, don't leave yourself open," Ari teased.

Maya held her fists up and blocked her face. She bounced from foot to foot before she moved forward and gave Ari a lethal uppercut. Ari felt it connect to her chin, and she flew through the air. She probably looked like the cartoons she watched on her Delphus pad.

But instead of cartoon characters, it was two dark-skinned girls fighting on the playground.

Something hit Ari in the head. It was Tim with his mace. She felt the connect, and stars swirled in front of her. She was in the air. She seemed to fall for a long time. When she finally hit the ground, she rolled over and saw the katana. Her head swam with a possible concussion, but her will to win pushed her toward the katana.

She unsheathed it and swirled it over her head. She sliced through Tim and caught Maya with a foot in the air. She sliced the foot off and in one motion twisted her wrists and drove the katana through her body.

"Mercy," Maya groaned. "Have mercy."

"Not how the game works."

"We're gonna get you next time," Maya said as she fell to the ground.

"It's Hide and Seek, not double up attack."

"Didn't have much of a choice. We needed to win." Maya coughed up a bit of blood before Ari moved on.

"Mai! I see you under the slide," Ari said. "Step out. I see you!"

Ari slowed her pace. Her head hurt, but that's how it felt to get hit with a mace, she guessed. Real mace or not. Her legs wobbled beneath her as she made it over to the slide and grabbed the side to hold herself up.

Mai remained hidden. She didn't give herself up. Ari jumped to the back of the slide and shouted, "Ha!"

She didn't see Mai.

"Where'd you go, Mai? Where are you?" Ari walked around the entire unit. There was a short rope climbing wall, a type of closet beneath, two small slides, and some dials filled with beads that rattled when they were turned. Wherever Mai hid almost assured her a victory.

In her peripheral vision, she saw the swings move. Behind the high swings were more bushes. Those bushes had thorns and the thorns hurt. Ari slowly moved toward the bushes and stabbed her sword inside them.

She continued until she reached the bench at the end of the bushes. She stabbed and heard the sound of metal hitting metal. Mai was right in front of her, and she was invisible.

"You modified, and you cheated!" Ari said.

"You cheat all the time! I mean, you always win. My brother did my upgrade because I wanted to—"

Ari swung and sliced Mai's head off her body.

She reviewed the attendance in her head: Tim, Maya, Mai, Sudi, Quan, and Perri. Everyone dead on the playground. She jumped up and down. She shouted out her victory, again. She heard a whistle and reached up to pull the plug out of her jackpoint.

Mrs. Anderson kneeled in the space beneath the stairs and sucked her teeth. "How many times do I have to tell you guys not to mess with your units? This is why we can't have nice things. Give them to me. The plugs. I see them!"

She held her hand out as all the kids slipped the plugs out of their jackpoints. They dropped them into Mrs. Anderson's palm. She thanked each of them as they stood from their circle and made their way to the classroom.

Mrs. Anderson pulled Ari aside and whispered, "Is this supposed to be your project for the Quad Science Fair?"

Ari nodded.

"Well, I think you'll do well. I know it's hard to compete every year and lose. Close isn't first, is it?" Mrs. Anderson ran her thumb over the jackpoints in her palm. "This seems to be a much better and stronger project than before. Other kids have easier access to materials and supplies. I know it's hard for you to get anything. The work you've done on this shows. I'm proud of you. Good luck."

Ari stared up at Mrs. Anderson.

Mrs. Anderson winked. "Now back to class. You can pick these up at the end of the day."

As Mrs. Anderson droned on about lariats and weapons, Maya cleared her throat and puffed out her chest. Mrs. Anderson reprimanded her with a glance.

Ari wanted to make her father proud. She thought of him as she worked on the small cube under her desk.

ILLUSIONS OF THE DE-EVOLVED

by Linda D. Addison

Consider
frenzy in
ridges and grooves
of hemispheres within
apparently evolved *Homo sapiens*:
jealously blocking sanity from waking
those hungry to revise history, cage children,
stand on the throat of another when no tree is found
to fulfill the need to dominate, burn, stone, bludgeon denied
humanity. Feeding the need for meanness, so many ingredients mixed
to create the bitter meal force-fed to the next generation: babies
born without hatred, taught difference is dangerous,
danger requires reaction to fictionalized
Others, even as their split skin,
heart and brains
bleed red red,
denial is
easier to
swallow
fueling
broken
souls

BLACK SCREAMS, YELLOW STARS

by Maxwell I. Gold

We think we are pushing, but we are being pushed.
   —Goethe

SIX MILLION BODIES carried off on demented railways, where chimneys of ash and blood expelled their last hopes and dreams. Simultaneously, fifteen million bodies, wrapped in chains of iron and bone, were ferried along oceans of greed and gore. These middle passages, these nightmares, wrought by the few defame machinations of sinister men, were the last thoughts flashing through my mind.

Soon, white hands, coarse voices, and orange flames crowded the last spaces over the horizon. Towers of white cloth, red hats stained in blood, cigarette smoke, and fornication mixed with the scent of death and cheap liquor clogged my nostrils. There was no discriminating human features on the figure in the white hood, cotton shadows outlining a pallid face; while callused fingertips pulled the rope tauter around my neck, my sterling silver mezuzah bouncing against the thick twine.

My body twitched under the heavy pressure, jolting in the opposite direction only to be met with a deep, resentful growl: "Quit moving, Jew-boy." If I hadn't known any better, I could have been fooled into thinking it was the voice of a disgruntled father, disheveled husband, or annoyed brother, though I knew all too well the source. Something inhuman, dressed in man's clothing, snarling with the voice of a monster.

I didn't answer him; my body stood resolute on a flimsy deck chair under the cool shadow of a dying willow tree in the middle of a parking lot in some unknown midwestern town. The rest of the city's law enforcement, wherever they were, seemed too concerned with quelling civil unrest, rioters, and right-wing agitators. It all happened so quickly, I'd no recollection of past or present. Only the end. Sweating, breathing, cowering, wishing in those last few breaths.

Leo Frank, S. A. Bierfield, and now me. How many more would follow, and to what end? How many willow trees and parking lots? More screams, jeers, and ruffling shadows ruptured the sweet silence as another pile of disheveled flesh was tossed to my right.

"Come on, you get your Black ass up there too," the Hood said, unfolding another chair, tying another rope, following the same deadly steps. They don't have names, nor do they deserve them. The other group of white hoods and red crimson faces watched us, judged us as if we were creatures behind iron bars and the Hood was the bold lion tamer putting his own life in danger. Surely the world hadn't lost all its senses, had it?

My Black brother shook off the fear and the terror easier than I—at least it appeared that way. "Walt," I said, and a confused look graced his brow.

"Shut it, you two," the Hood barked.

He continued to fluster and fiddle with our nooses as the wailing of sirens went on in the background, faint blasts and explosions as if small buildings had collapsed on some lowly main street or power lines were buckling in an unlucky cul-de-sac. Time was a funny commodity, misshapen and odd in the moment. Minutes lasted for years, and seconds ticked away like days as embers floated in the smokey night air.

"Paul Scott," he whispered, hands tied.

"Walter Goldstein," I said, eliciting a sly grin from Paul. "What's funny?"

Paul flashed a cheeky half smile. "So, that's why you're up here."

I couldn't help but chuckle aloud with him, and our momentary happiness caught the attention of the Hood. "I thought I told you two to shut it!"

It hadn't been that long since I heard laughter, maybe a few hours before being taken away to Hell. Still, those hours seemed more like decades ago, and Paul was the only man, the only human I shared a laugh with in such a long time. I'd never been happier. The Hood stepped away for moment. Not like we could make a run for it.

"Don't worry, there's plenty of it to go around," Paul said, cynicism biting at his tone.

"Isn't that the truth," I said, nervously attempting to clutch my necklace, but my hands too were tied.

Noticing my trembling, he adjusted his gaze. "What's the charm? On your necklace."

"Oh, it's not a charm. It's a mezuzah. It's kind of like a good luck charm for the home, a way to bless it. Same principle for why we carry it close to our hearts. I've never been religious, but honestly, this is all I have right now. I've had this since I was thirteen," I said.

Paul sighed, turning himself a little bit facing me. "Not much luck can do for us now, but it's a pretty nice thought to have. Keep it close to your heart, away from them. Close to your heart for as long as you can." Even with hands tied, he lifted his arms, pointing them toward my heart and the mezuzah.

More explosions, thunder pulsed in the background as something was drawing closer. The marching of red hats and white hoods could be heard throughout the city, and a chill raced down my spine as I wondered how many more of us there would be before someone finally stood up to this insidious evil.

"Are you scared?" Paul said, interrupting my thoughts.

"Terrified," I replied, my body feeling cold, rippling with anxiety.

"Me too, but I'm ready though," he said, deep brown eyes looking directly into mine, a whirling infinity of light and truth seething across the expanse of my brain.

"I—I'm beyond terrified. Words can't describe, but I am ready too." Staring back, I saw everything. Hatred, love, life, everything pooling together under the terrible entropic weight of history's sagging fat body. Without any regrets, a smile graced my lips, meeting Paul's when dreadful footsteps tromped over the browning grass.

There were hundreds of them, red hats and white hoods, but the Hood was leading the charge. Torches, cell phone flashlights, underscored by the roar of car exhaust pipes and engine booms.

"My patience is now at an end," the Hood said.

My heart pumped with the force of Hoover Dam, as if it were going to explode, sweat flowing down my pale skin and the world no longer making sense. Everything without truth or meaning, except Paul. The coarse voices rose in a furious orchestration of sinister melodies flowing with raucous glissandos, up and down as the Hood stepped closer.

"Hey," a familiar voice said, "keep it close. Close to your—"

"Close to your heart," I finished, one last tear rolling down my cheek as the Hood placed a boot near the chair.

"I am ready."

Six million and one bodies, carried off on demented railways, where chimneys of ash and blood expelled their last hopes and dreams. Simultaneously, fifteen million and one bodies, wrapped in chains of iron and bone, were ferried along oceans of greed and gore. These middle passages, these nightmares, wrought by the few defame machinations of sinister men, were the last thoughts flashing through my mind.

KALKRIESE

by Larissa Glasser

for Dave Thomas

OI

It wasn't my first time being burned, but this time I wasn't alone. The fire hadn't caught my field clothes, but the flames from a lit torch held by one of the revenants was pointed at my face, and no matter how I cringed, they jabbed, and there were cruel intervals when a piece of my arm, leg, or hair were singed by my captors.

When you're in fear for your life, time itself slows down, and your awareness of your surroundings becomes granular to the point of privilege. Emotion becomes secondary to those tiny but sharp points of focus—a loose thread in your clothing, a worm in the noodles, an empty beer can in your car wreck.

My enclosure this time was not the steel or chrome of a vehicle, but a mass of sticks and twine that, although crooked and hurried, had been lashed together with such determination that only fire or edged metal could loosen even a section of it. I gripped one of the thicker columns, its bark still steadfast although moistened by the downpour. There was no getting away, but I was at this point beginning to understand a little better why this had all unfolded.

The rope around my neck tightened as I pivoted toward the soldier before me. The afternoon sun hit his decay and lit up the bones beyond the maggots and their hatchlings. This one was the tallest of the group, but maybe he was standing more erect than any of the others of the legion who seemed to be weighed down by the air itself, or the decomposition had gotten to them so badly that their bodies lacked the strength to maintain their dutiful march. I could also tell by then, part of their listless stature was possibly diminished by sorrow, maybe even disillusionment. On some of the worst of them, though, their armor looked pristine, intact, polished.

The wide-open landscape was just as the excavation team had left it before the rainstorm, with a few important exceptions: the roof of the visitor center was no longer visible; the museum displays and commemorative paving stones had also vanished. The late-summer air and the enclosing forest were maybe the only common threads between sanity and whatever this carnage had turned into. We can fantasize and nerd out about opening portals, summoning or unleashing ghosts or curses, or discuss funding initiatives until we're blue in the face—I expect nothing less—but the crucified body of Ivan was real enough as we passed by it along the track.

Yet the man I'd hated the most, he who had given me the most shit, seemed to have been the only other survivor of this rout. His survival and the realness of the decayed corpses of Varus's legions were enough to drive reality home for me: This was no dreaming state, no abstraction of the ethics of what Ivan had attempted to fool the team with. The very fact that my wheeled prison had been fashioned after a wolf rather than a man standing upright solidified my understanding—the soldiers were real, their pain and humiliation of defeat were real, and to treat us invaders as the German tribes who had themselves routed this army, it was a purgative exercise through which they sought release.

Ivan had summoned something he could not send back, but the thought of Peg snapped me back into my own determination, and as the fire got closer, drying the tears that had betrayed my already terrible face, I recalled my own experiences with near death and as in some (but not all) nerd circles, I steeled myself back to presence of mind and the adage that takes so little real effort: "Not today."

I leaned toward the tallest soldier and began to speak.

02

It wasn't my first time falling off the sobriety wagon, but this time I wasn't languishing in a desert. The Hotel Osnabrück had a bar where I didn't have to worry about the lighting plowing my face into even more grotesqueries. Dealing with customs and the TSA had been bad enough, but the jet lag compounded by my humiliation in front of the excavation team had me spiraling to the point of just not caring. If I had to return to rehab back in the States when I got home, then that was for later. Right that evening, I'd needed a drink even more than I needed the income contracted to me by Craig and the excavation team.

In fairness to Craig, he'd done all he could for me during the orientation. But being heckled with a bunch of nonsense during my presentation to the team had made me more sad than angry. I decided that if a drink would kill me worse than the transmisogyny, then that was a chance I was ready to take.

But also, I sure as hell didn't expect to find Peg Bishop sitting there at a table in the hotel bar, big as life and seemingly without a care in the world other than the piles of notebooks that surrounded her.

"Jesus," I let out. "No way."

Her eyes dashed right up, and we beamed. Even from across a room, we know the tells. I'd only met Peg online, so we may not have memorized each other's voices, but we'd both geeked out about our projects at university. She was a linguist teaching at Oxford, and I wondered what she'd be doing here in Lower Saxony.

We got the "nod" and the hug over with, and after, I sat down across from her. I squinted into the murk for any signs of Jäger-meister. I was back to my old ways already, but this finally felt like the time, and the place, for which my drinking might involve having less judgment hurled at me from without.

Right out of the gate, I asked Peg about the notebooks. This didn't look like the type of work she'd been known for.

"I'm on my way to Hamburg," she said past a stray tuft of hair.

"Seems far enough from Britain."

I took my first drink since my so-called car accident. I needed it, after only a half hour of being laughed at by people I would be working with outdoors in September for a couple of days; being there with Peg galvanized me to abide.

She went on to tell me she was moonlighting away from her linguistics research.

In Hamburg she was interviewing several trans women who were verified granddaughters of the also-trans courtesans John Lennon had reciprocated during the Beatles' residency in St. Pauli. Although I had reason to be skeptical of the veracity of this oral history passed down, I was only then just beginning to under-stand the logic behind it: Even if it turned out to be a complete bag of lies, at least we were talking about us instead of waiting to be seen and heard from the outside yet again. It was going to be an actual book rather than a post on social.

"I'm just sick of the hypocrisy," Peg went on. "I mean, we're talking real trans history here."

"What about rock history?"

"Fuck rock history."

"You're going to piss some people off," I told her. "Maybe at *Rolling Stone*."

"And then a decade later, they'll do their own feature with the same transcribed interviews." Peg looked down, crestfallen. "Even if I'm still around."

"Be around."

I remember moving a little closer with my drink when I saw Craig coming into the hotel bar. He scanned the crowd and then locked his eyes on me. His shirt was untucked, and his hair looked scraggly at one end, as if he'd been rolled through something outside, across the quaint cobblestones and dog shit.

Or he'd gotten into a fight.

Peg shifted a little in her dress, but I held my hand out to her, at stomach level. We were safe.

Craig had hired me for the project and had shown deference since my arrival. He hadn't met me post-transition and had proved as respectful as my trip from Mexico City had been long, but his silence during the heckling by the team during my presentation about the Kalkriese battlefield is what had driven me into this state. It turned out to have been a mixed blessing.

He glanced at Peg only a moment. She had packed her piles of notebooks into a bag and set them aside. Craig wasn't part of our network, so I doubted he'd recognize her, Oxford cred notwithstanding.

Craig's eyes were downcast as he approached the table.

"You can save it," I told him. "If this team of yours is just here for the ride, then I hope we don't find so much as a chicken bone in the ground."

I introduced Peg, and they both just shrugged at each other. Craig had his agenda, but with Peg there, I was beginning to grow my own. She could tell, and we exchanged another pair of small but knowing smiles.

"I spoke with them after you left the suite," Craig began. "Sofer had some choice words for Ivan and Dieter, especially. He offered to send them on the next bus out of here, and that shut them both up."

Werner Sofer was curator of the Varusschlacht Museum, and was the one to oversee us. A citizen science team had uncovered the skeleton of a mule and a few buckles, but their time had been limited, so Sofer decided to commission a dig team before winter set in.

Craig had known me from way before I transitioned, when we were on the Anasazi project in Arizona. That hadn't gone so well, mostly due to the greed of a few team members who got away with looting. But Craig now had a leadership role with this contract, and knowing my background in Roman history, he called me in.

But I sure as shit wasn't going to stand for what had happened during my PowerPoint, and I told him this right away.

"Also, it looks like you've been mugged," I went on. "Was it Ivan?"

Craig saw I was looking at his mussed-out hair, and he tried to flatten it down. "You should see Ivan," he grunted.

Ivan hailed from Adelaide, and was open\about his penchant for Nazi memorabilia. A real class act. He didn't seem to care what the legalities in Germany were, so I wondered if he'd brought some along for his new pal Dieter's benefit.

"I don't know why you hired these two," I said. "Neither of them knows any Latin, and Ivan doesn't speak a word of German. Did you pick them out of a randomized Google search?"

"Their networks," Craig said.

"Follow the money, yes," Peg offered, then demurred. Craig wasn't an intimidating presence, but she seemed to sense he'd been hurt. I gave her a little shush, because better things were about to happen anyway.

"Look," Craig recovered, "you're the real consultant on this. Anything we find in the ground runs by your appraisal. I made it clear to the rest of the team. Sofer knows that too."

And this was for the money, by all accounts. When you lose your tenure just for deciding to go on living, that really puts the zap on your head. I could abide some more transphobia for a few days for the sake of making an equivalent almost-year's income.

Here's a state secret: Most transition costs burn a white-hot hole in our pockets. So despite the upset, I needed the income. And seeing Peg, another veritable unicorn, quite by chance in that noisy, dark, and stunted hotel bar, I can only attribute to planned happenstance.

"And Sofer told me he's definitely in your corner. His niece is trans."

I furrowed my brow at him.

"You're second in command," he said.

"But without the agency to send anyone packing." My reply was as much a statement as a question.

"Leave it to Sofer," Craig tried to assure me. "But keep your ears open."

"And your eyes," Peg said.

I was glad the Jäger shots were wearing off.

"We have another day before going out," Craig said, standing up as if in salute. "Relax with your thoughts."

And he was off to relax with his own. The crowd noise had died down into a tired rumble. Peg and I looked at each other, and you couldn't have shot us out of a cannon fast enough to get us out of that bar and into her room.

03

Battlefields live on, long after the dead and their wares and tactics and reversals have gone, recovered or lost, remembered or forgotten, and the same goes for the Battle of the Teutoburg Forest, where Varus's seventeenth, eighteenth, and nineteenth Roman legions were led into a Germanic trap and decimated.

Apart from brief footnotes in history, knowledge of the Varian Disaster at Kalkriese had only been in the public consciousness a few decades. Peg herself had questioned me on this.

"I don't know why you're bothering with this," she'd said after our thirteenth orgasm together. The booze had worn off, and I was feeling impeccable, natural elation from the companionship of someone like me.

"Clunn already uncovered the lion's share of this battle," Peg went on.

Unlike me, Peg was a Brit, so Clunn's discoveries at the battle site in the late twentieth century had been a point of English and German pride for as long as we'd both been alive. Rome had fallen, so I cannot speak for their own affinity for Kalkriese, despite the lion's share of artifact recoveries being of their own imperial pride, two millennia on.

NEXT MORNING, SOFER gave us a quick tour of the displays in the museum. Although I'd read the histories and guidebooks and pretty much devoured the website, being there made the difference, not only because of how well put together it is, but we were in actual proximity to the recovered objects. The massive Imperial mask replica greeted us with a resigned solemnity that made Peg's words echo through my head: *Perhaps, just as the Roman attempts to subjugate the German tribes during the first dynasty of Rome, this was all for nothing.*

I didn't pay much attention to Ivan or Dieter during the meeting or the tour. To them this was merely a diversion from a pub or a trip to an Osnabrück Chick-fil-A franchise.

On the other hand, having Peg and Craig there with me was enough to rouse me for the purpose of our few days of excavation, which if it didn't turn up so much as a bone fragment, at least I got to experience a battle site that had haunted and intrigued me for so very long. Seeing so much of what had been uncovered already and preserved with such professionalism and care for the collective memory of the battle stirred me deeply: Even the loss of my tenure due to the bigotry of my so-called peers seemed like a turned, maybe torn-out page of my past, and the rest would take care of itself for a young trans woman's hope, or folly, or faith.

"This place," Sofer told me as an aside, "is like our way of trying to make the wrong right."

"I'm not sure you can achieve something *that* human," I said, glancing at the displays of Roman formations, tiny doomed soldiers dotted in blocks of discipline. "You can pay tribute to them, but honor is kind of their own call. You don't honor the spirits of the dead with replicas."

"These are exhibits," Sofer countered. "And Rome knew how to put on a show."

"In the arena."

Sofer nodded, and we left it at that.

Peg told us that had it not been for the Kalkriese battle, Germany may have been assimilated into the Roman Empire, and the history of humanity could have been altered in some magnificent but perhaps stunted ways.

"It's not up to us," I told Sofer. "But if we find anything here, I'll be glad to see it curated."

Craig smiled, shrugged.

We were then led into the observation tower where you can see a panorama of the entire site, field and forest verge alike. As it was early September, just as the battle itself, we had the dregs of late summer, and Sol Invictus seemed to favor the entire project ahead of us, brief though it would be. The complex was plated with panels of rusted metal, giving the whole place an aptly sanguinary look that complemented the verdant greens and imposing blue skies.

The others had left, and it was just Peg and me gazing out at the horizon from the tower.

"This was like September eleventh for the nascent god Augustus," I told Peg, probably for the hundredth time since we'd first hooked up. The battlefield stretched out before us in a midday fuzz of paganized avowal. "Literally."

"How many on this team, besides you, speak any Latin?" she asked.

Peg was great with her Latin, but she was about to embark to Hamburg for her own excavation, trying to cull the deliciously scandalous dalliances of an immortal rock star from storied granddaughters in the Hamburg St. Pauli district, trans women who, like their ancestors, were just trying to eke out a living among the screwheads, jackoffs, and imposters of this world.

"Cis" is not a slur. It's Latin: "the same side of."

I smiled at her, shrugged, and, glad for a moment alone again, we kissed deeply and held one another, enjoying what we could in what remained of the late-summer heat. If anyone else came up into the observation tower, we didn't notice them. There was plenty else to experience.

THE NEXT MORNING was just as hot early on as it had been midday of the museum visit. I didn't notice I was setting out with a hangnail until we began digging the initial layers. Before embarking on my connecting flight through Portland, the TSA had confiscated my nail clippers after taking me aside into a room, where they made me expose myself just for the shits and giggles of it.

I knew my biting at the nail would only make it worse, so I asked members of the team if they had any clippers. If in reaction to this blank stares or smirks were dollar bills, I could've taken the next flight home with more cash than this project's guarantor.

These people were nerds but not *my kind* of nerds. Even Craig seemed out of his element this morning, aloof and not running at one hundred percent.

Sofer had marked well where the previous excavators had uncovered the mule skeleton, and a few yards farther along, the buckles that had been appraised as true of Roman legionnaires.

The flags were not far from the famed swamp that had winched Varus's forces against the Kalkriese hill. The Romans had been harried for three full days not only by Arminius but by the place itself. Also the gods had not favored them—the downpours had ruined their shields and arrows, and their sense of duty had only served to play into the hands of the "barbarian" Germanic tribes. The whole thing had been a rout and a deceit. Not many appreciate this in hindsight, but these soldiers were people, not robots. Many days' ride from home, I could speculate for their terror and bewilderment as I stood surveying the site. It brought to mind the fictionalized depiction of the collapse of the Marines in the xenomorph hive in *Aliens*, and that was maybe twenty soldiers compared to the nearly twenty thousand who'd met their demise here.

Panic, disorientation, and the Roman way all forsaken to the sticks, mud, and ancient mounds.

A tiny chipmunk darted in front of me after I passed the paving stones meant to approximate the forest track made by the doomed Romans.

I hoped it was a good omen.

Instead, the distress of the small, furred courier transferred, and took my physical dysphoria to a level I hadn't experienced since arriving in Europe. *There is no army in across-the-Rhine Germany*—

"What's up?" Dieter asked at my shoulder. "You've been staring at that area since we got here."

I shook my head.

"It was the swamp," I said. "It was drained hundreds of years ago, but in the time of the battle it was a pinch point. I keep thinking of how many of them tried to make for it when they were outnumbered."

"Or how many bodies were recovered."

I wanted to ask if Dieter was from Hamburg, but was still wary of him because he and Ivan had been such fast friends. He looked like he was about to ask me something else when someone cried out to us.

The layering had begun slowly, so I'd have been surprised if they'd found anything already. I'd bitten at my hangnail all morning despite any strength of will, and I'd not even glanced at a trowel. There was some effect the place was having on me—back in Arizona, Mexico, or even in Ohio, you couldn't have dragged me away from the soil until I'd turned up some kind of artifact, a link with someone who'd lived epochs before and might have even been trans themselves (or were wondering about that, despite jaded edicts of the time). But at the field I was tentative, cagey, as if our actual tread was a form of rape. The landscape of the preserved battlefield was too beautiful to disrupt, even though it had been curated and landscaped for our modern, timid, condescending gaze.

I caught myself biting at my nail again and was about to look for the first-aid kit when Ivan came running up.

"We found some things," he panted at us. "Small pieces."

I tried my best not to see him as a dark shadow, but nevertheless, the light in his eyes told me that this might indeed be a successful project and there could be more money coming.

Dieter picked up what Ivan put down.

"Where?" I asked.

"Base of the hill," Ivan said.

Right away I was suspicious, but we followed him to the place he'd flagged. Despite the acreage and scope, the site had been raked over so many times, one had better not expect a Sutton Hoo breakthrough. And yet we rounded the verge, and there the team had flagged five pieces on the tarp.

Craig was already there and motioned me over.

"We need to get these out of the sun," Craig said.

I glanced down, my hangnail already forgotten.

"You're . . . Fuckin' A," I muttered, heedless of how baritone I sounded.

The fragments screamed of breastplate armor and hinges. They seemed too good to be true, but Craig was right about the urgency—exposure to the late-morning sun was not going to help these objects that had lain in the earth for so long. Thankfully the appraisal tent wasn't far.

Before Ivan could get his paws on this stuff, Craig and I bunched them into the bins and hurried off. We rounded the same corner I'd come from when I noticed the bushel.

Stripped bark and branches had been lain at the juncture of the drained swamp and the paving slabs.

I stopped a moment and wondered if this was part of the museum landscapers' duties. But I hadn't seen anyone else working the site other than our team, and this had to have been placed recently. Surprisingly, it measured several feet in diameter and hadn't been tied, so it was more of a pile than a curated mass.

Craig and I made for the appraisal tent, where we could get ourselves out of the sun along with those little finds. The rest of the team were out, and I was glad to have some time to watch Craig work. We unfolded a table and set the fragments down.

"These look period," he offered after brushing their edges. "No insignia."

They appeared a little too pristine, but I didn't want to say for sure without Sofer also having a look. I felt incredulous because we'd not been there an hour and already our excavation had unearthed finds that Clunn with his trusty metal detector was unlikely to have missed all those years ago when he first identified the battlefield, and especially in such a major feature in the landscape. That enormous hill was notoriously important to the whole memory of this place.

Dieter traipsed in and told Craig that Ivan wanted a word with him. I was too busy examining the fragments to pay much attention to this at the time—I was measuring and comparing the stuff with my notes, and the authenticity of the pieces un-folded moment by moment. I began to question the very concept of time, of memory, of my very own dysphoria.

Would this find get my tenure back? Was this success? Was this defilement of the restful dead?

My thoughts raced in this manner perhaps because of my disillusionment with how badly the Arizona project had turned out. The museum itself prostituted objects sacred to Anasazi scholarship and then lost all trace of the material (so they'd said). After that, I was determined not to let it happen again, but even here at Kalkriese, anxious to get my so-called career back together and desperate to get my derailed transition on track again, I felt like a grave robber. What was I supposed to do with all of those years of study and fieldwork? What else could I do? Where else could I go?

A slow patter of rain began on the tent canvas, and I looked up to find Dieter had been staring at me the whole time. I squinted past him and outside where the weather shifted into a heavy downpour. I hoped Craig would come back alone, but Ivan was at his shoulder. They weren't that drenched.

"Great." Ivan brightened at seeing me. "Just us guys."

"Oh, go fuck a kangaroo," I spat back. "What's your malfunc-tion, anyway? Why are you even here? You're unlikely to find any panzer shit in the ground."

This only encouraged Ivan, and he went on to ask about Peg, and what kind of sex trans women are supposed to pretend to have, but I expected this from him.

I kept at him regardless.

"I saw you on the subreddit. You know all that Nazi shit's not legal here anymore, right?"

The rain really came down hard then. Some of it hit my arm through a rent and instinctively I began chewing at my nail again. I'd forgotten to look for the first-aid kit.

Dieter just shrugged.

"Like, is it frotting, or what?" Ivan grinned as he stepped closer to me. "You rub yourselves together?"

"Only your mom," I snapped back.

Craig gestured toward the finds.

"Hey, both of you, I didn't travel halfway around the world to waste my time like this. I can just send the lot of you home and Sofer and I can get on with this ourselves."

Where was home?

The rain let up slowly but steadily, as if from a tap. Craig told me to cover the finds and that we should all get back to the dig. That the sooner we finished surveying, the sooner we could move on to the next section Sofer had assigned. Craig had my back with Ivan's harassment, but I wished the curator was there too. I wondered what he'd have thought of what we'd found, which was more than I'd expected. The site had been picked over so many times over the years. And yet I felt we had spoiled history itself. It wasn't just Ivan's being a bastard—I felt dirty.

We stepped out, and my eyes had to adjust. The storm left just as suddenly as it had come. The brightest sun now shined, and yet it felt *unsafe*.

"It smells different out here," Craig muttered.

"Well, maybe it's something pagan," I quipped. "Or rain."

"No rainbow."

I wasn't looking for that anyway.

My eyes were drawn back to the old drained swamp, not so dry anymore as the rainwater had formed a vernal sea that stretched beyond the forest verge, but there was something else—the bundle of sticks I'd seen at the junction earlier had *tripled* in size. I shielded my eyes against the glare to see, and then wondered if we were being punked by the museum, or Blair-Witched by some freckle-faced student filmmakers.

My boots were squelching in mud, and I was about to turn back to the tent when Ivan started again, waving his arms from the verge.

There was a point of light there, aspiring to the sun.

I had no wish to get closer to Ivan. Craig got there before me. I knew I had to maintain my appraisals if I wanted to get my share of the stipend, so I quickened my pace.

What Ivan picked up from the turned grass and mud looked anomalous to the rest of what we'd found: a fully intact baton, ivory-white handle, about the size of a small lamp, topped by a cast golden eagle with its wings fully spread out.

There was no fucking way.

"The nineteenth legion," Craig told us. "SPQR."

"The Senate and the People of Rome," I muttered. "And maybe eBay."

Even from that distance I knew it had to be a replica. Maybe Sofer was testing us to see if we'd be able to make the call, as if this whole thing was some odd scavenger hunt rather than an excavation. If so, that would've been in poor taste, and I wouldn't think the curator would want to waste our time and the trustees' money like that.

"That's not real," I told them. "It has to be a facsimile from the exhibits."

"How do you know?" Ivan sneered.

"You haven't found anything real. If you'd read Tacitus and Cassius Dio you'd know all of the *aquilae* were recovered when Rome came back to bury what was left of the bodies. And the standard of the nineteenth had been the very first one. Germanicus recaptured it from the tribes."

Again, vacant stares from Craig, Ivan, and Dieter.

"Ask Sofer himself." I shrugged. "That thing may as well have just come from a Happy Meal."

I ran my index finger along the headpiece, which, despite its dubious origin, reflected the afternoon sunlight with some defiant glory of lost empires. It wasn't cheap; it was solid and cast in steel, but so unweathered and unblemished that it had to have been planted only just in advance of our arrival that day.

Ivan kept after me.

"How are you so sure it's not real? Maybe someone put some of them back, or we only have the histories to say so."

Indeed all traces of the seventeenth, eighteenth, and nineteenth standards had been lost to obscurity, but there was a small matter of the very gradual decline and fall of an empire to contend with. Two millennia had passed, with Rome shunting itself eastward to Anatolia before ultimately acceding to Mehmed the Conqueror in 1453.

All told, none of my so-called team members had taken Clunn's thorough excavation of the site into consideration. And by this time, I could tell there was no talking to these people. Again, these were nerds but *not my kind of nerds*. Even Craig as he held the object seemed entranced by it, as if he'd found something sacred and singular rather than counterfeit. The *aquilae* had held as much importance to the "barbarians" as it did to the Roman military, this was undeniable.

I turned back toward the appraisal tent, and there was the landscape, not forgotten but lost, hostile, fucked up.

"Where's the museum?" someone behind me asked.

The observation tower that had stood meters above the tree line had vanished. This wasn't some trick of the sun— I'd glanced at the hulking column in my eye line throughout the morning, of course not thinking much about it except to wonder if Sofer had stood up there and watched us occasionally. Any trace of it had gone and made me wonder if the thing had collapsed during the rain, but I think we'd have *heard* that take place. The grinding of those pre-rusted plates would not make a subtle commotion.

I was incredulous Craig could have been hoodwinked so fast and easily. Ivan or Dieter (or both) could have bought the replica online, or even at the museum itself. They'd had all morning to plant it at the hill. The more this dawned on me, the less I thought about the missing tower.

There had to be some other explanation for that. Unless the wanton desecration of the site, or the juvenile attempt to deceive Craig and myself had disrupted some semblance there of time or space. I shook the notion away as soon as it had entered my mind, but when I tromped closer to the tent I got a better look at the trees, a thick line of late-summer shade, a shelter against the blaring and heedless Sol Invictus.

I didn't recognize the faces. They weren't attached to bodies, or even necks. These were human faces, though, defiled to the quick: each piked to a trunk, some through the mouth, some the eye, the farthest gone to decomposition through the forehead.

I turned back to the others. "Is this supposed to be—"

Craig's eyes were still as wide as saucers as he held the counterfeit *aquilae* aloft, as if he himself had won some great victory over the ages and mysteries. But if it was a hollow gesture on his part, perhaps he wasn't entirely to blame. The replica was indeed very pristine and beautiful, and I considered searching online for a copy to place in my own apartment (especially from the nineteenth legion), when a javelin point pierced Craig through the sternum from behind, killing his enthusiasm, then his breath.

The replica tumbled out of Craig's clutches and disappeared into the shrubs just west of us. I watched Ivan's eyes follow the eagle as it flew off, but before I could lunge away, an edged metal bit the skin at my throat.

"Deinde te," a broken voice whispered, wheeling me around. *You're next.*

The forces arrayed before us looked closer to a cohort than a legion. The latter would have filled the visible field, but this was more than enough: four of us against hundreds, and what soldiers! Each stood at full height once their heads fully reattached. It was something to see, this resurrected army.

It didn't take long for my fascination to give way to terror as the rotted heads popped off the trees, wriggled from the soil, and rained from the sky. Absurdly, I wondered if all of the heads matched their origin.

When the unspeakable happens, when the world turns upside down and the ground feels like it's swallowing you up, time slows to a grinding halt, and you wonder if you're just abiding a waking nightmare. This had happened during my tenure hearing, when the people I'd thought supported my decision to live had reversed themselves overnight and painted me as a criminal to the board. Unfair doesn't even begin to describe it.

But the concept of fairness hadn't even been a dream in the cheapened lives of these soldiers. They'd allowed themselves to be deceived and routed in unfamiliar terrain. Their commander Varus himself had been warned repeatedly of the impending disaster.

The soldier with the sword at my neck ordered me in Latin to step forward.

The eyes were the worst of them. The mud, the twine, and the sticks aided the soldiers' bodies to stand erect. But their eyes burned with a red light that pierced me to my innermost dream-world, my chromosomes, my wishes to see Peg again, and any hope that had driven me to stay alive up to that moment felt useless, shrunken.

04

It was our turn to be routed.

The revenants stepped over Craig's prone body and made to dispatch Ivan and Dieter in short order.

My disassociation went into hardcore overdrive—everything I'd built up to then had all been for nothing. My decision to stay alive had in itself been folly—the tenure hearing, my catching shit for clothes shopping at Target, the randomized harassment by TSA, mall cops, and customs officials just to get to this part of central Germany, where all it was amounting to was having these creatures come out of the woods and torture us to death. Perhaps we deserved it—we'd disturbed a place of sacred history, not in the religious sense but historically. Archaeology is a very *white* pursuit that more often serves to perpetuate colonization and dominion. The Romans had been taught this lesson, and I was only just beginning to learn its egregiousness and futility. Let sleeping corpses lie.

But no, there had also been Peg.

To have spent so many years lying to myself, deciding that the best way to deal with searing dysphoria was to ignore it and drown myself in histrionic studies that others had written in the field (often badly enough to remind me that this approach wasn't working). And to top it all off, the social aspects of my closet—to be constantly wondering what intimacy or even a dinner date would feel like for the deserving and lucky among us, and still to keep hitting that wall where people who haven't lived through the shame and guilt at not feeling right within yourself won't deign to look across a table at you, much less hug you when you're down. Maybe it is like having a hangnail that only gets worse the more you bite at it.

Spending a day with Peg, though, someone not just like me finally but someone who understood the pitfalls of navigating academia as a trans woman, was enough to have galvanized me during this terror, but it also filled me with regret that I hadn't just dropped everything and gone with her to Hamburg.

But I also knew better on three fronts: First, I'd have been a distraction to her. Peg was off on a project that would shine a light on one of the most famous celebrities of the latter twentieth century, himself a murder victim, and that was highly emotive stuff if not plain dangerous. She needed her focus. Second, I'd lose the stipend Craig and Sofer had promised me, and without my tenure, I had no savings to fall back on. Third, the lovers who burn twice as bright risk burning twice as short, and I didn't want that. It had taken so long to find someone like Peg, and all told, I didn't want to blow it.

And yet there I'd blown it, by not going with her and staying behind only to be swallowed by nightmare and slaughter in that late-summer daylight.

Ivan turned to run but only just right into more ghouls who glided up from the soil and clutched his legs. He fell with a thud right into the still-forming limbs of our captors, their solidity ever-burgeoning with the sticks and weeds that flew into them as if pushed by a tide. Their red, glowing eyes never blinked once.

Dieter just stood there in shock as one of them grabbed him from around the neck, easily enclosing it, and grunted something unearthly as it marched him back toward the appraisal tent. That place had been the last semblance of the real by then. All else had unleashed some uncanny vortex of violence so sudden and hostile, I wondered if this was what it had felt like for the soldiers in the quick of the ambush itself at Kalkriese.

I thought I heard the guard who held me fastened to his own sword laughing as Ivan was then brought to his feet by five of the opaque creatures. One of them then whirled the Aussie around to face me. The creature's strength and agility was astonishing. I saw no mouth hole as it nodded sidelong to its prize, and then it addressed me in Latin.

I saw no movement in its face composed of soil and bracken, but its voice was clear, albeit sounded like gravel tossed down through a harvester machine.

"No more lies," it said, in the most erudite Latin.

With one hand it yanked Ivan's head back by the hair, and then its other shot lightning-quick into Ivan's gaping, ridiculous mouth, twisted a moment, and tore the tongue out with the finality of a scythe. Ivan's eyes clamped shut, and his gurgling scream was met with greater violence as the entity slapped him upside the head with the denuded tongue and then shoved him back down into the mud.

No more lies.

Were they trying to purge what had happened to them all that long, long time ago?

Ivan's burbled screaming increased as the other soldiers dragged him by his boots toward the tree line where I'd first seen the heads. The museum tower still wasn't there, or at least not in the time and place where this was happening to us.

Dieter was marched out of the tent, artifacts cradled in his arms. He saw what was left of Ivan and let out a cry of his own. The revenants weren't done with their liar.

More sticks, leaves, and mud gathered to the creatures as they fastened Ivan to one of the bigger trees, his rent and bloodied face to the bark. It looked like they were trying to crucify him. It takes a long time to die from that.

And now it was our turn.

Ivan's squealing died down a little, maybe out of exhaustion. Dieter called me by name as some of the company turned to face him. He dropped the small pieces we'd first unearthed and turned to run. The afternoon was getting on, and as he tried to make distance from the creatures, I saw him silhouetted against a break in the clouds. The sunlight caught him just right before a soldier stepped out from behind the appraisal tent and with one stroke lopped his head off. Also not a quick death, but perhaps more merciful than what Ivan was compelled to endure.

I'd read plenty about how the tribes had dispatched the captives from the seventeenth, the eighteenth, and the nineteenth legions, and as the ripshit and malignant spirits of those same victims turned in my direction, I finally realized the atrocities they had in mind for me.

05

The wicker enclosure they'd crammed me into wasn't upright. I was in fact lying prone inside the hull of a wolf bitch, constructed with twine and wood and sod that when spirited together formed a cage that felt harder and colder than my own car where I'd tried to kill myself in order to avoid facing the truth of my being. The rope around my neck tightened with every breath. The landscape had also continued to build these vengeful spirits. Their flesh hadn't grown any more human—the mud and soil made them darker than midnight—but by that time, most of them towered almost to the tops of the trees, and how they had constructed the wheels that bore me inside the wicker construction, I couldn't tell you. Whatever force had made it, was keeping it together, and preventing me from escape (to where?), it was the only reality left to me by then.

Until the fire came.

They started at my feet; and although it wasn't my first time being burned, it's the worst pain every time. Perhaps it's the dehumanizing aspect of the element; it takes all of your features away, perhaps even one's own memory—the ultimate fuck-you.

I'd have gladly forgotten my suicide attempt, but the fire brought that night back in a flood of sorrow. Not only did I feel regret for just not going along with Peg, but I was dying for something that didn't make any sense. All told, I'd never consult on a dig again.

Through a gap in the rib cage of the wolf, I saw Ivan drooping against the tree they'd crucified him to, still facing the other way. But then, I also saw the replica—the sunlight hit it with such precision, pollen danced about it like fireflies. I screamed at the petty little bastard, imploring Ivan to tell these beings that the eagle was counterfeit, to admit that he'd ordered it online from wherever.

Then I stopped myself—they wouldn't have understood him, even with his tongue.

Right then, a torch was thrust at my head through a gap in the wolf. The right side of my hair singed, and I let out a short curse, in Latin.

The fire carrier stopped short.

Its glowing red eyes narrowed, and the revenant muttered something about cleansing me with fire. Beautiful fire.

Over the grass, dirt, and twigs, the pieces of armor that we'd initially found were fastened to the being's torso. This mattered to them more than any fascination with the dead past mattered to me, in the end. I wanted a future, if not with Peg, then to be happy living in my own skin, to be alive-for-real in the truest, deepest, most *human* sense.

The being continued staring down at me, its torch powerful and pointing skyward.

To avoid another jab, I cleared my throat, and in Latin, I asked its name.

Fraxinus Antonius, it said. *Of the nineteenth legion.*

Fraxinus—ash trees, of the family *Oleaceae*. Ashes are also a symbol of rebirth. The lost soldiers had come back to Kalkriese, just not as *human*.

The other soldiers looked back at me, heedless of the seeming delay in dispatching me to the flames. One of the taller ones, seemingly in a panic, thrust his own torch at my shoulder. I winced, and with my limited mobility in the enclosure, it was difficult to dodge these attacks. Upon his withdrawal, I saw the twine at one of the hinges stay aglow and curl into itself.

"I am Tamora," I told them in Latin. Their hesitation was the only expression I could glean. This was all guesswork and desperation to buy time.

And of course, I began to fuck it up right away.

I thought the eagle, fake though it was, might somehow appease the revenants.

The twine at the hinge burned almost through. It was an advantage that I needed. I kicked, shouted, and rolled out of the wicker wolf and onto my side in the grass. The momentum was unstoppable, my desire for a future, to see Peg again. To start facial electrolysis back home and abide *that* burn. Perhaps even to gain tenure again at a seat of learning that would actually put into practice its non-discrimination policy, *some concept.*

Clouds set in again. All the soldiers' eyes were on me as they shuffled closer, and then I saw *PEG.*

There she stood, realer than the Hamburg dalliances of the nascent John Lennon, and she was holding the eagle standard replica aloft. Beyond her, Ivan had stopped wriggling.

SPQR.

Senatus Populusque Romanus.

We both said it together, like a beguiled couple who eat, drink, fuck, love.

A sword crossed her throat. I screamed and fell to the ground with both the replica and Peg. I was overwhelmed as the legion surrounded me and watched me sob into nothing.

After a while, it began to rain.

They all just stood there, staring at the *aquilae* languishing in the grass. Some of the more soil-based among the dead things began to sag, but Fraxinus stood tall, his armor gleaming against the elements.

I wiped my eyes and glared at him.

"It's not real," I told him. "Fraxinus Atoninus, all of the eagles went back home, to *Rome*. This one is a replica. It's *fake*."

Ivan thankfully was toast by then; he was the one to blame for all of this happening. Not me. I just wished his suffering had gone on for longer.

Peg had stopped moving.

The afternoon was getting on, and once more the rain let up. Late summer is a motherfucker. And so is Kalkriese.

I gripped Ivan's cheap replica stunt, stood up, wiped the dirt and rain from it against my torn and singed dress, and offered the thing to Fraxinus.

Senatus Populusque Romanus.

SPQR.

As soon as the being grasped it with its wooden fingers, the whole army blew apart in a quiet sigh of borrowed components. The fake standard fell into the very bundle of what Fraxinus had been approximated into, himself a replica of the lost and the, yeah, forgotten.

They had all been lied to. That was the shit memory of this battlefield. It was a humiliation where duty had stood for precious little else than futility, except perhaps for changing the course of European history.

Peg rolled over in the mud, her hand pressed against her neck. She sat up amid the piles of sticks and the broken wolf of wicker interstices, and then asked me what had happened.

Elated she survived, and exhausted, I slumped my shoulders and pointed to the eagle.

Just then, Sofer's frantic voice could be heard from just beyond the verge. Ivan, Dieter, and Craig remained just as they had been when they'd been ended. The curator's face was a sun of outrage. The observation tower of the museum stood just beyond the scene in all of its rust-plated glory.

"Was zur Hölle ist hier passiert?" he demanded.

Peg picked up the eagle replica from the bundle of what had been Fraxinus and scrutinized it a little more closely. She didn't look too bad; like my burns, the wound across her neck also seemed to be a thing of the past. Perhaps she remained alive because she didn't die during the rout—at least not in the real sense, any sense that would've otherwise made sense at that battlefield.

Peg let the fake thing fall back into the mess of sticks, and asked Sofer if he had any wine for us.

I shrugged, and bit at my hangnail anew. It didn't hurt as much. We try for these little things, although they don't usually work out.

After our benefactor ran back screaming toward the museum, flailing his arms like a child, Peg and I decided to stay there and wait until sunset before deciding whether or not to continue our journey to St. Pauli in Hamburg.

THE DEVIL DON'T COME WITH HORNS

by Eugen Bacon

I T WERE THE second day of summer, a sunny day that cast its own shadow, when you seen the devil. He slipped quietly into your neighborhood. He stepped out all hair, sunnies, and a bandana. A ghost dog and a moving van too.

THEY CAME IN a rush.

You were running down the road, the wind giving you speed as you cut through the field toward Baridi's house at the end of the neat suburb when the boys jumped you. One minute they were sullen, smoking ciggies on the stump that was once a red oak by the footy field. Next, they were swinging fists at your ribs as you writhed on freshly mown grass in a forgetting town that the council and volunteers kept spotless.

Forgetting. Because that's where your pa fled to forget.

"What you gone hit me fer?" you cried, shielding your face.

Mad, the Cormont boy—a good-looker, but all mean—spoke through his puffs. "Ain't no dawg but me," he said, and chewed on the smoking dart at the side of his lip.

Neat wore white shorts and a grubby mop on his jet-black head. No big-name heritage—he were a Clanger, and his mother part of the neighborhood watch. His brother Langdon, also in white shorts, had orange curls so tight they were a fist. The littlest Clanger, Jowls, had friendly eyes that asked fer a ciggie, offered you a puff, but he were as random as his socks, one beige, one crimson-striped, and a don't-argue vest that tradie folk somber about their business wore.

All this went through your head in slow motion as the punches fell in real time.

Soul Parchment, the compact one, had the body of an ox. He yelled *Fucketty!* as he whooped you. He were the angriest of the pack, made him the meanest. But Mitch Lightfoot unsettled you. His folding knife had an ebony handle. He wore a rucksack and stayed away from lil' fights—just big ones where he flicked open and closed the glint of stainless steel, the blade's flicker as gray as Mitch's danger eyes.

Waterman stayed away from fights too. He were a Nielsen lad, skipping tricks on a hemp rope. Alternate foot, jump, jump, cross, boxer step, jump. He kept skipping as his mates smashed you.

You tossed a kick that connected. Neat yelped.

"Got loose at the right time," hissed Mad. His fist flattened you *slam bow.* "Lie down, kid," he said, as you started to rise.

Something smashed into the pack, and Baridi was fighting your war. The boys fell away afore she spoke. "Let him go." She stood there in leggings and a tank-top. Heart face. Tiny eyes. Braids.

"Or what?" Mad rubbed his lip with a thumb.

She stared him down. "Yer the courageous one?"

"Weak 'uns run from this." He pulled a bodybuilder pose, muscles ripped through a pale polo shirt. The way he said it, you knowed that he liked her.

She ignored him, gave you a hand.

The bravery in a small girl surrounded by big brutes awed you, and it stupefied the boys, except Waterman, who was still skipping, and Mitch, who dropped the rucksack from his back, pulled out Metal Glo and a rag, and polished his blade.

The sound of the pocketknife's flick as you walked away, then: "Wait up!" said Mad. "Ye forgot yer ball."

"Toss it," said Baridi.

"Nah. You come git it."

She ran back, but he dribbled, bounced away, and then sprinted. Baridi chased, chest out in her leggings and tank-top. She ran hard and fast, little legs rolling. Mad gave his best to keep the ball, turned it over to Langdon.

Baridi held the heat, Mad dodging. Soul Parchment got involved, then Jowls, the boys outnumbering Baridi four to one, then five to one. She plowed through body traffic, dragged the ball with her foot, scooted away with it.

"Fortune changes," she called out, laughing.

"I ain't never change fer nobody," shouted back Mad.

"Is everything about yer?" She rolled the ball on the ground at speed. "Then come steal it. I'm *weak*." She hit a long one into the distance, raced after it.

Mad gave up first, then the rest.

She were full of panting when you reached her. "That's how it's done."

"Kick a ball?"

"Beat bullies." She tumbled the ball, grinned at your laughable attempt to catch it with a foot. "Want me to kick it to myself?"

"I got two lefties."

"They's *club feet*."

"Is that what yer think?" You positioned, paced to the ball and back.

"Don't reason with the ball. Just kick it."

"Sometimes, yer got to reason." You gave the ball another look, searched fer a target in the distance, and shot. The pack behind howled at your flying boot, the ball on the grass still.

Baridi took the kick. She thumped, strong shin to boot. Bent the ball across the quiet street to the cottage at the end of the world where death happened.

YOU SEEN DEATH. You fell into it. Happened when you rushed into the kitchen in Downs where you lived, when you burst onto Maw lying on the floor. She pressed a hand to her stomach as if pushing back guts. Her hazel eyes held deep surprise, maybe at the smell of wet soil and metal.

So much blood, and it were growing. So much, you could sail a boat in it.

You dialed Emergency and they cleaned her good, put her in the hospital bed, white sheets and all, then Pa came. But there was nothing left of your maw's strawberry and freesia scent, just a dying smell of nail polish and bleach. Gray lips replaced her glitter smile that made you think of a large diamond. You held her cold hand. Her eyes were half open, teary. There was no gentle tinkle of her laughter, just gasps, then a rattle. When her skin went porcelain, a nurse came and pulled white linen over Maw's face.

THE MOVING VAN was up by the cottage's driveway. A three-seater cabin with a ramp. Somewhere near the cottage—*ting!*—the peal of a bird.

"What yer bring us here fer?" you asked Baridi.

"Now yer give me stupid? I got yer out of a tangle!"

"Wouldn't call it that."

"A spectacle then?"

"Only a small one."

"That were some desperation, kid. They was killin' yer back there."

"Nothin' of the sort. And yer a kid yerself. Ye git me out of trouble, put me back in it with that ball. What we doin' here, anyways?"

"That's what I'd like to know," said the Black chap with sunnies and a bandana who'd crept out of nowhere. He stood on the stone steps that led up to the derelict cottage and its stained wooden door peeling paint the color of olives or mold. Halloween windows with the eyes of a ghost looked out at a wilting dawgwood tree on the yard.

"Need help finding something?" He tawked with a whole cherry inside his underlip. That's how he sounded. He held out the ball, but neither you nor Baridi moved to take it. "You got a good look, did you?"

"Nana said—" Baridi cast you a glance. She raised a brave face and announced: "We don't tawk to strangers."

"Nana is wise. You like Skittles?"

"Why Skittles fer?" you asked.

"Settle nerves." He pulled a tin can from his pocket, pried open the lid.

You helped yourself and popped a sour mandarin in your mouth. "If yer scared, why move here?"

"Who said I'm scared?"

"They dug up all them bodies, some whole, some hacked," you said.

"A year back," he said. "The real estate bloke told me already."

"Shrouded in them burlap sacks," you said.

He raised a brow.

"Nana said they found bones of seventeen pepo, the tiniest a bub," said Baridi.

"Tiny hole packed like a pyramid," you said. "IDs, jackets, rings, teeth, crosses, watches, a gold necklace."

"What are you talking about, nigger?" It weren't a question.

"Is it okaywise?" asked Baridi.

"Okaywise to do what?" he asked.

"Callin' folk niggers that ain't Black pepo."

"Aren't you a nigger?" He looked at you.

"Oh, no, sir," you said, and shook your head firmly.

"Who is, then?"

"I don't rightly know, sir."

He stooped to eye level. "Then I say you are." He poked you on the chest with a beautiful finger, perfectly shaped. Held your gaze, then straightened up. Offered you another Skittle. "What else Nana say?"

You swallowed a pinkie—sour raspberry. "They was dining chairs, coffee table, queen bed, carpet—ain't good no more."

"I like pineapple—the yellow one." He studied as you popped the Skittle in your mouth. "What if she got it wrong?"

"Who did?" Baridi stretched a hand and he shook a perfect rainbow—red, orange, yellow, green, blue, indigo, violet—onto her palm.

"What if Nana got it wrong?" he said.

"She my grammy," said Baridi.

"And that's enough?" He laughed.

Baridi folded her arms. "Yer ain't seen her."

"Place still smells rotten," you said.

He turned his beard face on you. "I bet you can conjure some magic with this ball."

"She can." You pointed at Baridi with your chin. "Give yer a good run."

"Show me." He tossed the ball and Baridi caught it.

Right foot, the ball sailed. It curled toward the footy field. The watching pack didn't stir or grab the ball. Mad smoked. Waterman skipped. Mitch flicked the knife.

Baridi ran to fetch.

"And she's a left-footer," you said. "What yer reckon she got if she put a left boot to it?"

"I won't argue with that," he said in that cherry-lip voice.

"She don't miss, Mr. . . ."

"Baba," he said. "Just Baba."

"She don't miss, Mr. Baba."

"I thought an accident brought you here."

Were he tawking about your maw's dying—how could he know?—or Baridi's ball? You shrugged. "She don't kick that ball no place she don't want it to go."

The silence felt off, so you broke it. "What happen to yer dawg? I seen it in when you moved."

"She's having a dream."

"Kin we see her?"

"Come by tomorrow."

"Chill."

"Make it early."

"How early?"

"Real early."

BARIDI PUT THE ball on the boot and kicked it home. "What were yer tawkin' about?"

"Nothin'." You looked at her. "He could be yer fahver."

She laughed. It were easy to forget she were different—her mixed race weren't there till you looked fer it. To you, she were just Baridi. A girl with plentiful courage to take one or all them brutes out there, and they knowed it. "Pity my maw's not here to tell."

"You kin find her in the city."

"Maybe. But yet again . . ." Her eyes challenged you. "What if I ain't got no maw?"

"Like Nana make it up? About yer maw run off with some Black boy and leave yer here?"

"Maybe Nana *made* me?"

Your eyes grew big. "With a spell?"

She laughed, and ran into the house. But you wondered if Nana could grow creatures. You'd seen her power, how she could heal. What if she had more power inside?

You stepped into a fresh whiff of baking. Nana's house was full of softness you never got from your pa, and it were nothing to do with the vintage velvet on her dining seats, or the turquoise plushness of a Persian rug rolling all the way from the doorway, or the perfect ribbons that held the waists of quilt curtains, hand sewn. Perhaps it were more to do with the powder softness of Nana's skin, despite her smell of vegetable soap—freshly cut greens. Hers were a softness that promised home, or its memory.

"Something's off with you two," she said, but didn't press.

She had barometer eyes that told of her mood. Warm green were what you wanted. It got you square donuts, iced like heaven. Candied fruit—clementines mostly. Prune tarts with custard cream. Peaches in white wine syrup. Ice blue, not so much. When Nana's eyes got blue, you knowed to scoot.

Today her eyes was lit green. "Give me something to work with," she said, like she did when she wanted a yarn.

You thought of Baba and his dreaming dawg.

Nana shuffled on one leg around the chestnut table, served iced tea and new croissants filled with homemade chocolate and hazelnut butter. You and Baridi wolfed them down. Nana was a Shield, so you reckoned that made Baridi a Shield too. It weren't public what gave Nana the shuffle.

"What someone gone drive all the way to Alexandra fer?" you asked on the third gobble of a second croissant.

"Same thing that brought you and your pa from Downs," said Nana.

"Ain't the same. Pa were grieving when he took a turn yer don't take at the freeway."

"What's wrong with turnin' in to Alexandra?" asked Baridi.

"The sign's all broke."

"It didn't stop your pa," said Nana.

"Yer know what makes a person who works fer a finance company called Coin swap the suit fer a rain cheater and a bicycle to pedal them letters?"

"Grief." Nana's green eyes stayed warm.

"Damn right. The kinda grief that makes yer hide from truth, even yer own self."

"Maybe fate brought you and your pa to Alexandra," said Nana. "Look at you and Baridi here. And your pa, remember when the fever took?"

Yeah, a year ago. Your pa were cooking, sweating a stew when Nana rang the doorbell, shuffled up the stairs to his bed, and put a touch on him. She muttered, her eyes all bug, big toads in her throat, and a blue ocean pushed from inside wanting to come outta her skin till your pa went cold.

"I knowed he weren't gone," you said quietly now to Nana. "Same way I got them feels, and knowed Maw weren't gone stick long in this world."

PA WALKED THROUGH the front door, no happy postman smile, nobody saying, "Darling, I'm home!" He came home like a funeral. He wore the long face of a ranger, eyes distant through invisible sights. Maw was dead and that was that, but Pa didn't get it.

"Nana say hello." You pointed at the big microwave. "She make truffle-buttered quiche fer yer."

He grunted.

You watched, hand on cheek, cross-legged on the floor in the open living room. He dropped the satchel from his shoulder, opened the fridge, and popped a beer on the fridge door. Unlike the apartment in Downs, your place in Alexandra was sparsely furnished as if you'd just arrived or were leaving. No one threw a carpet over the wooden floorboard. Pa slumped into the lone two-seater, cold beer in hand. He flicked a glance at you, and then away. There was no television or dishwasher. The fridge, mostly packed with beer, was all that counted. The microwave too, a little, and maybe the toaster. The walk-in pantry was nearly always empty.

Upstairs, Pa slept in his room on a futon, and you on a stacked mattress in the attic.

They said robbery. It were theft, all right—stole your maw fer good. Your pa, too. First, he were confused, slept a lot. Then he took one last heave, packed a bag fer himself, a bag fer you, hesitated, then allowed you to snatch a pillow, and drove, drove, till he seen a wonky sign that led off the freeway toward the lip of a town called Alexandra.

It were a town where pepo nosed into other pepo's business, and dead ones like Maw became everyone's business. What they hadn't reckoned on was that many deaths would happen right under their noses. A serial killer bested them. Chose to live in this quiet town that had neat tarmac walkways and grassy curbs, one café called Messy Chef, a newsie call Quik Ezy at the corner near the roundabout where the Cormonts sold cheap ciggies. Waterman's mother, a registered nurse, did births, needles, prescriptions, footsies, and dontics, but was unable to help your pa. Nana could. It weren't a plush neighborhood with its Pattersons, Nielsens, Lightfoots, Parchments, Cormonts—Belgian or Swiss heritage, Shields . . . and now a Baba. It were Alexandra, the town your pa chose to go walking dead.

Up in the attic, you sunk your face on the pillow that was your maw—it felt like her, brought back her smiles, smells, and glitters. You fell asleep and she visited wearing purple-gray skin inside a collapsible coffin.

YOU WAITED FER Pa to shave and chomp cereal. You heard the bang of the door, then a bicycle's bell. You brushed your teeth—Maw wouldn't like it if you didn't—threw on shorts and a T-shirt, pedaled out on speedy feet, and whistled.

Baridi flew from her house, bouncing the ball on her boot. She flicked it, and you gave it a thumping kick that drove it closer to the wooden chalet and its weedy lawn.

"I'm better than you think," you gloated.

"That were just a lucky break."

The ball went off her foot, bent and zipped right onto the stone steps of Baba's cottage. You stopped short. The yard looked as if an ogre had stamped it in a rage, made careless mounds in a corner over there.

Ting! The bell bird again, somewhere in hiding.

Baba was bustling to and fro with a wheelbarrow, tidying up or making a mess. A ghost-coated dawg loped about in playful leaps with a waggy tail.

Baba took off his sunnies, clear black eyes looked at you straight, and he smiled.

"Her name's Killer. A big softie."

You whistled and Killer paddled to the road, tail wag-waggy. You dropped to your knee, and her body relaxed to let you scratch her neck under the collar. The sand on her tongue found your face, all licky.

"What dawg is she, Mr. Baba?"

"She's a mastweiller."

Baba put a scraper to the wood on the door and stripped down the peeling paint. You watched as he dragged the scraper top to bottom along the surface, then began sanding.

Baridi was all quiet, uneasy around Baba. Occasionally, she bounced the ball on her foot, danced with it, ball whispering along the vacant road, as Killer panted happily around your face. She were a fat-pawed two-hundred-pounder with pale moon eyes, her mouth all droopy.

"Watch out, nigger, she's a heartbreaker," said Baba. "You like her too much, she'll say see you later!" He grinned. He looked at Baridi and stretched out the scraper. "Want to help?"

"Sure." She dropped the ball, her heart face unreadable. She tucked the hands of her unzipped jacket, exposing her wrists.

Pa grunted when he came home, and you tried to tell him about Baba and the dawg, how Killer was good-natured and keen to please. He nodded without listening as you told how she got up on two legs and hugged your face. Maw listened, head bent, silken hair over her face. When she lifted her head, black holes instead of eyes looked at you without expression.

YOU SOLD YOUR soul to the devil and his Killer. You were smitten with the sturdy dawg and spent much of the summer helping Baba. Killer brought you twigs to throw and loped heavy-set after them, her face wrinkled, white drool falling from her lip. She wore a soft sheen, velvet gray like Nana's chairs, and her coat glistened like a racehorse's. She put her head on your knee, nuzzled into the crook of your arm, and shed a lot. You reckoned you smelled of dawg—Nana said as much, but your pa didn't notice.

When Baba joined you to scratch Killer's neck, she went all floppy-eared, tail a high waggy, tongue licky, and holding his gaze. You noticed his immaculate hands, long handsome fingers, and you knowed the devil don't come with claws or horns.

What you also noticed was how Killer avoided the dark patch of the yard soil near the dawgwood tree shaped in a witch's claw. The tree was all curled and gnarly right about where they'd pulled out body after body in burlap sacks falling apart. Nothing else grew there near the tree—because deadness poisoned the soil, Nana said. But, strangely, mushrooms began to sprout. They started right after Baba stood near the dawgwood, scurried bark beetles that looked at him and fled, and he finished the rest with a pesticide. He patted mulch around the patch, and what do you know?

It shook mushrooms out of dead-people ooze in the post-apocalyptic house, as Baridi called it. "Zombie mushrooms," she said.

Weren't long afore Nana started shuffling by. She dropped Baba pickles and dills in jars, crumbed oven-baked tomatoes in casserole dishes, even brought trays of baked potatoes and smoky chicken, skin all crisped, lemons tucked inside.

One day she took some mushrooms and made a mean pie right there in Baba's home. You didn't want to enter the kitchen, because old sixpences stuck in your throat and a taciturn darkness overwhelmed you as soon as your feet crossed the threshold. You stood with a black circus and a clock in your head, not knowing if the shadows and their funny-voiced finger puppets were inside or outside you. All you knowed was that the three-bed with awning windows, grill-barred, was just another story with a terrible hush that a blade cut, and somebody's dream became other people's nightmares.

They started tawking mushrooms, Nana and Baba. The shrooms grew from deadness and put paradise in your stomach when Nana cooked them. Earth flavor, sea flavor, meat flavor—all of it came from demon gods. Shrooms carried all the dead-people vitamins. You could eat all the carrots and spinaches, gobble salmons and livers, and not get as much nutrients as came from those shrooms, Nana said.

"This here are button mushrooms," she explained. "See how plump they get."

They were dome-shaped, pale brown, different from the cup mushrooms, which were larger, partially open, and intense-flavored whether you ate them raw or cooked. The oyster mushrooms were nice to look at, flute-capped, as were the forest mushrooms with their dark, broad hats. But pine mushrooms got you and Baridi squealing—they grew wilder than the rest, saffron milk caps all bright orange, the taste rich and nutty.

"Strong bone, too, less sick," Nana said. "Shrooms make your heart beat right."

Ting! The bell bird agreed.

All this while, the lads at the footy pitch gave you no mind, just looked from the distance as if plotting something. Waterman skipped: alternate foot, jump, jump, cross, boxer step, jump. Mitch: the sound of scraping as he honed his knife. Only smoke, not much words, came out of Mad's mouth. He didn't need to shout, "What you doing with that nigger?" cos you seen it in the contempt in his eyes. Sometimes Mad spat when you passed, but you knowed he still liked Baridi even though her pa were Black.

Your pa still drunk beer and stared at the walls.

You slept in the attic, hugged your maw as she embraced you back with mottled skin. Blue-black beetles fell in and out of the holes in her stomach.

IT HAPPENED AT the cottage yard three days afore the end of summer break. Started with Nana's midday casserole, washed down with a cuppa and walnut-crusted cheesecake. The taste of mountain lemons and fresh earth lingered on your tongue.

Nana was inside Baba's house, washing up, and Baridi was helping to dry them. You didn't want to get inside the house that killed people. So you kicked the dawg a ball but, like always, it were a wonky kick that didn't go as planned.

The ball rolled to the cursed ground near the dawgtree that now had yellow-green leaves. This tree that never bloomed till Baba showed were beginning to sprout blood berries and snow-white flowers.

"They're just pretty leaves," said Baba in his cherry-lip voice. "Not real flowers."

The dawg chased the ball a bit, but was fearful, you could see. She perked up ears as she approached the darkened ground.

"Killer!" You clapped your hands. "Fetch!"

She whined, whimpered, and stopped moving. You had to fetch the ball yourself, and her by the collar. As you stepped away from the ground's pulse, a branch raked your face. You touched your cheek, and your hand came out wet.

Away from the tree, Killer was still shivering as if stained with the mark of death. Baba walked out with a first-aid kit. "Here." He put a smiley Band-Aid on to stop the bleed.

"Only the devil wanna live in a place like this," you said.

He considered you fer a long time. "That what you think?"

Killer stayed all mopey. She refused a treat, her yellow moon eyes all squinty. Even the bell bird was quiet.

YOU WHISTLED AT dawn, and Baridi tumbled out of the house with her ball. You scattered to the day, white mist in the air. A single *ting!* of a bell bird in the distance. Rain started to form, a drizzle in the vista. You pedaled on your feet, as if you were carrying demons on your backs. A torrent chased hard. The fingers of a damp demon touched you, first on the forehead, then on the neck. You raced up the stone steps, huddled by the door washed in a silence of the weather's pout. Then flood-gates opened and, with it, a rush of sound. A distant buzz of racing cars. A chorus of chimes, cheeps, warbles of the rained birds. Then *gribble!* Frogs. You lived fer the summer, and this day held a curse.

You seen it first—a blob of tar hanging down the branch. The dawgtree leaned from its weight. The tar disintegrated as the rain arrived, the buzz louder as large blowflies dispersed in a cloud that changed itself and soared into the sky. You leaned closer to look at what was left behind. A worm beast. Fat writhing things, wriggled in and out of its body, skin and intestines.

Baridi threw the ball up in the air, knocked it with a boot as it fell. It whistled—*slam!*—into the worm beast, and some of the worms fell off in a splat. The ball lingered, stuck to the squishy insides of burst maggots. Then it bounced to the ground and you seen what the hung thing really were. Killer, dead. Hanged with a noose roped on the dawgwood, her stomach clawed open. Maggots crawled onto each other, in and out of the dead dawg. You knowed whose rope it were that noosed, whose folding knife slit her all the way down her stomach to her butthole.

You fainted, but you didn't, because you were still standing. Baridi ran, and you looked at her sprinting toward the boys starting to gather and stare in the rain as if trapped in the same summer curse. Baba fell out of the house, came running toward the tree and strong hands carried you from it.

Your lips trembled. You pressed a hand to your stomach as if pushing back guts.

Baridi lost a boot running, but she flew at the boys, uncaring of the folding knife. She barreled first into Mitch, and then Waterman.

Soul Parchment yelled *Fucketty*.

Baridi was hitting at anyone in the wet. The boys just stood as she whipped at them, and Mitch was shouting, "I didn't do nothing!" and Waterman, "It weren't us, honest to gawd."

And Mad . . . he just stood in the wet as it pounded.

NANA DIDN'T LAY hands on the dawg, mutter, her eyes all bug. No toads fell out of her throat in incantation, so there was no ocean pushing from inside wanting to come outta her skin to bring back Killer.

"Why can't you?" you begged.

"Some things, boy, you don't bring back."

You watched full of empty as Baba disturbed the shrooms with a new hole in the ground.

THE EMPTY FILLED with something that burst when your pa got home. You gasped, "Pa."

His brown eyes fell on you. He dropped his satchel of letters, and the strides that reached you were big and long. The hands

that held you were strong and tender. You choked and hiccupped
as he said, over and over, in his awkwardness, "What's this, is
this." His chest was out of place, his hands disconnected from
his mind.

Maw was there with Killer when you slept. The dawg panted,
good as new. She lay all floppy on your stomach, her black
tongue licky-licking your face out of a droopy mouth. Her eyes
were a pale blue moon that filtered light under your door. Once
or twice, you woke to Pa's footsteps climbing up the wooden
steps to the attic. He stopped on the last rung, a shadow under
your door. Each time he went away without coming in.

You leapt soon as morning broke and didn't whistle fer
Baridi. You kept running, full of foreboding. Then you saw it:
the moving van purring on the driveway, with Baba inside—
clean-shaven, a bandana around his tight curls. He wore a neat
jaw like you'd never seen afore on him, sat with sunnies at the
wheel. You looked at his mouth, wide and honest, and you
knowed you'd trust anything that came off it.

"Mr. Baba," you said weakly, and he slid down the window.

"'Sup, nigger?"

You pointed at the van. "Movin' already?"

"Yessir." There was deep sadness in his voice.

He swept a final look, reached for something in his pocket,
tossed the tin of Skittles, and you caught it. He rolled the van
onto the road. And you knowed that he were no more a devil
than you.

INVASIVE SPECIES

by Ann Dávila Cardinal

JOSÉ MOVED THE café con leche to his right hand, then took the mail from his PO box with his left. Good God, could there be any more? Walking toward the post office door, he dumped the printed catalogs into the recycling bin and stepped out into the warm Old San Juan morning with a manageable pile. As he stepped off the curb, he stumbled over something in the gutter. He looked down to see a gutted iguana, its golden eye with the weirdly human round pupil staring up at the sky. They weren't indigenous to the island; seems they came from pets that were let loose in the seventies. He even heard that some people had begun to cook them. But iguanas in the old city? In the country or the suburbs, maybe. José stepped over the reptile with a shudder. *They don't belong here.*

He glanced through the correspondence and bills as he walked. All but one, his mortgage payment, were addressed to "Joseph." Why was it so hard to get them to switch? Women get married and change their names all the time—you would think it would be easier. Even the forwarded mail from his mother had "Joseph Murphy" scrawled in her shaky hand. He sighed and tucked the pile under his arm.

As he made his way up Calle Tetuán, he looked up at the bright sky, the electric blue accentuating the deep sherbet colors of the buildings of the old city. He breathed deeply, wanting to take it all in. The morning air smelled of roasting coffee, baking Mallorca pastries, and, underneath it all, rum. They could do all the street cleaning in the world, but José suspected that the smell never went away, that it might be soaked into the very foundation of the walled city he called home. It was a bit of a party town, after all. But that was not his scene these days; no, at forty-five those days were behind him. He had too much work to do and books to write. Speaking of which, the current deadline was not going to reach itself.

He crossed Calle de San Francisco and waved to Carmen, his regular waitress at Caficultura. He'd lived in the city for two years already and loved being a local. The shop owners and their employees knew him, and he was certain the local writer's group was about to ask him to teach a seminar. As he made his way up Calle O'Donnell, he noticed a series of work trucks parked in front of a neighboring building. That building, like so many others, was left abandoned after economic crises, hurricanes, and unrest in the city. Small palms grew in the corners of the cement blocks, vines and graffiti crawling up the crumbling exterior walls as if competing to see which could reach the partial roof first. He stopped, sipped his coffee, and waited for one of the workmen to come out.

"¿Perdóname, el edificio fue vendido?" he inquired of the portly mustachioed man.

"Yes, a corporation has purchased and is restoring many buildings in the city."

José hated when they answered his Spanish with English. Why did they assume he was a gringo? His grandfather had been half Puerto Rican, and he had been secretary of the interior! But he'd learned to hide his disapproval. It was a waste of time anyway. "What corporation?"

"They're called El Colonial."

"Ah, so they *are* Puerto Rican! Wonderful! I would hate for more of our real estate to get into outsider hands."

The man just looked at him, shook his head, then went to the truck to grab large cases of bright yellow paint.

"Yellow, huh?" But the workman didn't respond. José stepped down onto the blue cobblestone street and tried to peer into the two-storied building. There was a hive of activity inside, the rumble of many voices, and the tinny sound of salsa. He hoped they wouldn't be playing that too loud all day every day. He had writing to do.

He resolved to introduce himself to the owners as soon as he had the opportunity. It was best to know your neighbors.

The next day, after a morning of revising, he decided to treat himself to a nice lunch at El Convento. He hadn't been there in a while—he'd been eating at home, or close to it, for weeks. He started walking along Calle de la Luna, enjoying the hot midday sun on his head and the sounds of the ocean waves hitting the seventeenth-century city wall not three blocks away. He did a double take when he passed a formerly abandoned building and saw that it was completely restored. The walls were smooth and finished, the wrought-iron balcony repaired and freshly painted. There were even flower boxes along the railing, spilling orange and yellow blooms.

"Nice, huh?"

José jumped a bit at the voice of Joaquin, a neighbor from up the street who appeared at his shoulder. "Yeah, but I walked by this building, two, three weeks ago tops. How is it even possible to have renovated this quickly?"

"Anything's possible when you throw this much money at it. I hear they hire an army of contractors for each building they renovate so it gets done in record time. And they pay well. Nice work for local builders."

José stared up at the building. He looked for some flaw he could point out, some shortcut taken, but it was perfect. "Are they fixing them up to sell? Because then we have no control over who might buy them . . ."

"Nah, that's the thing. Irma, my real estate friend, says they're renovating all of them to live in, full time. Seems they like the climate and the center courtyards for privacy. The bonus is, we no longer have all these sad eyesores. It's really the best of both worlds."

José chewed his lower lip, working a piece of loose skin there. "I'm just not sure. There's something creepy about this."

Joaquin shrugged. "I'm just glad the buildings aren't empty and decaying anymore. The streets were starting to look like mouths with rotting teeth. So depressing. Well, hasta luego, Joseph."

José was so distracted that the misnaming didn't even register. He started walking, but there was something . . . wrong about this corporation, this land grab. He ended up turning the corner to head home again, forgetting about his sandwich. His appetite was gone. And that afternoon he didn't write a word. Instead, he spent hours searching the internet for information on El Colonial, some history or press pieces on the company's real estate dealings. But each time he thought he'd found something, he ended up back where he started with no new information. It was all he thought about as he ate, showered, attempted to sleep.

OVER THE NEXT two weeks, more and more buildings were bought and speedily renovated, and even José had to admit the entire city started to look brighter, livelier. But there was a dark undercurrent for him, like a beautifully frosted cake that looks pretty but is decaying from the inside. It was all he could focus on. He tried to write for the first few days, but only ended up staring at the blinking cursor on his screen, his concern about the new neighbors always running in the background of his mind like a soundtrack.

Instead of working, he would find himself standing outside the buildings for hours, staring at the façades, chewing his lip. There really was something untoward about the entire thing, and as he stood in front of the newly restored building on San Sebastian Street, his gaze wandering over the washed-on aqua paint, he decided that it was up to him to bring this to light. And that night was the monthly Old San Juan Community Resident Committee meeting. He would get on the agenda and bring it up. He barely slept that night, planning what he would say and how they could mobilize to stop this.

JOSÉ PACED THE back of the room, waiting for the meeting to start. Though it was time to begin, people were still meandering around, drinking coffee and chitchatting. The Poets Passage, the local business that was hosting this month's meeting, was filled to capacity. Good. More people to rally to the cause. Finally, the chairperson, Ileana, called the meeting to order, and people took their seats like a slow-motion game of musical chairs.

As usual, the agenda was in a PowerPoint that was projected against the wall behind the stage. First on the list was the proposed new event guidelines that would impact how alcohol is sold during the San Sebastian Festival. Parties. They're worrying about parties. Why do people get so wrapped up in this petty stuff when their city was being taken over right under their noses? After what seemed like hours of blabbing about liquor licenses, water pressure, and the iguana situation (during a normal month that one would have been of interest, but he had his mind on El Colonial), it was finally his turn.

"And now"—Ileana clicked forward a slide with her remote—"José Murphy has an issue regarding the restorations being done around town by the El Colonial corporation."

Eye-rolling from a few of the people in the rows ahead of him. Eye-rolling? Really? He didn't have time for such bullshit. He stood up and headed to the front of the room. He needed the mic for this. As he passed by the other attendees, he heard murmurs.

"Did you see the beautiful job they did on that building on Fortaleza? It was such an eyesore, especially on such a tourist-heavy street!"

"I know! And the gutted one where the junkies hung out on Norzagaray? Totally restored!"

José grabbed the mic from Ileana and turned to face the crowd. "I know you're all aware that one corporation has been buying up the abandoned buildings in our city. However, it seems that no one really knows who these people are, what their intentions are."

Mayra raised her hand. "I thought it was for their employees to live in. That was the first thing I asked about, whether they were going to Airbnb all these spots and we'd end up with armies of drunken twenty-year-olds. I mean, more than we already have."

Murmurs of agreement, heads nodding. How could they be so shortsighted?

"Have any of you actually *met* anyone from El Colonial? Any of the people who will be living next door to us? Across the street from your families?"

At first, they all just stared at him, then looked to each other, heads shaking. Yeah, he thought so. "I think before we allow them to buy any more buildings, we demand a meeting!"

"Wait, 'allow them'? 'Demand'?" This from Carlos Ramirez, the group's treasurer, a buttoned-up type with darker skin and perfectly coiffed hair. Every meeting, José resisted the urge to tell him to lighten up on the cologne. Carlos stood up. "Do you have any idea what this island has been through, Mr. Murphy? Recession, corrupt politicians, earthquakes—" He counted them off on his fingers as if José hadn't read all about them. He wouldn't pick up and move to another country without doing his research.

"Of course, I do. If you'd only—"

But Carlos cut him off. "Oh wait, you came *after* Hurricane Maria, didn't you?" He had that look that said he knew all along when José had moved there. "Something to do with the tax breaks for millionaires, perhaps?"

José lost his temper. "I don't need to listen to this from you, Ramirez! And I don't see what that has to do with these concerns!" A bunch of people started talking at once, and several voices were raised. It wasn't the first time in one of these meetings; they were an emotional group compared to his previous neighborhood, but he wasn't usually at the center of the drama. It felt so . . . unseemly.

"Enough!" Ileana's voice raised above all others, like a mother with a wayward flock. It was about time someone reasonable stepped in. "Carlos, sit down."

Carlos threw his hands up in pseudo surrender, then dropped into the folding metal chair with an audible huff.

"Mr. Murphy, he's right, we cannot police every person who purchases property in Old San Juan. After all, there's a reason those buildings were empty and in disrepair. We are not in a position to look gift horses in the mouth." She gave a slightly patronizing smile.

"Yes, but we've worked so hard to keep the city's atmosphere a certain way, keep it honest to its historical roots!"

Carlos let out a scoff and mumbled, "Colonizer problems." A chorus of giggles followed.

"Besides," Ileana continued, "I was told they prefer to keep to themselves, stay at home, even get their food delivered. That's why they wanted the buildings with the private interior courtyards."

"Told by whom?" His voice sounded almost pleading, but he needed to go to the source, get some direct information if he wanted to get to the bottom of this.

"It would not be appropriate to reveal my sources."

"Wait, they don't leave their homes?" José scoffed. "How can you think that's normal or acceptable?" He stared at the sea of faces before him. "Can't you see that something is really wrong here?"

Mrs. Sanchez spoke up from the front row. "Why? What's bad about that? Less people crowding the streets, neighbors who keep to themselves. Sounds like heaven to me." Laughter and humming agreement.

"You see?" Ileana continued. "It seems you are worrying for nothing, Mr. Murphy."

José felt chastised. He didn't like feeling chastised. "Well, I'd like to take a vote."

Ileana nodded in surrender. "Okay, all those in favor of demanding a meeting with El Colonial about their purchase and restoration of abandoned buildings?"

José's hand shot up before she'd finished the question. He looked out on the group of about twenty-five or thirty members.

Nothing. Their eyes avoided his, and no one raised their hand.

"All opposed?"

Every hand in the room shot up, including Ileana's. "Okay then. Let's close this issue and move on to the next item on the agenda." She looked over at José with a smug look. "You can sit down now, Mr. Murphy."

He stormed over to his seat, sat down with a clatter of metal on ceramic tile, and folded his arms across his chest. The rest of the meeting was just white noise, the voices a shapeless droning like cicadas buzzing in his head.

When the meeting ended, he swallowed his pride and made his way to Ileana. If she had information about these new residents, he was going to dig and get more. After she finished talking with the owner of the local bookstore, he pushed his way in front of her. "Ileana, I wondered if you could tell me where you got your information? I've been trying to discover more, but—"

"Mr. Murphy. I think you'd be better served worrying about your own business. You seem to have an unnatural obsession with this issue, and I will not be a party to it." Then she lifted her chin and walked away.

"Bitch." He hadn't meant to say it out loud, but judging from the looks he was getting, he had. José couldn't get out of there fast enough. He brushed by people as he rushed to the door. There was always a mixer afterward, sometimes going on for hours with music and laughter. He'd enjoyed them on occasion, but there was no way he was going tonight. He stormed up Calle Cruz, pushing through the gaggles of sunburnt tourists who wandered the streets, and turned onto San Francisco.

He couldn't stop thinking about how no one else seemed to care. Well, fuck them. Let whatever Tom, Dick, or Harry move in and see how much they like it when they don't recognize their city anymore. They'll move in like locusts, using up all the re- sources, taking their place in line at Café Cielitos.

He'd walked about five blocks when he came to a maze of scaffolding that blocked half of the sidewalk. He looked up at the buildings and saw two of them were being seriously reno- vated, the ones where the weeds grew as high as the windows inside the house, and the exterior was so covered with graffiti its original color was indiscernible. José glanced at the permits and signs on the scaffolding.

"El Colonial." These new signs included a graphic logo of an old-style hot air balloon in stark black ink. Charming. No one appeared to be working onsite, or José would have gone in and talked to them, squeezing information out of them before they knew what hit them. He sidestepped the scaffolding, kicking an empty box hard as he walked by.

He turned the corner and stalked up his street. When he looked up to check traffic before crossing, he noticed the lights were on in the second floor of the yellow El Colonial building. He stepped back up onto the curb and retreated into the shadow of the laundromat's storefront since the view was better from the other side of the street, and more discreet. A couple, dressed up and clearly a bit tipsy from dinner, turned the corner and started walking up his side of the street. He took out his phone and pretended to be absorbed in it until they passed by. Once they turned the corner, he went back to staring into the open shutters beyond the balcony. You couldn't see much; despite the heat of the evening, they had only opened the upper shutters instead of the entire doors, but he was determined to get a glimpse of the new owners. And since, as Ileana said, they didn't leave their homes, that left him no choice but to stake them out.

Time ticked by, and occasionally he saw a shadow pass by the door, or heard the clatter of cookware, but that could be from anywhere. His feet were starting to hurt from standing still for so long, his skin was itching terribly, and he could probably use some dinner, but with or without the backing of the neighbors, he was going to get to the bottom of this. His eyelids were starting to get heavy when a figure stepped in front of one of the open shutters.

José jolted to attention and squinted, trying to get a better view. They were probably not going to be there for long; he needed to get a better look. His phone! He pulled his phone from his pocket, and shakily pulled up the camera app. He pointed it at the window and spread his fingers out from the center of the screen, magnifying the image. He was halfway there when the figure stepped forward and out of view again.

Dammit!

He held the camera there for a moment, the lens still in macro mode. Maybe if he just held it there for a while . . .

The figure reappeared. José had to put his other hand up to steady it when the significance of what he was seeing hit him. It was shaped like an average-size man, head, shoulders, arms, but the skin had been removed, and the brick red of exposed muscles stretched over the chest, around the head in strips. Areas of bone showed through in bright white striations.

José couldn't breathe, couldn't move; fear had turned his insides to stone. Shaking, he snapped a photograph, the electronic fake camera sound echoing on the quiet street. The figure's head snapped, and its bulbous eyes seemed to stare right at him. *Jesus Christ!* José's skull was buzzing, the skin suddenly too tight for his head, and he shoved the camera in his pocket and took off back down the street. He couldn't shake the image of those lidless eyes looking at him . . . looking *into* him. He wasn't going home so that thing would know where he lived, no way. He was going to prove that he wasn't crazy, that there *was* something to worry about with this El Colonial business.

There were too many partiers milling about, blocking up the sidewalks, so he ran up the side of the parked cars, dodging traffic on the narrow street as he went. He almost got hit by a car on Calle Tanca, and on the next corner he stepped into a puddle, breaking the rainbow oil-slicked surface. He didn't care—he had to get there before the social part of the meeting broke up. Finally, he stumbled into the back entrance of the Poet's Passage, almost knocking over bony old Mr. Altieri in the process. He pushed his way to the stage on the far wall and was relieved to see the mic was still live. He grabbed it and spun around to face the group once again.

"Neighbors! Neighbors!"

Conversation trickled down, until there was only the sound of ice tinkling in glasses, and all eyes were on him.

"I have proof! Proof! A photograph of the monster living in the new El Colonial building on O'Donnell Street, right next to my home!" He triumphantly waved the smartphone over his head.

Ileana stepped forward from the confused crowd. "Mr. Murphy, what is this all about? This is highly irregular . . ."

While she blathered, José plugged his smartphone into the projector and pulled up his photo app.

"I'll show you; I'll prove to you that I was right!" People were quiet as he adjusted the projector's lens, focused on the photograph he had taken just moments before. "You'll see, I—" But the image wasn't getting clearer. "What the hell?" He looked at the phone, zeroing in on the image on the screen. With his shaking hands, he saw that the photograph was blurred, the figure at its center unintelligible, a cloud of muscle-red and bone-white.

His heart dropped into his belly as he fussed with the phone, trying to get it clearer. "I swear, I saw it . . ." But he realized that nothing was going to make it readable to others. He looked up to find anger spreading across some faces, pity on others. No, he did not want pity. His mind skittered. "Wait! Why don't you come with me? You can see for yourself."

"Mr. Murphy, I think—"

"Maybe if we went there with la policía, we could get them to answer!"

"Mr. Murphy, you have to—"

"I know what I saw!" His shout was loud in the high-ceilinged room, and all sound ceased. He said it again, but quieter. "I know what I saw." He looked at the black and white tiled floor and wished he could melt between the tiles and slither out the door, reconstituting only when he was clear of this place.

"Mr. Murphy . . ." Ileana's voice was gentler then, but careful, as if she were talking to a child . . . or a lunatic. "Perhaps you should go home and rest."

"Rest? Rest? With that monster just down the street?" He was gesturing wildly with his hands when Carlos appeared at his elbow.

"Time to go." And then he was dragging José toward the door, talking in his ear. "Let me give you some advice, José. You're new here, you need to listen more and speak less to understand how things are done here, and—"

José whirled around to face the younger man. "Don't treat me like I'm just a gringo! I'll have you know, my grandfather was—"

"Half Puerto Rican and secretary of the interior, we know. You've told us a thousand times." They had arrived at the front of the building and José wondered if Carlos, who had about six inches and seventy pounds on him, was going to throw him down the two steps and onto the sidewalk. *Just because you're, what, one-eighth Puerto Rican, it does not make you a native, pendejo.* Carlos didn't need to say it: José could see it in his eyes.

But Carlos just walked him down the steps, let go of his upper arm, and pointed up the street. "Go home, Murphy. Go home." His voice sounded tired instead of angry. Carlos Ramirez put his hands in his pockets and walked back into the store.

After Ramirez disappeared back into the party, José turned on his heel and headed home in a daze. He didn't see anything as he walked, just moving downhill by gravity, a discarded hermit crab shell dragged along by the tide. He was almost startled when he realized he was standing in front of his own building, key in hand as if in autopilot. He hadn't even remembered to look up at the second floor of the other building to see if he could catch another glimpse of the creature.

He turned his key in the lock and pulled the heavy door closed behind him, throwing the series of locks with a ringing of metal, a comforting sound. He tossed his jacket over the couch and kicked off his shoes as he walked. José was suddenly so very tired. It was this feeling that inspired him to leave his previous community, to make this place his home. He didn't expect others to follow, especially not these . . . beings. As he made his way back through the building, he undressed as he went.

Well, everyone in that committee will see, and they'll be sorry.

He dropped his clothes where they lay, his pants landing over the small palm tree in the courtyard, hanging there like thick khaki vines. He'd have to take that off in the morning so it wouldn't kill the plant, but tonight he was just too tired. When he got to the bedroom, he completely undressed, and carefully hung his skin on the custom-made rack in the corner. It felt good to take it off.

"Imagine. Not ever going outside. Not trying to blend in at all."

He scratched the long red muscle on his arm and shut off the overhead light.

"Fucking monsters."

THE ASYLUM

by Holly Lyn Walrath

The world is full of enemies.
There is no safe place.
  —Anne Sexton

It is only after one is in trouble that one realizes how little sympathy
and kindness there are in the world.
  —Nellie Bly

PROEM

Men are called insane, but women are called lunatics. The word
means "moonstruck." A woman's madness is unpredictable,
cyclical, like the gray moon. Women are driven by its light like
tides—full of cracks and flaws just threatening to let the light
show.

ADMINISTRATION AND RECEPTION

One of us practiced lunacy every night in the mirror to get
here. We feel quite bad for her, because Nellie is a journalist
and she merely had to act crazy to get here by pretending to
believe she was poisoned (this is not so bad by itself—some of
us did this as well because we were hungry and poor), but also
because Nellie seems to think she will be allowed to leave when
she tells them the truth. You see, she treats this place like a game,
but it's much more than that. We must admit, Nellie is a rather

good actress. Even Ida agrees, and Ida saw Sarah Bernhardt die on stage (in French, no less!) at her first performance in America, with twenty-seven curtain calls. Ida's family is rather rich.

In the entryway, there are hair-cloth sofas, and we are asked to remove our jewelry for safekeeping, our pearls laid neatly in a box labeled with our names. The doctors ask us why we are here, and we never know why, not the real reason. We are not sure where here is, until we are locked in the ward by the overseers, who are plain older women named Miss Davis and Miss Brown (no decent married woman would be caught dead in here—that is the message they send).

The night they brought Nellie in, we heard her ask, "What if there is a fire?" as Miss Davis locked her door with the little key ring she carries at her waist. We laughed along with the overseers like hyenas. "Then all of the women would burn up," Miss Davis said, and retreated to her desk in reception. (It has not escaped our attention that Miss Davis and Miss Brown are women too, but for some reason we are the ones referred to as such.)

Nellie begged to God the first nine nights, having only planned on being here for ten. Until someone, we believe it was Ethel, said, in the darkness, in a low and honestly threatening tone, "She'll not last till morning—"

Then there was a strangled noise, and the voice went quiet.

In the morning, Ethel would not speak. When she saw Nellie, she shook her head in terror and tried to run and had to be tied down. The doctors were very curious about the silence, and so they cut out Ethel's tongue so they could study it.

"Barbarians," said Hattie, who is a scientist, or was before her colleagues had her committed for being a woman with too many ideas.

Later, Ethel had convulsions and was sent to the dead house.

But of course Nellie did leave, and we are told she went and recounted her story to the newspapers. It was not our story, because we are still here. We did take small comfort in the fact that after her little tryst here, Nellie was never quite the same again. She kept it with her, you see, that viciousness this place bred.

Oh, there is one thing we forgot to mention about reception, which is the oiled bronze plaque dedicated to the man who donated the money to build the place, which says:

WHILE I LIVE, I HOPE.

We think it's kind of funny, which is the only reason we mention it here.

THE BATHS

After newcomers are thoroughly stripped (sometimes forcefully), they are given a bath, which is always full of icy gray water, and washed all over with soft soap by the Irish woman, who is so old, we think she must have always been here; perhaps she was installed with the other fixtures.

The water is not changed between us, so it is better to go first, but when one is last, one feels a kind of kinship—a mystical burning sensation all over the body. We are dirt together. We may die together; at least we can endure the hardship of having bodies together.

One woman would not consent to being stripped. We found her later in the ward, chained to her bed. She said she didn't feel right in her body because it was female, and she had worked so hard for so many years to hide the parts of her that were female, the body that would not be right no matter how she tried to make it so, and it drove her nearly mad to have everyone see it on display. She wished she could strip away all her female parts. We had all felt that way at some point or another, so when Hattie asked if she'd rather we refer to her as a man, the new girl nodded, and we all agreed to call her James, which was her brother's name, and James was very calm after that.

At least, we believe he was.

We only saw him for the short while before he was sent away. Someone said his family came to retrieve him. For a long time, his story was a kind of rallying cry, a mythology built around escape and freedom, and some of us insisted on being called men too. Hattie, in particular, preferred to be called Doctor. This reclamation among us, even if it was only between ourselves, was comforting in a small way.

But after the incident with Hattie and the scissors, we stopped telling stories altogether, even among ourselves.

We became soft doll women. Nothing could poke or prod us.

THE INFIRMARY

Dear God, we need death like we need doctors.

Mary is addicted to the young doctor like we all are, needle-smitten. She purrs in his hands when he takes her pulse, cries when he must leech her or if he asks for it, like we all do, and she is the first to join his retinue of so-called special cases—the most hysteric of hysterical. My young hussies, he calls them when he thinks no one is listening. He is flirty, making the chosen feel holy as he opens their thighs to make his little incisions. What is it about a white coat that makes us salivate, makes us long to throw ourselves in his strong arms, to fog up those tiny incomprehensible spectacles with the ghost fog of our female brains?

Perhaps it is the way his brow furrows in consternation when we hurt ourselves (for him—it is always for him, dear heart), or the gentle way he says our names—Gladys, Henrietta, Ethel— like a sexual sibilance—Ida, Gertrude, Annie—soft and yet pulsatingly, entrancingly hard—Hattie, Nellie, Maria, Katarina, Isabella.

He puts yellow powder in our tea that sits on top of the brown water like the bloom of algae, the young doctor, and we moan; he is learning how to use a scalpel, and we are learning the method of calming a woman involves hands and privacy curtains. God, give us the young doctor every day, every hour.

The older doctor, Dr. Smith, performs two types of surgeries at night: lobotomies or hysterectomies. Neither seems terribly effective. In the case of the former, the women become . . . if not more comfortable, then more docile. They lose some spontaneity, some sparkle. Something about their eyes goes dim and dark. No longer speaking in tongues, or Spanish, or Italian, they are like mice. You can tell which ones among them have been lobotomized by their gait on the rope gangs—the others often drag them along across the lawn when we go out for our walks. Dead baggage.

The latter is even less popular, for it sometimes is accompanied by a sweating sickness. Those who awake in the night strip naked and stand moaning in front of their windows, begging for a knife. Complications include death.

But they no longer flirt with the doctors, the hysterectomized. So it is often considered a wild success. Parties are given. Tea and hard cakes. Then we are shuffled into the baths again.

It must be a lot of pressure to serve this many women.

We don't blame the young doctor. After all, he's not much more than a boy, under all that white and gloves. No, we don't blame him at all.

THE TERRACE

The trouble with the doctor's girls, as we call them, is not all of us are chosen, so the left behind are angry. Literal rapture has occurred, and we are left in our bodies with only our sin. Whoever believes in sisterhood is gravely mistaken and must be corrected. We don't know what day it is—some of us still don't believe where we are, we are cold and smell like rotten flesh, we are hungry, goddammit. Give us entertainment—God, if we had the power to kill, what wouldn't we do.

For example, let's just say for illustrative purposes, we might ambush Mary in the night with the keys we stole from Miss Brown when she was napping after her nightcap and drag little Mary, kicking and not exactly screaming with her knickers between her teeth but not exactly quiet either, to the terrace, where we imagine they once gave parties for the celebration of the opening of this fine establishment—secret parties, of course, because it is a secret institution. It is a white-columned, beautiful place looking out on the midnight stillness of a silvery-gray moon-decked and manicured lawn, a lovely place to die. And convenient, with its open rafters accessible with a ladder stolen from the workshop.

This is merely an example, of course.

In the morning, when the young doctor comes to us wearing his white gloves, redolent of sex and cologne, we can only shrug.

"What utter disgrace," the young doctor says softly. "What utter lack of regard for their common man."

Common woman, dear doctor—give us at least that. We have so little left to love, after all.

She was kind of alarming—Mary hung by her red curls in the moonlight. Sometimes we still see her in our dreams. However, most of us sleep soundly now—when we are allowed to get any rest at all.

We are so very tired.

THE LAWN

Sometimes at night we see long shadows on the lawn. The light-house beam sweeps over them, and struck, they freeze like iron idols. When darkness returns the shapes move on—into the woods or perhaps down the wharf to the sparkling moonlit sea.

Gertrude says they look like lost women. She believes they are escapees. But we know that's just Gertrude being crazy; we know this place is easy to get into and impossible to get out of.

"Maybe there's a male ward on the island," says Maria hopefully, and we laugh.

Hattie takes a burning fag from the fire, hand reaching through the grate that is meant to protect us and fingers coming out red and blistered. She draws the shapes on the floor and numbers them, trying to puzzle them out in that scientist way of hers. Perhaps they were here before us all. Alien. Creatures abandoned in the midst of cities growing up around them, on islands more distant than this one. Children among wolves.

Annie puts a hand on the charcoal and wipes it away. "The only children here are us," she says. "Because we never grew up."

Still, we watch the grass move and listen to its whispers. When we go for our walks, like birds on a line, we peck at the ground, searching for some evidence of the shadows in the hot sun, sweating under our flannels. Sometimes we roll in the grass like crazy women, breathing in the scent of the shadows, something bitter, salt-wrecked, bloody like the sea.

THE LAUNDRY

Clara rubs lye in her eyes and stands on the bins, screaming, "Hurrah! I have killed the devil!" We scream too, and Grace laughs while the Irish woman tries to catch Clara, whose eyes are melting down her cheeks like butter left on the windowsill on a hot day. Even this makes us ravenously hungry.

When consulted later, Clara tells us that she couldn't stand it anymore, the smell of pig fat and the blood washing out of the white linens.

"It's like I was washing away any proof of her—of her body. That she had one, and it was a good, clean body given to her by God hisself," she says between sobs.

She is speaking of Pearl's body, of course. God rest her soul. Pearl, who would take spells and had to be sent to the surgeon. Pearl, who Clara loved most of all, who would pick flowers to leave on Clara's bedside after a walk, who we saw carted off to the dead house.

We tuck Clara into bed and try not to look at her face very closely. We know her by touch, after all. We know all of us by touch.

In the morning, Clara is gone.

"It is good she is with God," Eleanor whispers. "It is good they are together."

THE DINING HALL

We eat boiled meat and potatoes and oatmeal and molasses and tea and unbuttered black bread and fresh fish unseasoned and unsalted beef tea and spiders and tobacco juice and hard cakes when we can get them and rats that Annie catches with her traps and mussy butter and muddy tea and ginger cookies and yellow water and gravy and mutton and white winter radishes and quince sauce and soup and bread pudding.

There are no knives or forks.

We eat with our hands except those who cannot because they have palsy or no teeth or cannot abide the taste of spiders— God, what we wouldn't give for an orange. There is a kitchen but the door is locked and we can't see inside. If we do not eat what is on our dreadful plate, we are force-fed, and very often it is Ida who is led to the pump. Her face is quite terrible to behold when she is given back to us, wide-eyed and blanched like a turnip. Her mouth is bloodier and bloodier. She tells us she swallowed a tooth. She is deemed to be particularly troublesome and vicious by the staff.

Becoming coarse, massive women takes a lot out of us.

The very good girls who are the young doctor's favorites are given fresh fruit and greens from the gardens and live apart from the rest of us, in individual rooms very near the infirmary, where the doctor can supervise them in case they have any need of him at night, which is when things always seem to go wrong.

THE WORKSHOP

Fifty-two women in leather and iron, pounding hammers over wood like gods of thunder. The shoes themselves are beautiful things, red and blue and peacock green, shoes we would have worn to go dancing in our lives before the secret institution. Magic shoes which could have transformed us. Who among us had not dreamed of putting on the shoes and dancing across the ward, into the arms of the young doctor, out across the lawn and down to the wharf, under the moonlight, out over the waves until we were alone at sea?

It is Hattie who squirrels away some tools, hidden in her slip and tied around a string at her waist, tools that are used to treat us when we are sick, or to remove a troublesome tooth, or when one of the doctor's girls gets pregnant, which happens more than we would care to admit.

That's what surprised us about Hattie's death. She was studying us. "A human rat trap, this place is, and rats are meant for experiments." We would go to her with our worries, our sleeplessness. She put these problems in jars kept under her cot, and at night they glowed like fireflies. Ebbing, weeping from the rubber seals.

So when Hattie killed the young doctor with a pair of scissors and had to be sent to the dead house, yes, I believe we were surprised. Or we felt something, anyway. And maybe our ability to still feel is what surprised us.

THE DEAD HOUSE

If one of us dies, she is sent to the dead house for postmortem examinations and dissections. The dead house is a small building set off from the lawn under the gentle overhang of trees, and it is painted black. None of us has been there so we can't say what it's like, but we see the doctors going there, white coats like ghosts on the lawn, and they stay there until very late in the evening, past supper sometimes. Hattie explained to us that in an autopsy they cut open the body and inspect its organs to determine cause of death. (She will go on and on about it if you let her, down to the very grimmest of details.)

"It doesn't seem right," says Eleanore. "To cut open our Christian bodies."

THE CHAPEL

On Sundays, we are rope-led to the Catholic chapel to pray, even though very few of us are actually Catholic. The surgeon, Dr. Smith, is also the priest. He is a rotund and jolly man with gray whiskers and a black ensemble suggestive of the devil.

Dr. Smith will hear our confessions, which are either small and pebble-shaped or, if one of us is feeling bored, large and sweating like an elephant. The big lies get Dr. Smith excited, as if he thrives on our wildness. Some women use this as an excuse to receive more opium, because the bigger the sin, the bigger the dose we are given back in the ward. This is a double-edged sword, though, as sometimes the good doctor mixes his vials and the woman is left speechless or blind. We have not decided if the thrill is worth it.

We have so conflated church and the administration of drugs in our minds that there is not one among us who upon entering the church does not catch the scent of belladonna.

We were not witches before we came here, but how we sizzle when we step into the holy dim now, our skin under our slips burns. Carrying the ghosts of those who died before us is so very tiring. There are so many names to recite. If we didn't try to kill ourselves, then we must try something to stop their wild whisperings in our dreams. When we first came here, the doctors asked us, Do you hear voices at night? And like sane people, we insisted we did not.

Now we burn bits of leather and rotten meat and red flannel and fingernails and hair ripped out by the roots and whatever flowers we can find and ghosts—we burn all the ghosts, even the ones we do not know personally.

"I heard Miss Brown say they are bringing in bodies from the tuberculosis outbreak to be buried here, on this island," says Annie. "I bet these aren't just the ghosts of women from the asylum."

And soon enough, the longer we are here, the more medicine we take, the longer we are forgotten, the harder we try, the colder we become, the thinner our bodies thin—

We begin to hear children and men among the voices.

Human overflow on Damnation Island. A senseless mass of humanity. God help them, we feel lucky not to be among them. But what does that say about us?

POTTER'S FIELD

One summer we are conscripted into burial crews by the overseers (it has not escaped our attention that this is an act of desperation), and we are sent to dig graves—not a right word for the massive pits filled with rows of rectangular wooden coffins, unmarked, un-named, unloved. The small ones are the worst; they are so light.

And yet something good does come of this digging, because we are given better fare than our normal repast and we grow strong. Our shoulders bulk beyond what could be considered ladylike (we have long since ceased to be ladies, we are crazy women, Filipino and Spanish and Black and Irish, nameless like the graves).

To cool off, we are taken to the water, where we strip naked like fish (after all, the mythical men are on the other side of the island); we think we are in love with the water.

"Maybe the men work at odd hours from us," Minnie says hopefully, picking the dirt (dead dirt) under her nails. "There are more graves dug than we can have done."

At least we aren't burying our own kind. The kind that is crazy.

After a few months of this, it is Gertrude who arrives at a plan, for she is the one who took over when Hattie left, and we admire her brains and her bravery. Gerty whispers the plan to us between shovelfuls of dirt, and we pass it on at night when we sleep, during the morning meal, and while walking in the sun on the rope gang.

The bodies arrive at the wharf every day at noon, just as we are taken down to the water by Miss Davis and Miss Brown. Gertrude and Minnie rush the overseers and crash two smuggled jars over their heads at once; there is profuse bleeding. After that, it is a mere matter of keeping them from getting up again, which we achieve with an impressive amount of relish and beatings given how little we had for supper. We take their keys to our shackles.

Eleanore says she knows how to steer a boat, and then we are fifty-two minus twenty women and a whole lot of ghosts on a boat, brandishing irons and shovels at the poor, unsuspecting ferry captain, who is, bless him, alone on the boat! (When we think about it, it does seem odd how lucky it is, just this one old man alone on a boat with no one to help him unload the corpses?)

Then it is a short ride to City Island, around the perilous reefs, which the captain says have claimed many a sailor. He gives us ale, which we split among us, and some sandwiches from his lunch pail, which are liver but taste like the best thing we've ever eaten in our entire, very long lives, for all that the oldest among us is thirty-two.

"Crazy women, ehh?" He spits tobacco juice into the sea and grins a gap-tooth grin. "You can't tell by your faces."

We are no longer unsure that we are in love with the water. It is blue and glorious and a symbol of freedom, no matter what we will do when we step onto solid ground. (What will we do? None of us has a home to go to or family that does not already think we are insane or dead.)

Ida laughs and gives the captain a kiss on the cheek and calls him a doll. Minnie watches behind us as if expecting the police to show up at any moment. (We were told escapees would be hunted down like rabid dogs. Once, a woman escaped, and a policeman came to the reception and told Dr. Smith, "If she doesn't come quietly, I'll grab her up like a kitten and shake her," to which Dr. Smith nodded in grave agreement.)

Each of us looking on the sea wears the far-off, dreamy expression that landed us in this human rat trap.

Suddenly, Ethel says, "While I live, I hope," and we all look around at her in surprise, our eyes watery from the fresh bright sea air, because for now, on this boat, we've allowed ourselves to hope.

POSTSCRIPT

(You didn't think we'd end it there, did you? Of course we didn't escape. We died there and are still dead and will be dead for years to come. It wouldn't be right, would it, to rewrite the truth of that place, a terrible haunted island from which no one escapes? It would cheapen our ghosts, like rotten copper.)

Tiddlywinks

by Stephen Graham Jones

Okay, before we get all carried away, yeah, sure, I did kill those five other seniors that Friday night in March, and yes, we were out by the lake at the old campgrounds, and no, of course I didn't use a gun, so I guess you can, technically, if that matters to you, call me a slasher.

You've got to admit they were asking for it, though.

Where it starts is after school. We're all piled into Missy's dad's big four-door truck. There's six of us, so it's one seat belt per, completely safe, and all the coolers and camping junk are under a cargo net in back, just in case Missy hits a bump too zealously or whatever.

I'm in the middle of the back seat, and Kendra's sitting right in front of me. Since I'm six-four and she's barely five feet, I've got a pretty unimpeded view of the road coming up to meet us.

At this point everything's hunky-dory, fine, perfect, ideal, couldn't have been one speck better, or more normal. I don't have any killer compulsion, no big revenge arc, everybody's insides are still on the inside, nobody's having any mortal thoughts. We've got beer in one of the coolers, sure, but we're not drinking yet. Drinking while driving would be asking for it, wouldn't it? Neddy even insisted on bringing that little potbellied firepit thing from his backyard, because it's got that rounded iron grate on top to keep us from burning the whole forest down.

All in all, it's shaping up to be a great weekend. Four guys and two girls, but two of the guys match up, so the numbers are just right—no one's odd man out, no one's going to be slamming third-wheel beers and watching the fire die down.

Behind the wheel is Missy, and short little Kendra's beside her—not saying anything bad about her height, either. To a person, she can smoke each one of us on the basketball court. Well, I mean, she *could*, before I used that hatchet on the back of her head until it opened like one of those radish roses.

That's later, though.

Beside Kendra is Lobo, the party animal of us, always looking for a good and better time—he picked that name for himself— and then to my right in the back seat it's Neddy, the air between us sizzling with possibility, and to my left is Tom-Tom. And before you get to thinking we're being racially insensitive calling him that, let me just say that it's what he writes on his English papers too. I know because he lets me cheat off them.

So, the six of us, jamming to whatever country music Kendra's playing through the speakers, barreling around the edge of the lake, Lobo's face not at this point split in two with a logging saw—I tried to catch his tongue with those big metal teeth, but he was still alive enough to keep that from happening—Missy's left leg still attached to the rest of her, with no idea of how delicate its ball joint was, my hands not even *thinking* about being chunky with gore, when—

"Oh, oh, there's one!" Tom-Tom says, bouncing in his seat.

I lean forward to see what he's talking about.

"You're right, you're right," Lobo says, catching Tom-Tom's bounce.

"What?" I kind of mumble out loud.

Highway stripes? Trees?

And, no, I didn't at this point—or ever, I guess—have any misperceptions about Neddy being the love of my life or anything. The love-of-this-weekend was all I had in mind. Or all I could hope for, I should say.

I don't think I'll be forgetting the tongs I would later jam into his left eye and then wrench open, that little kitchen-strength hinge somehow strong enough to widen the bone of his eye orbit. It cracked in there—that was such a distinct feeling in the palm of my hand—but his skin would still be elastic enough to stretch with that widening, making that crack in the bone something I never actually saw, only have a tactile memory of.

Sorry, Neddy.

Could have been a fun weekend. I mean, for both of us.

But, barreling down that road, you're the one who leans forward, cups his hand on Lobo's bare shoulder—this got every last *ounce* of my attention—and says to Missy, to the whole front seat, to all of us, like the best secret ever, "*Do it!*"

"Do what?" I kind of mouth, not even putting any voice behind it.

"Tiddlywinks, tiddlywinks . . ." Lobo says, and everyone but me in the cab picks it up like a chant: *Tiddlywinks! Tiddlywinks! Tiddlywinks!*

If I can explain: Imagine a poker chip. Or, a whole game of mostly poker chips of different colors and sizes. Kind of like marbles, you could say. Just, with poker chips. What you do when you're a kid and still think this kind of stuff's fun is you pinch a big chip between your thumb and forefinger really hard, until the blood's all pushed back from the bed of your thumbnail, and you push the very edge of that poker chip against the edge of another poker chip lying on the hard tabletop, such that that second poker chip finally has to explode up, become this flipping projectile. There's some points or target system or goal,

I don't remember, but that's just because every session of this game is pretty much just poker chips shooting around everywhere, and getting lost.

Get it?

That's Tiddlywinks.

How to play it on the road, *evidently*, is, first, you be part of the big camping trip from last summer that I wasn't around for, and, second, you be in a truck on a road where turtles sometimes are.

The goal is to catch a turtle right on the edge of its shell with your front tire, and "Tiddlywink" that turtle up higher and higher, everybody in the truck screaming with delight.

Well, everybody but one.

Saying my heart dropped when Missy got this just right would be something of an understatement, taking into account my response.

When I was gone last summer, couldn't make the camping trip? It was because my parents had taken me and my brothers down to the coast to protect just-hatched baby turtles from seagulls and raccoons. Because my parents wanted my brothers and me to maybe have a chance at being good people.

I like to think it worked.

Except, now—well, *then*—sitting in the middle of that back seat, in the cab of this impossibly heavy truck, I was . . . I was party to the badness. I was part of the problem.

"No!" I scream, fighting for the front wheel.

Neddy, dear dear Neddy, holds me back, and then Lobo helps him. Tom-Tom is cringing away, and Kendra is trying to protect the driver from whatever fit I'm having.

"Again, another one!" Lobo calls out, somehow able to watch the road ahead of us *and* keep me from stopping this.

Missy grins one of the most evil grins in history, adjusting her steering slightly, and this time she misses.

But we all feel the bump.

Tom-Tom looks back and kind of dry-heaved. Not because a cooler had bounced up and shattered—cargo net, remember?—but because something much more important was now shattered, something much more innocent was splashed and smeared across the yellow stripe.

"No! No no no no!" I scream, my eyes hot, my legs pedaling, arms thrashing, and . . . I don't want to blame it on Neddy or Lobo. I'm the one who decides I can fake them out by pushing backwards, the direction they aren't expecting.

It works. And the result is that I jam the back of my head hard against the frame around the sliding rear window, and like that I'm out, I'm gone, checked out, the panic is over for me.

And no, I have no idea how many more turtles might have gone flipping into the ditch that afternoon, their shells splintered around their dark red muscle. But I do know this: Their shells shattered after they'd done the one thing that had protected them their whole lives. They pulled their head and legs in to wait this approaching threat out, and . . . it didn't work. Their house came down all around them.

At least it was fast. I hope.

So, yeah, I came to when everyone was out skinny-dipping.

From the trees, looking through the two eyeholes of the mask I'd improvised, I watched their naked bodies in the water, and considered whether this was a thing I actually had to do or not.

But all I had to do to wipe that indecision away was remember the distinct feeling of that turtle under the tires of the truck at sixty miles per hour.

My hands balled into fists.

I didn't plan on the hatchet, the saw, the tongs, the pipe, but it turns out that when you're out for revenge, those things just, like, *present* themselves, don't they? Who knew?

It was a couple of hours of running and screaming, of apologies come too late.

And, yeah, I say I improvised a mask, but I'd also strapped a lounge float thing to my back. A green one, because they needed to know, in their last moments on this earth, why this was happening. It wasn't just me flipping out, it was a giant *turtle* dealing this justice to them.

Missy, Kendra, Lobo, Neddy—they went down like dominoes.

When right is on your side, you can't miss, and nothing works against you.

Sounds pretty slashery, I know. Believe me, I know. The mask, the gore, the skinny-dipping, all of it.

I'll cop to that, sure.

But part of taking on the burden of a revenge thing like this, evidently, is that one of this guilty party will be strangely resilient, or lucky, or just plain old tough.

I'm talking about Tom-Tom.

And this isn't about him being Native, please understand that. Who knows—maybe a few centuries of being hunted instilled some survivor in him at the DNA level, but for the purposes of this weekend, at least, I think it's really just about him being last in the pecking order.

Well, the hacking order.

Because he was last, when I finally loomed over him—he was trying to use a cooler lid as a shield against my pipe, which I planned to jam into him until it was stacked with plugs of his meat—when it was his time to *die*, a thing started happening.

Blood leaked from his mouth, surprising us both.

He touched it, then touched higher, past his lips, under his top lip.

Teeth?

His incisors had enlarged, were enlarging, looked like costume stuff all of a sudden.

Instead of killing him then—it would have been easy—I watched.

He screamed when two comically large ears erupted through his human ears.

These new ears weren't furry, were just his skin under that blood, but now I could see what was happening.

On cue, his knees broke backwards with the worst sound, turned into ankles for his now-huge feet, and his thigh muscles bulged out.

"No, no," I said, swinging that pipe down now, with all the rage I had.

I only hit lake shore.

It splatted that black mud up onto my face.

When I cleared it, Tom-Tom was bounding away. He took a few tentative, desperate steps at first, trying to wrap his mind around his new shape, but there was some instinct coming on too.

Using both feet at once, and all those new muscles in his thighs, he accelerated, burst ahead of me.

To run fast enough to catch him, I reached back to pull this inflatable lounge chair of a turtle shell off my back, to peel this make-do paper plate mask off, but—

They were attached now. Or, not just attached: They're part of me. They *are* me.

The transformation that had happened to Tom-Tom, it had happened to me as well, but it had been happening all night, with each heart I stopped, each head I split, each scream that threatened to call help in.

This lounge chair on my back was inflatable no longer. It was, and *is*, a hard, durable shell. And my face was bony and alien to my fingers, and my fingers were even ... They're sharper now.

Worse, when I took off to run Tom-Tom down—you're ahead of me now with all this, aren't you? Somebody read you fairy tales when you were a kid, right?

I could only walk, and slowly at that.

Very much like a slasher, yes.

In the larger sense, though, aren't slasher stories themselves fairy tales? Final girls are the damsels in distress, and the slasher is this lumbering, misshapen ogre. So, yes, Tom-Tom can, in his assigned role in all this, put on burst of speed after burst of speed, run laps around what I've become here, but I have justice on my side, don't I? Justice and tenacity.

More important, I just keep on trudging ahead.

It won't be tonight, I don't think, and it might not even be tomorrow, but soon this race will be over. I'll find Tom-Tom napping under a tree, so confident I can never catch up with him that he's using his floppy ears as a sleep mask.

When he wakes, though—when I *wake* him—it'll be with the end of a four-inch metal pipe driving his mouth open, unhinging his jaw, and forcing the back of his skull out. Kick your big fancy feet then, Tom-Tom, see what difference that makes.

If I do it right, too, his eyes will be locked with mine until he's gone, I know.

And then?

Ten years later, twenty years later, there will be a story of the Turtle Man of Bridger Road, I think.

He haunts the ditches, tasting the air for his freshly burst kin.

And he memorizes the taillights that did it as best he can, but, really—honestly—sometimes he won't be there soon enough to see this or that carful of campers, right?

In which case, it's safest just to assume that anyone in a cabin or tent or hammock around the lake, or even just at a picnic table, they more than likely committed murder out on the highway to get here, and then just kept driving, because . . . it was just a turtle, right?

At which point I'm the shadow looming at the edge of the campfire light.

I might not be fast anymore, but I'm steady, I'm constant, and when you try to hit me with whatever you can scrounge up from the tall grass, I only have to turn my back, take that impact, then come back with my own slashing claws, sending your precious teeth flipping up into the air like poker chips.

And let's just let those teeth hang there, shall we?

It's more important that you keep an eye on the road, after all.

I don't want to have to come visit your campfire.

WHERE THE LOVELIGHT GLEAMS

by Michael Thomas Ford

THE DEW-DROP INN hadn't changed in twenty years.

As Andy stood outside, shivering in the December cold and wondering what the hell he was doing there, he could hear the sound of AC/DC playing on the jukebox inside. "Back in Black." It was the same song that had been playing the last time he was in the bar. Probably, he thought, it hadn't stopped playing in the two decades since he'd left Newtown and never looked back.

Until now.

Again, he wondered if he'd made a mistake in returning. There was nothing here for him. Nothing good, anyway. His family certainly didn't count. They'd made it very clear on that long-ago Christmas Eve that he was no longer welcome, no longer one of them. There was no reason things should be different now.

And yet something had compelled him to come. He still couldn't say what that was. All he knew was that he'd woken up two days earlier with the thought in his head. He'd dismissed it, but it had returned, again and again, until finally he'd gotten in the car and started driving. When, almost thirteen hours later, he reached the edge of town, he found he couldn't bring himself to drive to his parents' house. Instead, he'd come to the Dew-Drop.

This is ridiculous, he thought. *Just go home. You're not going to find what you want. Not after all this time.*

"I don't even know what I want," he said aloud, and pushed the door open.

As he entered the bar, the patrons already inside glanced up, as they always did, to see if the new face was a familiar or unfamiliar one. Andy felt himself tense as he was scrutinized. After all, he probably knew everyone in the bar's single large room. He'd grown up with them. Gone to school with them. And then he'd left without so much as a goodbye to any of them. Not even the one who deserved one.

He looked around, seeking out faces he recognized. His mind raced as he attempted to remember names, attach them to the people seated at tables and standing around the bar's lone pool table. He felt himself begin to panic. Then instinct took over and he found himself heading for the men's room.

He found it mercifully unoccupied, went inside, and shut the door. The single bolt used to keep it closed had been knocked loose countless times by drunks determined to get inside, and each time it was reattached just below its previous position. At chest height when Andy was last in there, it now sat just below his waist. He slid the bolt home.

The room was large enough for just a toilet and a sink. The walls were papered with centerfolds from men's magazines, glued on and covered in a layer of varnish. Andy was both shocked and strangely relieved to see that they were still there.

As he ran the water in the sink and washed his hands, Miss July of 1982 watched to make sure he did it correctly. She wore cowboy boots and a filmy white barely-there dress, which she held open to reveal her charms. Her blond hair curled around her angelic face, on which someone had scribbled a black ink mustache.

"Hey, Lynda," Andy said. Lynda Wiesmeier. Her name came to him unbidden, floating up from his subconscious.

He finished washing his hands, drew a length of brown paper towel from the roll standing on the edge of the sink, and dried them. As he was finishing, there was a thump on the door as someone tried to open it. He slid the bolt back just before the door was shoved open. A young man, probably not even legal drinking age, not even born when Andy had last been there, stood outside.

"Sorry, man," he said. "Gotta piss."

"All yours," said Andy, stepping out as the other man came in, already unzipping his jeans. Andy heard the heavy splash of urine hitting the water in the bowl and pulled the door shut behind him.

No, nothing had changed.

He made his way to the bar. AC/DC had been replaced by Joan Jett's version of "Little Drummer Boy," and Andy was suddenly sitting in the passenger seat of Trevor Cuddy's Firebird. They were parked by the creek, it was snowing heavily, and Trevor had just kissed him for the first time. Trevor, pulling back, had his eyes open, filled with questions Andy was about to answer. The Joan Jett song was playing on the stereo.

"Hey, A.J."

Andy, snapped back to the present, looked at the man behind the bar. "What did you call me?" he asked.

"What I always fucking call you," the man said, laughing. He set a bottle of Budweiser on the counter.

"Sorry," Andy said. "It's just that no one has called me A.J. in a long time."

The man laughed. "At least not since dinnertime," he said. He narrowed his eyes. "What happened to your beard?" he asked. "Cathy tell you to shave it or something?"

Andy put his hand to his face. He'd never had a beard. "Cathy?" he said. "Are you talking about Cathy Gilkyson?" Cathy. His high school girlfriend. Another memory. Another one he hadn't said goodbye to.

"Are you high?" the man asked. "Yeah, Cathy Gilkyson. Until you married her and saddled her with your fucked-up last name. And what are you doing here, anyway? Isn't tonight the big Rakesbill family Christmas party?"

Although Budweiser was the last thing he would order in a bar, Andy picked up the beer and took a sip, trying not to grimace. It bought him time to figure out what was going on. He'd IDed the bartender now. John Grace. They'd been in the same grade, although they weren't exactly friends. John, a stoner, had spent most of the school day dealing weed out of his locker. Now, pushing forty, he was a much heavier version of his high school self.

"What's with the jacket?" John said.

Andy looked down at himself. He was wearing a red-and-black plaid wool jacket. "What about it?"

John shrugged. "A little fancy for driving a snowplow is all," he said. "Cathy trying to update your wardrobe again?"

"Snowplow," Andy repeated.

John snorted. "You forget about that too?" he said.

Somebody called John's name and the man walked away. Andy, alone, replayed the last few minutes. John had called him A.J. Andrew James. His given name. Technically, Andrew James Rakesbill III. But his grandfather had been Andy, his father Drew, and so he had become A.J. He'd long since dropped the III part of his name, and had gone by Andy as soon as he could, far preferring it to the initials.

John calling him A.J. made perfect sense. But what about the rest of it? Married to Cathy Gikyson? A snowplow? He had no idea what to make of that. And why did John not seem surprised to see him after so many years?

Somebody punched him in the shoulder. Not hard, but enough to get his attention. He turned his head and found himself looking at a short redheaded woman. She didn't look happy to see him.

"Thought you had a family thing tonight," she said. The words sounded like an accusation.

"Uh, yeah," Andy said. "The, uh, family Christmas party."

The woman rolled her eyes. "Then why the fuck aren't you home?"

"Oh," Andy said. "I, um, needed to pick something up."

"And you just happened to end up here?" the woman said. She peered more closely at him. "And what happened to your beard? You look weird. Kinda like you did in high school."

Before Andy could say anything, the woman took the beer out of his hand and drained it. She set it down hard on the counter. "Come by later tonight when you're on your run," she said. "Park the plow in the school parking lot, not in front of the house."

She walked off, rejoining a group of three other women, who looked over at Andy and laughed. He decided it was time to leave. He took his wallet out, put some ones on the bar, and walked out into the cold.

It had started to snow. He stood for a moment in the bar's parking lot. He looked back at the door. *It's a joke*, he thought. *They're playing a joke on me*. That must be it. John, or someone else, had recognized him when he walked in, decided to have some fun at his expense, and spread the word around the bar. They were all in on it.

He got into his Forester and started it up. He couldn't decide if he should be angry or amused. He also couldn't decide where to go next. There was one obvious choice, but it was also the one he wasn't sure he should make.

You came this far, he told himself.

He drove there without thinking. Muscle memory, aided by the fact that the streets hadn't changed at all in two decades, took him to the house in which he'd grown up. As he approached, he noticed that a snowplow was parked in the driveway of the house next door, where once upon a time the Millingtons had lived.

The lights in his parents' house were on. He parked the Subaru at the end of the street, got out, and walked down the sidewalk. When he got close enough to see inside from the street, he stopped. He stood in the snow, looking through the large front window into the living room. Framed in the window was a Christmas tree. It blocked much of the view, but on either side of it he could see people moving around.

Drawn across the lawn by the twinkling lights, Andy walked closer to the house. He stood to one side of the window, peering in. Inches from his face hung the angel ornament he had made for his mother in Sunday school at Calvary Baptist Church when he was seven. Cotton balls glued to popsicle sticks. Tissue-paper wings and a pipe-cleaner halo. Glitter everywhere he could put it. It was always given a place of honor. He was surprised to see it there, assuming his mother would have removed all traces of him after their abrupt separation.

He turned his attention to the people in the room. He saw his grandfather first. Now in his eighties, he was a thinner version of the man Andy remembered, stoop-backed and balding. He stood beside Andy's father, who instead of shrinking had expanded in size, his belly extending over his belt in a way that Andy had recently started to see himself when he looked in the mirror. Both were positioned near the stairs leading to the second floor, talking to a teenage boy who eerily resembled Andy at the same age. The boy said something, and the older men laughed.

Before he could wonder who the boy was, his attention was taken by a woman walking into the room carrying a plate of cookies. His mother. Seeing her, both his heart and time seemed to stop. Although he thought about her less and less over the years, when he *did* think about her, he always pictured her the way she was on that last night, the disappointment on her face as she turned away from him and didn't tell him not to leave, although he'd waited for her to speak even one word that would stop him.

Now she was all smiles as she walked over to the stairs and held out the plate. Three hands reached out, each taking a cookie. His mother beamed, in her element, feeding the people she loved most. Once, Andy had been one of them. Once, he had been the boy on the stairs. He wondered if she ever thought about those Christmas parties from before, if she ever wished things had turned out differently.

Then another entrance. Another ghost. This time Cathy Gilkyson. She looked almost as she had in high school, just a little softer in some places, harder in others. Seeing her face, Andy realized that the boy on the stairs didn't entirely resemble him. He had Cathy's nose, her chin, a combination of the two of them. Cathy paused, looking around, and then Andy appeared behind her. Andy with a beard. He put his hands on Cathy's waist. He leaned forward and kissed her on the cheek. On his left hand, a gold wedding band circled the ring finger.

The Andy inside the house looked up, toward the window, a peculiar smile on his face. Outside, Andy stepped to the side, out of view. His thoughts whirled like the snow tumbling from the sky. Then, almost instinctively, he started to move toward the front door of the house.

"Don't."

Andy looked toward the sidewalk, where a figure stood in the darkness.

"Don't go in," a man's voice said.

"Who is that?" said Andy. When there was no answer, he walked back across the lawn. The figure remained where he was. When Andy got close, he saw someone whose face was hidden by the hoodie he wore. Then the glow of a cigarette provided momentary light.

"Trevor?" Andy said.

"I was at the bar," Trevor said. "I saw you. When you left, I followed you."

"Why?" Andy said. "And who is that in there?"

"You," Trevor answered.

"That's insane," said Andy. "That's . . . someone who looks like me. But it's not me."

"It might as well be," Trevor said. "As far as anyone here knows, it is. Come on. We can't stay here. He'll know."

"But who *is* he? Why does he look like me?"

"Come on," Trevor said again, turning and walking away. "Meet me at my parents' place. You remember where it is?"

"Yeah," Andy said. "Of course. But—"

"Just meet me there," said Trevor. "I'll tell you what I know."

Trevor walked off, got into a pickup parked up the street. He did not turn the lights on as he drove off, which explained why Andy hadn't noticed him arrive. Andy got into his own car and followed.

The Cuddy house looked exactly as it had the last time Andy had been inside. The kitchen had the same worn linoleum in a fake brickwork pattern. The round table had the same Christmas-themed tablecloth on it, patterned with smiling Santas and elves carrying stacks of presents that threatened to topple.

"Have a seat," Trevor said as he opened the refrigerator and took out two beers. He popped the tops with a bottle opener, set one in front of Andy, and took the chair across from him. It was the chair his father had always sat in when he drank his coffee and read the paper.

His black hair was now shot through with gray, and he needed a haircut. He'd grown a beard, which suited him even as it aged him. His eyes were the familiar green that Andy remembered, but now there was a wariness in them that hadn't been there before, as if he was forever expecting bad news.

"Are your folks home?" Andy asked.

Trevor shook his head.

"Did they move?"

Trevor took a long sip of his beer before answering. "Dead," he said. "Not long after you left. Just after the new year."

"Jesus," said Andy. "I'm sorry. I didn't know. What happened?"

"Somebody shot them," Trevor answered. "While they were sleeping."

Andy waited for Trevor to say he was joking. He didn't.

"Did they catch who did it?"

Trevor nodded. "Thought they did, anyway."

"Who would do something like that?"

"Me," said Trevor. He tipped another cigarette from the package on the table, lit it, and set the lighter beside the same Niagara Falls souvenir ashtray Andy remembered Mrs. Cuddy using. "According to the police, anyway," he continued. "My fingerprints were on the shotgun, which makes sense since it was mine. I spent fifteen years upstate for first-degree."

Andy didn't know what to say. "But you're out now."

"Somebody else confessed to it," said Trevor. "Guy who killed a girl over in Harlow. Knew some details about the scene no one else could have, so I got out. I had nowhere else to go, so I came back here. My mother's sister had been living here since I was sent away, but technically it was mine. She didn't want to live with a murderer, so she left."

"Why come back?"

Trevor shrugged. "Where else is there to go? Besides, I want to keep my eye on him. One of these days he'll slip up, and I'll take him out."

"Who?"

"The guy who really killed them." He tapped his cigarette on the ashtray. "You."

"I didn't—"

"I know," said Trevor. "I meant the thing that looks like you."

"'Thing? What do you mean?"

"I don't know what it is," he said.

"Why did he kill your parents?"

"Wondered that too. Then I found her diary."

"Whose?"

"My mother's." Trevor got up, opened a drawer in one of the cabinets, and pulled out a small book. He came back to the table and sat down. Opening to a page marked with a scrap of paper, he began to read. "'The man came again tonight. He told me and Chuck we could have the life we wanted if we just agreed to give him what he wants. We said no. He told us this was our last chance. I think we should go to the police. Chuck says that nobody will believe us. He says we just need to pray.'"

Trevor shut the book. "That's the last entry," he said. "They were dead by morning."

"I don't understand," Andy said. "What kind of deal did he offer them?"

"Don't know," said Trevor. "But I guess he made your parents the same offer. Only they took it."

Andy shook his head. "None of this makes sense. Who *is* he?"

"I don't think it's so much a who as a what," said Trevor, blowing out a stream of smoke.

"He looks just like me," Andy said.

"I think he can look like whatever he wants," said Trevor.

"So, he just came along and took over my life?"

Trevor nodded. "Married Cathy. Had two kids. Girl is Jessica. She's thirteen. Boy is Jamie. He's sixteen. A.J. drives a snowplow in the winter, works for the county road crew the rest of the year. Oh, and he's fucking Brenda McGowan."

"Brenda from school?" Andy remembered the redhead in the bar. "Wow. She looks rough."

"It's not an easy place to live," Trevor said. "Especially for those of us who didn't leave."

Andy looked at him. "You blame me for leaving?"

"No. I'm just saying you did."

"If I'd stayed here, I would have died," Andy said. "You know that."

Trevor nodded. "We all made our choices," he said. "And now here we are."

Andy looked at him. "I couldn't stay here, Trevor," he said. "After I told them what I am—who I am—they made it clear that wasn't going to work for them. I couldn't stay. Not even for you."

Trevor took another draw on his cigarette. He held the smoke in while he looked at Andy without saying anything. Andy, watching his face, saw an entire film unreeling behind Trevor's eyes, as if he was replaying their short time together. Then he realized that, no, Trevor was thinking about what might have been. This was worse somehow. *All this time*, Andy thought. *All this time, he's wondered what things would be like if I'd stayed.*

Finally, Trevor exhaled. He stubbed out his cigarette, then stood up. "I'm going to bed," he said. "You're welcome to share."

"Is that supposed to be some kind of invitation?" said Andy.

"You need more than that?" Trevor asked.

Andy looked at him for a long moment. "I'm going to stay up awhile."

"Suit yourself," said Trevor. "I'll be up in my old room if you change your mind. Otherwise, there's the couch."

Andy was about to ask him why he hadn't moved into the larger master bedroom downstairs. Then he remembered. Of course Trevor wouldn't want to sleep there.

He heard Trevor go up the stairs. He remained seated at the table. Part of him still thought everything that was happening must be some big practical joke. *Right*, he thought. *A practical joke the whole town is in on.*

He got up and walked into the living room, then down the short hall to the master bedroom. The door was closed. He put his hand on the knob, turned, and pushed the door open. The inside of the room was illuminated by winter moonlight, pale and cold. It took Andy a moment to realize that someone was standing in there. His back was to Andy, and he seemed to be looking at the bed.

He turned. It was A.J.

"Wondered if we'd ever meet face-to-face," he said in Andy's voice. "Kinda surprised it took this long. Guess you really meant it when you told them they weren't your family anymore."

"I believe that's what my father said to *me*," Andy said.

A.J. shrugged. "Same thing, in the end."

Andy felt rage course through him. "Who are you? What are you?"

A.J. sighed. "The obvious answer is that I'm you. Well, I'm the you your family wanted."

"I don't understand."

"Your parents made a wish," he said. "More or less. Maybe I should call it a prayer. They wished you'd never turned out the way you did. They prayed for a different you. One who fit into their lives better. I just heard them and granted it."

"So you're what, some kind of genie?" Andy laughed at the ridiculousness of the idea.

"Let's just say I'm someone who likes to be worshipped."

"Do they know?"

"No. As far as they remember—or anyone remembers—you never left. This is the life you would have had if you weren't, you know, the way you are."

"What about Trevor's parents?"

"What about them?"

"He says you killed them."

"I didn't. Not directly, anyway. I suggested it to the man who did." He held up a hand with his finger pointed like a gun. He aimed it at the bed and made a soft exploding sound. He moved his finger over a fraction of an inch and did it again. Then he smiled. "I'd like to say they never knew what hit them," he said. "But I might have told him to wake them up first."

"Why?"

"I don't like being rejected. I offered them a life with the kind of son they wanted. They said no. Guess they weren't as upset about having a queer boy as your parents were."

"But why let Trevor go to prison?"

"That was just for fun."

"You're a monster."

"Am I? Why? Your family has the life they wanted. And you have the life you wanted. Don't you?"

Andy ignored the question. "What about the kids? What are they? Cathy is human, but you're . . ."

"They're human enough. They'll live out their normal lives."

"And you?"

"I'll appear to age. And when it comes time to die, it will look like I did. Then I'll move on."

He spoke so casually about it, as if the lives he was toying with meant nothing. Andy felt the rage inside him turn to something else.

"You want to destroy me," A.J. said. "I can feel it. You'd tear me apart if you could. Why?"

"You stole my identity. You stole my life."

"As I said before, I took the life you didn't want. You still have yours."

"I'll tell them."

"If you do, your family will meet the same fate that Trevor's did."

"You'd kill them? But why? Cathy is your wife. The children are your children."

"There are other wives. Other children. Other husbands, for that matter." He chuckled. "Your parents would be disappointed to hear that, I know. But it doesn't matter to me what form the adoration takes. Only that I am worshipped."

"Show me what you look like," Andy said. "The real you. The one that lives inside *my* skin."

"I no longer remember what I was."

"Try."

A.J. fixed his gaze on Andy. Something in his eyes changed. Andy saw a blackness that went beyond darkness. A void. And inside of it, glimpses of something even worse. Something very, very old. Without form. Hungry.

Andy looked away. A.J. laughed. Then he walked past Andy and into the hall.

"Where are you going?" Andy called after him.

"Home," he said. "I suggest you do the same."

Andy watched as A.J. disappeared around the corner. He heard the sound of the kitchen door open and close. He hesitated a moment, then left the bedroom, shutting the door behind him. He went upstairs to Trevor's room, where he found the door open. Inside the room, Trevor was stretched out on his bed. He was shirtless, wearing only a pair of white boxer shorts. He was reading a Batman comic book. For a moment, Andy saw seventeen-year-old Trevor.

"He was here," Andy told him.

Trevor laid the book on his stomach. "Figured he'd show up."

"Can we kill him?" Andy asked.

Trevor shrugged. "I don't know."

"I'm leaving," Andy told him. "Come with me."

Trevor looked at him, and for a moment Andy expected him to say yes. Then he shook his head. "I can't," he said.

"You mean you won't," said Andy.

"Not until I find a way or die trying," Trevor replied.

Andy started to argue, but he knew it was no good. Trevor had to stay because he loved his parents. And they deserved his love. Andy wouldn't stay because his didn't. Not anymore.

"It's not fair," he told Trevor. "They rejected me and still got the son they wanted. The life they wanted."

"No one ever said life was fair," Trevor said.

Andy looked at his old friend. His first love. He'd left him once without saying goodbye. Now, he wondered what their lives might have been like if he'd tried to get Trevor to come with him then.

"It's not your fault," Trevor said, as if Andy had spoken his thoughts out loud. "Now go. And don't come back. Forget about this place."

"I don't think that's possible," said Andy. "And I'm going to look for a way too. To kill him. When I find it, I'm coming back."

They both knew he was lying. He wouldn't be back. Trevor was right. He had spent years trying to forget this place, these people. Coming back now had been a mistake.

Trevor picked up the comic book and opened it. "Goodbye, Andy."

Andy lingered for a moment longer, looking at Trevor, trying again to see in him the teenage boy who had first awakened the man inside of him. But that boy was gone forever now.

Andy went downstairs. In the kitchen, he went to take his jacket from the back of the chair and found that it was gone. In its place was a worn blue Carhartt jacket, stained and patched. On the left breast the initials A.J. were stitched in white thread, now gray with dirt.

He left it there and went out into the snow. It had picked up, and now swirled around him in thick clouds. As he opened the door of his car, a snowplow drove past, its lights flashing.

From the open window, an arm extended. An arm wrapped in a red and black plaid sleeve. At the end of the arm, the hand was raised, the middle finger extended.

The plow disappeared, the snow parting before it and leaving a cleared path on half of the street. Andy got into his car, started it up, and backed out of the driveway. Instead of following the plow, he went the other way, driving on the snowy side. At the end of the block, he turned right, heading out of town. As he passed the sign thanking him for visiting Newtown and encouraging him to come again, he turned on the radio.

"I'll be home for Christmas," Bing Crosby sang. "You can count on—"

He switched the radio off. In front of him, the snow blew straight at the windshield. It was difficult to see the road ahead. No lines were visible. No mile markers. He was driving head-long into a wintry oblivion.

He stepped on the gas, urging the car forward, his desire to get away outweighing his customary caution. Behind him, the town slept, the momentary intrusion into its dream already forgotten. Tomorrow it would wake up and remember nothing.

Andy would try to forget. But he knew that he wouldn't.

He would remember.

It Comes in Waves

by Jonathan Lees

WE FACE THE *night, all fists and teeth.*
You had all day to linger. Then you go to sleep.
That's when *our* eyes open.

We are drawn to wild screams in the shadows, while you run for the false security of a locked door and a light. We kick down the cracker-thin walls you frantically try to build around us.

They'll have you believe that we act as if we are invincible. That it is incorrect. We know we can die. There's a thrill knowing that the next punch, jump, drive, flight, or bite of food could be our last. If anything, we are more aware of death than you are. We just might be more attracted to it while you cram your chapped fingers into your mouth to trap the throttled screams in your throat, afraid others will hear you lose control. We will not cower and crouch in a circle, praying for it not to touch us. It is coming for us all. We'd rather be standing up, facing it, as it dances around us, and we'll laugh when it makes its move.

If there's one thing that unites us, it is darkness.

Can't see the eyes of the man in front of you darkness.

Being digested in the soft gut of an animal darkness.

At the time the sun dies and slips out of sight, we arch strychnine spines and slink down the strip searching for something new to destroy.

❖

BEHIND THE DUNES, a crackling of wood surrounds us, a hobbled dance of drunken youth begins in front of the flames.

Needing to be anywhere but here with *them*, I yank my sweat-stuck shirt over my head, push down my shorts, walk onto the beach, stare at the angered face of the ocean, and wait to see myself. There are no reflections on a restless surface.

I wish for something to happen. An airplane falling out of the sky, burning metal searing my flesh in seconds. The rabid snarl of a dog bounding from beyond the dunes to rip up my throat and suck out the sinew. An approaching silhouette whose intentions are only revealed in the final moment with a circle of moonlight in his eye and a glint off the steel before the knife plunges into my stomach, poking around my guts.

Like all of the moments that came before this, nothing like that happens. Nothing ever happens at all.

I squint into the horizon—a black sky meets black waves, and a blacker shape rises in the chop. No fin, no mouth, just a shadow. The silhouette of a man.

I've seen him before. His shape sculptural and still in the distance. I have seen him waving from above the depths, always at an impossible distance from me, waiting for me to join him on an island I can't see.

This water has an edge. You can feel it harden around your skin like the flat side of a blade as it slides across you. Severing each limb until you are just a head, floating.

I glide in to the chilling void and swim toward the stranger until it swallows me.

ALL I HEAR is my heart.

My eyes are open, and I see nothing.

Once you're underwater long enough, your most common senses dull, but you start to feel the pulse of other life surround you. Even with your eyes closed, the slightest movements can be detected, minor waves alerting your skin. Something is in here with me.

I can't breathe.

The water feels heavy, conspiring against every thrust of my arms and legs, grappling me, holding me in place for what's next. My chest is tightening. All this liquid around me doesn't feel loose anymore; it constricts, like a bicep on my throat and hard legs crushing my midsection until it isn't even water anymore, just a myriad of limbs strangling any movement I try to make. Powdered armpits and heavy thighs. Pectorals and knuckles press into me. Sharp cheekbones and chiseled jaws lean on my shoulders, pushing me further into a maelstrom of flesh, eyes, and teeth, wisps of hair tickling my nose in hopes I'll choke.

I say goodbye to myself as I cease treading and sink.

It can be said there is no light here.

There is no warming touch of a long-gone family member. There are no welcoming kingdoms or punishing pits of fire. There is only nothing. I am ready for it unless someone saves me. No one does, so I breach the surface, gulping air into my lungs. I look around for anyone watching. Scream to hear if anyone is listening—if anyone cares I am about to disappear.

THE FACES OF my so-called friends stay buried in the sand, their bodies a mass of swollen arms, tattooed with tribal markings, crossing over pelvic bones and extended across lowered shorts. Bare chests with faint hairs curling around nipples. Fingers vanishing within folds of skin. The bonfire is dead and so is the music, judging from the broken guitars.

Even in the pale morning light, I can see the pores of their skin gasping. Whether acne-scarred, dark, tan or damn near translucent, all their skin is perfect, screaming to be used. To be touched. To be abused. I imagine the skin of their future bodies, the birthmarks rotting, the ingrown hairs and angry scars, the worrying lines of age, the droop of dying flesh, the rolling pustules where former muscles lay stacked, the hard bulges turned to somber sags. Then the rot sets in. Blackened inside and out, the blood spoils, and the skin is sallow, darkens, ripe no more. Until the edges of bone push out and the gaseous pockets bloat and flutter, the monstrous shake-rattle-and-roll of the final breath. Then stillness until their skin rustles again from the scurrying of the insects within. The guys belch, roll around, moan, smack their lips. They're ready to do it all again. It's 1:45 p.m.

The air is a furnace. A hot, constant breath on my face and, in contrast, the shore feels cool and unbalancing like stepping on sloughing skin. Like the flesh of the girl they found last weekend washed up among the jellyfish. We've been having a particularly nasty summer of them, dotting the Massachusetts coastline with translucent blemishes.

The cops come for us first. The burners of the boulevard. The fuckups. The waste-oids. What did we see? Who were we with? What were we doing? Like most times, we knew nothing. We saw nothing. Yet they still asked where we were all night. If I have to be honest, she did look a little familiar, but I didn't tell them that.

She also kinda looked like the other boy they found earlier this summer. The way they died, I mean. We had just finished a show at the Arc and could barely see straight from the whiskey and weed. The screams coming from the beach brought us face-to-face with death. We overheard them say they couldn't tell if the tears in his body were from teeth or something else. Either way, he wasn't getting up again.

—◦—

I CAN'T HEAR myself think with the caution tape we tore down, flapping like a loose tongue in the wind. I couldn't hear myself think over the distant dizzying screams from the Midway. Couldn't hear myself think over the day-to-day chatter of these *people* I surround myself with.

Frank, all guns and gums, always talking, always trying to overpower a conversation with poor attempts at humor or some ill-timed remark. Bobby, this sad sack right-hand man who "yups" himself into every bad situation Frank can get him in. Sam, whose wild eyes spin like slot machines and, god forbid, if they land on you, his fists always follow. And me, the guy who they all grew up with, just always there by their side for amusement, argument, or worse.

THE WATER IS black with little interruptions of foam, bursts of white static on a dark screen. I often wonder, as in tonight, if I am the only one witnessing each wave as it crashes and dies. Life gone just shortly after it is born, observed by one. If so, it deserved better than me watching over it.

I turn from the ocean, look to the street, devoid of life, absent of movement, and within a flicker of the sodium vapors, I spot a curl of smoke and follow its trail dancing out of the cracked window of a midnight-blue truck. The streetlamps backlight the lone figure in the driver's seat, until the cigarette's cherry glows, brightening his eyes, and I feel like he is watching me. No. I *know* he is watching me.

MORNING BECOMES LATE afternoon, and I put two beers in my tote along with a piss-scented paperback covered with demons.

The strip is filthy. Detritus from the night before clogs the sewer drains, and stoned teenagers are replaced by manic children with sugar-spun grins and sticky fingers. The arcades bleep and bloop in protest to the maniacs banging their fists on its buttons. Families with bad teeth and scorched skin lurch up and down the strip in hopes for the excitement that, judging from their faces, will never come. They're all smiles though, faces painted with sickening lights, so I move on, stone-faced and silent.

I'm stuck in a loop. Watching myself walk down the same street, drink the same swill, and get in the same trouble. It's my own fault. I can't blame stupid Frank and his penchant for fucking and fighting. Can't blame the tool bags we hang out with who go to the same places and repeat old stories so often that I wonder how they have time to create new memories. Can't blame my own sad, squirming brain for wanting something different. No, not wanting. That's a choice. *Needing* something different. I can blame myself for not doing something about it.

At the end of the strip, where the new condos shove the wilting cottages aside, signs on the boardwalk mock everyone with slogans such as IF YOU LIVED HERE, YOU'D BE HOME RIGHT NOW.

I think, If I lived here, I'd be dead right now.

I jump onto the sand where the jetty rocks carve a long tooth into the ocean's face. With each step forward, I slip on the seaweed snot clinging to their surfaces, and in one bad move, I envision myself twisting, falling fast, and splitting the crown of my head open. Then I see it happen again, faster, and this time a pointed rock pierces my eye, punching through my brain. In the next vision, I fall backwards, slap my skull, and slide into the ocean where big fish with rolling eyes wait for me to slip into their mouths. None of that happens.

I close my eyes and imagine the expanse of the ocean's underworld, past where the light dies, and what lives below. These deities existing without a care for what happens to any of us above. I envy them.

❖

FRANK, SAM, AND Bobby stalk the arcades, bare-chested and blasted, the neon lighting up their sun-kissed skins. Girls' eyes devour every detail from the sculpt of their abdominal muscles to the creases in their shorts. Frank will eventually pick them up and lurch back to our cottage to impress with his skills in bed. Thing is, I've watched him go at it before with a bunch of dialogue yanked from porn films, and ill-advised offbeat thrusting techniques that probably gave the girls a migraine more than an orgasm. They shouted anyways, and heaved and hawed and praised him, but usually avoided his eyes when they left.

Anyway, this girl that had washed up on the sand, her mouth overflowing with the head of a bloated jellyfish, definitely was one of the girls from the night before. The one who'd said Frank's lips tasted like cotton candy, and he'd told her no fucking way: *It's for little shits and fags like Whittier.* He'd pointed toward me.

I leave the pack by their dying fire and go for my walk, watching the ocean, staring to where the sky meets the water, trying to decipher where the night ends and the sea begins. I turn and see, under the streetlamp, the midnight blue truck, idling, its window cracked, and a curl of smoke dancing out. The engine growls in the dark. I can't see in, but I know he can see me. I can feel his eyes on every part of me. I return my gaze to the sea to discern if the horizon was even real.

IT'S ANOTHER DAY though it doesn't feel like it, and I'm three beers down. I strip down and dive in the water. My head bobs in rhythm with the waves as I float away, letting the current do what it will with me.

A piercing light catches my eye. On a small island, there is the figure again, this time a brownish blur, shimmering in the waves of heat, distorting my view. I hear the slight backbeat of a drum. A drum that gets louder, the beat heavier, closer ... my heart. He stands high, impossibly tall, growing in length each time a ripple of water breaks over my brow, and I tread closer, no longer caring that with each push toward this figure, I am further away from what I know. I squint, and his form becomes defined. An impossible body, growing, thickening, and standing tall above the surface.

This figure waves to me and I no longer feel alone.

I hear a muted shout from the shore. I dip below and close my eyes, knowing I'm in too deep to see a bottom. Another shout from land as I surface. This time I squint toward the island and the brown blur has definition, muscle; it is waving its limbs that look too perfect to be real. They wave faster now, and I go under. When I surface he is closer, his limbs engorged, and the shouts get louder when my head rises again, and I realize I am far from the jetty and even farther from shore when the shouts crystallize and I hear the familiar word too late. The last word you want to hear while floating above endless darkness.

Dagger-long teeth punch in and out of my chest and stomach with the impact of fists, their heft tearing me, gnashing my guts, everything moving in and out, emptying around me; everything that is me disperses in the churn of the water, and the only screams I can hear are my own. It rips me back and forth so hard, the water is no longer liquid. Past the point of help, I am witnessing my own final moment and wondering, as it all leaves me so quickly, how it happens so easily. I finally see my reflection in the black eye of the shark before it rolls back into its head and its mouth opens. A final bite severs my neck, and more of me floats away. I look to the island, where the man, his naked back to me, retreats until I can't see him anymore. I sink as sunlight and foam turns red and the final tug pulls me below.

THE NEXT DAY, the beach is closed. Empty except for a line of cruisers and some new yellow tape, fighting the wind, batting from the blades of the copters scanning the water below. The signs warn the swimmers even though we all know they will be ignored. Frank and the boys are stoned, asleep, nursing deep purple bruises on their knuckles that some kid's face messed up. Within close proximity of these monsters, wheezing and inhaling the hot stench of their own breath, I down my first beer and walk outside to breathe again. I pull out a cigarette, light it with the flash snap of a Zippo, cough, flick it away, and keep moving before they realize I am gone.

Two more beers go down quick on the walk, so I have a nice buzz that's morphing into a headache. Feels like I have a soaked washcloth covering my forehead, the kind my mother dressed me with during a fever when I stayed home from school. For a moment, I wonder how she is, and then I take two more pills to forget and watch the kids whip around in janky coaster carts until the bolts come undone and the cars plummet off the track, slow enough I can see their smiles turn to screams, but fast enough that the impact with the beam smashes their teeth clear through the back of their skulls, their scalps landing at the feet of little girls with fists of dripping vanilla ice cream, eyes stuck shut with blood.

The pizza stand is overrun, so I will have to wait to eat even though my stomach is turning and I'm thinking of the dead girl with the jellyfish stuffed in her mouth and the dead boy and Frank and his jawline and his terrible tattoos and the man on the island with the long limbs.

I feel the crush of the crowd, their breath on my shoulders, while I change my dollar for tokens. They all close in, their gums smacking, their red and purple skins sliding against each other, piling up, faces in each other's armpits, smiling and laughing and screaming, their eyes jittering around in their sockets like electric, haunted house skeletons.

Nothing feels comfortable: these people stare at me; these guys look like they want to fight me; these girls laugh behind closed hands; these parents shield their children's eyes from me as if they have read my thoughts. As if my eyes project the images of all of them dying in the hideous accidents that loop in my head. I just want to be back in the ocean, dark and cold, slipping beneath the waves, sinking, and then I see the truck. I've never seen the midnight-blue truck in broad daylight. No silhouette, no cracked windshield, no curl of smoke. The sun pounds down on all of us, every detail of this circus brightly displayed, no shadows to hide in, and I couldn't be more frightened. My throat is closing, and I'm afraid if I make a sudden move he will be there by my side, waiting for me to take his hand, to join him, and everyone will see it happen and understand.

I am not one of you.

THE MAN ON the island never returned. He might have never been there. I sink beneath the waves into the black waters, so deep that even the light glinting off the surface has the appearance of luminescent minnows so far from my reach. I can only hear the muffled pound of surf punishing the land.

The somber slap of my heart in my head.

I am still, holding my breath.

Eyes open, stinging with salt.

Expecting a dark shape to appear from the darkness below, with its eyes rolling back, and its jaws open to take me in.

If I can fit between its teeth.

These white daggers.

I tighten my legs together to descend quicker. I open my eyes and see nothing below the pale ghost of my imperfect body, and I expect my last vision will be to disappear into its gullet, whole.

I wake to a rumble, and I believe I am in its stomach.

I hear the chug of a motor, and my eyes open, and I see his tanned, tight chest and my chin moves against the soft hairs, my cheek brushes his throat. We hear the cries of the children at the amusement park. I can see the crackle of a bonfire as Frank and his boys splay out with a group of strangers, telling the same stories, drinking from the same bottles and singing the same songs. The window is cracked and the stranger is smoking. The curl of smoke trails his nose, around his cheek, and swirls outside the midnight-blue truck parked under the streetlight. We are backlit silhouettes to anyone watching us from the shore, wondering who we are and what we are doing here.

My name is John Whittier. He is still a stranger. For now, that's all I need.

THE VOICES OF NIGHTINGALES

by M. E. Bronstein

AFTER DAY ONE at the Accademia, Lynn needed two things: a drink and quality time with the ruins. And so Jenny grabbed a bottle of cheap grappa, and Lynn and Simon followed her downhill. They passed the bottle back and forth, took long swigs as the night's first stars slipped through the teal and orange dusk.

They came to the sunken amphitheater carved into the hillside—the last real remnant of the Usignoli's original presence here. It was full of scattered columns, jumbled piles of gray brick, tufts of yellow-green grass. A bubble of history, loudly different from the telephone wires in the distance, the bright lights that glowed in the Accademia's entrance uphill.

The three of them stretched out in the grass while the cicadas buzzed and the wind stirred their hair, and they mimed, raising cups to each other.

"I really hope you'll change your mind," said Simon.

Lynn shrugged and hoped he'd leave it alone.

"Simon's not wrong," said Jenny. "You know you'll learn the language better if you try producing it actively. Whether Traccia's your end goal or not, taking at least half a whack at it'd be useful."

Simon nodded vigorously.

Lynn didn't answer for a moment, but made a mental note to reprimand Jenny later for taking Simon's side. "Maybe," she said.

"I'll think about it. I'll admit I'm starting to develop some weird affection for pieces of it, anyway."

"I have decided that I love the shit out of Traccia," said a slightly drunken Jenny. "It's so fucking weird. Potent feelings, you know? Love 'em. Even the bad ones. Fear and hate. Look at the gross and pretty pictures they've given us. Scaly words with forked tongues. Nightingales' blood staining the sunset. Lactating monks."

"Love me a good lactating monk," agreed Lynn. She aped the tenor of Traccia: "'Thou shalt suckle at the breast of the true man's word, rather than the teat of the poisonous Nightingale.'"

Jenny collapsed against Lynn as she cackled, and Simon had to rescue their bottle of grappa so it didn't all spill in the grass. He looked a little confused, but chuckled along anyway. Probably thought he had gotten his way.

EARLIER THAT DAY, their first lesson had taken place in an airy gray room lined by pale and bony columns, snarling faces carved into their capitals. Their instructor (Paolo) introduced himself. He paced before a chalkboard and summed up what most of his audience already knew: how the medieval writing system known as Traccia first evolved from an elaborate censorship project (though he didn't call it that), an effort to suppress the writings of a small group of Apulian poets generally known as the Usignoli.

Abbreviations were standard form in Latin manuscripts. For instance: "puella" meant "girl," while "puellam," in the accusative, situated "girl" as a direct object. Paolo wrote on the board, his chalk chirping:

"Puella canem timet." The girl fears the dog.

"Canis puellam mordet." The dog bites the girl.

However, in a medieval manuscript, to conserve space, you were likelier to see "Canis puellā mordet"—no "m" after "puella," but a line above the final "a" instead. "That macron serves to mark the accusative ending," said Paolo. He wrote "arbor" ("tree") and the final "r" trailed off into a squiggling tail, and he pointed to it and said, "This abbreviation, meanwhile, stands for 'ibus,' the dative and ablative plural ending. Forgive me, gentlemen, I don't mean to bore you; I know many of you are frequent guests in the manuscripts reading room, and your Capelli's are already well thumbed."

A chuckle radiated between the pillars and the vaulted ceiling.

"Capelli's?" whispered Jenny.

"A reference book—it lists all these abbreviations," said Simon, who knew his medieval Latin (and many other languages) much better than either of them.

Paolo went on:

Traccia started off as a joke. Abbreviations supplied where they didn't belong, to change the meaning of Usignoli verses (so that dogs bit girls rather than the other way around). They added new heads and tails, new odds and ends of meaning. Then the joke took on a new life. Signs that had once belonged to an established system of abbreviations became tangled carpets of script that covered the songs of the Usignoli. As it corrected and gobbled up all it could, Traccia became a kind of language unto itself.

Paolo distributed photocopies of poems in the old southern Italian dialect of the Usignoli, facsimiles of manuscripts containing Traccia, and several reams of tracing paper.

He guided them through a few preliminary exercises, deciphering first the antiquated Italian, then the Traccia, and then he led them through the process of transforming the one into the other on tracing paper. Twenty or so heads bowed through the room, noses and hands hovering over the intertwined texts.

Then Paolo approached Jenny—she glanced uneasily toward Lynn, as though to say, Why did we sit in the front row again?

(Good question, thought Lynn, as she slid her own work into her lap, tried to hide the fact that she was pretty lost and had just doodled some of the faces grimacing on the capitals.) Paolo asked to see Jenny's progress, and she gave him her tracing paper. He nodded, then crumpled her work up into a ball and gave Jenny a new piece of tracing paper. "Again," he said.

A nervous muttering through the room. "Not just this young lady," he said. "All of you. Again!"

A rustling, crinkling as they all discarded their first efforts.

"The repetitive nature of the exercise should come to feel rather like prayer," said Paolo.

Scattered smirks indicated that the comparison wasn't exactly inviting to everyone.

Just when Lynn figured her dereliction had been overlooked, Paolo's hand fell on her shoulder and he asked her if she needed any help. She shrugged him off. "No—sorry, I'm always a slow study at first," she said, "but I'll catch up. Just watching and learning." She jerked her thumb in Simon's direction; his hand darted across the page fluidly, like he'd been possessed by the spirits of the old monks who had inhabited this place back when it was the Monastero di San Giosefo del Ponte all'Oca.

Paolo said, "Don't be shy. It is natural to make mistakes when you first attempt it. That is why we must try again, and again."

Lynn nodded, like oh yeah, of course, never would have occurred to her that you learn languages through trial and error. As Paolo surveyed the rest of the room, she tried to look busy, scrawled some nonsense. She could already tell that this routine would become difficult to maneuver around as the summer advanced. But Simon would probably let her copy his work if the situation ever got desperate (she'd just be in for a disappointed frown or two).

Soon, Lynn's pencil quirked its way into doodles again. There were little birds in low relief, she noticed, all over the room: on the vaults, spiraling downward around the columns, even a few scratched into the flagstones underfoot. Nightingales or doves or something else? And then the carved landscape seemed to vibrate around them, full of sinuous and curling shapes.

While everyone else left for lunch in the refectory, Lynn lingered. She sat on the floor, then stretched out on her back, and studied the ceiling.

Serpents. Very faint, but you could make them out if you looked closely enough. Clouds of carved snakes, coiling around the birds.

THERE WAS NO such thing as an Usignoli "expert," and that was really what Lynn wanted to be. Traccia was just a gateway she had to pass through to get there.

They knew so little about them, but most of the Usignoli appeared to have been women (or at least liked to write in women's voices), and they wrote each other strange and beautiful love poems. Overripe fruit, bursting blossoms, ecstatic birdsong. A lyric register somewhere between the Song of Songs and Sappho and that weird Catullus poem about the sparrow.

While the Accademia had put some effort into compiling and editing a few samples of the language of the Usignoli to serve as classroom materials and model the leap from one language to the next, most of the original texts still remained hidden beneath heaps of Traccia. When Lynn asked why nobody had yet put some effort into extracting the whole known corpus of Usignoli poetry, Paolo told her that the exercise was unnecessary; they had all they needed already in order to understand Traccia.

PAOLO SHOWED THEM fragments of a sermon in Traccia, built on top of a song about nightingales and swallows. Romantic birdsong turned into prayer, feathers became quill pens, kisses on bare arms became the kiss of the divine logos.

Lynn noticed "filomena," a word for "nightingale," through a wriggling overlay of Traccia, which transformed it into a word for "sculpture." As though the monks had tried to petrify the Usignoli's song.

As the days passed, Lynn could relate.

She noticed that Paolo and his cronies never cold-called her. They preferred Simon and his ilk (not that that was anything new). Probably for the best. Lynn mastered the art of guarding her work with a forearm and a curtain of loose hair. She didn't need any extra scrutiny.

THEY WERE A couple of weeks into their work when their photocopies of Usignoli texts dwindled, then disappeared. They had exhausted their slim supply, and so they turned their attention to Traccia by itself. They traced, they transcribed.

"It's like prayer," insisted Paolo.

Low grunts of agreement.

Lynn nodded along, feigned attention while she struggled to unknot something: "sole." That could be a substantive ("the sun"), or it could be an adjective ("alone" or "lonely"). She couldn't tell without disentangling the preceding or following words, which were pretty buried beneath Traccia. Sometimes this whole process felt like trimming an unruly hedge. She could almost feel the thorns of the scribes' unruly script prickle against her palms, resisting her efforts.

Maybe if she cut around the weeds of Traccia on the next line up or down, she could find something, she could figure this out. She looked up from her work and Paolo was off on a tangent about Alan of Lille and his great admiration for the monks of Ponte all'Oca.

Lynn jumped ahead and recognized the edges of a word she had freed once before. Dawn.

The hidden line opened up as she picked at it. The nightingale's dawn-song, waking up the sun; Lynn's hand wavered. The nightingale's song invites the sun into the sky. Without her notes, it would always be night. She could almost hear it—feel it, a fluting, sweet rhythm, hot with new sunlight . . .

"Lynn?" said Paolo.

Her reverie broke.

"Could you remind us what this sign represents?" He pointed at a white square on the chalkboard.

Was he joking?

That kind of simple geometry rarely occurred in Traccia. Simon nudged his notebook with his elbow. Lynn tried to figure out the answer by herself; it wouldn't come—what with the singing sun-dazzle in her head. She let her gaze lick across Simon's notes.

Oh.

"It's a common marginal note, right?" said Lynn. "A reminder to the scribe that there's a word or a line he still needs to write his Traccia over." The square was supposed to evoke a veil, to drape across the text.

"Very good, Simon," said Paolo, earning a ripple of hearty mirth in response. Lynn glowered down at her notes. Nightingales and dawn, she thought, willing herself elsewhere as she pictured a blushing sky and birds' silhouettes darting across it, their dark beaks pen nibs, writing the sun into being.

SOMETIMES LYNN NEEDED to be loud. That was how she came to the chapel. Lighter than the rest of the Accademia, with its bright plaster walls. Bucolic molding: grape leaves, ivy, songbirds. Wooden rafters crossed the ceiling overhead, and sparrows sometimes roosted there (Lynn found some bird shit among the pews).

Although the monks had done their best to cover up the language of the Usignoli, they had neglected the neumes, the musical notation, that hovered around their words. Faint memories of choir practice murmured at the back of Lynn's mind, and sometimes she would tap out an imagined rhythm on her knee while she read. It wouldn't hurt to try out some fragments of Usignoli song in the chapel.

But she swallowed her reconstruction as Simon entered with a fat textbook tucked under one armpit. Lynn waved. He waved back and settled into one of the pews.

She slipped into a seat in front of his and peered at the open textbook in his lap; he, meanwhile, studied the rose window above the altar.

"What's that you've got there, Simon?"

He showed her a page with a reproduction of a miniature from one of the manuscripts. Above lines of Traccia: an illuminated roundel, tidy petals of red and green ink. Lynn recognized it as an illustration of the chapel's rose window.

"I've switched between various seats in this place," said Simon, "trying to find the best angle, so that my view of the window will match the version on this page. That way I'll know that I am sitting in the same spot, more or less, as the monk who drew this image so long ago."

Lynn stopped herself from laughing when she saw the wounded twitch at the corner of Simon's mouth. "But the chapel must have changed so much since then," she said. "I mean, the pews are definitely new, for one."

Simon shrugged. "I'm just trying to get as close to them as I can," he said. "Close to Traccia. Close to history."

"I get it," said Lynn, though she wasn't sure that she did. "Didn't mean to make fun. Your dedication is . . . admirable."

He offered her a faint smile. "As is your singing," he said quickly. It became clear that part of his staring so fixedly at the window had to do with working very hard not to make eye contact with Lynn.

Later, she would hear something in the classroom, a faraway kind of music. If she didn't know better, she would have said that it was like echoes of the tune she had started and then stopped in the chapel had gotten stuck in the Accademia's walls. Still resounding.

PAOLO TOOK HIS flock along for a visit to the Accademia's archives. They stored their treasures in what had once been the crypt.

The class descended, filed through the chilly dark.

Paolo stood at the head of a long table and showed them a trio of codices full of Traccia: imposing volumes bound in aged scarlet leather that put up some noisy resistance as he pried them open. Not pretty books, but stained with water damage, riddled with holes, tears stitched together with pale red and white threads. The volumes' history had left them with scars.

Many lines of Traccia looked more like wounds in person than they tended to in photocopies—rubricated to catch the reader's eye, letters underlined or filled in with bright, messy crimson.

Paolo invited the students to the reader's table one by one, had them touch the corner of a folio, to feel the old parchment, study the dead calf's hair follicles, like shaving stubble.

When it was Lynn's turn, something like static bit at her skin.

"Something wrong?" said Paolo.

"No," said Lynn, pinching the book.

WHEN THE PROGRAM first started, Paolo would make bad cranky-grandpa jokes, which the room largely shrugged off. He'd wonder aloud what the inventors of Traccia might suppress, if they were alive today. (Except he never said "suppress." It was always something like "reinvent" or "rewrite.") Trashy films, pop stars, godless politicians, all wrapped up and digested in Traccia, their discourse reshaped.

But lately, a number of students—maybe in a misguided effort to ingratiate themselves—acted like they got what he meant, stopped groaning and sighing.

Simon kept interrupting Lynn at her work.

She would set up shop in the common room between the students' cells, arrange a quilt of papers on the table. The corners of her pages shifted slightly whenever a breeze crept in through the wide arched windows; she weighed them down with stones she found in the cloister garden.

She was onto something. She knew it. The dawn-song. She'd cleaned up a few new patches of text: Let us echo through, the sound of us will still resound . . . There is a cure, made of stone and sound . . . She needed to figure out what came next. But then the photocopied ink got blurred and unruly, and the language of the Usignoli drowned in it.

Simon appeared in the common room; he stood at one end of the table and watched Lynn as she jotted down ideas, scratched them out, rubbed her temples. Then he picked up one of the stones idly, and she lunged as the page it had anchored floated on a wayward breeze.

Simon sat down, attention tugging at her.

Lynn clicked her pen. "What is it?" she asked.

"Nothing," he muttered. But it didn't take long for him to burst out: "Do you know why I want to learn Traccia?" She could tell even before he answered his own question that a flood of tangent was about to carry him off, and she couldn't stop him. "I want to hold the abstract substance of the language in my head, to pretend that I'm one of the monks, that I'm lost in the act of writing their words down myself, as if they were my own. I feel like, if I do this, if I transcribe everything, then I can feel the very sensations that they must have experienced when they first generated a new language, when their ideas first lay cradled only by thought, before being filtered through the pen." He stopped. Breathed.

"That's nice, Simon," said Lynn. She didn't like herself for the vague embarrassment she felt for him—his passion too transparent. Sometimes she worried his ideas would overwhelm hers. She studied her notes, hoped he would leave.

He didn't.

"Simon." She turned to face him. And the person she saw didn't look like Simon anymore—or he did and he didn't. She saw two faces, a new Simon inscribed on the old and faded one, a palimpsest; he had the same features—dark eyes overlarge in his gaunt face—but there were lines that didn't belong, as though a pen had etched new and angry ridges between the eyebrows, across the bridge of his nose.

"You never listen to me," he said. "Listen!"

He slammed his palms down on the table. The stones atop Lynn's papers rattled.

Lynn closed her eyes for a moment, gathering herself. "Simon, that's ridiculous," she said. "Of course I listen to you."

The worst part: seeing her own contained rage these past few weeks sketched across his face, mirrored back at her, distorted.

"No." Simon inched closer, loomed. Lynn tried to shrink away from the wrong lines on his face. "Where are your passions, Lynn? Do you feel so strongly about anything? Why do you refuse to learn Traccia properly? Why are you even here?"

Lynn faltered, tried to remind him that the Usignoli were her real project—once, he had understood and respected that—but Simon wouldn't listen.

And then, to Lynn's relief, Jenny drifted in, hair shaped like an amoeba. Her cell was right next to the common room, and apparently she had been sleeping.

"Would you two stop bickering like an old married couple?" she begged.

"Old divorcing couple'd be more accurate," grumbled Lynn. Simon glanced sharply at her, frowning.

"Whatever your imaginary marital status may be, shut it, pretty please," said Jenny. "Or divorce more quietly."

They apologized, said their good-nights. Lynn tried to unhear the curse Simon muttered darkly, before he left.

PAOLO HAD BEEN doing his rounds of the room and Lynn hadn't even noticed him, creeping up behind her desk.

"You are here to learn Traccia," he said, "not the nonsense underneath it."

And this time he actually grabbed her hand, wrapping his fingers around her knuckles until he could clutch her pen and guide it across her tracing paper; he dragged her through a line of Traccia. Lynn squirmed; his palms were damp and hot, like something's maw had clamped around her rather than a hand.

She studied the room and all its eyes looked back in silence—including Simon's and Jenny's. Blank-faced, not a single sign of empathy, horror, anything. Was she crazy? This was inappropriate, right?

Paolo let go of her hand.

The meaning of the line he had forced her to trace sank in: Drink not of the poisonous song.

"There," said Paolo. "Isn't that better?"

AS LYNN CHANGED into her pajamas, something flickered into view in the shadow of her nightshirt, tented over her head—

She shrieked, banged her tailbone against her bed frame, then twitched in a ragged circle, scanned all the walls of her cell. But—nothing out of the ordinary. All empty.

Lynn crumpled in a corner by the door, pressed her forehead to her knees, squeezed her eyes shut. She breathed, reined in her galloping pulse.

She went to the mirror, just saw herself. Circles below her eyes, hair a mess as usual.

But before.

There had been a snake—something like a snake. Draped around her neck, across her shoulders and chest—a tangle of bright bronze and mottled black, like an ink spill. A head just beneath her collarbone, and it had been writing something across her with its dark tongue, her skin its parchment. Calligraphic text mirrored the sinuous curves of its own tail.

A waking dream. A misplaced nightmare. It had to be.

AFTER THAT SLEEPLESS night: a numbing fog. A welcome change, sort of, after coming to class every day with a bundle of tension in her gut.

Lynn abandoned her old notebook, the one that had offended Paolo, and brought a fresh and blank new one with her to class.

She paid attention while Paolo lectured.

He spoke about a passage of Traccia and the hortus conclusus, the enclosed garden. The lamb roams the garden to drink from fountains of light, and so forth. The monks had built the image atop a more sensual garden space in the verses of the Usignoli. The Usignoli were fond of fruit trees; they described dipping needles in ink to write each other love notes on cherry leaves.

The overlapping narratives didn't unnerve Lynn as they once had. In fact, something amused her about the shift from cherry trees to fountains of light. Like amorphous riverbed stuff turned into workable clay, that could become a jar, a brick, something useful to build upon, to build with, to contain.

While Lynn listened to Paolo and took notes, her left hand probed an itch near her breast. Damn the tiger mosquitoes of southern Italy.

Her other hand traced something new of its own accord on the page. A serpentine line of script wended its way across her notes.

A sharp shriek.

It took Lynn a moment to recognize it as her own.

Jenny leaned over, draped her hand across Lynn's.

Good old Jenny.

"Would you shut it?" she hissed. Something was different about her voice. Like she had caught a cold, but not quite, ragged edges around her words, the ghost of someone else's intonation. "You're making a scene."

Lynn's chair screeched backwards across the flagstones.

She apologized for the upset, said she was unwell. Needed to go lie down.

HER NOTES. SHE had to get to her notes. She could find some secret that could help her fix . . . whatever this was, the weird madness bleeding through the Accademia.

Lynn loped down the hall, then froze.

Her door was already ajar.

Ice at the base of her spine, in spite of the oppressive summer heat.

She shoved the door open and stumbled into her cell.

At first she thought someone had torn open her pillow and filled her room with down. Then she recognized shreds of paper fluttering through the air, stirred by her passage.

And in the middle of the floor: her notebook. Or its corpse, rather. All wrong. Ragged. Someone had opened it up and eviscerated it, torn its pages to pieces.

Lynn nudged the damaged notebook with her toe. Revulsion shuddered through her and she kicked it toward the wall.

She sat down on her bed, her limbs heavy. A flurry of torn paper shifted around her. She swept it all away before collapsing against her pillow.

LYNN TRIED TO remember. The lines she had exhumed. There was one that liked to linger:

There is a cure, made of stone and sound . . .

Those horrible lines on Simon's face, Jenny's changed voice.
A cure?
And there—she heard it again.
A thin song, vibrating through the room.

THE SUNKEN AMPHITHEATER looked different after dark.
Its columns taller, lengthened, their shadows stretched out by
the moon. Lynn shook in the cold while starlight simmered
overhead. She stood in the quiet. Then, she opened her mouth,
and let the one verse of Usignoli song drift out of her.

And there it was. A bit of music echoed around her, uncon-
strained by the monastery walls.

Lynn followed the voice's lead, though she wasn't sure at first
how to follow an echo that filled so much of the space around
her with a shimmering shadow of sound. She recognized one
word, then two. "Sole." "Cura." They were words she had sung
herself, carried on now by strange voices. And a vague, background hint of birdcalls.

And the amphitheater did not, in fact, appear to be quite so
sunken anymore. Its fragments of pillars had become arches,
like broken bones grown back into place.

Lynn rubbed her eyes, dizzied by the overlay of past and present.

She saw people, a procession filling into the space around
her. Women in long brown gowns. They all wore masks, puckered around the nose: little beaks.

One woman paused, turned to face Lynn, tilting her head.
She held out her hand.

Lynn hesitated a moment, then accepted the invitation.

The procession wound its way between columns, then formed
a neat ring at the center of the amphitheater. Song reverberated
through the circle; Lynn realized it had become a tune she
did not know at all, and she shifted uneasily.

The woman who had invited her stayed by her, placed a hand on her shoulder.

Then, one by one, couples broke away, to dance in the middle of the circle. They moved lightly, barefoot, on the balls of their feet. Just like the pizzica, the taranta, the southern Italian dances meant to shake out tarantula venom.

Soon, Lynn understood they were teaching new verses to her. Words she hadn't yet unearthed.

The woman who first invited her leaned in close, fingertips brushing against Lynn's collarbone.

When Lynn glanced down at herself she flinched at the sight of her snakebite. On either side of it, lines of an unfamiliar text glimmered darkly just beneath her skin, like misshapen veins around her breast.

The woman's hand lingered for a moment, as though she wanted to wipe away the line of unwanted text. Then she tugged Lynn toward the center of the ring.

"Oh—oh no," said Lynn, digging her heels into the earth. "Can't dance."

She found herself confronted with a distinctly avian pout, though she couldn't figure how the woman managed it around her mask. And how to say no to that? Instead, she let herself be led into the music by the ghost of a nightingale.

As they danced, the sun rose—brought into being by their song.

And when the procession filed out of the amphitheater, Lynn followed them. She would sing with them. Their words would resound through the walls.

There would be a cure.

She flew through the refectory, the old vestry, the chapter-house, followed the nightingales' voices as they tugged her along.

❖

PAOLO CLAIMED THAT Lynn no longer cared to study Traccia, that she had decided to go home. Jenny and Simon weren't too surprised, though Lynn could at least have said goodbye—whatever the tension between them recently.

But then, Jenny was the first to hear it—a faint murmuring, lost bit of sound. The cadence of it somehow like Lynn. They used to hear her sometimes, practicing in the chapel. Lynn had a lovely voice, a flutelike soprano. She'd shut up in an instant of course if anyone ever came in to listen to her, so they had to be sneaky and hang out outside the chapel if they wanted to hear her.

And now. Some remnant of that.

Day by day, it mounted. Soon, the others started to hear it, too.

Voices wrapped around trilling birdsong. Louder this time. Impossible to ignore. And drumming, tambourines, pipes.

Paolo lost their attention as his students glanced around the room, studied the walls and ceiling, searching for the source of the distant music.

And there it was. Lynn's voice.

Paolo hissed, curled up on the floor as he covered his ears, but it grew, a flood of sound, filling the room.

The music of the Usignoli radiated outward from where it had lain frozen, petrified beneath the monastery's walls. Paolo stopped struggling. A wild look frozen on his face, his eyes wide and bloodshot.

Later, the students would be hard pressed to describe the change in the air. A shimmer of feathers and birdsong, diaphanous as spider silk, fluid as smoke, everywhere, thrumming.

And somewhere in that song, Lynn's high and pure voice, ringing and wavering, begging them to listen, to sing the poison out.

What Blood Hath Wrought

by S. A. Cosby

K EISHA HATED WORKING nights at the Pancake Shack. She hated the dry, barren hours between eleven p.m. and three a.m. when the third shift crowd from the mill poured into the little diner like ants. She hated the flickering streetlamp at the corner of the parking lot that threw strange shadows onto the asphalt. She hated the creaky sign that advertised the Pancake Shack as a twenty-four-hour eating establishment. The sign hung from a rusting arm on a pole that rose ten feet into the air near the street. When the wind blew, the sign would let out a mournful squeal like a banshee.

She especially hated the lights that illuminated the mill three blocks away. Huge plumes of steam poured out of smokestacks that reached into the sky like towers on an ancient castle. The lights that ran along the steel fence and were positioned at various strategic locations across the plant's campus gave off a ghostly green glow. The droplets of water in the steam could play tricks on your eyes when they hit those eldritch green lights. Then there were the truckers and mill workers that constantly hit on her as they shoveled down greasy hash browns and doughy pancakes. Some were a little more insistent than others. Their greedy eyes appraising her body the way a wolf stares at a deer unnerved her sometimes. One night she had gone out back to throw away a bag of trash and one of the truckers had been hiding behind the dumpster. He had walked out of the shadows with his dick in his hand. She had run back inside after hurling the contents of the trash bag at the man. She hadn't told her manager, Vicky. There was nothing she could have done, and the guy was probably a hundred miles away by the time she got back inside the building.

Most nights the Pancake Shack was a spooky, stressful job, but she had to pay the bills. She was a single mom and in Pittsville. If you didn't work at the Lowenfield Pulp and Paper mill, you took what you could get. Keisha was a waitress. Troy Green was a waiter/busboy. Shavon Mitchell was the cook, and Vicky Jones was the manager on duty. Sometimes Troy was a waiter/busboy/ assistant cook and sometimes Keisha was a waitress and janitor. The employment structure at the Pancake Shack was as flexible as a contortionist.

Tonight was a perfect example of that malleable hierarchy. Vicky, who was supposed to be working the eleven p.m. to seven a.m. shift too, had given Keisha her keys. Vicky had then slipped out the door to go bang the married guy she had been seeing for the past four weeks while his wife worked the graveyard shift at the mill.

"I'll be back before the till has to be counted, okay?" she had pleaded as she had thrown Keisha the keys on her way out the door. Troy had watched her go and just shook his head. Keisha was fairly sure that if Troy just glanced in Vicky's direction she would rip off her pants and screw him in the bathroom. Vicky and Keisha had both applauded Ike Hathaway's business acumen when he hired a luscious piece of eye candy like Troy. Ike owned the Pancake Shack with his wife, Hilda. Vicky was his niece.

Troy was built like a Greek statue dipped in chocolate. His megawatt smile could elicit flirtatious repartee from even the oldest churchgoing grandmother. Troy would hit her with that smile from time to time, but Keisha did her best to disregard it. Troy was a sophomore at Colson College on the other side of town. Guys like Troy graduated and never looked back. They settled down with a nice Becky or Madison and raised a gaggle of badass children. Eventually they forgot the pungent smell that the mill belched into the sky—the omnipresent stench of burning pulp and wet wood. Locals liked to say it was the smell of money, but Keisha thought it smelled like servitude and dreams deferred. That was why she was taking online courses in the mornings and working at the Shack at night. She was going to get the hell out of Pittsville or die trying.

"Tell me you got an order up, Keisha. I'm bored to death back here," Shavon said through the sliding rectangular window that separated the kitchen from the dining area.

"You could dump the grease trap," she responded without looking up from her crossword puzzle.

"I said I'm bored, not suicidal," Shavon said with a laugh.

Keisha shook her head. Shavon was funny and quick-witted. He had a subtle charm that drew you in like you were warming your hands by a fire. He reminded her of her son's father. That alone was enough reason to steer clear of him. Shavon had shoulder-length dreadlocks that he tied back with a red bandana and a set of deep dimples. He also had a record for possession with intent to distribute and assault and battery. He might have been fun for thirty minutes, but Keisha knew she and her son deserved better.

Shavon came to the window again.

"Why you so mean, Keisha? Can't you at least let me see them pretty eyes when you diss me?" he said.

Keisha felt herself smiling in spite of herself. She put down her crossword puzzle and walked behind the counter to poke her head through the window.

"You could clean out the grease trap," she said before batting her eyelashes. Shavon laughed.

"Forget you, girl!" he said. His words seemed harsh, but his tone was playful. Keisha saw Troy walk in the kitchen through the rear exit. He had an empty trash can in his hand.

"Troy, go through the side door! You can't have that in the kitchen!" Keisha howled. Shavon laughed again.

"For a college boy, you mighty dense," Shavon said.

Troy started to retreat. "Yeah, but in two more years this college boy will be an accountant, and you will still be flipping omelets. Guess we'll see who is dense then, huh?" Troy said.

"Yeah, but you still gonna be dense. Probably be doing books for the Russian mob, thinking they just really successful caviar importers!" Shavon said.

"Whatever, Treasure Troll," he said.

Keisha shook her head as Troy slipped out the back door. "Why do you pick at him? It just gets him all worked up," she said to Shavon.

"That's exactly why I do it. He always walk around here like his shit don't stink." Shavon pushed an errant lock of hair out of his eyes.

Keisha shook her head again and turned back to her cross-word puzzle.

Shavon cleared his throat.

"Yeah?" Keisha said.

Shavon smiled, dropped his head and looked at his shoes for a moment before catching Keisha's gaze. "So, I noticed we both off next Friday and, well, I mean, you know Kevin Hart is coming to the Scope, and I got some tickets, and I was just wondering if you wanted to go. I mean just as friends. Unless you wanna get buckwild, which in that case, I'm definitely down."

"Shavon, you know I got my online classes and homework, and I'd have to get a sitter for Arian." She crossed her arms.

Shavon put his chin on the bottom sill of the sliding window. "So that's not a no," he said as he gave her puppy-dog eyes.

Keisha rolled her own eyes and was about to say something else when the roaring of an engine drowned out her thoughts.

Keisha turned and saw a big red rig ambling into the parking lot. It was just a rig with no trailer. Keisha watched as the trucker's headlights illuminated the entire diner and chased away the shadows that seemed to congregate in the corners of the Shack. A tall, rangy white man got out of the rig and began a stiff-legged trot over to the Shack. Even though it was a cool autumn night, the trucker was clad in summer attire. A black T-shirt, a worn pair of blue jeans, and a greasy baseball cap completed his ensemble.

"Well, glad to see the redneck nation has sent their representative," Shavon said just before the man entered the diner.

Keisha shot him a wicked glance but said nothing. The man sat at the counter and stretched his arms. She pulled out her pad and prepared to take his order.

"Hey there, how you doing, hon?" she said.

The man gave her the slightest of smiles. "All right, I guess. Can I get some scrambled eggs and hash browns and a cup of coffee?" His voice had a bit of a southern twang.

Keisha wrote down his order and turned to give it to Shavon. Troy entered the diner through the side door that led to the storeroom and began wiping down the tables that lined the walls.

Shavon took the order. "Hmm . . . the breakfast of champions," he whispered.

The trucker yawned and extended his arms straight out behind him, lacing his fingers together as he stretched again.

"Huh. You mighty flexible there," Keisha said.

The trucker smiled. "Twelve years of yoga will do that for you."

Keisha raised her eyebrows.

"Yoga, huh?" she said with a smirk.

"Yeah, my ex got me started. Best thing she ever did besides leaving me," the trucker said with a weary laugh.

The diner went quiet again save for the pop and sizzle of Shavon's griddle. The Felix the Cat clock on the wall ticked away the minutes as the night chased the dawn. Keisha was trying to think of a four-letter word for physical discomfort when she felt goose bumps run up her neck. It was the unmistakable feeling of someone staring at you. She raised her head, fully expecting the trucker to be staring a hole through her. She instantly regretted making small talk with him. But when she did raise her head, the trucker was playing a game on his cell phone. She looked at the sliding window over the drink machine. Shavon was finishing up the trucker's order. She looked to the right. Troy was concentrating on cleaning the last few tables in the back of the Shack.

Almost as an afterthought, she glanced toward the front windows of the Pancake Shack. What she saw made her jump.

There was a man staring at her through the window. He was wearing a long, weathered trench coat over a dingy white dress shirt, and loose-fitting black slacks. His face wasn't pressed against the glass, and he wasn't doing anything lascivious. He was just staring into the Shack. Staring at her. His sallow brown face was covered with a kinky black beard that looked like a map of England. His bald head was peppered with large, angry pimples. His eyes were bloodshot with watery gray pupils that seemed ready to float away.

The man noticed her noticing him staring and quickly dropped his gaze. He took his hands out of his pockets and entered the diner. He walked quickly but with a pronounced limp. He grimaced as he sat two seats down from the trucker and placed his palms on the counter. Keisha didn't move immediately. There was an odor coming from the man that made her stomach quiver. Finally, she swallowed hard and went to take his order.

"Hey, hon, what will you have?" she asked.

The man closed his eyes. She could see his eyeballs moving behind their lids. It was like watching someone viewing a dream.

"Yes, I'll have coffee and a grilled cheese sandwich. I would like that very much," the man said.

Keisha was shocked at how smooth and melodious his voice sounded. It was like listening to a DJ on the radio hosting the Quiet Storm. Keisha wrote his order down and turned to give it to Shavon. Shavon had the trucker's order ready. They traded, a plate for a piece of paper.

"He look like Ving Rhames on crack," Shavon whispered to Keisha. This time neither one of them laughed. One of the perils of working at an all-night diner was drugged-out armed robbers. Meth- or coke-addled zombies who thought their next hit lay in the cash register of a second-rate chow spot. Other than the steak knives and a baseball bat in the storeroom, there were no weapons in the Pancake Shack.

"Just cook it up and let's get him out of here," she whispered back.

"Fine college you have here in this town. Fine institution of higher learning. I used to teach history at a school very similar to it many years ago. Back when I was Professor Knight," the bald man said. His booming voice made Keisha jump again.

The trucker glanced at him, then returned to his phone.

The coffeemaker began buzzing, indicating it was out of grounds. Keisha was silently relieved. It gave her an excuse to go to the storeroom and get away from the "professor."

"Be right back, fellas. Gotta get some more coffee. Don't know where my mind is tonight." Keisha turned and headed for the storeroom.

Professor Knight raised his hands and undulated his fingers in front of his face. "Perhaps it has better places to be. Your mind, that is. Sometimes our minds need a break."

Keisha stopped in her tracks. She fought the urge to turn and scowl at the professor. She didn't know what she might see in those watery gray eyes. Somehow she knew whatever it was, she wouldn't like it.

Keisha entered the storeroom and pulled the string that hung from the porcelain light fixture in the ceiling. She grabbed a bag of coffee and a filter. When she turned around, Troy was standing in the doorway. Keisha let out a startled cry.

"Hey, you all right?" Troy asked. He put his hand on her shoulder.

She patted it and then gently pushed it away. "Yeah, I just hate when those homeless crackheads come up in here. You never know what they gonna do."

Troy put his hand back on her shoulder. He moved it up her neck until he was cupping her cheek. "You don't have to worry. I'm here." His brown eyes caught the light from the ceiling fixture. They seemed to crackle with light gold sparks.

Keisha nodded and tried to gently move Troy's hand again. It didn't budge.

"Troy, I'm good. I gotta make some more coffee," she said.

He held her cheek tight. Seconds ticked by as they stood there in a strangely awkward semi-embrace. Troy rapidly shook his head from side to side and took his hand away from Keisha's cheek.

"Yeah, okay, good. Just checking on you," he said. He hit her with that megawatt smile.

He stepped aside and Keisha hurried past him. She took a deep breath. First Shavon asked her out, then there was a trucker doing yoga, then a homeless guy was trying to stare through her soul, and now Troy was acting creepy. The night couldn't end soon enough as far as she was concerned. Keisha put the filter and the coffee grounds in the machine and then turned to pick up the homeless guy's order. Shavon leaned his head out of the pick-up window.

"You good? I saw college boy heading to the storeroom. I mean, you all right, ain't you?" he asked.

Keisha didn't fight the smile this time.

"Yeah, I'm good, Shavon. Troy just can't believe every woman in the world don't wanna fuck him."

Shavon touched her hand.

"He didn't . . . he didn't try anything, did he?" he asked. His normally passive face was suddenly as tight as a drum.

Keisha frowned.

"No. He know better," she said. She hoped her lackadaisical response calmed Shavon. He hadn't exactly tried anything, at least not like the trucker who had shown her his shortcomings. Still, that lingering touch had been strange. She pushed the incident to the back of her mind and turned to hand the homeless man his sandwich. The coffee would be ready soon.

"Here you go, hon. Your coffee will be ready in a few." The man looked up and smiled.

Keisha almost retched right there on the counter. His teeth were black, bloody stumps of bone. His tongue was a mottled gray eel squirming in his mouth. She gagged. She couldn't help it.

"I'm sorry, my dear. It has been a long and circuitous road that I have traveled in this life. My body bears witness to the miles," the man said. His gray eyes brimmed with tears.

Keisha felt her face get hot.

"Naw, I'm fighting a bug, that's all. Hope I ain't made you sick," she lied.

The man nodded. Then he stared down at his sandwich. He took a deep breath. Steam from the sandwich spiraled up his nose.

"Mmm. We take food for granted. We consume it without a second thought. We throw away in one month more than some people will eat in an entire year. Yet we are oblivious to the incredible freedom we have when it comes to food in this country. If you have as little as one dollar you can find something to eat. You can eat whenever the mood strikes you. If the food you have purchased does not meet your standards, you can dispose of the entire portion, safe in the knowledge that you can purchase something else to satisfy your hunger.

"Did you know that during slavery, some slaves were only fed once a day? Their choices were limited to what the slave owner deigned to give them. Slaves were often fed the scraps left over from the butchering process. Pig knuckles, hog maws, chitterlings, turkey necks, chicken gizzards, and other assorted offal, considered unfit for human consumption, but was tossed to the slaves. It is a testament to their fortitude and ingenuity that they took what amounted to garbage and made it into edible cuisine. We truly are a spoiled and lost society today," the professor said.

No one in the diner spoke. The man's soliloquy had been delivered with such elegance and passion that they all felt guilty for their past dining habits for a few minutes.

The trucker began to gobble up the food that he had previously been picking at disinterestedly. Keisha said nothing and returned to her puzzle. She just wanted this night to end. Professor Knight took a bite out of his sandwich. He pulled his head back and chewed slowly. Finally, he swallowed and wiped his mouth with the back of his hand. He leaned forward and put his head in his hands. Keisha could hear him mumbling, and for a moment, she thought he was reciting some sort of prayer. As she listened closer, she realized he was repeating the same phrase over and over again. It made no sense to her.

"What blood has wrought, blood will rectify. What blood has wrought, blood will rectify," he whispered again, and again, repeating the strange mantra.

The trucker finished his meal and motioned for Keisha.

As she walked past the professor, he vomited. A torrent of black viscous liquid exploded from his mouth and splashed over Keisha's right arm and part of her thigh. She reflexively jumped backwards. She held her hand out away from her body and shook it wildly. She felt her own gorge rising as she felt the warmth of the liquid soaking through her pant leg.

Troy came running from the corner of the diner and Shavon came trotting out of the kitchen. The trucker stood and took a few steps away from the professor. He pulled a twenty-dollar bill out of his pocket and put it on the end of the counter.

Troy handed Keisha his rag while Shavon began pulling napkins out of a dispenser sitting near the cash register. Keisha wiped her arm with the rag while unconsciously moaning. The black vomit smelled like something fetid and rotten had burst inside the homeless man.

"Just go to the bathroom, Keisha, we'll take care of this," Shavon said.

Keisha didn't argue. She started walking to the bathroom as Shavon approached the professor. He grabbed him roughly by the collar while Troy grabbed the man by the arm.

"Come on, Cracky McCrackerton, you gots to go," Shavon said as they dragged the man off the stool and toward the door.

"Let me go. I am a professor of African American history," the man moaned.

Shavon ignored the man and continued toward the door.

Keisha went into the bathroom and turned the water on until it was scalding, then scaled it back a few levels before scrubbing her arm. Her mouth began to fill with saliva, but she pushed the urge to retch away with grim determination.

"This is so much fucking bullshit. I am not getting paid enough for this shit, for real!" She rinsed her arm and then scrubbed it again. She washed her pant leg, then rinsed her arm again. She turned to the hand dryer and waved her hand under the sensor. Short of going home and changing pants, this was as good as it was going to get. She felt on the verge of tears, but she pushed those away as well. She took a deep breath and headed back to the floor.

At first, she had difficulty understanding what she was seeing. Shavon, Troy, and the trucker were sitting side by side on the stools with their heads down, facing the kitchen. Their hands were clasped behind their backs. Keisha realized their hands were bound with zip ties. The professor was standing in the middle of the floor holding a huge black pistol. The fluorescent lights reflected off its polished barrel. He didn't point the gun at her, but motioned her over with his free hand. Her legs didn't seem to want to work.

"Come on over, my dear. This won't take long. I am sorry for this, I truly am, but some things just need to be done," he said.

Keisha didn't move.

"Now!" the man screamed. There was something wrong with his voice. It sounded like there was more than one person shouting. As if he was speaking in unison. She hurried to the counter and sat on the stool next to Shavon. She was trembling like the last leaf of summer at the end of autumn.

"Put your hands behind your back. Good girl. I really am sorry they yelled at you like that. You can't understand how horrible their rage is. Justified, but horrible," the professor said. His voice was once again smooth and erudite.

Keisha winced as he pulled the zip tie tight around her wrists. The man inhaled deeply. Something wet rattled inside his chest.

"Look, I have five hundred dollars in my wallet. Just take that and the money in the cash register and go. We won't say anything to anyone," the trucker said.

Professor Knight sidled up to the trucker's right side and whispered in his ear. "If you are the one, there is only one form of currency they will accept."

The trucker shuddered.

The professor stepped away from him and began to pace back and forth.

"Poets will tell you that love is the be-all and end-all of emotions. They will tell you it is undying and everlasting. But they are wrong. When everyone who has ever loved you has died, so does their love. No. The strongest emotion man has the capacity to feel is hate. Hate is generational. It is handed down like an inheritance from one twisted soul to another. It persists even into death. It never sleeps, it never tires. Hate is everlasting, not love." The professor spoke with such sad assurance.

Keisha felt utterly and helplessly defeated. *We are going to die. This crazy motherfucker is going to kill us.* The crazy thing was, she actually agreed with him. Keisha had long ago realized people hated more passionately than they loved.

"It's hate that I found among the ruins of Green Hills Plantation. I had gone there taking pictures for a symposium I was putting together. I walked where men and women who were treated worse than cattle walked. I came upon the ruins of an old barn. That was where he killed them. The slave master Bartholomew de la Chance. He killed them there instead of letting them go as the Northern troops closed in," the professor said. His voice was breaking, and Keisha realized he was crying.

"He locked them in that barn. Men, women, and children. Some of the children were his offspring, conceived during his casual raping of his female slaves. He locked them in that goddamn barn and set it on fire. I heard their voices crying out as I stood among the ruins. Their voices filled my head. The pain—oh God!—the pain was like nothing I had ever felt. I fell to my knees. I heard a voice say 'Dig.' So I dug until my fingers were bloody and my hands ached. Until I found the first bone. A femur," the professor said. He had stopped crying.

"Just stop. Please. Just stop," the trucker whimpered.

"I ate it. I put it in my mouth and ate it. I felt my teeth breaking and my mouth filling with blood and I ate it. Then I found another bone, and I ate it. I filled my belly with their bones, and my mind was filled with their pain. And their rage," the professor said.

Without warning he spun them around on the stools so they were facing him. Troy yelled, and Keisha screamed as they rotated on the stools. The professor stood before them with his shirt unbuttoned.

His belly was distended like a starving child. There was . . . something moving inside him. It traveled under his skin from right to left, slowly but continuously, across his stomach. The skin there was riddled with oozing red sores and pulsating veins. The professor patted his belly with his free hand.

"Their hate is implacable. It demands satisfaction," he said.

"What blood has wrought, blood will rectify," Keisha whispered. The professor nodded his head.

"What the fuck do you want, man?" Troy said.

The professor cocked his head to the side and gazed at Troy.

"It isn't what I want. It's what they want. And what they want is nothing less than the eradication of the de la Chance bloodline. Wipe it from the face of the earth." Black ichor dribbled out of the professor's mouth and ran down his chin.

"One of you is a descendant of Bart de la Chance. One of you carries his corrupted genes," the professor said.

Shavon snorted. He couldn't help himself. "Well, I don't think we need Maury Povich to figure this out. No offense, white boy," he said.

"Hey, fuck you, buddy!" the trucker said.

The professor laughed. The sound was dry and brittle. Both Shavon and the trucker grimaced and stopped talking.

"Do you think Bart de la Chance stopped his extracurricular activities just because he no longer had slaves? Oh no, that monster continued raping and abusing women and men until he died and boarded a train straight to Hell . . . He sired dozens of bastards both Black and white. Just because your skin is brown doesn't mean you're not filled with his perverted DNA." As the professor spoke, his belly rippled. He moved toward them and grasped each of their stools and turned them around to face the kitchen again.

"One of you is a branch of that rotten family tree. Their hate has drawn me here on this night at this time. But I don't know which one is the right one. I just don't know," he said. His voice had dropped an octave, and Keisha had to strain a little to hear him. She was staring straight down at the counter. She started to pray but figured it wouldn't do much good. God had never tried to intervene in her life up to that point. She didn't think that was going to change now.

She heard the professor's footsteps as he walked across the black and white tiled floor. He stopped directly behind her. She could feel the warmth of his breath on the back of her neck.

"I don't know. But I'll find out," he said.

Keisha let out a shrill cry as he touched his palm to the back of her neck. His grip was surprisingly light, almost tender. Her eyes fluttered, and her breath came in ragged gulps. The professor stroked her neck.

"You hate this job," he said. "Your son's father is in prison. Your mother is dead, and your own father is a drunk. You find Troy sexually appealing but are turned off by his arrogance. You burned your hand on a frying pan when you were three and have had a fear of fire and burning ever since. You love the scent of honeysuckle. It reminds you of your grandmother," the professor said in a stilted, robotic monotone. He exhaled deeply and pulled his hand from Keisha's neck.

"You are not the one. I must admit I am glad," the professor said.

The tears that had been threatening to fall since this ordeal began sprang from her eyes and landed on the counter. She could hear the professor take a few steps to her right. He stopped directly behind Shavon.

"Man, I ain't who you fucking looking for. I ain't never heard of this Bart you talking about!" Shavon said. His voice was strained, and Keisha could see him rocking back and forth on his stool. The wind must have been blowing outside because she could hear the Pancake Shack sign creaking. It's mournful cry was like nails on a chalkboard.

"Shhh. It will be over soon. One way or the other," the professor said as he laid his palm on the back of Shavon's neck.

"You lost your virginity at ten to your mother's friend. You feel a dichotomous repulsion and attraction for older women. You read voraciously but hide this from your friends. You long for a closer relationship with your father. You had a dog when you were six who ran away, and you cried for an entire week whenever you looked at his water bowl. You wish you could build things with your hands." The professor exhaled and stumbled a bit. He put his free hand on Shavon's shoulder to steady himself.

"It isn't you," the professor said. He licked his lips and tasted the black bile that had spilled out of his mouth. Time was short. Shavon let out a sound that was half laugh, half scream.

"Ha ha! That's your ass, white boy!" Shavon exclaimed.

The trucker pushed himself off the stool and took off for the front door. He only made it three steps. The professor's arm whipped out like a snake and grabbed the trucker by the throat. Effortlessly, he picked the man up and held him the air. He tilted his head and peered at the trucker. The man's feet were kicking like a newborn baby's as the professor held him tight.

"You . . . you're a homosexual, but you have not told your family or friends. You meet men on the road for sex and then drink until you pass out after the act. You feel . . . ashamed. You were a scuba diver working on a salvage crew in Florida when you saw a creature in the water that looked like a sea serpent.

You convinced yourself it wasn't real. You like to pop bubble wrap whenever you see it. You count the steps on stairs and escalators. You don't know why you do this. Your grandparents came to this country from Ireland in 1934. You have always wanted to go and see where they were born." The professor opened his hand and the trucker fell to the floor in a heap of twisted limbs. He rolled onto his side, keening like a wounded calf.

The professor stumbled toward the counter. Keisha raised her head and looked over her shoulder. He was standing behind Troy. The black fluid was pouring out of the professor's mouth now. It had stained his shirt and was dripping onto the floor. Troy looked straight ahead.

"Don't you fucking touch me, man," he said. Troy's deep voice rumbled out of his chest like an avalanche of sound.

The professor's hand hovered above the back of Troy's neck. Keisha saw the professor close his eyes. He took a deep breath and grabbed the back of Troy's head. Keisha saw the fluorescent lights in the ceiling flicker and create a strobe-like effect. The professor exhaled and staggered back from Troy.

"Those poor girls. You cut them open while they were still alive. You . . . you did things to the wounds. You killed your neighbor's dog with a tire iron. You just beat it to death because they wouldn't let you pet it. You want to do horrible things to Keisha. Unspeakable things." The Professor's voice was weak, barely above a murmur.

Keisha and Shavon glanced at each other. Over the last four years, three girls had gone missing from Pittsville County. The youngest had been eight years old.

Keisha knew what the professor had said about her was absolutely correct. Not close, not in the ballpark, but completely accurate.

"You don't know shit about me," Troy whispered.

"Troy . . ." Keisha said. Her voice quivered as she spoke.

"Troy, what the fuck, man?" Shavon said.

The professor put his pistol in the pocket of his trench coat. He wiped his face with both hands. Sweat and bile spread across his face and beard like war paint. Moving with surprising speed, he closed the distance between himself and Troy. He spun Troy around and grabbed him by the collar of his T-shirt and pulled him off the stool. Their faces were only inches apart.

"You look like your ancestor. It's the eyes, I think," the professor said. But his voice sounded different. It sounded feminine with a hint of a French accent. The professor closed his eyes and threw Troy to the floor. A wet crack echoed through the diner.

That was Troy's arm. Keisha thought. Shavon and Keisha swiveled their stools and saw Troy lying on the floor. The professor was standing above him. The trucker had scooted himself over to the corner.

The professor opened his mouth. Wide. Much wider than should have been possible. Black smoke began to billow out of his throat like a furnace was in his gullet. Keisha's eyes were bugging out of their sockets. It wasn't smoke. Not really. It was some kind of semisolid material. Like a liquid that somehow floated in the air. The black floating liquid smoke glowed intermittently as if a storm was raging inside, and red flashes of lightning could be seen amid the black cloud. The dark, formless shape expanded as it flowed out of the professor. Keisha thought it looked like some type of floating lava.

The dark material fell out of the air and engulfed Troy. Keisha, Shavon, and the trucker watched helplessly as Troy's body thrashed and twisted inside the viscous cloud. Shavon could hear more bones crack and snap like two-by-fours in a tornado as Troy's form twisted and bucked within the gelatinous globule.

Keisha heard Troy scream. Not with her ears, but in her mind. It was the mad howl of someone experiencing a pain that was beyond her comprehension. She looked at Shavon and knew instantly he had heard it too. At last, the form on the floor was still, but Troy's cries continued to echo in Keisha's head.

The professor began taking harsh, deep breaths. The skin over his belly was loose and flabby. It lay against his thighs like a leather apron. As he inhaled, the gelatinous material flowed back into his mouth and down his throat. His belly roiled and undulated as it once again became distended. It left behind a man-sized black stain on the floor.

The professor turned and walked toward the door. As he put his hand on the handle, he paused.

"I prayed he was the last of his line," the professor said. His shoulders slumped, and he hung his head.

"But he has a son," he said before stumbling out into the night.

INCIDENT AT BEAR CREEK LODGE

by Tananarive Due

THE LAST TIME I saw my grandmother was at her lodge in 'seventy-three.

It was also nearly the first time I'd seen her, unless you counted when I was a baby and then another time when I was about four, but all I remembered was long, glittery nails. She and my mother weren't what you'd call tight, meaning they barely talked to each other. So I was shocked when Mom started selling me on staying at Grandmother's for a few days that fall, saying I could miss a couple days of school and sleep in a cabin and meet Grandmother's famous friends. Their whole relationship was birthday and Christmas boxes, swathed in bright, pretty wrapping. But that was it.

"You can see *snow*," Mom said, which was tempting for someone who'd never lived anywhere except Miami. But then she sealed it. "She says Diahann Carroll will be there."

"You're lying." I loved the TV show *Julia*. Diahann Carroll was my first crush. I knew I was too young to marry her, but I was jealous of that kid playing Corey because he got to see her every single day. In person.

Mom glanced over a letter she'd kept taking in and out of her pocket. I glimpsed the lined paper, both sides crammed with slanted, jittery handwriting that felt urgent. Desperate.

"Diahann Carroll. Lena Horne. Maybe Joe Louis, if he's up to it. He was having some health issues. Her lodge used to be like a resort in the forties and fifties."

"You. Are. Lying."

I didn't care about the other names, only Diahann Carroll. I was trying to make sense of how someone I watched on TV could be hanging out at my grandmother's house in Colorado.

"You knew Mother was an actress, Johnny," Mom said wearily. She said *actress* like our Cuban neighbor would say *shit-eater*: comemierda. Mom folded the letter and slid it back into her pocket with more force this time, as if she wanted it to disappear.

"Why don't you want to come too?"

"I've already seen snow," Mom said, ignoring the obvious question. So I ignored it too. Sometimes I wondered if she hated Grandmother; her voice changed when she talked about her, small and soft. "You just spend a few days there, get to know her for yourself—understand a few things better. You're old enough now." Ever since I turned thirteen, Mom acted like I was ready for the draft.

"By myself?"

"Of course not. You and Uncle Ricky will share a cabin. I can arrange it."

Uncle Ricky lived in Amarillo, Texas, and knew how to ride horses, which basically made him a cowboy to me. Seeing him would *almost* be as great as meeting Diahann Carroll.

Mom fumbled in her pocket for the letter again. "So what should I tell her?"

THAT'S HOW I ended up on my first solo airplane ride, which should have been the scariest part of my trip. I was terrified to use the bathroom because the plane was shaking so much. (I tried to focus on my comics, but even Spider-Man can't fix everything.) When the plane landed, the misty mountain range through my window was so pink and gold and surreal that I wondered if I'd crashed and gone to Heaven.

Uncle Ricky was waiting at the gate in a thrift-store army jacket that made him look like he'd just come back from the war, but his big, toothy grin assured you that he'd never killed anyone or been shot at. His bad knee from an accident in high school had kept him out of Vietnam, Mom said. Uncle Ricky gave me a soul shake I messed up all the way through, but he only winked and rubbed my head instead of razzing me.

"Ready to hobnob with the bourgeoisie?" he said.

Whatever *that* meant.

"Is Diahann Carroll here yet?"

Uncle Ricky looked down with sad eyes. "Mother just got her letter, kid. She's shooting a movie in New York. She thought she was done, but she got called back to the set."

"What movie?" I said, challenging his story. Praying it wasn't true. "What's it called?"

"*Claudia. Claudine.* Somethin' with a C."

The name of the movie, however vague, made it real. I almost cried on the spot, and he could tell. He squeezed my shoulder. "Listen, you'd better learn it now: People in show business ain't shit. They'll disappoint you every time. You hear? That goes for your grandmother, too. She ain't the peppermint candy and gimme-some-sugar type. But I'm here to look out after you. Don't you even worry about it."

Looking back, I wonder why I didn't ask why I needed to be looked out after with Grandmother. Maybe I'd stuffed that question away with my questions about why Mom didn't want to come too. Or why she and her mother spoke so rarely. Maybe I didn't want to know.

"Where's the snow?" I said. Denver asphalt looked no different than Miami's, except for the mountains in the distance.

"Not at this altitude," he said. "Just wait till we get higher. You'll see so much snow, you'll never want to see snow again."

He was right about that part, at least.

I climbed into the passenger seat of Uncle Ricky's powder blue Volkswagen Beetle, which he'd driven from Texas and had the Burger King wrappers to prove it. My feet were cushioned by the pile of Black Panther newsletters he'd told me to push from my seat to the floor. I tried to smile at his jokes about Nixon as he toked on a joint and the smoke blew back in my face from his cracked-open window.

But as far as I was concerned, snow or no snow, my trip was ruined already.

I'D FALLEN ASLEEP to the rhythmic coughing of Uncle Ricky's engine as it climbed the steep road, so by the time I woke up we were in the woods. I jolted awake when his tires skidded, unsteady on the packed gray slush. At first I thought I was back on the plane.

Snow! I sat up, electrified. Every window in the car was filled with the sight of white clumps of snow: draped across craggy branches of fir trees, piled in what looked like hills on either side. A few flakes were hitting the windshield like pale butterflies before the wipers washed them away. Uncle Ricky was grinning again too, infected by my excitement.

"Pretty when it first falls down, ain't it?" he said.

"Can I get out and touch it? Please?"

He turned on his blinking yellow hazards and let me jump out of the car to catch snow on my tongue and kick at the snowdrifts to watch them scatter. It was a fairyland. My clothes were soaked by the time I got back in the car, but Uncle Ricky turned up his heater and let me sip warm coffee from a thermos—I didn't care how bitter it was because at least it was warm—and my heart was full of excitement for the next twenty minutes at least. And I was with family, which was no small thing, since my father lived in Jacksonville and my mom's family lived in Texas, California, and Germany, so I didn't see any of them often. Mom blamed the distance on "bad memories," but they weren't *my* bad memories.

The drive was the good part. The best part.

"Here it is," Uncle Ricky said, slowing the car.

I only saw the snow at first, a sheet of white, so I wiped away the condensation on the windshield. We were approaching wooden cattle fencing topped with snow, the sagging gate hanging open. As the car crawled past, I made out a tall, rusted insignia discarded against the side of the fence rails, written in fancy script: *The Lazy M.* I almost asked Uncle Ricky about it, since Mom always called Grandmother's place Bear Creek Lodge.

I wish I had. If I had, the whole incident might never have happened.

Twenty yards ahead, as we drove past the low-drooping fir branches, a long wooden porch came into view, light shining from behind the curtains. I felt my second big disappointment: Mom had called Grandmother's lodge "a resort for Negroes" during segregation, but it looked just like a regular old two-story house, only made of wood. The cedar was an uneven gray from age, not pretty at all. Three or four shiny visitors' cars parked on the side of the house were the only evidence that anything inside was worth seeing.

Two lights stared down in golden yellow from twin second-story windows. Below, the porch wrapped around the house like a ragged grin, gapped from missing porch rails. I tried to think of a way to convince Uncle Ricky to drive me back to the airport, but no excuse I thought up could change the fact that my ticket wouldn't be good for another three days. I was stuck. The house looked dangerous for reasons I couldn't explain even to myself.

"Are there bears here?" I looked for a clue in its name.

Uncle Ricky laughed. "No more'n anywhere else in the woods. We don't see killer grizzlies this far south, just black bears. Don't feed 'em and you'll be fine. Doubt you'll see none anyway. Bear

Creek doesn't have bears just like Atlanta doesn't have peach trees. Every other street is Peachtree down there, ain't it? I bet every street in Miami named for the ocean."

I shrugged, annoyed by his small talk about Miami when Mom always complained that he never came to visit. He was a plumber by trade and made good money, she always said, so why didn't he come see her more? Then he'd know all about Miami's street names.

"Listen . . ." he went on, voice assuring. "Some years back, Mother got her feelings hurt by Hollywood and holed up here by herself. For five years, she wouldn't see nobody. And I mean *nobody*. If she made it alone, you'll do fine with all of us here."

"Got her feelings hurt how?"

"Folks decided she was too old-fashioned, that's all. Times changed. They treat her like a curse, like she sold her soul. Half the folks who'll talk to her only have their hand out."

Uncle Ricky parked, careful to keep several feet between him and the mile-long shiny red Caddy closest to his space. Beside that Caddy, Uncle Ricky's car looked like it belonged in the junkyard on *Sanford and Son*. Uncle Ricky kept his hands on his steering wheel, staring at a door on the side of the house with frilly white curtains. Like the house had put him in a trance.

I was in my own trance, staring beyond the three steps leading to that back door, trying to understand the snow. A small mound rested there, soft and white, not like the grimy snow ground into the road. A few flakes puffed out as if the mound had sneezed. Was it settling? Mr. Ramos, my science teacher, said we should consider the world with a curious mind, so I tried to figure it out without asking Uncle Ricky. I waited two seconds, and the snow puffed again; this time, a dark hole appeared at the center of the mound. Could a cat or small dog be buried there?

The snow itself seemed to come to life, shivering flakes free, and then the entire mound moved in a shimmy, undulating away from the porch, snakelike. A twig snapped beneath its motion, or I might have thought I was imagining it. Then the mound fell flat. No cat or dog emerged to explain it. The snow just settled to stillness.

I slowed down my heart by telling myself that must be a normal thing, that it was childish to be scared of snow. But I think I knew better even then.

Uncle Ricky slapped his palms against the steering wheel, making me jump. "Well?"

I realized I was holding my breath. My socks were still damp, so my toes felt tingly. I wondered if I'd only dreamed any fun, just as maybe I'd dreamed the dancing, breathing snow.

"Well what?"

"Ready to go in and see Mother?" He could have been talking to me, or to himself.

I nodded, shivering.

It was a lie.

THE SIDE DOOR led to the kitchen. A piece of luck. Old-timey band music and loud laughter were floating from another part of the house, but I didn't hear any children, as I'd been promised when Mom said, "I'm sure somebody else's grandkids will be there too, baby." There was a party, but it wasn't a party for *me*. You couldn't call it a party if they were playing some old horn section in an orchestra instead of the Jackson Five.

Although it was empty, the kitchen was a party all its own, the tile counter lined with an array of casserole dishes under loose aluminum foil. Uncle Ricky grabbed a plate from the stack right away, so I did too. Each surprise under the foil was better than the last: Roast chicken legs. Macaroni and cheese. Greens with turkey necks. Peach cobbler. I hadn't realized how hungry I was until I used one hand to hold the chicken leg I was stripping with my teeth while I spooned cobbler on my plate with the other.

"Slow down, boy. Your mom'll never forgive me if you choke to death on my watch."

By silent agreement, we stood hunched over the counter to eat instead of joining the party right away. Mom would have been mortified that I wasn't sitting at a table with a proper place setting: salad fork, dinner fork, butter knife, the whole nine, like Grandmother had taught her. I couldn't even eat a bowl of cereal at home without a napkin in my lap. But we just lived in a two-bedroom apartment near her job at Miami Jackson High, not in a big house in Baldwin Hills ("They called it the Black Beverly Hills") like the one Mom had been raised in. I was glad Uncle Ricky didn't care about greasy fingers.

Uncle Ricky finally slapped cornbread crumbs from his palms and filled a water glass from the sink to wash down his meal. The pipe under the sink whined like it was in pain.

"I'll have to take a look at that," Uncle Ricky said, mostly to himself. "All you gotta do is nod and smile and be impressed with everything they say. And don't call my mother anything except Grandmother—not Granny, not Grandmama especially. She'd hate that. She needs everything a certain way."

"Okay."

He studied me closely, frowning a bit at my faded sweater and jeans. He took off his army jacket and hung it on the hook. Underneath, he'd dressed in a black sweater and slacks, instant formality. He glanced down at his cowboy boots and meticulously wiped mud from the tips with a napkin. He patted down his 'fro. Then he took a breath, jouncing his shoulders like he was about to run out on a football field.

"Let's do it," he said.

Uncle Ricky pushed past the wooden swinging door from the kitchen and we followed the music and laughter down a narrow, wood-paneled hall. For the first time I noticed his limp, how he slightly favored one leg.

The lodge was more impressive inside because of the decorations on the wall: rows of signed old photographs, some of them with Grandmother as a young woman in a ball gown posing with other well-dressed people, some close-ups of almost every famous person I could think of. Duke Ellington. Bob Hope. Lena Horne. I stopped in front of Diahann Carroll's photo: her head thrown back, smile wide and full of joy. I wanted to cry again.

"Well, *there* he is!" a woman's voice said ahead, and I realized that Uncle Ricky had left me alone in the hall.

The laughter stopped. Someone turned the music down.

"Goodness gracious, what have you done with your *hair*?" the same woman said.

"That's how they wear it now, ma'am."

"Well, if everyone jumped off a bridge, would you jump off behind them? Imagine if we'd been running around with these bushes on our heads."

I was glad that Mom had trimmed my hair short before the trip. I took a few tentative steps and saw Uncle Ricky face-to-face with Grandmother: she was tall for a woman, reaching his nose, in a sequined dress that could be in one of the photos. Her hair was black and straight, hanging loose in a girlish fashion, but the dark color looked like dye. Grandmother was in her seventies, although you couldn't tell from her smooth brown skin. I'd never seen anyone so thin, and I wondered if she was sick. Those same long, long fingernails sparkled in the room's light.

Uncle Ricky looked like he might want to hug her, but Grandmother wouldn't come close enough. "Sadie's boy is here," Uncle Ricky said instead, motioning to me.

The living room was elegant, with a white baby grand near the double door and a lively fireplace big enough to warm the house. Three other people were there: one man and two women, all of them Grandmother's age or a bit younger. The man was husky, sitting in a chair as wide as he was. His face was familiar, but I couldn't place it right off. The women were fashionably dressed, one in a fur wrap, but Grandmother was the queen of the room.

I walked toward the queen, trying to remember to smile. I don't know why I was so nervous with everyone looking at me, but I could barely keep my head raised. She took a small step back, so I stopped short of her like Uncle Ricky had.

Grandmother did not smile at me. "Spitting image," she said to the room instead.

"Isn't it spooky?" one of the women agreed.

"Where's your mama, boy?" the man called out.

"Had to work," I mumbled, then I raised my voice to project it like Mom was always telling me. "Grading papers. She teaches English in high school."

The others seemed impressed, but Grandmother frowned. "She'll barely make a living on a teacher's wages. I told her to keep up her voice lessons. I could have given that girl the world."

Grandmother suddenly glared at me like I was everything that had let her down in life, her eyes so angry that my skin prickled. Then her face softened to a mask: not a smile, but less severe. The transformation was so fast and convincing that I had to remind myself that Grandmother had been a famous actress, after all. Her eyes were as flat as the settled snow.

"How old are you now?" Grandmother said. "Ten? Eleven?"

I winced, insulted. "Thirteen."

"Thirteen! You're small for your age. Your mother needs to put some meat on your bones. And I'll bet she coddles you like mad. We'll have to get to know each other, Johnny. I need to teach you a few things about the world."

Uncle Ricky's hand landed firmly on my shoulder. It felt like a prompt, so I said, "I'd like that, Grandmother."

"I'll be getting to know him too," Uncle Ricky said. "Out in the cabin."

"No, I don't want him out with you in that drafty cabin," Grandmother said, floating away toward her friends gathered on the plush twin sofas near the fireplace. "You stay out there and smoke. He'll stay in the main house. My old powder room has a bed."

I glanced up at Uncle Ricky. He looked actually *scared*. But he didn't say a word.

"Ain't you gonna come over, or you too grown now?" the man teased Uncle Ricky.

"Nah, Uncle Joe. You're lookin' good, man."

The fear was gone from Uncle Ricky's face and his voice. But it was too late: I'd seen it.

Someone had one of the new Polaroid cameras that took color photos on the spot, so I posed with everyone in the room like I was long-lost family. Uncle Ricky called all of Grandmother's friends "Aunt" this or "Uncle" that. I learned later that "Uncle Joe" was the legendary boxer Joe Louis, so that photo would become one of my most prized mementos on the days when I could forget about the rest.

But I didn't know who he was yet. And in my only photo with him, I wasn't smiling.

"YOU NEED ANYTHING, I'm right across the way," Uncle Ricky said, pointing vaguely as he walked me to my room. "Right outside. Head out the kitchen door and keep walking straight."

I couldn't imagine anything that would tempt me to walk past that snow pile beside the steps, especially at night, but I nodded.

Uncle Ricky handed me a heavy flashlight. "For seeing in the dark," he said. "*True* dark. Trust me, you don't know nothin' about that."

The closed door at the end of the hall was Grandmother's room, he told me. The narrow powder room door, also closed, was at a right angle. A small silver star shined from a nail.

"If there ain't enough room in here, lemme know and I'll see what I can do."

The main light switch didn't work, so he stepped in and flipped on the lights on the mirror and vanity table that took up most of the space. This room was all tile instead of wood, so the bright mirror lights made the room look like noontime. Three or four of the bulbs were missing, leaving a few darkened spots in the reflection. I saw myself standing there puny beside Uncle Ricky, my face lost in a shadow.

"Not much of a bed," Uncle Ricky said. He quickly began hauling piles of fashion magazines to the vanity table, uncovering folded blankets and a cot underneath. "We used to have to sleep in here if we were on punishment. It's a little claustrophobic, but it's all right. Mostly it was the *idea* of being on punishment that made it bad. Know what I mean?"

The windowless space looked more like a cell than a bedroom: Of course it was a punishment room. It was only slightly larger than a walk-in closet in a slight L shape, leading to a second closed door painted white.

"Where does that go?" I said.

"That's her bathroom," he said. "Don't go in there. You need to pee in the night, run to that other little bathroom at the end of the hall. When you need a bath, use the one upstairs."

The idea of being that close to where my grandmother would be sitting on a toilet—or taking a bath!—made me want to puke. "Can't I sleep in the cabin?"

"Lady's house, lady's rules. Remember what I said about how to find me. Use your flashlight instead of turning on a bunch of lights. She don't like you burning up her electricity."

When he turned to go, he was already patting his pocket for his lighter. If the car ride was any indication, he couldn't wait to light up another joint. And now he would have the cabin to himself. When he hugged me good night, I could see how relieved he was to go.

As soon as I was alone, I wanted to cry again. The lodge didn't have a telephone, so I couldn't even talk to Mom. Uncle Ricky had promised to drive me to town to talk to her sometime, but my real life already seemed far away and long ago. Mom always said action made her feel better, so I dug into my backpack for my stack of comics and my cassette player from Christmas, my survival plan. Six new comic books, most of my best cassettes, and headphones to make my music my own business.

The cot was stiff even with three blankets beneath me, but I managed to get comfortable enough. I turned off the bright lights and read my comics by flashlight with "ABC" playing on my headphones. Soon I forgot where I was, lost in Peter Parker's adventures.

When the vanity lights flared on, I gasped and nearly fell out of my cot. Craggy tree branches were only Grandmother's nails before she snatched the headphones from my head.

"Get some sleep, Johnny," she said in a honeyed voice. "You have these turned up so loud, you didn't hear me knocking. You'll hurt your ears. Rest up so you'll be fresh tomorrow."

I was stunned, but I thought fast enough to push stop so the music wouldn't come blaring into the room when she yanked the headphone cord free, because then she would have taken the cassette player, too. And maybe the cassettes. It was clear on sight that no one was supposed to have any fun in this room. I nudged my flashlight under the blanket so she would forget about it now that the too-bright vanity lights were screaming.

"Yes, ma'am," I said, mimicking Uncle Ricky. "I'm sorry I didn't hear you."

The flashlight made a tiny click when I turned it off. I hoped she hadn't heard it.

"Don't forget your prayers," Grandmother said.

When she turned off the light and closed the door behind her, I realized my earlobe was stinging from where her nail had caught my skin.

When I touched it, I felt a spot of damp blood.

I WOKE IN a tomb. My room was cold despite the blankets, and the darkness made it impossible to tell what time it was even though my glow-in-the-dark Timex said it was seven-thirty in the morning.

But my watch was wrong, I realized when I crept into the hallway from my room. The sun had barely risen outside, casting gray light. It took a couple of sleepy, confused moments to remember that Colorado was in a different time zone, an hour behind. The quiet house was a mercy, freedom I hadn't expected. I rushed to dress, ate leftover peach cobbler from the kitchen counter for breakfast, and ran out of the kitchen door. The cold slapped my face and made me miss the down jacket Mom had bought me, but I didn't dare go back inside.

The snow piled near the steps looked different in new light. Ordinary. Light snowfall had buried any signs of the original mound I'd seen, and evidence of movement. I even poked at the spot with a stick. Nothing. Feeling silly, I tossed the stick away.

I surveyed the property, which was easier to see in rising daylight. The fence ring seemed huge at the time, but her property wasn't much more than five acres. The main house sat at the end of a snow-covered driveway, and three small cabins lay beyond it, blending in with the stand of fir trees. The two rear cabins looked like shacks, with boarded-up windows and part of one roof under a tarp. But the closest cabin looked okay, with a shiny axe standing beside the door and a nearby pile of wood that looked freshly chopped. I admit I tried to peek into that cabin's window, but the thick curtains were pulled closed except for a tiny slit that revealed only a small wooden table with Uncle Ricky's thermos.

Still, I knew where he was now. And compared to the powder room, Uncle Ricky's cabin looked like a palace. I wondered if I could get on Grandmother's good side so she would let me sleep there, but my sore ear told me she might not be the type to change her mind.

I tried not to let my sneakers sink too deeply into snow as I walked inside the fence, reveling in the sight of small animal tracks and frozen spider webs and knotted tree trunks shaped like open mouths. At the end of the driveway, I came back to that large metal insignia, *The Lazy M*, nearly as tall as I was, leaning on the fence. It was now obvious that this had once been posted on the driveway gate, but maybe it had fallen. Maybe that was one more thing Uncle Ricky would need to fix.

I didn't notice the red droplets on the snow just beyond the Lazy M sign until I saw the dead thing. Actually, it was a dead thing's *head*.

I was so startled that I fell backwards, landing on my butt in the snow. But I jumped right back up again to get a better look at the matted fur, open black eye, and bloody mess where its head had once been attached to its now-severed neck. Maybe it was a raccoon, but hardly enough was left to tell, especially to a boy from Liberty City.

But I knew it was dead. And I noticed from a pinkish trail in the snow that it had been *dragged* to that spot. Parts of the trail had been covered by snow and sometimes disappeared, but I kept following until it took me back to the kitchen steps, beside the Caddy. A sound like shifting sand behind me spun me around fast, panting like I'd been running. My eyes looked for movement everywhere, and finally I saw something under the snow slither around a tree trunk, out of my sight except for a few loose flakes spraying away. *Fast*. I ran to where I thought

I'd seen it, but all of the snow was flat again. The one mound I kicked was only a buried tree trunk.

I went back to the Caddy. The trail didn't originate exactly where I thought I'd first seen the snow move, but close enough. I picked up the stick I'd thrown away and scattered the snow beside the steps until I uncovered a blood-soaked center, maybe as big as a car tire. The blood spot was almost purple.

The way I stood there staring, I might have been frozen solid. I wasn't sure myself.

A thump on the kitchen window made me look up. Grandmother was standing there, her hair covered by a bonnet, which made her seem much older. She cracked open the kitchen door.

"Johnny, come inside!" she said. "Get out of that cold without a coat. What's wrong with you? You'll catch your death out there."

That was something Mom said a lot too, so now I knew where's she'd gotten the saying: *You'll catch your death.* But that was the first time it sounded real. I threw my stick away and hurried to do as I'd been told. But as I walked back to those kitchen steps, I was sure something was slithering under the snow behind me. On my heels.

Tracking me.

"WHAT KIND OF animals move under the snow?" I asked Uncle Ricky when I cornered him to myself. I'd spent most of the day like a mascot for the ongoing party, answering prying questions about Mom and Dad I was pretty sure Mom would *not* have wanted me discussing with Joe Louis or his wife or anyone else. (I figured out that part of the rift between Mom and Grandmother had to do with Mom having a baby—me.) The rest of the time I'd sat stiffly trying to pretend I wasn't bored, since I was afraid Grandmother would confiscate my comic book if she saw me reading one. I was deep in my head, wondering about what I'd seen outside.

Uncle Ricky reeked of grass when he finally emerged from his cabin. He gave me a red-eyed stare. "Oh, like mice?" Uncle Ricky said. "That's all that was. You'll see all kinds of mouse tunnels out there. That's how they hide from foxes and such."

"Bigger than a mouse."

"Foxes, too," he said, and my heart sped up. "They'll sleep in the snow sometimes."

I was both intrigued and relieved. Now it was making sense. But I wanted to be sure.

"Did you . . ."—I lowered my voice—". . . chop off a racoon's head with your axe?"

I was sorry as soon as I asked, since he looked at me like I was smoking grass too. I went on: "So . . . that was probably a fox, then. Right? Hunting under the snow? Moving like a snake?"

Uncle Ricky shook his head. "That's not how foxes hunt. They leap up and dive—"

Laughter swallowed whatever he'd been about to say. The group was moving toward the card table in the corner. "Come on over here, Ricky," called a woman whose name I still don't remember, but she was an opera singer. "You be on my team so Joe and Martha don't clean our asses out." She winked at me. "'Scuse my French, Johnny."

"Two people you never wanted to play cards with . . ." Grandmother began, and everyone fell silent, eager for one of Grandmother's stories. "Billie Holiday, rest her troubled soul. And Clark Gable, that cheap SOB. I had to tell him, 'You know you're getting paid more for this picture than I am, don't you?'" Everyone laughed, so I did too.

"Were y'all *just* playing cards?" the opera singer teased, and Grandmother swatted her.

"You should write a book, M," Joe Louis's wife said. "We keep telling you. You should have your own star on the Hollywood Walk of Fame. It's long overdue."

Grandmother made a motion to dismiss the thought, but her eyes twinkled with pleasure.

"Spades or bid whist?" Uncle Ricky said.

An argument ensued over which game to play while Grandmother fussed with her stereo console, fanning through a pile of records. Seeing her with her music reminded me that she'd taken my headphones. I sidled behind Uncle Ricky and whispered in his ear, "Can you ask her to give me my headphones back?"

"She'll give 'em back when she's ready." He sounded sorry, but not enough to help.

I glanced up at Grandmother to see if she'd heard us, and she was staring right at me. Smiling, for a change. Her smile was cruelty, not comfort. Oh yes, she had heard.

"How about Sam Cooke?" she called out. "I can't stand this new music today. Just sounds like plain old noise."

Her friends agreed that Sam Cooke would be a wonderful choice. While Cooke sang "A Change is Gonna' Come" and the card game was in full swing, I escaped to my room.

THE POWDER ROOM wasn't big enough to pace in, so I explored. Uncle Ricky had warned me not to open Grandmother's bathroom door, but he hadn't told me not to open the cabinet built into the wall under the vanity table. The tiny door was paint stuck, so I had to tug on it for a couple of minutes before it gave way and opened with a belch of musty air. Even the vanity lights couldn't brighten it, so I grabbed my flashlight, crawling halfway in, which was as far as I could get. Three large filing crates were piled on each other, filled with yellowing pages. I skated my flashlight beam past those, looking for something more promising.

I found it staring right back at me: a framed movie poster against the far wall. My grandmother's name was in large red type: Mazelle Washington. From the size of the type, bigger than anyone else's, she could have been as big as Barbra Streisand. A true movie star!

I shifted the light to see the faces: not photos like the modern movie posters I saw at the theater, but realistic drawings. The only Black face on the poster was a young woman encircled by a white man and two white women who were laughing against the backdrop of the Empire State Building. But the Black woman wasn't laughing—her mouth was in a wide-open O, her hands clapped to her ears in exaggerated shock.

It took me a long while to realize that the woman in the sketch was Grandmother. She was Mama's age, and she wasn't in a ball gown like I'd seen her in every other photo. She was wearing a frumpy black dress and white apron, a maid's uniform. Her hair was in short, thick braids in bows flying out in every direction, a crown of spikes on her head. If it weren't for the way the artist had captured her eyes and sharp chin, I'd never have recognized her.

The movie title was just above her hair: *Lazy Mazy Goes to New York.*

My surge of pride upon seeing her name wilted when I saw the whole poster, then sank to a dull throb in my stomach. I didn't understand everything then, but I knew that Grandmother wouldn't have hidden the poster in the darkest cubby in her darkest room if she ever wanted to see it again. She would have hung it on her wall.

I'd found a true secret. And it felt like power.

I scooted out of the crawl space as fast as I could and jammed the door closed again, hoping she would never notice that I had opened it. Between the mysteries in the snow and the treasure in my own room—which I planned to dig into more late at night, when everyone in the house was sleeping—I was starting to think the visit to Grandmother's house wasn't so bad.

Then I turned back my blankets.

My cassette player was gone.

"EXCUSE ME," I said, and the card game came to a halt. Uncle Ricky looked at me with one eyebrow raised, on alert.

"We've got a game goin', Johnny," Uncle Ricky said with a note of caution.

"Can I please talk to you alone, Grandmother?"

She took her time turning her head to acknowledge me, and this time she didn't disguise her simmering eyes. I'd embarrassed her, and she was enraged. I might have been more afraid of her if I hadn't found her secret.

"Have you ever heard the saying that children should be seen and not heard?" Her voice was still sweet, a show for her friends. "You can see the adults here are busy."

"It's all right, M . . ." the opera singer said, but it didn't soften Grandmother's eyes.

Uncle Ricky tapped on my foot so hard with his boot that it hurt.

"Some stuff is missing from my room," I told Grandmother, accusation in my voice. "My tape player my mom gave me for Christmas. And most of my tapes. Can you give them back, please?" After frantic searching, I had learned that my Sly and the Family Stone and Ohio Players were gone too, along with the Jackson Five tape still in my player.

"Did your mother buy you those?" Grandmother said. "Has she listened to those lyrics? Those lyrics aren't for children. Half those band members are out of their minds on drugs. Did she tell you that? None of that so-called music you like is worth a damn. I'll teach you better. You need to learn about Ella Fitzgerald and Billie Holiday. Louis Armstrong. *That's* music."

I don't know what Uncle Ricky saw in my face to make him jump up from the table to grab me by the arm, but I couldn't remember ever being so mad. A *stranger* had stolen from me, was lecturing me. Was saying I had a bad mother.

"I'll talk to 'im," Uncle Ricky said, and he pulled me toward the kitchen.

"You'd better," Grandmother said with bland menace. "Marching in here like . . ."

"Just hush," Uncle Ricky said when I complained about his tight grip. He steered me past the kitchen and out of the door, to the steps. He closed the door carefully behind us, his breath hanging in clouds. "What are you doing? You don't talk to my mother like that. *Ever.* No one does."

"Somebody should," I said, defiant. "She doesn't have any right to—"

"She has the right to make up whatever rules she wants in her house, and *never* forget that. When you go back in, you apologize."

"Why are y'all so scared of her?"

Uncle Ricky looked away from me, out toward the gate. He and Mom had that in common, at least. Neither of them wanted to talk about Grandmother.

"Look . . ." he said, sighing a fog of breath. "We'll stop at a record store on the way to the airport. I'll grab you a new player, whatever you want. Cool? Just . . . smile. Get along."

"You mean pretend."

"What the hell you think?" he said. "You're gonna' spend every goddamn day of your life pretending. Get good at it. She's doing you a favor. *Shit.* What do you think this world is?"

He went back toward the kitchen door. I thought he might slam it, but he didn't. He slipped back inside, leaving me to my anger.

I glanced back down toward the bloody spot I'd uncovered, or where I thought it had been. My own circling footprints were there, and my stick, but the purplish blood ring was gone.

Buried again.

THAT NIGHT, GRANDMOTHER brought out her film projector to show off for her friends. I thought we might see one of her movies, but instead she showed interviews of famous people talking about her. Someone must have collected every nice thing anyone had said about her, as if we were at her funeral. A tall white actor in a tuxedo who was in that movie about a flying car I'd seen with Mom said, "I'll tell ya . . . if you want to learn about comedic timing, find the work of the greats like Mazy Washington." A white woman with short orange hair was on *The Tonight Show* and said to Johnny Carson, "I grew up loving Mazy and those terrific pratfalls, so it never occurred to me that a woman couldn't be funny." I noticed that everyone praising her was white, until at the end Muhammad Ali was ringside in boxing trunks saying to Howard Cosell, "Get in the ring with me, you must be crazy. I'll dance and I'll jab and I'll dodge you like Mazy."

Everyone laughed and applauded, Joe Louis loudest of all. "That boy still talks smack."

"He can back it up," Uncle Ricky said. Everyone laughed again. Uncle Ricky looked back at me: "Uncle Joe helps train Ali, you know." He winked at the way my mouth fell open.

"But we're not here to talk about me," the retired boxer said. He raised his glass in a toast. "To Mazelle Washington—one of the greats."

"And fuck anyone, Negro or white, who doesn't think so," the opera singer muttered, but I don't think anyone else heard her except me.

Everyone toasted Grandmother with champagne flutes while I drank apple juice. When Grandmother put on her old-timey Duke Ellington, I let the opera singer lead me in a dance. I was smiling so much that I fooled myself into thinking I was having a good time. I was blood kin to one of the greats, after all.

Grandmother's seizure of my music didn't seem as upsetting as it had been at first. Maybe any grandmother would have done it.

Besides, I wouldn't need my music that night. I had the cubbyhole to explore.

Once again, I excused myself early to be alone. Grandmother stepped in front of me just when I was almost clear of the room. Her approach felt like a performance.

"We need to know each other better," she said. "Tomorrow we'll walk in the yard."

"Yes, ma'am."

She patted my arm, the most affection she had shown me. I missed the way Mom hugged me like she didn't want to let go. Maybe that was another way Mom made sure she wasn't anything like her mother.

"Sadie says he does well in school . . ." Grandmother bragged to her friends, which sounded like another performance. I thought about asking if I could sleep in the cabin with Uncle Ricky while she had an audience. But I wanted to see what was in her files.

I read my comics until all of the noises in the house were gone: the footsteps from guests trudging upstairs, the shower running in Grandmother's bathroom, her toilet flushing for the last time. When the house was still, I climbed back into the cubbyhole and pulled out the first case of files to scour with my flashlight. Most of them were notices about Lazy Mazy, and photos of her with that same hairdo and oh-shit expression, or some with a grin so wide that it seemed too big for her face. One headline from 1935 said: WHAT HAS LAZY MAZY GONE AND DONE NOW? Beneath the stack of articles, I found reels of film. The true treasure. Since she'd already set up her projector in the living room, it felt like fate instead of prying.

I had to see for myself.

I moved quietly and made sure the projector volume was turned all the way down before I flicked it on. At first, I threaded the film wrong and it spun with a flapping racket I was sure would wake the whole house, but nobody came out while I fixed it.

Lazy Mazy Goes to New York began to play.

The film opened with Lazy Mazy dead asleep at a kitchen table, slowly stirring a mixing bowl while she dozed. A white man in too much makeup walked in wearing his work clothes, and I didn't need the sound on to know he was mad to find her sleeping. Lazy Mazy fell back in her chair and rolled to her feet like a gymnast. The bowl she'd been stirring had ended up on her head somehow, dripping batter on her face. That only made the white man madder, and he spanked her butt while she ran away.

I tried to be quiet, but I laughed. Her eyes were so big, nothing like Grandmother's. The expressions on her face! The way she could contort her body in unexpected ways. Every moment on the big living room screen was a revelation. *This* was Mom's mother? My grandmother?

I'd been watching the film for maybe ten minutes, laughing louder than I should have, when I realized someone was standing behind me. I felt a presence before I turned around, the same way I had in the snow. I hoped it was the opera singer, or Uncle Ricky.

But it was Grandmother, framed in the living room entryway's blue light from the projector in a fancy robe with her straight hair loose, fanned across her shoulders. She'd been pressing her hair; she was holding a hot comb. Instead of looking at me, she was staring at herself on the screen.

"Grandma!" I blurted. "You're Lazy Mazy! Is that what 'The Lazy M' means—"

That was all I had time to say before her robe's sleeves fanned out like a night creature's wings as she swooped toward me.

"*How dare you,*" she hissed in my ear before she grabbed my arm with shocking strength.

And then I was in the worst pain of my life. I had to look down to realize she'd pressed the hot comb into my upper arm *hard,* applying more pressure the more I tried to pull away. It wasn't orange-hot, but it was hot enough to stick to my skin and make me yowl. Hot enough to leave a scar I would carry into adulthood.

"Stop! It hurts!" I yelled, and wrenched my arm away.

She was standing in front of the screen now, the film playing across her face, the ghost of her forty-year-old grin mocking from her forehead while she stared at me with tearful loathing.

"I'm sorry," I said. To this day, I don't know what I was apologizing for. She was the one who'd hurt me, yes, but I'd hurt her too. Scarred her, too. It was as if I'd dug up a dead body and dragged it in her living room the way our cat brought us dead mice. I saw it in her eyes.

I ran as fast as I could to the kitchen door and outside, to the snow.

"IT'LL BE FINE," Uncle Ricky said after he'd dressed my burn with a cold, damp cloth from his cabin's tiny sink. "Stay out here tonight."

The burn had turned an ugly red, with a rising bubble on my skin I'd never had before.

"I wanna go home." I'd stopped crying, but the tears were still in my voice.

Uncle Ricky sighed, but then he nodded. "Okay. We'll figure it out tomorrow. But I don't drive out on these roads in the dark."

"Did she ever do that to you?"

"Not that, exactly." I thought he would leave the story unspoken, but after a moment he went on. "One time I was about fourteen and I gave her some lip at the store. When we got home, she pulled a tire iron out of the trunk and whacked my leg good a couple times. I had to stop playing football after that . . . but it kept Uncle Sam off me."

His story was so much worse that I almost felt better. Almost.

"What about Mom?"

"I tried to protect her. But when you get home . . . ask."

"How can you not hate your mom?" I asked. "She's the worst person I've ever met."

Uncle Ricky sucked in a long breath. "I used to," he said. "I guess your mom still does. But nobody's born like that, Johnny. One day I realized . . . everything has a price. A burden. So I just started feeling sorry instead. There but for the grace of God. You know?"

I didn't know. And I hoped I never would. As I nursed my arm, I was mad at all of them.

Uncle Ricky went right to sleep on the bottom bunk of the cabin's bunk bed, but I stared through the curtains toward the house, the kitchen door. I expected her to come after me.

About an hour after Uncle Ricky went to sleep, as I'd feared, the kitchen light went on and the door opened with a shaft of light. Instinct made me crouch low in the cabin window.

Grandmother was still in her robe, carrying an aluminum tray of food. She looked like she was taking out the trash. But instead, she sat on the frigid steps with the tray on her lap. She looked so sad and alone that I almost felt sorry for her too. Her sob was a barely muffled wail. She could catch her death out there.

Grandmother opened the tray and tossed a chicken leg on to the snow. And another.

The snow near the meat *moved* . . . and something popped out, showing itself as it shook off a layer of frost.

It wasn't a fox. It wasn't a dog or a cat. It was white but didn't seem to have fur, just pale skin cleaved to a frame that looked more like an insect's than a mammal's despite a bony tail lashing from side to side. Long, too-sharp teeth chomped at the offered meal, grinding meat and bone alike. I gasped with each snatch of its powerful jaws.

The terrible, nameless thing slid closer to Grandmother, ready to keep feeding. But she didn't run. She didn't even flinch. As the hideous creature burrowed its snout in the tray in her lap, she let out childish laughter, her cheeks puffed wide with Lazy Mazy's mindless grin.